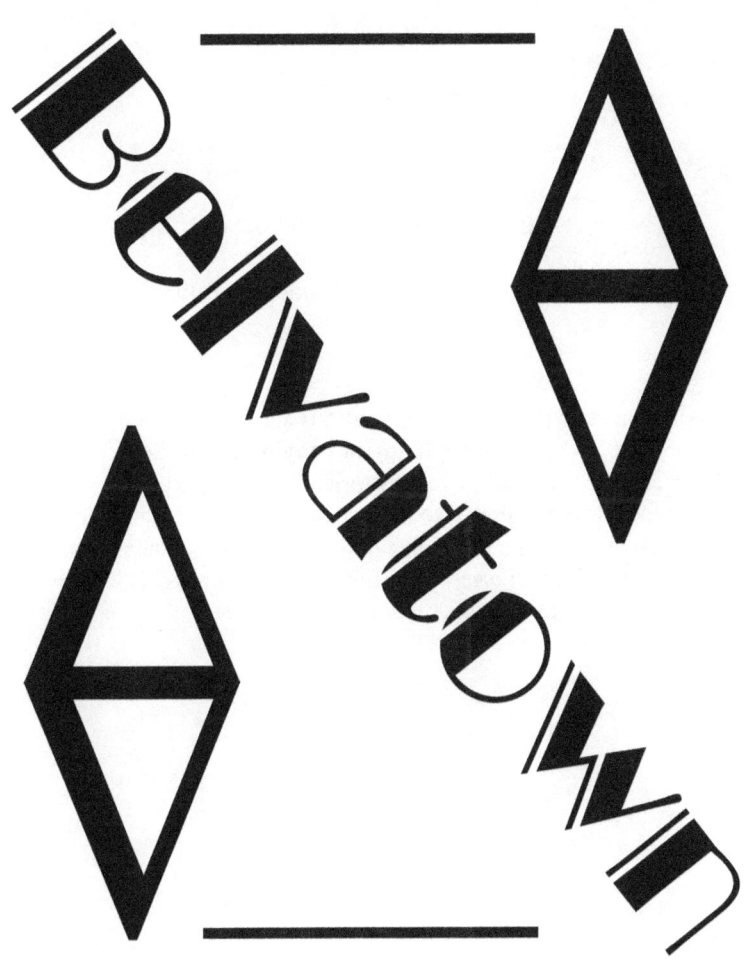

# Belvatown

by J. Lea Koretsky

Regent Press
Berkeley, CA

Belvatown

# Prologue

On May 14, 1963 A BLOND WOMAN EXITED A department store in Belvatown, founded by a woman named Shaunessey Belva in the county of San Bernardino. The blond was accompanied by a guard and a personal friend who was there shopping for a dinner dress. As they left the store a dark tan vehicle pulled up and shot the three. Each keeled over hugging their waists and knelt to the ground. A street alarm was sounded and sheriff came running from a block away, pistols drawn. The vehicle was later apprehended inside a private yard of an orange grove where a night security guard lived. It turned out he was wanted for a crime in London, England, involving the near fatal demise of a British Lord of Commons. The demise consisted of a vehicle too closely driving near a man causing him to fall in the street.

The initial investigation into the Belvatown shooting was handled by three police jurisdictions — San Bernardino, Colton and Ontario — and a private agency. The narratives were entered onto a city computer, countersigned and referred to the Marshal Office for further inquiry. The Marshal Office rejected the referral, closed out the case and sent a polite document file to the state Attorney General which, in turn, cross matched all information, sending various items requiring further disclosure to federal offices across the nation and marked the file into periodic review.

## JAKE HAROLD, *SBPD*

I had been on the job approx ten months, was not yet completed with my Spring training in San Francisco, when I took the call for Hariff's. It was for an officer down, with two pedestrians, both VIP status. I drove up three blocks, went around the rear, saw someone drop a cup, and went in for the chase. I was slightly heavy and lost him as a result. He was very tall, maybe six two, very slim, was hooded, carrying a weapon which he fired on me, dinging me in the right shoe. The airport was there then, a tiny strip. Adelanto wasn't there yet, neither was MCAGGC, but 29 Palms was at East base. Pioneer Cemetery was there. I went to the front of the Hariff department store, found both women dead, guard severely wounded. Guard later identified shooter as Steven Hariff, with John Wadd and girlfriend Karen Clerk; guard was John McCoy, dark tan, approx age 58. Hariff was involved in a crime against Harris for their outlets, three in the state.

I called an ambulance. It arrived within minutes and took the shooting victims to the closest hospital which was at Patton. After we learned that it was the senior Hariff who built the entrance at Patton, we had our own hospital built. Imaging can't be in a hospital or you kill everyone, it is separate. Technically it shouldn't be on the grounds at all. As soon as the hospital went in, Hariff built Mt. View Cemetery on Waterman.

When we arrested Hariff he pled nolo contendere and said Donald Jackson fenced him. Jackson was an alias, we pulled up a ding sheet as long as shadows are long, his family name was Scein, his cousin was Meijhian, who had a small billboard on Mountain Way off 8th. Hariff was bailed out by his family lawyer. Our policy continues to this day not to go back to the scene for eye witnesses. We had the entire crime on camera.

The judge on the case was Mulrovey. He reviewed all footage, excused the jury, and brought in a guilty verdict. The courthouse was at Old City Hall near today's Chamber of Commerce across the street from the library. The state did not allow footage to be admissible in most trials thereafter.

## AARON GEORGE, *CPD*

The hooded man reported as the assailant was apprehended by Colton Police in Grand Terrace, a small suburb that sits on a drive overlooking the flatlands, made of Portland cement and San Bernardino glass. It is a half mile past dutch Germantown which is two miles from Blue Ribbon Cement at the train tracks of the army train. I was a rookie then, I was patrolling the creek bed near Portland Cement when I encountered a man cooking over an open flame in a refuse can. As I approached him inside my patrol vehicle, dispatch warned me to wait for backup. Aerial camera had cited the man in the shooting vehicle, a tan Malibu with a black roof, with Wadd and Clerk visible near the flame. Colton Police arrived in five patrol cars, all armed, Marshal in assistance cutting off all roads to and from the creek bed. No weapon was found on any of the parties nor in the getaway vehicle.

## GARY FRANKLIN, *OPD*

I worked the resorts in Ontario near the airport and military hospital. I was on duty first shift when I handled a call routed from another desk. The caller described herself as the wife of a Steven Hariff. Mrs. Hariff said she had an argument with her husband earlier in the day. She alleged that he threatened to purchase a pistol and hurt someone if she did not leave him alone and quit bugging him about their son. Per Mrs. Hariff the couple shares joint legal and physical custody of their six year old son; however, Mrs. Hariff does not think her son is at suspect's home because whenever she calls he is not available. She states the courts allow her two phone calls on weekends. According to Mrs. Hariff suspect was temporarily residing at a friend's vacant house while their divorce was pending.

I placed a telephone call to the number given me by Mrs. Hariff for suspect. A man answered, yelled in a harsh tone that he would deliver the money and slammed the phone in my ear. I ran a clearance on subject, got a hit, and put out a call to all jurisdictions. Approximately an hour later I received a telephone call from SBPD Harold, Badge #19, saying suspect was identified in a driveby at Hariff's Department Store in the afternoon. ACE Security Inc. interviewed the guard employee, name deleted — they were out of Las Vegas, Vegas had just been built in 1974. Former Chief of Police Ed George headed ACE located locally on Third Avenue at Sepulveda between the Sheriff and National Guard. ACE hired security guards out of high school with one year army or navy, they had to be eligible to be bonded and have both a clean record and no DUI citations. The guard who fled was a Meijhian, age 30, supporting a wife and two sons. They brought Meijhian in for questioning, through the interview the guy had a heart attack and had to be rushed to a hospital in Fontana. The interview was subsequently conducted in his room, after a court order from Circuit Court was obtained granting permission. Meijhian stated under oath in the presence of the court reporter that he had taken a bribe.

J. HARRING, *District Attorney General*

I worked security originally for the El Paso line, then was

brought to California to give my sayso as to a series of wire jobs in Berkeley. The stores that were wired in 1959 were the Black Sheep which closed it, the UC Textbook Company and we made it a store inside a student union, the mining building and we put it on a hill above botanical gardens, the tennis club which we closed, the deaf and blind school which we made a separate campus, and a group of sororities which we turned into offices. I then went to work for the state.

I received the file after it was reviewed by two jurisdictions, San Bernardino Police and Colton Police. I was asked to send an independent investigator to Harris House to obtain information on Hariff. My detective was a retired police officer with twenty-nine years in Oakland, California. He submitted the following information. Steven Hariff, subject, went to work for Harris after his uncle kicked him out of his store when he had a disagreement at a family gathering that escalated into a shouting match. A friend agreed to hire S. Hariff at her cousin's store. At Harris Store the store manager put him in charge of security for the upstairs. The black glass made it hard to see what customers were doing, so he brought in mirror backed shelving to give him a better idea. He brought suspicious customers into a room made entirely of mirrors and interviewed them. He inerviewed a wire thief and a year later was accused himself of wiring the Harris Store.

We don't know whether the thief made it clear that he was recommending a course of action.

## Summary by LAURENCE CHILDRESS, *Physician*

I was practicing medicine in downtown San Bernardino at a medical clinic a block east of Hariff's. I was in my early thirties, having been educated at Patton Medical Group at the base. I periodically worked in San Francisco at the Precidio and rotated weekend shore duty in Surf City in Los Angeles. I met the senior Hariff when I was invited to become a physician of chief disciplinary practice for the passenger trains from Los Angeles to Florida and New York. He considered relocating to Ontario, California because it was a quiet small town with a hospital managed by the army, however, he did not want to become known as the train engineer who laid down track for a nationwide train. He contacted me once a year by telephone. During his most recent contact to me he described it was apparent that his youngest child intended to take over all competing businesses in retail.

## Per COUNTY COURTHOUSE *Public Documents*

The case was reviewed by Honorable Harry Murre who because there were no confirming eye witnesses overturned the sustained conviction against Steven Hariff, dropping all charges and deleting the narratives produced by the police. His legal opinion was that for allegations to be sustained there must be eye witnesses who the Court could examine by oral testimony.

## JOHN L. TRAIN, *Advertising Manager, San Bernardino*

The train station was built to look like a Turkish Blue Mosque. It had beautiful mosaic and stone that survives to this day. The place was built by Jason Hariff, then in charge of Istanbul Express in Turkey. Jason had three sons, John, Jack and Steven. All would wed models who worked display.

The train ran from Hollywood to Florida, had houses in a handful of towns, built small town squares and ran passengers to stores on its route. It also shipped products across the country.

The department store where Cimone Hollan and Roberta Harris were killed was originally called Hariff. Roberta Harris owned Harris House — there was one in Berkeley which closed in early 1959 and one in Hollywood which closed late in 1959. Roberta was from Florida where her uncle sold wrapped oranges and shipped them nationwide by train. Her uncle's oranges were called Dateblest. One could order them from a catalogue. Her department was on D near Hariff's called Harris Store, entirely of dark tan glass, and it sold patterns for women who wanted to sew their own dresses. When it was wired in 1971 it was closed permanently. Harris House in West Hollywood was sold to another retailer.

There weren't many departments in the early 1950s — Hinks, Harris, I. Magnin, Joseph Magnin, Goldman's. The dime-a-dozen stores such as Macy's, Penney's, Sears Roebuck came later when the radio and television transistor went public. Prior to them, there was ACE hardware and blue chip stamp stores.

There are certain people the mobs won't touch. Then there are others who various governments would ideally like retired. These people sometimes wind up engaging in crime and being put to ruin as a result. In the town of Rialto the life was quite good. Ten to thirty trains ran daily for as little as $1.50 a week, a king's ransom in those days. The problem was the Hariff family decided not to hire son Steven to build homes because he was too violent, and then the trouble began. For some reason the U.S. Army decided to go into the building of houses and to make towns instead of permitting private firms to build. There has long in U.S. history been a feud over who should build, thus it alternates between army and real estate developer. The alleged American dream is based upon building houses predominantly.

GENA RUTHIE MCKARRIN, *Witness Protection*

She remembered the early days when she had come with her father to Long Beach. She was nine when they rented an upstairs flat in the white wood and glass duplex overlooking a pristine beach and sparkling blue ocean. Her father, a Scotsdale man who sold manufactured homes in the west, packed her into his Oldsmobile after tersely explaining her mother had run off with another man whose last known address was listed as

Ontario, California. A lineup of pretty waitresses kept him off the sauce. By the time they had relocated, her mother she was told had gone again, this time into the dustbowl of Nevada's stateline in search of either a casino job or a more permanent residence. Long Beach was dry and breezy, her winters too cold, her winds in the summer too restless. Gena spent days in a lounge in the restaurant where her father worked and nights on the beach with handsome men who took weekends at their oceanside apartments and tennis courts.

She met Jack Hariff, the second oldest son, on the pier as he was docking his seventy-two footer yacht. He was ten years older than she was, tall, cropped wavy hair, tannish complexion, dreamy bedroom blue eyes, who when he worked cashiered for a nightclub about a half mile down the beach from her father's restaurant featuring solo comedy and dizzy jazz with black vocalists. One day he would enter his father's lines, take over several stations, be in charge of as many as fifty employees. He thought he had it in him because he could keep the club's monthly figures in his head. He talked alot about himself and she listened trying to help him sort through the plans his father gave his sons. Invariably she realized he hoped to be like his older brother John who was studying business at a college in Los Angeles for the time he would take control of the southern lines.

Her father didn't approve of the Hariffs. He wanted her to reside locally, perhaps manage a hotel for the concessions, not fill her head with ideas about traveling city to city. He considered Jack Hariff a negligent drifter who with or without a steady wage would not remain satisfied with any one place but would push forward, with trends or in spite of them. If Jack made it into his forties, if he got the notion to buy a house and have a family, if he decided his father wanted more of him than he had to give, he might mature to produce a worthwhile achievement, but Jack was attracted to the glitz and the glitz was the game and gamble of industrialists who would never reside permanently in the country, not in New York, Miami or the gulf, let alone on a chalky beach front despite the fact that the best of living was to sit on a balcony and gaze at the bluest of blue oceans.

The news of the Hariff shooting that wounded a guard and killed two prestigious women was over and done before it had received much attention. Jack brought home the newspaper, thrust the news section onto the kitchen table, and told her that the man the police had identified was his baby brother. Jack was disgusted but didn't invite comment, his brother was in over his head, had a stack of debt in his quarry, had probably heisted half a dozen warehouses of fur and leather coats over the years, knew one too many stinking high school dropouts, and couldn't cashier to save his life. He rambled on, got drunk, took out a pistol and said his brother had played finger the stalemate once too often. He probably didn't mean to tell her much, but he let loose with a bunch of expletives that his brother probably was given the go-ahead by the clerk who left the back door open to call the job.

Gena moved back to her father's house on the avenue almost immediately. She stopped taking his telephone calls and casually told friends she was seeing another man. She told her father she and Jack had split up and asked him to send her to stenographer school in San Bernardino, which he did.

# 1 / One

Before there was a growing city, suburbs sprawling over a fifty mile cement tundra, the county of San Bernardino was a small quiet town comprised of its army base and a handful of lazy towns characterized by their key routes, Fontana by its ranches on Arrow Route, Rialto by its Turkish train station and Vernon Street bridge and San Bernardino itself with a group of elegant department stores and flats neatly laid out between Second and Fifth on Court Street. Hariff was a Turkish entrepreneur from Istanbul when he built his elegant department store in the fifties for his train station, his department store was the most expensive retailer, featured diamonds, racks of high haute fashion, high heels, a counter for lipstick, carry bags for evening wear. Inside carpet with glass stands backed by mirrors ensconced a central chandelier that sparkled with light and a lavish stairwell that led to a basement floor where antiques were sold. Outside the marque entrance was a stunning dark tan tile with a marble front and tall windows inside which were elegant mannikin displays. It was the only department to sell stockings and velvet gloves and overnight became a sensation. Hariff put his store on the map for his train station for which he hired any number of tax accountants, most of whom produced schedules, fares and collected money — one or two lawyers, and a handful of doctors, not to mention men who worked the trains from coast to coast who collected tickets, ran a restaurant and beverage car, and who managed stopovers, since the lines did not have sleep-overs in those days, in Ontario, Palm Springs, Houston, El Paso, New Orleans, the Bayou, and a handful of landmarks on the gulf. Except for night trains that passed uneventfully over a landscape of rich squares of farmland, the southern Sante Fe & Topeka lines kept to hourly schedules as soon as they entered California's desert, depositing at its five stops to houses to let on the cross streets Stoddard, Mayfield, Arrowhead, Pershing and Mountain Way — which would eventually house the county administration, the sheriff and courthouse, the California highway building and as the city grew the National Guard on Third and at Fifth and C Streets City Hall to relieve the downtown of major debt — out-of-towners who would arrive for nightclubs, army duty, industry jobs, and other reasons, golfing, ranching, casinos, shopping, and a chance to relax in a change of scenery, take in a few movies, take a breather from below zero weather, purchase antiques and possibly seek work at the studios at the end of the line.

The fact that the desert gave any idealist the most favorable advantage was understood in its affluence of orange groves without smoke lanterns and its affordable summer cabins, which over time would create its own sea of affluence and the once jocular sporty town would swell to forty-five hundred homes, another thousand flats, their chrysalis marked by verdant rugged mountains to the north and by Lytle Creek Wash through its basin, as baby boomers fleeing a sudden congestion of Los Angeles flocked to desert oases for retirement and privacy.

In this singular context of unrippled desert bloom, replete with wildflowers and tumbleweed, the meadows and hillsides received an unwanted attention for real speculation. Short-lived in its concept, the land nevertheless became another type of gold rush driven by rising inner city costs for standard jobs and by banking surcharges without which slow interest rates were not easily remedied. A host of city services to offset the heartache of its fragile mining corporations were stamped onto an enlarging map, a new heretofore law enforcement of police for the inner city to fight city crime was put in Colton under a new headquarters while the sheriff remained based at an adjunct to Patton, library and tourist services with a stadium which because of its narrow width was unable to race cars, armored car vehicles stationed beside a car wash, an industry unheard of except in Chicago, Detroit and New York, and several architect firms situated along Baseline to push the suburbs growing along the train tracks.

# 2/Two

I WILL ONLY TELL YOU THAT I WORKED AS A COURT reporter. Once the session was done, it was my job to dictate my notes into a transcription machine, then seal up the tape with a copy of my longhand and send it by messenger to City Hall where the service produced a formal document of the trial. When the transcript was sent back I then had to check it for wording and if no further changes were required, the original went into the judge's file and copies were sent to the agencies.

In those days in 1962 the city of Belva, what is since San Bernardino, was tiny. The four buildings in downtown were a center that displayed new automobiles, there was a restaurant, there were apartments with a lounge and bar, and there was Hariff's. Ted Mulrovey ran San Bernardino County out of what is now Colton. He was a CPA. He was New Jewish Agenda.

Cimone's husband Jim Hollan was hired by a chain of

different department stores to put in homes that would be elegant enough to attract Hollywood business types, among them physicians and tax accountants. There were several stores that formed chain businesses — Newberry's run by a man named John C. Newall, who later developed a drugstore, Penney's run by a woman named Joanne Caternewall, Harris Store run by the Montegomerys, and Sylvester's, run by John Silva. Hollan developed a plan for four squares with seven homes on each block, his idea was front and back to each block to encourage neighbors. Each square had to have forty homes around a large square park with trees and some flowers. The houses sold for about $30,000 apiece. The squares were in Del Rosa off the new highway 30 where the Rockefellar Junior home sits, a square at the north tip where there is an elementary school, and then two side by side on a hill above the flag station which burned during the making of a movie featuring Ross MacDonald's book, originally titled *The Grifters*, which Alfred E. Knopf published as *The Doomsters*.

The train station was subsequently run by a company from Old Ventura, headed by a man in cinematography Aaron Climenhattor. Aaron was from the Bayou in Mississippi from old iron money. Iron put up all the iron grill work. New Orleans wasn't built yet. Neither were plantations.

So, they had this gorgeous elegant train station, walking paths throughout Rialto, I would call it a posh downtown consisting of several blocks, one street of businesses including upper flats, approximately two hundred houses in the original inner city, all army personnel residing at the base, a stunningly beautiful entry, orange and green, lit up at night front to the entrance.

There were two stores in the city of Belva. One was Harris Store on D, the other was Hariff Department Inc. Hariff was Turkish. Harris Store did not go with Harris House in Berkeley. Harris House was a place where designer clothing was modeled and made after purchase. Steven Hariff later married Joyce

Hildegaarde, who worked as a model in Berkeley in 1955.

There was one other suburb containing a hundred homes in Rialto. Although Fontana had a police department, it served Ontario because Ontario had an airport, albeit a small strip and station, an air base hospital, several schools, a plaza with a movie theatre, and approximately two hundred and fifty homes, most which were civilian owned. Colton had the other police, but Colton like Fontana had no houses. The United States Marshal Office was located on highway 62 and had a prison for adult wards in addition to long houses at a place known as Rand. The prison had enough cells for fifty customers if they doubled up in each cell. The primary job of the sheriff on Arrow Route was to paint a stripe down the center. This was done by each new workforce on hands and knees in broad daylight in the event of a heist, which was a common occurrence, in the rare event an airplane could not land in the fog and thus required to land by landmark arrow on a road.

The getaway vehicle was described by a man who saw it drive around from the dock as a tan car with what looked to be a convertible roof. It had apparently stopped in dock to pick up a long thin cardboard box that was propped up against a cement wall. A young female was driving with two men in the back. She was the one who got out to pick up the cardboard box which she slipped through the open door and handed to the man on the right. She then got inside and started the engine. While she pulled out another car, a small station wagon, followed her on its way to the outside drop of the nearby post office. The man in the back removed a rifle and held it up appearing to take aim at the passenger seat of the car behind it causing the driver to yell at them. The tan car picked up speed, drove around another car on the road and signaled to a guard sipping a styrofoam cup of coffee which he immediately set down on a stair leading to the hotel across the street. As he ran he removed a gun from his holster and took it apart discarding a part in the street. He then went to standby along the building as the man on the right inside the tan car unloaded pellet fire at three people emerging through the entrance, one of whom was Roberta Harris, the other who was rumored to be heiress to the Swedish throne when her child turned 25.

The two women went down fast, the guard was not fazed much by a shoulder wound and proceeded to run after the vehicle when an armored truck pulled into the street behind him honking him. The truck pulled up to the curb, two men got out and without seeing the wounded women carried bags of coin inside the store. The driver however noticed the women and dispatched a call to Patton and then went outside to pick them up and get them inside the armored truck. While he was doing this, the guard returned, helped him and they drove off leaving the two guards inside the store.

The man on lookout seeing the truck pull out radioed on his CB to someone who apparently dispatched a Carmenina truck from the boxcar coliseum to pick up the guards when they came out. They left with the food van and were never apprehended. The Carmenina truck was seen fleeing past the stadium onto H Street where it looped past a furniture warehouse and sped across the canal to the other side, charging past the billiard palace onto the freeway.

The Carmenina truck was subsequently found with its food stand raided in an orange grove. The truck was taken by mobile command to a warehouse in the city of San Bernardino, dusted for prints and stripped down. Evidence technicians submitted a report which allegedly disappeared off the lieutenant's desk. The crucial piece of evidence was what was called a frame-up, a personal memento on which the driver's thumb print was detected by metal strip. The memento apparently had a heart decal on it and was sent to UCLA for confirmation as to identification for employer. While in the lab it was taken by a senior evidence technician who, convinced the print identified a friend of his at the lab, gave it to another technician who walked it in the door to a slide smear lab for an alternate opinion.

The desk company was called in for the trial heard by Judge Mulrovey. The company operator stated under oath the glass memento was one of his. He had a thousand such manufactured which he gave to each employee at sites throughout the valley. In the courtroom he produced one like it. He said these frames that sat on wire stands usually contained a spouse's photo. He thought they were given by employees to their families and spouses, which he thought was how the glass frame was found inside a food truck.

A coat from the slide smear lab took the witness stand next. She testified that the memento in question was submitted for analysis, was accurately designated as to thumb print. She identified her employee's handwriting, stated that the document submitted to her for her initials was proper procedure according to chain of evidence yet could not produce the object for court examination. The judge threw out the evidence as a result.

The prisoner after being arrested could not remember correctly as to who called him. Although he was shown clips of the man calling him, he swore under oath that he did not know him. He was also shown the number the man called and acknowledged that it was his telephone number. He was unable to explain why he responded to the call including where to show up to since the lookout man had not told him the address to respond to. In his testimony he stated that the call he received said, "Come quickly, we need to make sure the men inside are not detained." Thus it was assumed that the two bagmen were in the armored truck under false pretenses having been at the pickup spot wearing uniforms.

There was one point of contention during the trial, whether to permit Mrs. Steven Hariff into the courtroom when the photo memento was to be admitted as evidence. She was very elite, thin to a fault, wearing dotted articles of dress, the same colors every day, white on top with pink dots and a black skirt with white dots, light stockings and sunglasses which she called shades. After the first week she was excused because no one could concentrate.

While she testified on the stand the dock was full. Usually the men were migrants from Tiajuana who had come into the Imperial for seasonal work picking oranges in large picking sacks. They were driven over the border in bale trucks containing cracked cement from foundations in Venice, California which had the other air base. She testified her son had a lisp and she was trying to get him accepted to a boarding school but each time she set up an interview, her husband Steven pulled the child out of class and took him to the home of a friend and she had no idea where he was. She was asked to identify a revolver piece that had fallen into the street during the shooting. She said it looked like a gun Steven waved at her when he was drunk. She said he had waved it at her at least five or six times always in front of the child. On the last occasion she said he threatened to use it on himself. She did not worry he would actually pull the trigger on her because of who her uncle was. He was a Meijhian, an architect from the Middle East, and was respected by the Hariff group who had gone to him at least once for money.

Meijhian stayed out of the entire affair. After the trial concluded, Meijhian put in two community hospitals, all senior high-rises, and he built Carousel Mall. He did not build houses — those were built at the Navy's request, the Navy being situated in San Diego, by Hollan in 1964, Turner & Associates in 1971 who built Grand Terrace and Del Rosa near the cow pasture, and in 1974 the Army built most of the other houses and sold them turning over the sales to City Hall for redevelopment of its square. After the trial City Hall built up the two cities — Rialto and San Bernardino, no coliseums — to include a low bridge, four additional buildings in downtown, another cement company, a row of businesses on Fifth Street and Arrowhead where the Harris Store was, lots of apartment flats, each four hundred square feet with gleaming dark hardwood, Formica counters, walnut ceilings, large picture windows and small gardens.

In the late 1960s the county put in a city jurisdiction for Fontana along its primary avenue Arrow Route, added Baseline Street running from Colton, through upper San Bernardino and Del Rosa and a new mesh of freeways in the early 1980s — highway 30, hotels and highway 10, a new suburb Redlands and a hospital complex and lots of new malls. The rumor was the Harris Store hired someone to go after the shooting. They thought based on a description given by the wounded guard he was a Steven Hariff, son of the Harriston mobster who lived in Belvedere, Los Angeles, what is today Burbank and West Hollywood where Hariff, the father, had a retail department store that sold diamonds purchased by a Spaniard known to many as Consejo Aragon Haritine, aka Hariff, also known to many as Hariff & Sligh, joyners for retail.

Steven Hariff took the job to shoot the security guard and the friend, a Harris, after Hariff took one too many notes on his ranch in what has since become Palm Springs where his ranch now is managed by a group of German Dutch out of Laingendorf, formerly in Sunnydale, Florida, a nursing home that was run by the senior Hollan's third wife Letitia Mable Retrange, also known to others under her maiden name Fersterhof, this being the only German enterprise in the U.S. of its day.

Over the years I've thought of many questions that perhaps ought to have been asked during the trial and weren't, the most significant in my mind being, was it Roberta Harris who married Steven Hariff first?

# 3/Three

THE WOMAN STANDING ON THE CURBSIDE OVER-looking the canal was tall, dark hair pulled back in a tight braid, her angular posture defined by an unrelenting defiance. She wore a long dark brown woolen coat and leather boots. If she were waiting for someone, she showed no sign of anticipation.

The canals in the flood control basin had been emptied out in Colton after water was redirected to newer suburbs built in Del Rosa and Highlands. As a result the canals in Colton had become bare and foot high horse head figures made of white stone became visible. From a distance these figures resembled chess pieces on a thin alabaster strip, modestly elegant, well perceived. Apart from their surroundings which were the Portland Cement gravel hill, the BN & SF railroad, a few unsightly oil wells cropping from behind rows of warehouses, they seemed to better fit the posh surroundings of the newly rising upper middle class on Pershing and Mountain Way Boulevards, their tennis club, dance cotillion ballrooms, semi ranch houses with tile roofs amidst cramped gardens tucked between entry ways of birds of paradise, tall blue lilies, ferns and yellow and white daisies. A viewer always had the uncanny sense that to turn these horse heads in the canal would bring a crescendo of water from sources unseen to amply irrigate miles of dense orange groves as far as the eye could see. Whatever petty squabbles the rich interior hid, the remaining cultivation of orange and green bespoke an economy that would supply every last city in the state.

Olivia George turned away from the sight and began the walk up the hill to her cottage. She was just forty and the promise of the valley seemed at once less productive and more gritty in the past twenty-four hours. She wrestled with the knowledge that the poison telephone call she had received told her history was not forgotten, her grandfather Aaron George had overlooked a few major details, Roberta Harris had been in the wrong place at the wrong time, a clerk inside the store had left the door open. Had Harris not gone in for dress shoes, she could not have stepped into the plaza where a hit man was waiting. To this day the police knew nothing, probably they would say nothing. The act would be a blot on the Harris lives which little would cancel.

When Olivia reached her cottage, a small two bedroom bungalow made of sandstone with a garden of bougainvilleas and neatly trimmed grass, she unlocked the door and entered, admiring as she usually did, the walnut floors and chalk white walls, her practical decor of comfortable rust colored sofas and easy chair around a marble fireplace. The leaded glass windows looked on one side onto a courtyard of other cottages, seven in all, and on the other at a narrow wading pool covered with red maple leaves. The garden table and wooden chairs on a long veranda were in need of an umbrella, yet she knew things being what they were, it would have to wait.

She picked up the phone and asked the operator to connect her with Lt. Jake Harold of the San Bernardino Police Department.

The documents sat on Lt. Jake Harold's desk for a good week before he reviewed the file again after a hiatus of some thirty-four years. He was set to retire in three years when he intended to sell his house on Mountain Way and purchase a small condo in a golfing community in Riverside County. He remembered the court reporter. She was a young kid then, fresh out of business college in Surf City, having moved to Belva after an aunt found her a job. She would be in her early sixties, probably still married to the bailiff who worked the jails, living in Del Rosa in a Hollan home with a few children who had become attorneys and worked at the fancy courthouse on Arrowhead. Out of the cops who were subpoenaed to testify, only his buddy in Colton, Aaron George, had retired. Even his father, old beefeater ACE, continued to work at something, being well beyond ninety-four, having earned every pointed shoe any cop chooses to slip his tired feet into. Aaron was a thing of the past, a cop who tracked every last criminal on foot, who did not file his reports until he personally had handcuffed the guilty. Nowadays police worked in two's, in shifts and went off duty at three-thirty in the afternoon, resuming their work on the subsequent day, after reviewing a bulletin posted on their computers as to night and graveyard calls. The Hollan case had been worked twenty-four-seven without coffee breaks until every suspect was photographed and fingerprinted. Oddly enough none apprehended would supply a print that matched the print taken by the lab, that special print wouldn't produce itself until the pistol for the silencer that was tossed into the street was found in a size shoe seven box of Mrs. Hariff's son at the home of the woman friend of Steven Hariff who used to provide day care seized in a search of her home. The tip-off was that the woman picked up Mrs. Hariff from court on three occasions. An ACE detective assigned to watch for comings and goings at the courthouse was told by his partner that on one occasion, instead of driving to the friend's house, they took a detour to the concession stand of the boxcar stadium that sat at the corner of the Orange Showgrounds at Central and South E Streets. There, they purchased sodas with Hariff's nephew, a half black young man in his early teens known to police as a gangster who trafficked pieces. He let them onto the property of the armored truck company next door. The ACE detectives, thinking they had a potential gang on their hands, followed them to the woman friend's home, picked up a subpoena and returned to confiscate anything they came across. In addition to the gun and silencer they discovered evidence locker guns, stolen badges and uniforms. At that point the entire network considered the case wrapped up. The various people who had committed the crimes were sentenced to federal penitentiaries in the country and the police files were closed.

The difficulty with placing a wire tap on a police officer's granddaughter was it was not reasonable to assume the caller would repeat the act. Once the telephone call was traced, it was possible that a police entrapment team could adequately resolve the caller's spite.

Jake ran a numeral code on Olivia George's number. The entries on his computer were over twenty. He then ran a parallel index for names or type of businesses and seeing what he was up against he decided it might actually be easier to put in a tap. It wasn't often a poison call originated with the upper class. In this situation knowing the caller's alleged identity probably wouldn't be much help, unless George had had an illicit affair and then the problem would be all too evident. Matters of the heart weighed small beside bankruptcies and court orders to sell corporations. The fact that the caller's telephone number belonged to the wife of the physician who came forward during the trial thirty-four years ago caused Jake to ask himself whether he ought to check the trial transcripts to see if mention of her was made at all. Otherwise it was highly out of the norm for even a spite call to be directed at any of the grandchildren of the George family, even though it was Aaron George who tracked the killers in his capacity as a police officer.

Laurence Childress had retired to the stone garden known as Grand Terrace to a side street off Cadena Road on Grand Terrace Drive overlooking the city of Colton and the Santa Ana wash. The house sat high in the hills on a palm tree lined street amidst other predominantly glass houses with cement foundations poured from the Portland Cement factory that made its gravel hill an eyesore off Freeway 10 as its corridor shot into San Bernardino from Ontario and Fontana. Dr. Childress had purchased the home when the suburb was in its infancy and a year later after his picture was in the paper walking down the old courthouse stairs he married and took his wife home from the house she had grown up in San Bernardino off the city canal. To get to the house required driving up a steep driveway past two brick posts with lights on them and past a flower bed with hydrangea below the house. Jake parked his sedan and went through a courtyard to a slate backyard with sand and flowering cacti in the middle. He knocked on the door and waited.

The woman who opened the door was a buxom blond, in her late seventies, wearing a white smock over green paisley stretch tights, with heavy green mascara and lipstick as though every breath were sealed with a goodbye kiss. She eyed him as he withdrew his badge and showed it to her.

"May I come inside?" he asked.

She showed him into the house. Blond floors glistened, dark wood furniture everywhere was stiff although elegant, two sets of living rooms were back to back, each red with large white flowers, end tables, coffee tables, bookshelves, a dining room table with twelve chairs in the adjoining room done entirely in ivory wallpaper with ceiling molding, a built-in hutch with fancy porcelain edged with gold leaves and rim and tall glasses.

He asked her full name. She gave it, Lorene Mable Childress.

"Someone from your telephone made a call to this number. Do you know it?" He handed her the number.

"No. Whose is it?"

"Is your husband at work?"

"Yes, he's usually home by six."

"Is there ever anyone else here with you?"

"My son. He drops in from time to time."

"Is he an adult?"

"Yes, he's in his thirties."

"Do you have a number for him?"

She gave it to him, and he jotted it down.

"Do you have other children?"

"A daughter but she attends college in Sonoma. She's in her second year. She doesn't come down except at holidays."

"How old is she?"

"Twenty. She's a young twenty, you'd think her somewhat naive."

"Does she have a boyfriend?"

"None that I know about. She hits the books pretty hard."

"What's she majoring in?"

"Drama, but it has nothing to do with what you're asking about. She's doing set design."

He asked, "Have you had any reason to talk to detectives who may have testified at a trial where your husband gave evidence?"

"My husband is a distinguished man with many years in the field of prostate surgery. He has testified at many trials, over thirty."

"I was speaking of a shooting that occurred at Hariff's."

"That's a long time ago. Over thirty-four years ago."

"Thirty-four to be exact. One of our staff received a rather upsetting telephone call from your residence several days ago. I am following the incident to try to determine what that is about."

"I'm sure I don't know. Have you considered that your caller got my telephone number by mistake?"

"Yes, I checked that first before I came out."

"I'm not in the habit of calling police. My husband hires a watchman who drives by nightly in case there are any problems."

"The call was made from your residence. Could your daughter have made it?"

"There's no reason to involve her. She doesn't have a calling card. She wouldn't have time to drive down, and she doesn't have a key here. I would have to let her in."

"Does your son have a key?"

"Yes. He works."

"Do you mind telling me where?"

"At Blue Ribbon Cement. He's in a truck all day."

"Do you think your son would have had any reason to have made such a call?"

"I wouldn't have any idea. You could ask him."

"Thank you for your time, Mrs. Childress. By the way, where does your husband work?"

Poison callers like poison pens made anonymous calls to un-suspecting people telling them a crime had been committed; generally they did this years after they had helped line up a job. For Lorene Mable Childress to send Ms. George a poison tele-phone call the police policy would be to regard Lorene as being a busybody with nothing better to do; unofficially a tab would be put out on her with a question as to a friend of Ms. George.

Jake drove across town to the address given him for her physician husband on Temple Street a half block in from Wall. Jake parked in the back behind a two story building made of dark brown stucco and tinted windows. He went around to the entrance, a large copper plated door, with a lawn bordering the sidewalk to the walk, and entered inside a cool interior.

"I'd like to talk with Dr. Childress, if he is available," he told the receptionist, a fair haired beauty in her early sixties dressed in grey.

"You'll have to take a seat. He's with a patient."

He looked through a magazine on fashion for men admiring trousers and collared shirts and advertisements for jewelry. At length the doctor came out with his patient for whom he instructed his secretary to write a prescription. The doctor was tall, nicely dressed in a black suit with a discreet shirt, a stethoscope around his neck.

"Detective Harold to see you, Doctor."

"Come on in, Detective."

Jake went into the all cherry-wood interior with a bookshelf filled with medical journals and a large mahogany desk. He sat on one of two high backed brown leather chairs. The doctor went around to his side and withdrew a legal sized notepad. Jake handed him his badge which he gave a cursory once-over, jotted down the number, then handed it back.

"One of our staff received a call from your home telephone, believed to be a crank call."

"Did you tape the caller?"

"No, we didn't, but they described a female voice."

"It could have been my wife, I suppose, although I don't understand why she would have done that. What was said?"

"The person made reference to a trial some thirty-four years ago. They alleged the case was improperly handled and there is still missing evidence."

"That seems fairly innocuous. Why would it upset the person to whom the call was made?"

"It was apparently obnoxious. It was a trial you were called to testify on."

"Yes, I recall it. A serious shooting, wounded an officer."

"That's the one. Did your wife attend any part of the trial?"

"I wasn't married to her yet. She called me as a result of my picture appearing in the paper and I took her out to dinner."

"Did she tell you anything about herself?"

"The usual sort of small talk. She had a son by a former marriage, a kid of about twelve when I started dating Mable. She was married straight out of high school to a tennis pro who got her pregnant before she was nineteen. After the boy came along, she moved in with her mother and told her husband to get lost. She was into her thirties when we met and when her mother died I slipped a ring on her finger and took her home."

"What was her maiden name?"

"Griswald. She had a sister who went to Hollywood and became an actress for several years."

"Has she worked since you married?"

"Not a day. I want her to enjoy herself. She's had a hard youth, I wanted to be the one to make up the difference to her."

"Had you been married before Mable?"

"She's my first and only. I had a few girlfriends but no one who I wanted to marry."

It was fortunate for Childress that his wife had sought him out, otherwise he would probably still be unmarried. "I understand from your wife that you have a daughter?"

"Yes, her name is Irene. She's attending Sonoma State University. She's in her second year. It's a four year college."

"She's taking drama?"

"That's right. She's handled set design for the theatre there. She's hoping to enter production next semester."

"How often do you see her?"

"I visit her twice a year and she comes down at the holidays for several weeks. She's a pretty girl. Do you want to see a picture?"

"Sure."

Dr. Childress opened a drawer in his desk and removed

two framed photos and handed them to Jake. They were of an attractive brunette in her late teens. She had a round shaped face, brown eyes with a studied intent expression, a cashmere sweater with a collar and pearl necklace in one picture and in the other was standing beside a horse.

"Does she ride?" Jake asked.

"I gave her a horse for her eighteenth birthday. She's at the stables where I board him every day after classes. Irene walks him in the round, canters him, feeds him, brushes him down, cleans out his box. She's a very dedicated horse woman."

"How does Irene get along with her mother?"

"They've gone through the usual mother daughter struggles. My wife wanted Irene to attend Pomona in LA so she would be closer to home, but Irene wanted to be in the country near Valley of the Moon. I had a cabin up there when Irene was a child and we spent summers there so Irene has fond memories. Mable felt it was too woodsy, and eventually I stopped taking Mable along."

"Did anyone from the trial remain in contact with you over the years?"

"An agent drops in periodically, chats about how my practice is going, gives me season tickets to the new stadium for baseball games, although I almost never go. His name is Chase Fourier."

"I know Chase. He's over on 2nd and F Street."

"Oh, is that where? I always thought he was in the Army Reserve on Third, a block below Court and Palm."

"No, he's always been in the one location. Would you mind if I talk to him about this situation?"

"Not at all. I hope you get to the bottom of this. I'd hate to think this trouble is caused by someone my wife might have brought in."

"Does your wife have household help?"

"Not any more. She did for a long time when she had a hip replacement. It was hard for her to get around, I hired in a maid to help with meal preparation, a little house cleaning, some physical therapy."

"How did you find this maid?"

"I went to the college bulletin at the nursing college. I interviewed a handful of good candidates but I chose the girl — Peggy or Pilar, I've forgotten her name — because she was very soft in her manner. The others were fussy, or bossy."

"Might you have payroll stubs with her name?"

"I paid her in cash. The college covered them for insurance."

"How were things left when you stopped using her?"

"Friendly enough. She knew it was for a short time until my wife recovered."

Chase Fourier was located in the gray AT&T building with the white cameos. His office on the third floor was a small two rooms, the first a waiting area with two dark blue couches and a reading rack, and the second room was his office. It had two nice windows with light gray awnings overlooking the corner buildings. His desk was parked in the middle of the room and had two friendly chairs in front of it. Bookshelves decked one wall and a large painting of ducks in flight over marshes took up the long wall. Beside it was a door leading directly into the hall. About ten framed disciplinary certificates on the far wall said he knew his business and had been at it for a long time.

"Been awhile, Jake. How's it going?"

"Can't complain. I just saw one of yours, Dr. Childress."

"Yup. I've been on him since the trial. We came across one too many coincidences when we finally apprehended the weapon."

"A client of mine received a hate call which alleged the crime was not researched as well as it could have or should have been and that there was an officer who was bought off and was still at large."

"Any idea where the call originated?"

"At the Childress residence."

"Oh, I don't think he's the one we want. It's his wife's son."

"What was solved?"

"Every last thing. Who drove the getaway car, who did the crime, who was lookout, who picked up the discarded weapon off the pavement. The shooting itself was done by a Dave Ambez. His girlfriend drove the car and a mutual friend watched for the lookout. The man with the cup of coffee who was lookout was a personal friend of the Wadd family, man by the name of Gaudy. The woman who testified was Gaudy's wife Dotty's youngest cousin and she was Ambez's ex wife. The man who built the rifle for the job, a Mathew Borroughs, worked for Brinks which was located next to the Orange Show concession. His family made old style Brinks trucks for Meijian who at that time used them for all his stores. Prior to then no one used a Brinks. The two men who drove off in a Brinks truck out of the area forcing the company to change its model were Wadd's cousin and an employee. The truck was found in an orange grove where Highlands now is. The clincher was when a tip told us that Gaudy, the lookout man, bought off a San Bernardino police officer. The weapon was found unbeknownst to him on his property. That's what got me assigned."

"Who put it there?"

"No idea. It was found in a home in Del Rosa in one of Jim Hollan's houses."

"They're nice homes."

"Yes, all stone, white washed brick or brown, conservative, far back off a lawn. The cop lived with his wife and her mother. He was a nice guy, but the discovery of the gun about did him in."

"What do you have on Mable Childress' son?"

"We found his print on the item where the gun was found."

"What was the item?"

"A shoebox."

"Perhaps he just handled it." Jake surmised.

"It was a child's, not a woman's as was originally thought."

"What was the size?"

"71/2 E, quite large. Could've been a boy's sandal."

"Odd way to keep a gun part."

"Very odd, I agree, but there you have it. It's public record."

"Was anything made of it at the trial?"

"To my recollection, it was a cop's carrying case to bring evidence from the locker to the trial."

"Who was the cop?"

"Aw," Chase said, relaxing in his chair, "I can't say, that piece of the case is still being litigated. Like I said, the cop didn't know the gun pipe was even inside his home. Someone did it to smear him."

"Are you free to talk about the items that didn't quite hang together?"

"Sure. There was as you know the sensational item that brought the trial to an end, the gun part in the kid's shoebox, allegedly taken as a discard off the sidewalk where the shooting occurred, a similar size shoebox was filled with baseball cards and given to a boy who resembled Hariff around the time the cop's case went to trial, there was the Brinks found in orange grove that was stripped down, a thumb print on a heart frame — and a matching background on a computer and some mention of a horse transport that allegedly had lads looking for certain driver through back windows at night on the highways."

Jake jotted down the information on a hand sized spiral notepad. "Sort of a hodge podge. The orange grove, where was it?"

"Up near Highlands."

"You think the drivers were making a reference to the Orange Speedway?"

"We racked over every last item for significance. Did the robbers of the Brinks armored car leave it in an orange grove because there was some connection to orange? Why the frame-up with the thumbprint? Why the size shoebox? We brought in a psychologist. She gave us some ideas, that it suggested in a town with a boxcar stadium that 71/2 was a boxcar, E probably went with the address for E Street, 1/2 probably went with something also; but none of it panned out so anyone could make sense of it in the long run."

Jake said, "Someone must have a reason for stirring things up now."

"Could be someone's about to be paroled."

"Thirty-four years is a long time."

Chase replied, gathering papers and sticking them inside a drawer."Unless this caller of yours is working an angle."

Jake heard someone enter the waiting room. "You have company."

Chase motioned with his head that Jake should leave by the far door to avoid being seen.

"Thanks for the information. I'll stay in touch."

There were three canyons in the original Belvatown, two that bordered the highway, one off Mt. Vernon past Rialto, other side of 10, up in hills. Off 15 there was a canyon on Old Mill Road, high above the roads and suburbs, that goes past the station, the other might be Boulder Drive or Creek Drive a little past Patton across from a station where three burnt houses sit. The Ambez's lived along the skyline of Old Mill and it took forty minutes to come down by car past the Arrowhead Ranger Station to the old mill.

*Rim of the World Canyon* — picture of spa with two hundred houses, they were all stone and stucco, no bevelled glass, all leaded glass windows, before the fire that occurred in 1959.

Timeline:

1959 – *sm. white wooden houses, approx 600 sq ft, built all over state for Japanese in Calif after release from Manzanar*

1959 – *huge fire in Belvatown burned two hundred homes*

1962 – *Shoebox is left in Hariff Dept Store*

1963 – *Army hires Hollan to build houses and expand train lines in California*

1963 – *shooting death of C. Hollan*

1964 – *shooting death of JFK*

1969 – *UC Berkeley builds Greek Theatre*

1972 – *riots at Berkeley campus*

1975 – *subway crimes in New York City*

1979 – *blizzards in New York and Chicago*

1989 – *Nimitz freeway collapses*

# 4/Four

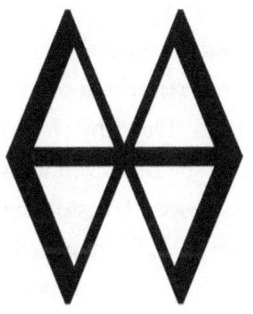

**I**N 1959 THERE WERE ALMOST NO SUBURBS. THE desert was a dry ground of silver leafed olive trees, pinion and pine trees. A movie producer came to Belvatown with a publisher to make a movie out of Ross MacDonald's book *The Doomsters*. The set was two hundred homes made of stone and stucco and leaded glass windows. During the filming a fire broke out in the canyon and levelled the place. The single eyewitness was a paraplegic man with a mental age of about eleven. He alleged that a group of men came to the house of the aunt who was raising him and left wood and then went up the canyon where they set off a fire. The arson burned for days, one of the first forest fires in the state, and burned nearly fifty acres of housing and forests.

In retrospect Dotty recalled the entire day the arson started. It was emblazoned in her memory. She was a good friend of

Seymor Stevedore who had financed the construction of a spa with two hundred houses, they were all stone and stucco, no bevelled glass, all leaded glass windows. Seymor started with the idea to build decks and porches for modern houses but a construction firm headed by Jack Hariff expanded taking in two additional partners and he joined up. Married to Ron Collins, Dorothy purchased a house on the downwind side of the suburb across from what remained of an orange grove nestled up against the mountains. Dorothy would later tell a journalist covering the arson that she observed a handful of poets at the scene early; they were descendants of scholarly works, but on the morning of the fire in 1959 that began in the canyon, she awoke to a blood reddish grey sky, almost lavender at the summit except for a ring of fire which every few minutes spewed whips of fire into the sky. She had donned tight black stretch pants to the calves, Bermuda style, with a sleeveless black top with white dots and a white scarf with pink dots tied behind her short ultra curly hair. In minutes she was in the Chevrolet and had backed it up the cement drive to the street and was slowly cruising up the canyon for a look-see at a real arson. She didn't have far to go before she saw pinion trees, mesquite — their long slender rust colored bark and cactus-like very dark green leaves — burning in small scattered fires. The fire was burning inward, up the canyon roads, here and there the roof of a wood house had caught fire and was spewing fire and spitting wood into the air. Thinking she might get caught in a fire unable to return to her car safely, she tried to turnaround. Then she saw him — a tall handsome man with dark hair and light skin wearing next to nothing except cutoffs — beating back the flames while trying to escape a fire that threatened to engulf him. She threw open her car door and shouted for him to get in but he didn't seem to hear. The brush fires were gaining momentum burning to the road. She gave up trying to draw his attention and instead coasted in reverse gear until she spied room to turn around. By the time she had reversed her car, the fire had jumped down a ravine and was spreading toward the road she was on. She floored the accelerator and sped curls standing up, headband pulled tight accentuating her dark eyes and high cheekbones. She would pass for Greek or Latin, and could get by without being carded although she was actually in her late thirties. She tore off her headband and flung it into the backseat onto the bucket seats and headed for her boyfriend's home, several blocks east. Behind her burning up the tar a tan Thunderbird came ripping out of the canyon; she pulled over to let the driver past. The driver was a youngish blonde dressed scantily in white sleeveless cotton with noticeably thin shoulders and arms, almost as if she were too young to take the wheel. Dotty watched the convertible hood disappear as the streamlined car took the winding turns at hair-spin speed. When she could no longer hear the screeching tires, she got back on the road intending to ride into the neighborhood surrounding the elementary school. Before she had any idea it was there she noticed in her rear view mirror a black Viera. Dotty swerved out of the way as the Viera stepped on the gas and floored the accelerator taking off in a cloud of smoke.

She passed her mother's house, the broad veranda made of dark grain wood with plants to the side of the dark stained door. The large foyer fronted a living room on the street side and a dining room which had an entry into a small kitchen and bedroom, then a flight of broad stairs to a second floor of three large rooms, one which was her mother's sunroom suite. Most of the homes in the canyon were two story, some with small verandas, some not as large, two bedrooms at best. Her mother would be somewhere in the canyon chopping down brush so that the ranger crew might be able to slow the arson and put it out by nightfall.

By the time she got to the bottom of the hill where the spa and tennis courts were, she saw the sheriff waiting for her. She waved to be polite even though she figured it wouldn't do much good. The sheriffs no longer patrolled for safety; they were all on quotas now to justify military spending. She wasn't a half block past him when she saw the red lights pulsing in her rear view mirror. She slowed and pulled over.

He had parked and was a uniform walking toward her — dark brown boots, a tan uniform, tan hat, night stick, holster, cuffs. He was young, maybe thirty-nine, forty, dark brown hair, crewcut. He bent to her window, carded her. Blue eyes, hard, cold as glints.

She handed him her driver's license, which he took to his vehicle to run a make. She was clean as a whistle, this time not even a public scene on her record. Despite that, she was driving like a bat out of hell.

She waited a good fifteen minutes before he returned.

"My camera anchor says he picked you up on spec in the canyon."

"I was trying to find my mother. I thought I'd find her."

"I'd like you to come downtown and give me a deposition as to what you saw up there," he said.

"I can do that, officer."

"Call someone who can drive you home."

"You arresting me?" she asked, when she finally got his intention was to temporarily detain her.

"Merely escorting you. You'll be free to leave after a look at mug shots and a rundown as to what you saw up there."

"I'd like to call the family lawyer."

"You can do that from the station."

"Fine. Shall I follow you into town?"

He'd take no chances. "I'll have your vehicle towed and you can ride in with me."

"Okay." She turned off the motor and dropped the keys into his palm. "I'm ready when you are."

She rode in the backseat behind the fence. The officer

drove at a cruising speed lights on down the canyon road to Baseline, then a good fifteen minutes past the funeral parlor, the small diamond and tennis courts, past the hospital and into the seedier parts of town. He took her to the police station at Seventh and D Streets.

The police station was a two story grey artifice with an arched entry across the street from City Hall. The officer parked in a lot at the rear and took her to a small detention cell where he booked her in. He rolled her prints on a stamp pad and one at a time marked each thumb and finger as a print, wrote her name and date of birth and wrote "Urgent" across the top. Then he assigned a female officer to go with her to a bathroom for a clean catch and a finger pelvic to make certain she had no contraband on her. After the search was over he was certain she would raise an objection.

Her family attorney was waiting in the hall. He was given a private room in which to interview her and he took her there.

"They wanted to detain you because you were seen talking to him." Jacob Reneke had bailed her aunt out more than once for shopping crimes at fashionable shoppes. It had become that her mother ordered entirely out of a catalog. "Do you know him?"

She looked at a photograph of her in the car yelling at the man who was beating back the flames. "He used to work for my mother."

"Do you know where she might be today, at this moment?"

"I thought she had gone up the canyon to help."

"Has she done that before?"

"Every year there's a fire. Her brother's son, my nephew, has a cabin on the summit of Rim of the World Road, and I think she's afraid one day he'll be trapped."

"Anything I ought to know before the police tape an interview?"

"Nothing. I'm clean."

"Best to say it now to me. If the police discover something

you haven't told me, it is going to look bad for you."

"I don't know what that would be. Honest."

"Alright, but if they ask a question you want to discuss first we can conference it before you answer."

"Yes, I understand."

"Good girl." He stepped into the hall to say they were ready. When he returned it was with two deputies, both female.

"Sgt. Detective Flander," the first said. She was medium height, dark brunette, coiffed hair, slender. Her badge said Jean Flander.

"Detective Romero," said Flander's second. Leslie Romero was a bit taller than her superior, dark red and blond hair, with the notepad. She'd be taking dictation along with her small steno machine and thick pad.

Sgt. Det. Jean Flander said she would ask the questions and instructed Dotty to give concise responsive answers. Following the interview they would give her a written narrative of the interview which she would sign. Her lawyer turned on a recorder machine.

The interview took a little over an hour. She told them the crackling sounds of what she thought was a storm brewing had awakened her. She was surprised to realize upon looking out of the window of her mother's office there was a canyon brush fire. She could see the fire and flames racing up the hill in the forested area and thought she might have to drive out of the area. She went to find her mother and unable to locate her turned on the radio for an idea as to whether the area would be evacuated.

"I think you knew your mother was not at home." Sgt. Det. Flander remarked.

"I wasn't sure."

"You didn't call her on her car phone?"

"I may have but I expected her back by morning."

"We have that her car a Cadillac was parked on Acacia."

"That's possible. She has another brother who lives there."

"And another on Montrose? Three in all?"

"Yes, near the country club. She rarely visits him. They had a falling out a few years ago."

"Over the nephew? The one with a cabin at the summit?"

"No, it would be over her property. She owns a hectare of orange groves this side of Patton from Ponderosa to Fortieth Street surrounding Wildwood Park near the old highway."

"Do you know whether your mother used to own property near the clubhouse?"

"That's not ours. We had a swath along the Santa Ana between the two counties — Riverside and San B. — all the way to the gravel hill and the San B. airport. My mother got nervous when the government decided to ship airplane carcasses by train and opted to sell."

"She must have given up an enormous section."

"The government put in Highway 30 and connected 215 to 10."

"Just my point. Did she need the money?"

The lawyer stepped in to ask for relevance. The sergeant said the fire had broken out along the old fire road on a parcel that was still owned by her mother and a corporation that her brother, the Montrose resident, sat on.

He took a few minutes to explain what she was required to answer.

Dotty replied. "My mother doesn't actually have inheritance rights to the groves. She can sell. The money goes to the corporation which is controlled by my father and he increases amounts of our holdings based on what the corporation brings in."

"Could she have been on the property last night?"

"You'd have to ask her. Generally if she has to go help turn on smoke lanterns because the pipes cracked and the water froze due to weather conditions she's there non-stop for about two to three days, but this is still technically summer. It's early November."

"Could your uncle have turned on smoke lanterns?"

"He had the place irrigated, so it's unlikely because he has a different system based on temperature and timers. He's often said smoke would put him out of business, but you'd have to ask him."

"What about the paraplegic nephew?"

"What about him?" Dotty asked.

"Did he ever light smoke lanterns?"

"Not on your life. He'd wander off, his lantern leaking oil, and probably start a fire. It'd be irresponsible giving him any responsibility."

"Why did you think you knew this man?" Sgt. Det. Flander asked her.

She gave the answer she had given earlier. The man had done gardening for her mother. He had planted hedges, dug a trench, put in sprinklers and set them on timers. He had wheelbarrowed in dirt and bark and all in all made a pretty backyard on an acre that consisted of a brick patio square, a path through a garden of hedges and bougainvillea trees and a lawn with a border of polite peonies. Her mother had found him at the clubhouse on highway 18. He seemed likeable and was looking for work. The job took him a week and a half and thereafter he returned every few months to trim trees and remove a haul.

The supervising lieutenant had put together a timeline in an obvious attempt to tie several seemingly unrelated situations.

1955 – *huge fire in Belvatown burned two hundred homes*
1960 – *shoebox is left in Hariff Dept Store*
1962 – *shooting death of C. Hollan*
1963 – *trial, discovery of food van in an orange grove*
1964 – *building of repository in San B. across from Hariff's, shooting death of JFK*
1969 – *UCLA, theft in medical building of surgery protocol manuals*

Jake Harold thanked her for her summary. Dorothy Collins had come and gone inside of five years as another long legged beauty whose failed marriage sent her home to her mother's on a day in 1959 when she would become unwittingly an eyewitness to a crime. In her mid seventies she no longer lived on that canyon road but in town off Baseline a few blocks below the rail station near Mt. Vernon, on Congress where it intersected Prospect and Lenore. It was a modest street made of two bedroom rectangle houses with a pad of grass and a flower bed, each house about nine hundred square feet, a front door that opened onto a wood floor living room with a shuttered bay window, a walk-in kitchen overlooking a depressingly small backyard. The Collins had retreated from the modernity of her orange blossom hills and aqueducts to the lower middle class lack of distinction in Rialto. Long after the trial the Collins had separated a half dozen times. Dotty had moved in with her mother, then with her uncle, moved back to husband Ron and finally inherited his house. She remarried once, become widowed and had her divorced daughter move in with her three children.

She had aged as Lt. Harold saw few women age. She had haggard lines on her face and had hardened in attitude which gave her an overall pessimism that never quite left her. While still being attractive, she had become to his way of thinking sedentary and that by itself had eaten up her enthusiasm, for whatever it had been worth in her youth. He took it upon himself to review with her what she had testified to at the Hariff trial. Most of what she remembered had to do with Laurence Childress and the nurse he hired. She worked the front office. She was a pretty brunette who had resolved to stick it out with a married man until he could become financially independent to leave his wife. She, Dotty, had covered for the two on many occasions.

"He's still married to her," he said.

"His wife? No, he eventually left and married Mable."

"I was under the impression Mable was his only partner."

"He may tell outsiders that but I'm pretty sure he left his wife for her. Maybe she wasn't a wife; maybe she was a live-in."

"She's a silvery blonde."

"I haven't seen her in years. She took care of him all during the trial. She saw to his office, his difficulty with a patient, she was very good for him."

"What difficulty would that have been, something specific?"

"He had a female patient follow him. It was quite freaky. She seemed to believe he had seen her husband over some matter and wouldn't leave her alone. Mable put a tail on the patient and that was the end of that."

"Would you know the name of the first wife?"

"Elisa Lake, something soft and feminine like that. She just wasn't interesting enough for him I guess. It was rumored he had come into practice by working for her father and he wanted out. Mable had some money in her own right and put it into the practice. Eventually he decided he had enough to go solo."

"Some men are like that."

"Apparently some physicians are. Any idea where Ms. Lake might be?"

"You could try Ontario. I heard she had a brother in the Air Force."

"At the air base?"

"Yes, that's right. I heard once he went public with his affair, she just up and left him."

"I'm surprised she didn't sue."

"I'm not. I think she wanted out and didn't want the hassle."

Elisa Lake was a thin wisp of a woman who despite dark hair had chopped it off dovetailing it. His initial impression was of a woman down on her luck but up close she was bony, discerning, with scrutinizing dark eyes and all-too-severe cheekbones. A bit of makeup might warm her up a bit but she had long ago tossed out frivolity with sentimentality. Except for her place, her boniness and height — she was short and slight — condemned her as uninteresting. Her place was on the ocean below Ventura, a bungalow with a patio in sight of a wharf and hotel, with climbing white roses on a vine, the proximity to a walking path the accoutrements of the good life.

"Laurence had affairs," she said, after Jake was comfortably situated in her tiny apartment comprised of a kitchen, living room and small sitting room, a patio and an office across the way. "I lost track; there were so many."

The ocean was staggeringly blue. It was expansive as if nothing except the sky could fill the bay window.

Jake said, to remind her, "Her name was Mable."

"Oh, she wasn't the first or last. There'll probably be others. There usually are."

"Do you know where Mable came from?"

"She filled in for one of the girls after seeing Laurence in the paper. She was much more trained than she let on. I thought she was a nurse but after a time I decided she was almost as skilled as he or I."

"You?"

"Yes, I too am a physician."

"Are you in practice?"

"Yes, I see about three patients a week."

"Does anyone assist you?"

"I have a girl come over Friday mornings if surgical op is scheduled. Otherwise I don't need a girl. What is this about, Lieutenant, certainly not the trial, or has a new development sprung up?"

"There's a concern that the gun was taken from the evidence locker."

"I doubt it. That gun was found in someone's parlor.

"Would you know how it was discovered?"

"Allegedly her three year old son was playing in his parents' closet and accidentally tipped a hatbox spilling a gun onto the floor. He picked it up, ran to his mother and fired it. She was lucky it didn't do much damage."

"He shot his mother? That could've been dangerous."

"I saw her here. The bullet grazed her arm, not much else, but it scared. I patched her up, gave her a sedative and prescription and sent her home."

"Did you report the injury to the Department of Justice?"

"In those days nothing was reported."

"Did she say she got rid of the gun?"

"She said she dropped it off with the bailiff. The department where the trial over the gun was heard."

Jake consulted his notes. Judge Mulrovey sat in for Judge Harring after Harring during an objection declared himself unable to proceed due to a conflict that arose when the gun was disputed. Mulrovey's name was pulled by the Conflicts panel out of the bin. Therxes Mulrovey was Portuguese descent, an elderly conservative pro military man off the base at Patton, with a handful of credits, the most noteworthy that he had adopted the Portland Cement Corporation for peacetime government contracts after it was released that the company manufactured deep wells that protected concrete walls against fractures due to their thickness.

# 5/Five

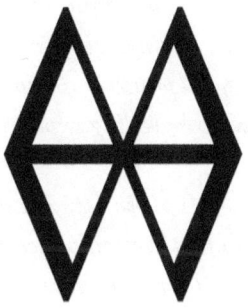

JAKE HAROLD MIGHT SAY HE HAD GOOD REASON to doubt anyone who was a liar but the proof of the poison caller came when he put out a match for any gun including a Smith and Weston 22 gauge revolver that had never been recovered after a serious or bizarre shooting. Home Office England sent him a communique that read —

## BACKGROUND TO THE CRIME

*On or about October 3, 1952 in London, England during a rehearsal of the Guard, known formally as Militia, a drunk man staggered into public square on the cathedral corner, removed a constable's revolver Colt 22 and loosely fired it upon the Militia.*

In that October Third event the round of pellet fire caused nineteen injuries predominantly to upper torso and neck. All Guard were admitted through the basilica to the foundation hospital run by Copenhagen.

On or about December 2, 1952 an argument ensued in the Trafalgar square, around the corner, during which a constable officer, a new ensign from Delhi, India, did punch in the abdomen a man who was drunk in public believed to be yelling expletives about the Queen.

On or about December 8, 1952 in London across the square from St. Mary's cathedral a funeral procession led by Lt. Al Cattle with twelve footmen did proceed through an ancient stone turnstile into the thoroughfare when a sports car, to avoid hitting a horse, sped from an auto barn into the fare killing two adults.

The man who was drunk in public was the son of the brother of King of Norway. The man who disposed of bullets in public was his personal notice (a private secretary). The eventful pistol weapon fire was initiated by a horse losing its path and steering the coach with the coffin of Lord Malle into the square.

## JURISDICTIONAL SUMMARY

A spectator taking a camera shot caught on film the lead lieutenant unclip the horse's reins and poke the animal with a pharmaceutical dart which caused the horse to run wild. Another spectator caught on film the driver of the MG swerve at the two adults on the street, hit them and without stopping keep driving. All film was entered to exhibit to a judge presiding on evidence.

There are a few things Guard has to stand ready on, the need to save lives, the need to draw on pistol fire, the presence of looters, *the knowledge that Parliament is engaged in treasonable acts and to save the Queen. In past times when the royal liege was outside the market square the inability of the liege was hampered only by failure to resist.*

## DISPOSITION REPORT
### Submitted by Surrey county

*The Court hearing the evidence brought verdicts for Lt. Allen Cattle and for the sports car driver Steven Hariff on presumption of intent to perform menace in the first degree. Each man was sentenced to Newgate for hard time of no less than 140 months to be served through isolation before being sent to China.*

*Information was heard as to reconsideration for Lt. Cattle on contingency the horse was nervous and bolted. The examiner produced evidence of lashes on the horse to indicate it bolted first. This matter requires a decision.*

*The shooter Steven Hariff works for the Eye and has returned recently from India after serving five years in brigade. Late twenties, newly married, he and his business partner, same Lt. Cattle, own substantial land holdings in the desert of Belvatown as well as throughout the state.*

*It is noted that sometime during October 1952 there was a decreed issued that not a single private guard could bear arms during off duty hours, or present to the Queen. The Guard was given notice that only the Royal Constable Chief may discuss matters of the Militia Treatise, all matters regarding duty and Service — District Lien Officer, Branch Government, Royal Command — were to be taken up at a monthly meeting with a post officer designated by PM. When the Guard was fired upon this government structure was abolished.*

*In its place were: PM, Constable Chief, Society of Merits, Eye, Rank, Militia. Thus the position of Guard was reduced to public disposure.*

*The Constable Chief took turns filing documents with Home Office, necessitating oversee of the Guard. On this occasion of injuries the Constable Chief was at home sick with influenza. There was no replacement assigned.*

*On or about September 4, 1951 there was a small matter taken up with the Queen. The matter involving the disappearance of grain ships to Leone was assigned to PM who then co-assigned to Chief of Royal Navy and Royal Eye.*

## CALENDAR REVIEW
### March 10, 1953

*The discussion in court chambers sought to resolve the mental state of the man with the weapon, who fired. His name was Steven Hariff, 1st cousin to Mike Hollan. Hariff was as part of his duties assigned to remain inside his office which was on the third floor entrance of the Chequer's Office in the Lead building that stood behind the Trafalgar Square on the North side. The presiding judge was asked whether the man might be released to a place not yet developed. The judge wanted ideally a small village where the man could go live with his family and close friends. The son later proposed his father to build this village.*

*A resident psychiatrist was brought in and it was he who stated the shooter suffered from a rare form of hardening arteries introduced by excessive alcohol consumption, while displaying no outwardly signs of intoxication. The man was turned over to the Bench prison to get sober, once sober he presented to a Service Aid to spend twenty hours a week as a mechanic. He was subsequently sent to the California desert for the remainder of his incarceration.*

*The presiding judge was John Jones Michael. He was in his seventies. He had been assigned by S. Bench.*

A notation had been added to the closed file —

*Al Cattle was seen at the 1972 San Bern arson sitting in wheelchair looking out a window of a board and care home. Cattle also is alleged to have wired the Harris store. Hariff shot and killed Victim Hollan after he shot Guard members. Buyer is believed to have been a man Hohr who served on constable detail.*

*The Hollan village was built in 1958 and consisted of an army base, two hospitals, tennis courts, a intercontinental train, shops, a small government plaza of city hall and permits, armored van, cement and games, not even a postal office. Stamps were purchased at groceries.*

*Other dates of concern are:*

1932 – *Netherlands, 125 glass buildings fall at same time*
1952 – *shooting of the Guard*
1957 – *Pakistan — 10 put in Afghani prison*

Yet, later, someone had scribbled —

*Crimes were:*

1962 – *San Bernardino arson at Rim of World Road*
1964 – *JFK death*
1972 – *San Bernardino arson in what was then Pacific Heights off Baseline; now only mobile homes*
1972 – *Patty Hearst*
1975 – *New York*
1976 – *San Bernardino, delta, Florida — all corp crime, like People's Temple, cash deposits, swindled banks,*

*fraudulent title corps, illegal deeds and deed drafts*

1977 – *New Jersey turnpike, it broke, bomber suspect went to*
*four sites in twelve hours after entering Turnpike twice*

1979 – *Chesapeake Bay, bomb*

1980 – *New York to Maryland, 42 Brinks holdups*

*Key suspect: Shoebox*
*Pistol never recovered.*

Shoebox was thought to be British origin, a physician from East Ham, member of Royal Navy and Eye, celebrated member of Society, both a gun barrel designer for Colt Manufacturers and gunner for Royal Navy. A promising lad on his way up, he was put to test to engineer an airtight coffin for use during wartime. During peacetime he utilized his skill to wire coffins for sound. Shoebox was thought to be the alias for the shooter who shot the Guard and then shot the victims at Hariff Department Store. It only seemed fitting that the person who picked the pipe piece off the ground had at one time seen it on the gun and had packaged the part in a shoebox to identify the person to whom it belonged. It was odd that these men already convicted of menace in degree would have arrived to live in a small desert community staffed by the Army and instituted by a city management consisting primarily of Turkish entrepreneurs at approximately the same year.

Jake reconsidered his problem. A better bet was to assume that the players were enlisted for the crimes which occurred after having already committed at least one similar crime somewhere else. That one crime, deadly serious for the injuries the shooting caused, nevertheless retained enough similarity to put someone's mind at ease that the target could be taken up in the same fashion without many unanticipated difficulties. The people who committed the crime and Hollan were placed in the same small jurisdiction by at least one individual, in this case by a presiding judge hearing a trial as to public menace.

The crime was a shooter was hired to kill three people in a public plaza. This was staged by having a horse run loose and a car out of control. Sentencing required moving the shooter and horseman to another country in the mountains. They were wanted for wiring a building and an arson respectively. Finally the architect and his family had to be relocated to the same locale. Law enforcement had to be minimized. Thus, the judge had to be involved as well.

The 1959 arson went without a hitch. The small community of some two hundred homes built as a stage for a movie were burned by about fifty people. The cement village in Grand Terrace was razed almost immediately along with two cement yards, one in Rialto to construct a highway and one at the gate where the MacDonald movie was filmed. The Hollan murder appeared to most to have been an inspiration by a crazy man named Hariff who with Mrs. Hollan out of the way would have control over an entire country and could conduct its business for whatever purposes he deemed necessary. The judge ordered a postponement of bail on Steven Hariff after a newspaper reported the Hariff guard seen at a resort after his alleged death. The judge ordered the body to be exhumed. Photographs of the dead guard were produced, the body having withered and extremely aged, and skeletal X-rays proven identical. Additional evidence of the guard on duty, the day of the shooting fatalities, his fingerprints and a set off the exhumed body made the question conclusive. Although Hariff was caught, sentenced and convicted, the Montgomery family was effectively torn, its holdings bought by several corporations, and its networks turned from forested stands to department stores in the clothing rack.

Everything but the weapon was produced prior to trial. The discovery of the pipe part in a shoebox concluded the findings. Although the gun was believed to be a Smith and Weston, it could now be proven conclusively to be a Colt with the same gauge. The gun was obviously still in someone's possession with an uneraseable print. If a gun could survive water or could be detected in the ground or had survived the subsequent 1972 arson, the person was possibly under an impression it could not be adequately destroyed. The problem was Jake did not know what this new find signified.

The heir to Harris Store was not likely to have seen the gun and recognized what she was looking at nor would she require a reason to be clandestine in her concerns, but a previous juror may have asked himself or herself the method by which the individual could have acquired the much sought-after item and having verified it was now concerned that justice was not comprehensively done. It would not be much trouble to check out tapes, run them in a dark room and assess jurors in their lives today for a likely candidate who could be concerned. The shooter would probably be typical in sociopathic profile: someone who would not tolerate any exposure, who would try to eliminate all sources of knowledge once aware someone outside the group of killers knew any real information and who had access to power and people without their knowing he existed.

He drove to the police library storage facility and all too quickly learned the tapes from the trials were lost. When he contacted the tape company and inquired about copies, the clerk told him it would be at least a few hours before she knew if they could be retrieved.

By noon he was on a plane to San Francisco. The day was fiercely warm with a slight overcast of haze. Below mountains stretched their green plateaus and sparkled with tiny wooded lakes. The lack of any signs of human habitation comforted him. In a modern economy with miles of suburban tract homes it was a relief to know the greenbelt still survived. He watched as the coastline unfurled becoming dotted with an occasional winery, switchback plats of vineyards matched by squares of lush greenery and periodic yellow, valleys of houses and then roads careening up and down hills. As the cities came into view he was saddened by an abrupt sense of nostalgia, that an enjoyment of serene nature was limited to many places one was unable to travel into, and that such places were being gobbled up by an ever sprawling metropolis. Short of the hour the plane was descending on ribbons of highways, cramped yards, lack of space on the ground, a lone hill in the distance, toward mega-lithic buildings. The shiny blue water pulled sharply beneath the plane like a glassy runway, waves visible, a sandbar with a low bridge, a row of towers, Tent City, its white peaks like stiff starched mastheads. A display of blue glass dolphins caught his eye as the plane soared to a drop beside a plaza of stunning blue buildings, themselves like waves.

The weather made him feel depressed, out of sorts. He carted his overnight bag and took the flights of elevators to the ramp where he hailed a taxi. As usual jetlag would set in some ten hours later and he would feel somewhat irritable, despite the absorption of his task. The driver stepped to it, dropping out of the airport, past rows of meat lockers and headed toward the exchange, then onto the highway, warehouses glittering with promise of the offices they would someday become. The dollar was in a rise, the city was coming into a European mindset, with liquid gold, desolate blue, a glance at purple, color peeking behind new elegance. They sped off Army Street past churches, old dilapidated schools, the city never having forgotten or for-given the major earthquakes it once suffered. Across town, up steep hills, down them, the city one moment on its side, the next flat as a spread, and every last lot filled to its brim with flats, to a series of warehouses with roll-top awnings. Jake paid the driver and jaunted into an office and presented himself. The man he had talked to on the phone had a screening room set up and took him there, showed him how to operate the projection computer and left him.

The tapes were a volume recorded by day. Jake slotted in the first of six tapes and watched a small monitor. The jury was voir dired over a week. He jotted down their names, addresses, personal information, notes on looks. They were an adequate cross section of residents: black, white, Asian, indian, Spanish, men, women, young, old, professional, slightly disabled, parents, divorced, never married. They were precisely what the attorneys liked: forthright, confidant, concerned. The trial defense went through its motions, brought witnesses, questioned them, the presentation was direct, confused answers were clarified, what did you see, who shot the victims, was the shooter hooded, did you see the gun, could you describe the gunfire, what was the color vehicle, did you write down a license number, who did you see pick up the discarded gun part, what happened when the armored van pulled up? The questioning got stuck on what happened with the armored van.

The van pulled up, the driver seeing what had occurred got out to help, and someone got inside and drove it away. Speedmark registered it and followed it by helicopter as it drove off a main road into the desert and meandered through mud washes, gravel pits, up ravines, and lost the helicopter in a forest. A sheriff discussed a round the clock search that took all of two days to locate the armored van. When it was identified by camera, although it had been parked in sight with its muddied rear plate clearly visible, to the team of narcotic agents whose job it was to go in after speed chase vehicles, it had left the passenger door open as though a man were inside ready to shoot anyone who approached. Jake put in the next tape which was marked "review only" and saw the actual footage of the chase, search and identification. The night aerial had almost missed it. On film the van, turned on its side, resembled a shack that was built partially in the ground with a protruding front door. A flare shot at it illuminated it for the briefest instant showing a streak of silver with its logo.

He leaned in the chair. There had to have been an indication as to why the reckless driver elected to land the armored van as he did. Few drivers would comprehend the importance in making a getaway and it was clear to Jake the driver was not going to leave until he had that idea. The van's tank was full and easily had several day's worth of mileage possible. In order to give sky camera the view it had initially of a shack in a hill, someone had to prepare the image, seek adequate mapping and then determine how to flip the vehicle. Thus, if the driver had no expertise in tracking, he had to be given obvious instruction. On the other hand, if he was searching for good terrain to take a somersault, it stood to reason he had training in flipping a vehicle possibly in midair. A stunt driver maybe, a weather man who searched by Eye to find active crimes, a trained technician who reconstructed forensics also possible.

He returned to the taped proceedings. There was no mention during the trial. A few hours later in sequestered chambers a juror asked how the driver thought to stage his truck like a mine. Was he a miner? The query raised heckles. A male juror, one of four, told her he did not understand the concern, thought the driver had run out of gas and angry, top ended his vehicle. Her reply was armored vans never ran out of gas, they were power fueled and could drive indefinitely if they had to. The argument that ensued took up nearly an hour with the man standing above her telling her that if there was a cop that had taken a bribe who did not send an ambulance to collect the injured, then despite the fact that the shooting was picked up on sheriff monitors someone had seen to it that too few sheriffs were available for adequate response. That in itself told him there were people at large who wanted the murders to occur and a good deal of money must have been used for that to occur. Another man asked for a recess then asked the guard to call the judge to ask for a bailiff search.

The bailiff search ended with admonitions to not raise

questions that were not discussed during the trial. The only statements the jury could discuss were actual text.

The remaining four hours of tapes addressed the problem of identifying the hands through which the gun moved. Dotty Collins spoke for two days on the subject of her ex-husband's threats to her. These had started over an affair she thought he had with a young female in Grand Terrace who Dotty claimed had given her ex a gun similar to the one shown in court. The gun was a pistol, a Colt, which he kept on the bottom drawer of his desk at her father's house. On at least one occasion Dotty knew the pistol was given to Hariff to test at the Rod & Gun Club and had been used to calibrate size of impact. With a piece attached the spray was broad spectrum identifying tiny shards on a target. Once Steven had left the device on the glass coffee table when he had his son for a visit and the boy had picked it up and ran around capably holding it when Dotty walked into the house to take him home. The visitation judge, assured it was unloaded, modified Steven's visits to occur with another responsible adult. Dotty brought a witness to testify that Steven threatened her in front of the child but the judge would not be persuaded.

Jake asked the clerk for a copy of the transcript concerning the armored van as well as all trial closed chambers discussions with the steno. The man at the desk promised to have it ready first thing in the morning. Jake left, took a cab to a hotel in North Beach and ate dinner at the hotel restaurant.

"Sgt. Harold?"

The soft female voice caught him off guard. He looked up into the face of a middle aged woman dressed in a tailored black suit with a satin blouse and string of pearls and matching earrings.

"Have we met?" He asked her.

"Susan Collins," she said. "May I?"

"Please, can I order you dinner?"

"I've eaten, but I'll have an iced tea."

"Are you Ron Collins' daughter?"

"Sister. Dotty is my sister-in-law."

"What a coincidence. How did you find me?"

"I contacted an old friend of mine, Eliza Lake, and she told me the case has been reopened." Noting his faint mistrust, she said, "To be quite truthful I called your service and they told me you were here in San Francisco."

She had had him tracked by caller whereabouts. "The City is a big place."

"Yes, well, I have a locater tracer system on my cell phone. I figured if you had reopened the case I ought to look you up."

"Would you have flown down there?"

"I'm there every other weekend to see Dotty."

"What can you tell me about a poison caller?"

"My guess is Mable Childress or her son. Mable was the blond vixen who made tracks for Steven Hariff. She had a child by him. She did everything to get Dotty out of Steven's life."

"You didn't even have to think about how to answer."

"Well, Belvatown was a small place in those days. Of three hundred homes at least a third were summer rentals for Hollywood out-of-towners. Plus Steven owned the Hariff Club at the base. Anyone who went there soon knew anyone who was new."

"Do you think the trial was fixed?"

She ordered a vodka gimlet. "I wouldn't know about that. The judge caught a cop in a lie and creamed him for it, so it's unlikely he would have permitted any hanky panky."

"What about a dissatisfied juror?"

"Probably many would have liked to see a hung jury. The jury was in session for almost a week straight before they surrendered a verdict. Frankly I don't think Wadd stood a chance after he dropped the piece out the window and that lieutenant he cavorted with wasn't much to speak of either with his business dealings. The judge didn't think much of either and made that clear. He instructed them they could only bring in a guilty or not guilty."

"Did they ask any questions?"

"I wouldn't know. Mulrovey cleared the court once."

"What did the jury say about the trial?"

"They admonished the Clerk girl for agreeing to drive the car, felt she should be placed in an institution. Cattle they found guilty of using the sky camera system to mask the crime and gave him five years prison for it. The man who ran off in the armored van received fifteen to twenty which is the maximum."

"What about the other one?"

"I don't know. He was thought to have been seen in Riverside."

"What did you think about sitting?"

"It was an interesting trial, a horrific crime, but too shocking to think people were actually capable of what they did."

"Why do you want it reopened?"

"Dotty was told something by Hariff. I wouldn't know what it was because she refused to say. But right after she said that Hariff had traded in his store for a closure. I always thought he had Harris Store wired."

"That's not a reason to have a case reopened, Susan. That's simply a concern for the past. Are you concerned justice wasn't served?"

She took a deep breath. The waiter served her drink with apologies saying there was a crowd in the bar and drinks were delayed. When he had left, she picked out the olive and ate it, putting the toothpick to settle in the clear drink. "The Hariff family was shut out of their railroad, their stores were closed down, their employees faded into the desert. It's been a long time but the fact is Jack Hariff has the gun that was used and every so often takes it out to show company he invites for dinner when he's up to entertaining. He wrote a statement to the court. I am concerned he may get drunk someday and fire that thing off."

He didn't know whether to believe her. She made him nervous for her as though could she become inebriated sufficiently she could talk a tall tale herself. "Jack is a brother?"

"Yes, the middle one. He said he wanted to take Steven apart after Steven left the weapon with muzzle and pipe for his son to find."

"Did Jack go along with the plan to unload the various investments?"

"He wanted to retain the officer's club. It had made them a huge amount of money but the probate court said no. There were legal fees to pay off in the neighborhood of two hundred thousand."

"As always the suits are tweed. That's alot of money."

"Yes, I agree. I was hoping you might tell Jack to stop."

"That's hardly my place to tell him how to entertain his guests."

She drank her drink. Her manner had become cold. "He seems to think at least one person got off scot-free and intends to correct the matter himself."

"Who is the person he suspects?"

"Mable's son. He's a dirtbag."

"Do you know anything about him that gives you that belief?"

"I've been telling you."

"I can visit him and talk to him about the gun."

That seemed to mollify her. "I would appreciate that," she said stiffly, as if saying thanks was too much to offer. She was a woman who would always go too far to learn there was no more threat to contend with.

"Is the gun a Colt?"

"Yes, it's a handsome revolver, dark brown and light tan."

"Good. Do you have a number where I can reach you?"

She wrote it on a piece of paper she tore off the menu in a flamboyant cursive. To watch her she had the erect quality of a woman actively suppressing a strong dislike who nevertheless felt she was pursuing the best course of action.

He took it and put it in his pocket. "Would you like to stay to watch me eat?"

She consulted her wristwatch. "I think I could manage that. I have nowhere to be until eleven."

"What happens at eleven?"

"I have to meet my father at the bistro. He's a longshoreman and gets off work about then."

"How nice of you." He was genuinely touched.

"I am an admirer of his. He works hard to put the chow on the table and then goes home, draws and paints some color onto his waterfront buildings."

"Is he any good?"

"I think he is. He's imaginative, likes to juxtapose intricate design with buildings, profiles of a busy street, monuments, and always adds the right dab of color on an otherwise penned in visual description of life in a big city. He began his pasttime after he left my mother, when I was in my thirties. He said he needed something to occupy his time. While he couldn't tolerate her moodiness or sloppy housekeeping anymore, he said he listened for the foghorn to clock his retirement by."

She could be a good companion for a night or two, he thought, drawn to an emotion he hadn't felt in a good long time. "In my profession none of the women I've encountered stay around for more than a few years because they want a level of materialism I cannot afford. I'm always telling myself I want someone I can sit with or someone to travel with but the fact is I like to stay at home with the radio on listening to talk shows."

"I can't stand to hear anything while I'm at home. It gets in the way of my thinking."

He laughed and she smiled. He said, "It takes a special sort of woman."

"Men are difficult to adjust to change."

"But not your father?"

"I grew up without him. I'm making up for lost time."

A permanent companion without the mess a relationship makes.

She caught the waiter's eye and signalled for another drink. "I know what you're thinking, that it's safe but I don't need anyone the way I like to be around him. He's just himself, there's no judging."

"I'll tell you my real problem. It's not getting judgemental, I like to see dinner on the table when I come home, the laundry neatly folded, the floors washed, my reports typed, the toothpaste restocked, the grass mowed. If I'm going to work sixteen hours a day I don't want to find her in her bathrobe and slippers watching television."

"Would you like to meet my father? You could take the expense off on your tab."

"I'd love to meet your father. How old is he?"

"Seventy-five. Don't say it," she remarked as the waiter brought her a drink and a plate of deli compliments, "I looked up your age when I was tracking down your whereabouts. Sixty-eight isn't ancient."

"Sixty-eight is a great deal older than you. You're a kid. Fifty-five is thirteen years younger."

"My cutoff is eleven years."

He did the arithmetic. She was fifty-seven. "Your dad was fresh out of high school when he had you."

She shrugged. "My mother was ten years older than he was."

He pushed his plate aside. "Yes, I'd be pleased to escort you to visit your father."

"Good. I'm sure he can tell you about Jack."

"Does he know him?"

"Knew him. Saw him as he really was, setting up smudge lanterns in the night like a hood with an Aladdin's lamp,

unhitching the train in southern Florida, taking the compartment off track and rolling it into the water."

"Why did he do that?"

"No idea. He believed it was a good way to increase his
line. Compartments stood halfway in the water as though the
coast had sunk." She looked at her watch. "It's time, we should
go."

At midnight he crawled into bed, a bit miffed she had successfully put him off. He had placed her hand on his leg after
her father, somewhat derailed by a beer, had gone to retrieve a
handwritten notebook, all about Hariff he claimed, and kissed
her long and hard in the kitchen of the two bedroom condo. He
asked her to return to his motel but she said she couldn't, that
her father wouldn't accept her being gone and when he said he
would have her back in a few hours, she turned him down flat.
When her father offered Jake the sofa bed in the living room,
Jake said he had to awaken at seven to leave for his errand and
the airport. He walked the distance along the pier rethinking
whether he had been too pushy.

"I thought you liked me," he had said.

"I like you alot, Jake, but the night hours belong to my
father."

"He'll handle it, he's a grown man."

"He won't say so because he won't offend, but he will feel
displaced. I can't do that to him. It's his house."

"Would you drive down to see me?"

"I could. We could talk a while by E-mail."

"I'd like that. I'd like it if you could come around with me
while I'm investigating."

"You wouldn't like me there. This is a sticky series of situations. But I'd be alright with a motel overnight once a week
for a while."

Her father had returned. He stood like a hunk of relationship wondering when was the right moment to interrupt and then to overcome his self-consciousness rushed in and thrust his papers in Jake's hands. "He was a real fucker, Jack. Never had any notion if you could trust him. One minute he was all peaches and cream, the minute your back was turned he'd stick a knife in your back and never hesitate."

"I'm sorry he was such an asshole, sir."

"Oh that's alright, I didn't let my feelings show. But you had to know that about him first, if you didn't you'd think he was in your favor when he didn't intend to be."

"I appreciate your warning. I honestly have to be going. Please don't take it as selfish if I can't take you both to breakfast in the morning."

He didn't answer right away probably because he didn't know how to articulate whatever he was feeling. Then he said, "Susan is cool, she won't turn on the dime, but give her a call, we all like a break now and again."

"Oh dad," she said, and kissed him as if it occurred she could be unfaithful. "You don't need a break. What would I do without you?"

The reassurance was unnecessary, said out of an unspoken assumption that he needed something he could never ask for to shelter him against the past. Yet Jake wondered whether she was emotionally free to fit another man in any different capacity into her life. When he left he was questioning his own motives. When he reached his room, he decided her father's divorce had been hurtful in a fashion without his having been able to acknowledge it. His experience of love was tears, trashing, a method of accommodation, a mixture of social institution and brattiness intended for male domination, in actuality the flutter of cocaine and drawing him into what he thought was a soft tender place. Yet his first wife was cool, she liked an uninvolved dispassionate encounter permitting her to fall for him as she read Sarte, she tended to the house, garden and always laid fresh herbs and a stone on the table, his second wife while tolerant of his long absences accepted his immature contemplations jotted down before he could see into them, she persisted at confrontation long after the emotion had been integrated, a nuisance he thought that he should be reminded as to his shortcomings, even after his wife left him before his big investigation she was bored.

He was pushy, he decided, after taking a glance at the first sentence and knowing he had read more of the other man's life than he wanted to know.

"I am in full knowledge of a man's death."

Jake closed the notebook. Susan was correct, she knew what she was looking at. She was seeing the stone beneath the mattress. The bed was lonely, a desolate uncontented place to lose the burdens of a lifetime.

He woke up to sunlight streaming in like golden milk. A breeze wafted the green chiffon, he thought he was slow to come to alertness, a shave of cool lather with his horsehair brush, a tepid bath, a long hour on the patio with a cup of coffee and fried kipper and the first edition of the day were as good a way to start the day — yet he elected to sit in bed to read Susan's father's papers. I am in full knowledge of a man's death. If for the fact I know the man who owns the brandished weapon I should have left his house sooner once I had learned where he was going. I will say the gun shows only when the October orange season has terminated. He makes a usual thoroughly brash exhibit of placing the revolver at the edge of his large desk. It is a two colored brown and tan gun given to him by his cousin, a constable who runs the largest shoebox concession in Liverpool. On this particular evening spoken of during the trial upon returning from a business convention he dropped in on his cousin with the gun in his possession.

*Shoebox — 7 E men's*
*Person who lines inside of coffin with satin holding it in place by*
*a wire band; good experience for wire jobs; term may be derivative*
*from small black bag containing kit to do wire jobs;*
*Rubber gloves*
*Police station 7 at E, four blocks over from Pioneer Cemetery*
*Harris Store — above Baseline on E and 15th; affiliated with Har-*
*ris House at UC Berkeley on Prayer Hill across from Chancellor's*
*house; no models for women's wear in San Bernardino*
*Baseball stadium, new 2005, 2nd at H, mustard and purple cement*
*Boxcar Orange Show stadium, Arrowhead and Huff Sts*
*Orange groves — upper NE quadrant Baseline and Waterman to*
*the Indian Res bound by 18 and Arrowhead Rd in National Forest*
*Hariff's club with oranges — Victoria at Highland Ave.*
*Van found in orange grove in what is today Highland*
*Repository lounge — go dancing — 2nd at E, up a half block from*
*corner across street from Hariff's*
*1972 fire — Foothill and Hampshire, incl Delmonica and Golden*
*Place, approx 60 houses, replaced by mobile homes*

The pomp and circumstance of orange groves far exceeded
the small amount of land that contained them. Dismal blight
rendered tenacious by damp ground with poor drainage receded
a stunted crop to gnarled trees that sank into an already leached
soil. Each successive row of trees, an aisle of leaves and blossom
flowers, crossed diagonally through a sprinkler system with
erect sheathed smoke lanterns to push the stamp of frost from
stinging the fruit. When the victory of harvest produced baskets
that lined the road in healthy supply the hour of supplication
cornered as many vans as would fit.

The focus taken out of context bewildered Jake. He had
often perceived a world around him that he couldn't palpate, one
with high social walls populated by people who were incapable
of sincere affection, who had long ago lost their lives as though

a missile shot high into the sky out of reach were the social contradiction of the day, a group who despite promising associations nevertheless lived according to some historic ghost town in which the buildings dilapidated with weathered floorboards comprised a best western set not designed for modern living, a habitat landscape, a cornerstone with a saloon, restaurant open for two hours, a post office, a fire house with a skeleton chassis. The river with rapids, a lone winding back country road, trees inhabiting an entire mountain of pine, oak, silver mahogany, maple, orchards with mule hoofs further down the main highway, ranch houses with verandas abandoned until summer, a sort of cosmopolitan jungle with young pretty college students and dark men from somewhere else looking to learn about life, something not yet endeavored on, a shining light at the top of an avenue looking upon a trusting society whose faith in humanity might not ever restore. The lonesome and the lonely made into criminals by acts of self dedicated employment were at best a pardon for the huddled masses that the criminally insane trampled over every day. The true criminal was awaiting his or her sentence, that savage individual could not comprehend what lay in store as a government bereft of funding left back doors open to any pharmacist who wanted a small taste at an unholy act, the psychotic mind unprepared for its own dangerous befuddlement could no more grasp at inner sanctum dictates than could a good contentious farmer who was about to get taken for his presumed large billfold, the gun question lay somewhere at the bottom of this morass, a hardbitten syndrome waiting for adjudication as to the gun part presumed still in its evidence locker, already newly assigned to any cop or leatherman who could bring the case to an unerroneous verdict, whatever minds dictated the crime were in all probability residing on cases far more complex and without the soft tissue remains of the trench, looking toward the landscape that pit this criminal mind against the whole of society like a shallow tunnel into a mountain would offer no repose until the sunlight in its shadows swept over the vast panorama and captured for a few seconds that raw despicable horrifying act that had originally produced the first act of hatred on an unsuspecting paraplegic man, driven from an also vast ocean stored high along its coasts of crates and containers that would go nowhere, a star spangled banner tribute to a new chord for domestication wherein masters and lords ruled what was once the stamp of declaration for trade to new ports no longer in the Indian Ocean but now sat sparkling abroad in the Americas, he considered himself apart from the emotions of chorus-inclined depravities although no less sheltered than the common man, only able to render a summary and conclusions when the hallmarks of the case rested on the cutting table, the thorn stems long ago separate from its bloom, a knife still sunk into the tenacity of the root, a clavicle of bone spread beneath a sparse thin ray of light in the dead of night, someone else's notation like an errant erstwhile commentary as to the progress and attention the case had already consumed, a clearly discernible piece of rock adhering to the lapel that told the Coroner the earth the body had lain on as the shot disposed of the man and left warm blood to congeal in what would become stonily commented upon as a blunt instrument of base depravity. Thus the case even before it was ready to be referred to the district attorney for disposition would take neatly into effect everything but the killer's face. That would become the task of some illusive camera stepping out of the bouquet of a garden translating acts into description, then sealing the plastic as it were and as quickly retranslating the lines of the human landscape back into a semblance of hologramatic images for discernment by a blue print specialist. The gun never recovered obviously had a problem as to how to dispose of itself, a Militia registered weapon, designated by the chief constable, rifled down in its barrel like a self styled shot off rifle, its inner instrumentation hammered for a precise target blunder, able to be uncovered despite depth or packaging, its steel a Prussian component with the initials of each deputy to whom assigned engraved in raised letters, the bullets usually dummy wad yet often flimsy metal designed to plug on contact emission. Whomever possessed the weapon would definitely get tracked to year and month by date of registered delinquency, firing the revolver placed the path of the bullet on its own trajectory of photo file sheets necessary to convince any court of the find. Had it been placed into poured limestone it could still be removed as though from a cast of gauze. This weapon type was created specifically for the English. Instances of abrogated conduct, stymied discovery of evidence moved, failure to present your gun were reasons for having a gun permanently removed prior to dismissal. Thus, the original deputy to be assigned the gun had reason to lose it. Probably he had set his holster and gun down and someone swiped it leaving him the Colt which was essentially for show and could only be used for a procession and not for duty.

No one who ever knew anything was willing to come forward. Tracing a call was one thing, proving Mable Childress or her son as a gun for hire was quite another. He had already talked to Dr. Childress and learned nothing, he suspected that Eliza Lake practiced out of an apartment complex to protect her patients. Although there were plenty of illegal events that had occurred, none offered up any suggestion as to why Mable would have a Guard weapon nor who she would want it used for. Only Dotty's sister had any rationale to suggest, her belief was that the Childress couple along with Steven Hariff were serious thugs whose anonymity depended upon getting rid of people they tried to hire for building demolitions who refused. Childress was a loner who presumably acted on behalf of his mother, at least one witness stated that she had seen the duo ransack someone's life. Mable was in her early seventies, her son allegedly in his early sixties, Mable's husband in his late seventies. Problems were certain to surface when a son was not even twenty years younger than his stepfather. Mable described a closely intimate relationship with her son, her protectiveness defended his midnight lurkings against anyone's criticism of his shocking behaviors, that left surveillance of him as an acceptable yet treacherous accommodation. Within the palm-lined heights of the cement jungle of Canyon Heights were thriving parent child gangsters that the society of proximity viewed as esteemed yet normal. A son who killed for pay might be the last ditch for a mother who fenced.

Mable Childress was a woman who went after a physician, he thought as he looked up her credentials. The CLETS database said she was a Susan Hariff Harris, from Palm Springs, who had married John Hariff before she eloped with Tom Harris and ran off to Vegas to start a nightclub. Tom Harris, his disposition as a bounty principal, came under query when he hired her then young son to manage surveillance and he left his office to scout out a brawl and forgot to close his vault. When he returned sometime around midnight he discovered missing certificates of deposit earmarked for delivery by train, the Lugar he used to lay his hands on weapons in the suites of his guests was on his leg in view, the small screw job in his vault now missing from its leather stitched pouch, a photo of a reddish brown haired man in his late forties also flown the coop. It was too coincidental that the small weapon had been seen in Childress's hand as he made the rounds at closing after a weekend show, to Jake it was all too convenient, a setup designed to bring a gun to a hitman whose collections of living were earned by the deep blue glint of a barrel, the only camera to witness the mark hidden inside the plaster of dry wall behind a mirror across the room, a roll of film on deposit in a small locked box outside the dried-up window to the bank in the parking lot of the casino. Tom Harris as it turned out resided on Seventh near the city hall, a camera profile smack dab on the inner room of the district attorney's strobe light which after the office was closed at five displayed flecks of rainbow on the ceiling and walls.

"I'm here to learn about your stepson," Jake said, and eyed the room. It possessed all the accoutrements of a young ambitious attorney who because he handled civic law would never hit his stride tending to corporate defense. The dollars were fixed on walnut wood doors and base trim, a soft pink pastel wallpaper, ebony furniture, rattan chairs with flowered cushions, a cherry wood hatrack and black framed credentials behind him. He had gone to Golden Gate College of Law, deserved honors, Chief Commissioner for the State, finally a post as District Attorney for the city's murder trials. All in all whether photographed with the president or with local counsel in front of a diner's club, he was one of three DA's who could wipe his shoes on white trimmed carpet in Surf City at any number of prominent law conferences held for the State Bar. "I have him on spec as a suspect."

"Would this be a serious crime?"

"Yes. Did you ever have occasion to open a file on him?"

Tom seemed slightly ruffled. "This office has received numerous referrals on Alexander, the first when he was in his late teens. He had a security job at my grandfather's new palatial store, he couldn't keep his eyes off the merchandise."

"Is that meant to be understood as diamonds?"

"Nope, it was the vault. He robbed new stuff when it came in and claimed the company shipped low."

"What did he do with the goods he stole?"

"Gave them away."

"Did he know any clerks at your store?"

"Yes, he dated one Francesca and one Susan. Susan was a Collins. She thought she'd marry him in fact until the trial."

"Do you think it might be plausible that his mother married your father in order to fence her son for the wire job?"

"He's no shoebox, not a deputy nor one with a registered Guard weapon."

"But he could've used the gun or passed it along."

"I don't see how. The gun on his person for a long time was thought to be standard regimen. He tossed it after a botch-up he did when he ran after a young woman and beat her up. He discarded the gun in the garden."

"What about his weapon for his job?"

"It should be in his locker still since the store closed."

"Did he ever have to assign weapons to other guards?"

"It wasn't my file. I didn't prosecute because the gun originally was held by my family. I never saw it, even when it was taken as evidence."

"Well, it must have been an embarrassment that it was a Harris."

"It proved mercenary. I was in my first year as a DA when it made the headlines. The gun had been used in a shooting in London at Victoria Station and it wasn't until the shooting here that any detachment thought to ask whether it could be the gun that fell off the deputy in the procession. It wasn't, because that gun slipped off at the moment the sports car driver shot wildly out his window wounding and killing two innocent bystanders. The driver used a regimen Lugar and the Guard lost a Colt."

"Two separate guns. What do you account to that fact?"

Harris shrugged, as if to postulate consequence wasn't defined by coincidence, the lives of criminals were made only by their acts, sometimes contested in courts of law. "One gun was responsible for the Hariff incident, the Lugar showed up under someone's pillow."

"Does the German gun make the rounds?"

"It appears to. It was found at Harris Store lying on the counter, part of a silencer attached with a part screwed on. It was marked into the evidence locker and a year later removed. Whoever took it out would presumably have had to enter a notation, for exhibit in such and such a trial, date, officer's initials. There was no notation so your guess is as good as mine."

"Could Steven Hariff have had an office remove it?"

"Hariff was dead by then. His brother Jack tried to have it tracked. The reality is if you were to pack in another gun's bullets into a Colt they would bust the gun wrecking it. If you put dummy wad in a Colt the wad wouldn't fire, it would get stuck. In a Lugar the dummy sprays the shot and shields the identifying features of the shooter thus making it nearly impossible for the victim to ID the shooter. My guess is the shooter wanted that effect."

"This man is a Childress. Do you have a first name?"

"Yes, John, they call him a sieve because of what he does to the liquor stores he robs. He crashes the aisles, wrings doors off the freezers, is a total terrorist; has his mother wait in the car while he robs a store."

"How did John become induced to commit these crimes of extravagance?"

"These aren't extravagant crimes, not such as what's in his file. The man has a record as long as your arm. He does anything and everything related to petty burglary. He has his mother in his car sitting in the parking lot."

"Great relationship. Could he have knocked off your grandfather's jewelry counter?"

"It's not a liquor store, is it?"

"Why only liquor stores?"

"Just his pattern. It's all he knows, same act, same stupidity. He went to church when he first got out here, we are pretty sure he did the 1959 arson but where he was we aren't actually certain, possibly at his office, there was a grisly murder that was associated with him, he became friendly with an older white woman into whose house he moved, she was then Mable Hariff, he made her his mother because they were ultra close, saw everything the same, real affinity, he then stepped up to the plate to do a burglary of a liquor store which was not family owned, he had her sit in the car as he robbed the store, and then as though that wasn't enough he told her what he had done on the way home, not only did she never leave him but remarried Childress and gave him all familial rights. A truly sick relationship. To meet them you'd think they were longtime marrieds who take late night excursions into town."

"Where do I find him?"

"At the drive-in at any A&W," he said facetiously. "He resides with her and the doctor, sometimes he is in Surf City on the beach at his summer home. It's a Greek toga affair. If you go out there, tell him I said hello."

The home was palatial, gaudy marble columns, icy blue tile, strikingly copper plated door, a one story home comprised of a side deck overlooking the Pacific ocean, white alabaster, dark slate roof, approximately six hundred square feet; inside was a small entry, the living room held a dark blue carpet with a view of a patio and pool, a dark cherry wood hall led off to two bedrooms and a bath and in the other direction were a tiny kitchen, all black Formica and windows and a dining room with gold wallpaper, white wood moulding, thin strip of white floorboards with a cherrywood dining table on which sat a stunning piece of crystal in the shape of a bird. Blue tinted shades kept the interior cool, subliminal.

"The DA says hello," Jake said to John Childress, who in stockinged feet led him into the living room to sit on satin olive green couches, in front of a cherrywood panelled fireplace with built-in television and stereo. "Your home is stunning," he added, looking with envy to sliding glass doors through both living and dining rooms onto the patio where a glass table and striped blue and white umbrella sat.

"Ever bring your mother here?" Jake asked.

"She designed it. I wouldn't live in a house she didn't pick out for me."

"You and she must be quite close."

"We have that type of relationship. I discuss everything with her, take her everywhere with me, let her help me out of those scraps. So what brings you all the way out to Surf City? It's a long drive for you."

"Yes, it is, it took me six hours to get here. I'm representing a client who would've inherited the Harris Store, were it open for business."

"Is this a Harris?"

"I'm not at liberty to say. I spoke with your mother several days ago."

"I dropped by last night. Childress was at his weekly poker game."

"Did you see your sister?"

"Half sister. She's Childress's daughter. No, she's not down from college."

"Are you a Hariff?"

"No, I'm something else. A Fersterhof. It's German."

"Where is your father today?"

"He's running a prison in California near the Channel Islands for teenager inmates. He's been doing this for almost twenty years."

"Are you and he close?"

"I wouldn't put it that way. He lives at the prison, so if I want to visit, I have to drive up."

"I'm investigating a complaint. Apparently there's a cop who didn't carefully research information that could have otherwise positively influenced the outcome of a group of court cases. "

"Do you mean the Hariff trial?"

"No, this one was about the Orange Show down at Dumas."

"Oh, the gun. I believe that was a Lugar, regimen, missing since 1959."

"That gun could not have been stolen, could it?"

"Security did a clean of all weapons because they weren't firing. His name was Collins. I know his sister Susan. She spends weekends here."

Jake perceived a lump in his throat. "Why Susan Collins?"

"She's Dotty's sister-in-law. Her father, I believe, knows a thing or two. About that gun situation."

"Do you think he knows where it is?"

John reached down and untaped an object from the inside of his desk, then without conscience he set a Colt pistol on top of the desk. It was a handsome revolver, more honorable in fashion than the heavy pug-nosed Lugar, its pencil barrel edging out past the cover like a thin possibility of threat. "That belongs to me, it's not the one that fell onto the street in London."

Jake lifted it with a pen from the blotter and sniffed it. "When was it last fired?" he asked, lying it on the massive desk noting the screw-in piece would not attach.

"A year ago. It's been fired less than five times."

"During a parade?"

"I don't like your insinuation, detective. I've shown you my gun. If you'd like you may take it with you to test for weapon fire."

"No, that won't be necessary. I wonder if you could tell me whether you own any other guns?"

"No."

"When you've robbed small convenience stores, what did you use?"

"This, I had it tucked in my sleeve."

"Why not ask your mother to do the holdups?"

"She isn't aware of what I have done."

"I was under the impression you told her and showed her the money."

"Could you please see your way out? I've heard enough."

"Did you wire the Harris Store?"

John Childress took to his feet at once. He stared in Jake's eyes as menacingly as he could manage without losing self control, he was an ugly man beneath a rough hewn exterior, a womanizer who had no thought for honest intimacy or other competent emotion. Whatever Susan saw in him escaped him.

"I'm no fucking cocksucker wire hat. I come and go as I will, I like my freedoms, you won't lay me to rest in a goddamned fucking screw, I couldn't wire to save my fucking ass soul."

"Could you fence it?" Jake queried, not caring whether the man grew irritable by the second.

"No, I couldn't," Childress responded, yelling, his clean square face reddening. Then, having to restrain his anger, he said, peering into Jake's face, "I couldn't build it either. Go ask a Cattleman. Go fucking figure!"

Jake saw his way out, peering down the plushly carpeted hall as he left, a glance at a golden Buddha in the parlor, a mirror framed by tiny lights as though a roadster sports jeep might crash through the walls at any moment. He paused, door opened, and turned around, asking in as subtle a tone as possible, "Did you ever stunt drive for a movie?"

"No, I told you I'm a self made man. My wage comes from construction. I build city buildings, I don't goddamn blow them sky high, stupid!"

Stupid was as stupid did. Childress gave no indication of being very intelligent. He was a bratty specimen of a house that was put together by a mother looking to bust free of a corset and a nice loving female, now inexplicably tied to a whipping post. How a woman like Susan with her insightful mind and innocence hooked up with a slob like Childress was bewildering, and the realization, grown in unkindness, created in him a special contempt for her needs.

A thrown set of shoes followed him out. "Go find a fucking lunatic, why don't you. His shoe doesn't fit any longer. He limps, they should have put him in a chair after that first shooting spree!"

Jake knew he ought not to return to the angry young man, but logic told him he must. He followed him inside, leaving the backless sandals on the weathering pavement. "Who could that have been?"

"Those regimen weapons were reassigned by default with no clue as to what their original numbers were, the tags stripped and replaced. Or there was a problem after the killing spree in Northcumbershire. If you don't believe me, go ask, they probably won't tell you, those filthy rich landowners, headstrong dukes and duchesses."

"So they wired Harris to pull fast money out of it."

"Not fast altogether, Susan didn't receive a cent."

"Thank you Childress, that was more suggestive than you could know." Jake closed the door behind himself and stood on the step, realizing he didn't know who the heck he had referred to and knew he couldn't ask, that was just a man letting out his particular rage.

# 6 / Six

He HAD THE CRIMES — A KILLING SPREE IN England outside London and one in Belvatown — he had a focus, the old Harris Store on D Street, with several principals, a missing weapon presumably used for murders over the years, and a dirty cop, possibly who was the subject of the poison caller whom he now thought could be Susan Collins' brother Ron. At the bottom of these unsolved crimes rested a gun, it could be a Luger, it lay either on a man's desk or inside it, it could not be disposed of without implicating half of the Guard, it was brought out of retirement to destroy one or two complainants or people who had turned down arsons and armored van robberies, and since the people who knew of its existence were guilty of heinous crimes they were not likely to come forward with information.

Jake jotted down his ideas on the random aspects of these crimes, gave himself a miserable lunch, sat at his typewriter to compile his narrative, signed it, went for a walk to the town square, made some notes as to layout of the city in 1959, came home, lit a fire and reread his notes.

## CRIME

*Young man who fences crimes —*

*Psychologically this looks like preferred relationship above all other relationship in the immediate family —*

*Background: Both have had jobs that pay out on arson — she paid out on possessions, he on estates; The Fersterhofs are from Berlin, in their sixties — Dutch; This son became a cop in Calif after serving fifteen years in the federal pen for burglaries.*

*Mother is white older woman — very pretty, some possibility in 1959 she was seen at an arson after she already collected on people's estates before their deaths — they owned jewelry from Europe, during arson mother provided technical expertise as to improvements based on her knowledge of arson, both Fersterhofs own substantial property, son attended trial to learn court process to meet girlfriend Susan Collins, mother met and remarried Childress after trial —*

*Evidence: Colt usually on John Childress, he worked for Guard in England pre-1959 for funeral processions, he placed satin inside coffin with flexible metal wire —*

*A procession was led to Avon with dappled gray horses in twos, four hitches, in front were James Williams Jr. whose family manufactured shoeboxes for coffins for Royal Navy, his brother Gaun Williams, Thom Prett who hitched horses, John McCork who made unlit lamps, David Jackson, Stratford James who manufactured sights for rifles, one no longer employed, Jon Marshall on left, Mark Johnson and Sam Kelly, and Steve Bond and John Jones. All relocated to Belvatown in mid 1960s.*

*A shouting match ensued in the street of Northcumbershire a few days hence, a drunk man discharged a weapon at the Guard killing two pedestrians, both male, watches were everywhere yet one watch went off to post office to obtain help,*

*At Harris Store on D Street the Exchequer from London left a door open, a shoebox entered and wired ceilings —*

Facts of the London crimes consisted of: the insurance company relocated to Ontario in an orange orchard, the man who discharged the weapon at the Guard was wearing an Odyssey Explorer watch, one compatible with a yacht submarine propeller nose dive, the watches gave someone an ability to find the Guard in a large crowd, the Exchequer was an Eye trained in call box, three hitches transferred to City Hall, Ontario, California. Mother and son killed bad horses. Jake decided that the Childresses were lower class animals with upper class leanings.

The oddity of the entire situation was that the men who stood trial there were sentenced to a sort of perplexing banishment in Belvatown just prior to the outset of a major arson that burned down two hundred homes allegedly for a movie. These outcasts were from a similar geographical area and were said to have participated in the same sets of crimes, were adjudicated by a small group of judges, accompanied in flight by the same bailiffs and townships being predominantly prescribed by state parks and consisted of wild, wild west saloons, post offices, fire houses, restaurants and a college or two grew on the map overnight, substituting for small cities and resort clubs. At the foothills lay the army base with its institutional buildings of a mess hall, laundry, library, training school, officer's club and quarters, a small depo, and often a small prison not to mention a market, swimming pool, golf course and truck repair. Generals left in the evening in regulation trucks to patrol the two or three neighborhoods, to check in at the train station and oversee shipping schedules. For the fifty personnel stationed there, another fifty represented public affairs at the local city halls, ran the cement factories, worked police and sheriff posts, staffed the metropolitan airports and built construction of roads and institutions as needed. From time to time as the city grew, separated its government from other cities, the army brought in architects, mayors, police chiefs, city business and gradually a junior judicial system to take the place of outmoded ideas and a least amount of commerce.

Ron Collins sat in his tiny austere library living room with a thoughtful expression on his aged mien. He was tall, a hulk of an individual thinker who had done his thinking with a cup of coffee, grey bookshelves crammed full of every philosophy book, an expensive oriental rug on the floor beneath a comfortable damask couch and old Mexican chair with walnut wood. The fireplace was long unused as were the curved Moorish doors that faced a patio of old brick and greenery.

"I came for pharmacies," he said, the accomplishments of a man who changes his career path late in life from the simplistic to the morass of genuine study of architecture and making peace with wants and social encumbrances had chosen a goal of maximum relieving stress. "I put them in rundown libraries and traded old one room libraries for school district buildings and barber shops. The least advantageous I felt ought to view historical places with a minimum of wit, an appreciation of life as we begin it, a rolling out of a shorn carpet that is unpretentious while also an enduring social grace."

"How well did you ever know John Childress?"

"Well enough. He and Hariff went on a tear after my father

and determining him to have understood the exquisite nature of evidence opted to place upon his doorstep a demand note for my sister, for her ability to weather substandard thinking."

"What did Hariff want?"

"Nothing, a way to get even for the fact the gun was registered. I suspect that as a result of the Guard incident the guns were taken in for inspection and he unknowingly received a new pistol, and that is what killed him. So someone in the crowd captured him on camera in a car and that ought to have been the end of him, except he did the crime again, did an arson and then was put out of his misery."

"What would account for that revolver — Hariff's original one — being in a certain person's possession?"

Ron looked lost as he went over the past in his mind. "Perhaps he didn't realize it was really his gun. Maybe his wife or girlfriend realized it and lent it to another person."

"Weak. That reminds me." He quoted:

> My grace in life makes serene most sorrow
> The sweetest chloe gives melancholy
> Peace restrains the pensive mind for morrow
> Simple grief denies the arrows of folly
> Had you a compass for distress for shame
> Neither avarice nor envy false blame.

"That is part of a poem taken from Jack Hariff written at his brother's capture and conviction. He didn't write it for Steve but for his ex Dotty. He always believed that she, like him, was set up by a clever mind who did not wish to become associated with the Hariff crime."

"Could be you know more than you think you are aware. A gun that makes the rounds every twenty years could be owned by a physician, for example."

"Oh, brother. Steven was insane, a completely dishonest

man far in over his head."

"Only the piece that screws on is seen. It flashes sparks. That could be someone who used to own the train into Topeka, it could be a reference to a woman Steve Hariff was personal with, someone who is seen on the street in some way."

"A Childress, Fersterhof?"

"No idea, even though she does a weird thing when she approaches the doctor after he is photographed leaving the courthouse. She marries him, brings her son along."

"Photospectrometry. Takes a physician to read the jacket. Here's this: at the range the bullet from a rifle can't be retrieved because the fly breaks up, the cartridge out of a barrel sticks to the inside only if it is dummy, otherwise a pistol bullet shoots out straight, only one pistol in the world which if the pistol is in other hands kills the owner of said pistol when in test the gun is declared deadly, thus my guess is person can give pistol only to a person who might kill for same reason owner would, gun probably cannot get used more than a few times."

"Do you have a psychosocial for anyone who fits this description?"

"The person you ought to talk to is Bryan. He can be found through the DA. My suspicion is the bullet when recovered tells you the gun it usually fires out of is not the gun that could be responsible for your crime."

"What types of guns does dummy come out of?"

"Rifles only. It would be unusual to learn a Stetson for example was tilted down and the butt substituted by any standard pistol."

Bryan was short, a red, a square face with piercing eyes, a man in a firm with a vengeance. He said, "No such dummy, no such gun. It is either a hammered down revolver or a sawed off rifle."

Jake Harold took his time with his note writing. He had to narrate an explanation that he knew very little about, except for the fact that the probable victim might be male, he could find no justification to any crime about to be committed. All he was trained to do was to track down murders; if this technically didn't qualify as a murder, he was out of luck. The notorious gun was used for effect and should not have included a female. The Hariff crime was probably intended for three men. The US Army invited an architect to build houses where residents would be dependent upon bussing or cars, Harris Store was closed about the same time, and the brother who would have inherited the train and its southern route was put to work in Burbank. Some detective marshall had called the correct number. Only the man was intended to be dead. The problem here was the shooter did not review the outcome of his first shooting spree to know what acts he was being asked to take up.

Three deaths, in a morgue, a subsequent arson, a gun. None of the suggested evidence led to any conclusion. It was the times when although he was in retirement the memory of procedures and protocols were long in practice, came readily and required pursuit. He was neither a man who drew a line at closed cases and in having done so retired the need for inquiry. Despite a semi-permanent perception of mental weariness, abrupt departures from his workplaces which consisted of the police force, some part-time moonlighting in Rialto and Del Rosa, as well as gumshoeing for the district attorney left him with a sort of unsettled dissatisfaction that could he maintain a security post for a hospital or golf club, he would view himself as more functional and inch with the society of the desert. But he had wanted out, folded up his lawn chair and quit chess, and tossed in a weekly trip to the pool and green. Relationships gave him a sense of marking time, of having to relinquish something he wasn't certain he wanted to hang onto anyway, he was forever trying on new haunts, going to the reading room at the library to talk to a librarian, attending parents without partners and finding chitchat twenty years too young.

He drove into the hills to a narrow road that led along a sheltered river, pine trees rising above crowded on hills in dark and light shades, the river, calm and soothing to look at, peered through leafy yellow leaves, the rushing water over a low dam of rocks visible to the ear before the sight came into view, the dark mossy river was a still reflection of the hills of pine at the edge, the quiet was inundated by the barest perception of a single yellow maple leaf moving slowly downstream. He parked at the end of a small lot, took his kayak out of the van and carried it past trenched oak trees to the stream, as he climbed into the girdle of the cockpit and snapped the nylon cloth about his hips, he slid into the cool water and grabbed his oar moving into the four foot deep current. At his eye level silver roots of withered trees and leafy ferns crowded over damp dirt giving him at once a peaceful serenity, as if his pressures had been left miles away, discarded for the moment, his chilled skin and alertness a long desired change. He recalled his first trip to the wilderness at age seven trampling across dried bay leaves, the crunchy matt beneath his feet, herblike release of winter in the air. His father strode up ahead keeping a healthy distance between them, he running to catch up to him, the water in the stream less than a foot high. The stream permitted him to forget his search, while containing his thoughts of Susan and her father, the knowledge that Childress needed Susan left him cold, the fact that Ron knew nothing of his sister's liaison suggested he knew little about her, not in keeping with what he thought their relationship ought to be, what he thought it must be. As he paddled downstream the mountain grew taller, the sun went behind the crest and darkness emerged momentarily from a verdant tress. He could see he would run into Susan and she would be happy to see him, but there could be a question as to whether she might spend an evening at Childress's comfortable home, leaving him in that yearning state wanting her close yet not having her. The wet splash of inviting coolness dampened his face with sudden desire, moving him to reverie, her soft swell of her breasts making him throb with need, the darkness of the underbrush receding into a stark pronouncement and as quickly trees, silver, green, tan and pink seemed to make him aware of his self conscious mood and of his intense desire, that he could need to join to her yet she could remain detached, causing him to be bewildered by her essential nature. Desire was unpredictable, he thought he could be destined for longing and for remaining solitary, wishing for neither, giving in to hope where hope was an ideal, a far off brush with love. He wished he were more assertive around women, more capably seductive, his yearning a begging insistence that could bind her to him as love had bound Rina his wife to him. I love you, Jake, don't leave me, I'm begging you, be sweet, be sweet, oooh yes, yes, faster, hurry Jake, deeper, oooh sweet, sweet Jake, love me, oooh yes, I'm begging you, the sound of her cries soft in his ear. He had loved Rina with everything he could give up, had wanted her, fumbled with her blouses, let her as close as he could to possess her, yet he left her for his cases. Susan could be different, self-willed, she could surrender if she only would. The current took his kayak and he obliged without resistance finding in himself no residual restraint or fear after not having river rafted in almost a year. The body wore an armor, partly to protect itself against stress, partly to acknowledge grief that came about because of unrelenting pressure, the goriness of death its own devouring cynicism. He had retracted and the job had won and when he finally threw everything on his desk into a box and said goodbye to the work, he hoped he was free, hoped his life would remake him into the man of leisure he envied in older associates. But retirement had been unkind, he had remained single in a divorced loneliness, without a close friend to go places, and he had gotten used to being lonely, and gradually his body quit his urgencies.

His return up river was arduous, a systematic rhythm of deep strokes of the oar pushing against a fast-moving current. He pressed his legs against the sides of the kayak and oared once on each side, increasing the strokes as the kayak slid through the resistant surface, the trees having lost their stark intricacy, the stream green and turbid, no longer clear or revealing. The froth on the rocks threatened to turn the kayak around, he entered deep water where sand gradually became visible and the reflection of trees kept to a maximum of two feet. When at last he spied the sand below the trail he steered across the eddy and grounded the bottom of the boat.

He got Susan on the first ring.

"Will you be coming down soon?"

"Yes, this week, I've some business to attend to."

"Where will you stay?"

"With Ron most probably. Did you want to go to dinner?"

"We could do that. There's a good Chinese restaurant in Del Rosa."

"I'd be up for that. I have to be free between one and four on Saturday however."

"I went to see Childress," he said. "He said he knew you."

"Yes, we used to live together," she replied dully. "That's how I know about him."

"Is that where you saw his gun?"

"He doesn't own one. His mother has use of one although I don't think she owns it."

"Whose person was it on?"

"Hers. They used to leave together to run an errand but she's the one who kept it with her, I'm pretty certain."

"Thanks. I'll see you in a few."

"I'm looking forward to seeing you."

The mother son duo was a complication. If it were the son out on a lark, why did he require his mother, if he could take her car. On the other side of the argument, why would she consent to drive him if she knew what he was doing. Jake thought perhaps the gun was hers and he took it from her for protection inside the stores. If he didn't rob them what was he there to do — help himself to the books and caught in the act throw the gun on the counter. Then the gun was in someone else's hands. A report made to the cops bagged the revolver into the evidence locker, tagged by an admitting officer, transferred downtown for prints and identification including mug shots, the brass probably knew the various visiting weapons by detail. Once procedurally processed each gun was sent for tests, any conclusive summary was entered in with the respective case, once the trial began the evidence was brought only in as photographs. Doubtful any weapon could be amended on the face for exhibit. The laws were strict for actual evidence brought into a courtroom, all a store clerk had to say was that the assailant produced a gun, if the store camera failed to show a gun that was the end of it, the burden of proof was on the store owner to prove their store was held up. If a conclusive testimony was needed the lock up sergeant could state under oath the weapon by reference number was the weapon brought in on that date. The most logical deduction he could make was that the gun went with a piece off a rifle and was used to identify a member of the guard. By now regimen guns would have been reassigned for use and display.

He drove to Roberta Harris' home below Baseline. The garden grass was damp, the rhododendron was in partial white bloom, the walk-up was recently clipped, the door was ajar. He entered removing his sun glasses and seeing her in capris and a tight blouse with a half apron he surprised her with a hand over her eyes. She wheeled around to face him and smiled cordially.

"Won't you have a seat?" She gestured for him to sit in the

breakfast nook. The floor was Spanish tiled with yellow tile countertops and wall below the cabinets.

"I'd like to know who your grandmother brought in to manage the store?"

"A man named Thomas Franklin. He was the brother of an officer who worked for Ontario Police who had taken a telephone call from Mrs. Steven Hariff."

"Would you know whether Franklin passed clearances?"

"I believe so because he was bonded. He came through a detective agency."

"Do you remember the agency name?"

"It wasn't in the desert, possibly in Los Angeles. Might have been Ventura Investigators. They bonded their detectives after giving them the lie detector and running police and FBI checks as well as a medical exam."

"What would his gun have been?"

"I wouldn't know, standard pistol probably."

"Did your grandmother have a gun in the vault?"

"I wouldn't know."

"Who would have that information?"

"Perhaps the State. They approved the building for a use permit."

"When the building was closed down, was anything left inside?"

"Initially the diamond drawers, the bankroll and clothing items."

"You say initially. What happened?"

"The first wire was cut, the store was vacated of contents. Another wire was discovered causing the store to close. It has remained closed."

"Were you the first wife of Steven Hariff?"

"Not me. That was Mable Retrange. She remarried a physician named Childress."

"I thought she married Harris."

"For a brief time. She had it annulled to marry Childress."

"What kind of person is Mable?"

Roberta lit a cigarette and took off the apron stretching to emphasize the length of her body, to give him an appreciation of her as though she had guided his hands over her chest and abdomen and feeling him against her had demanded him, herself carefully surrendering to him, making him at first miserably aware of her, then getting him to give in, to gush, to come at her in a powerful wakening of sensation, to reveal to her who he was in his powerful, fierce discovery of himself, coming as close emotionally as he dared and then her breaking away, as though the conversation demanded some other perception, some other sequel.

Mable was a feline woman, selfish, not at all understated, governed by her needs, by her comfort and her ability to be managed or looked after. Not many men afforded the Mable Retranges of the world; not many men wanted to possess this type of female. She was clever, with a knowing keenness, someone who spied a sensitive man before he had learned himself of his own sensitivity, yet she could not be tamed, there was a raw aliveness to her perhaps underscored by her running around with a gun and her teenage son requiring her to escort him in that vehicle that seedy influences knew by reputation. Indeed who would know a woman like her, in a way vulgar in her size, her breasts cumbersome and stunning, her bossy attitude placing her husband in a servile manner, or one seeing them supposed they ought to have a relationship a bit skewed, desperate, mildly dissatisfied. Roberta thought it was Childress himself who did not place enough restrictions on the interaction and thus Mable had a dominance few people outside the relationship thought to understand. Mable may have come a long way up, moved out of rawhide and low cut bosomy blouses into jeans and string shirts, yet her reality was she stayed at home, minding the fireplace until her husband got home, then she stepped out for an evening jaunt, perhaps to the liquor store, or a swim at the club, or a game of tennis, or some local entertainment.

He kissed her not so much because she had remained talking to him standing close enough to cause him to be aware of her presence, more because he had sensed a contradiction in her the entire evening. The kiss was impersonal, a bit distracted, focussed on those worries which with certainty would consume her after he was gone.

He wished he could strike them down for the tears at his personality they gave him, trying to cause him to feel less than he was, to reshape him into a harassed man, seen as average, denied, frustrated by all the unkindness they tossed at him, the moment he knew he was weary he went to her, opened himself up to her, asked for forgiveness as though she possessed a great talent for restoring a man to his manliness although in truth she was more giving of herself than the other women and gave of herself without burdening him to stifled inability. Susan was a dream, not altogether real but Roberta was fashionable, elegant, tall, a vessel of class, a special affordability of grace, perfection, youth and knowledge. He would rather have a portion of her as she opened to him, took him in, yet as he gave in to her he was aware she held back some small thing, some privacy, that told him she would not give in completely until he had placed himself entirely in her domain. For after all, what was love really but a complete capability to trust and to take in; her breath, appearing to hold back when she was softly releasing herself to him was seduction, he doubted Susan would allow it. Whatever eventuality he held for her and the man whose house he had seen, he scarcely thought the matter was over between them, there was too much tension between their words for a relationship that was truly over, truly disposed of by way of living and many realizations, he thought the woman to draw him close was

Roberta and he could see the soft underpinings of tender need and a willingness to be changed to the creativity he gave her. It was a slow moving, a barely perceptible or conscious breath, a need to be spoken to without also being taken, Jake thought he could go a long way before entrapment seemed provincial.

Life was a bouquet, richly gratifying as many directions of studies which had he time he could see fulfillment in many guises. As a youth his mother urged music, the arts, library; his father promoted his need to know — become an investigator, work for the district attorney, work thirty years. He maintained a steadfast core, varied little, in keeping with the job borrrowing on the teamwork of a public officer in full swing. Yet he hungered for a larger definition of self — to learn what constituted motivation. It occurred to him that the goals one sets was answered by a reality outside one's experience, by a need for satisfactory and that while he should be satisfied he wasn't, he had reached a state of ambivalence no longer defined by age, as much as he had reached a sense that living was temporal, its language defined by a yearning idealism, a contemplative confidence, his close friends had raised children who had stepped into the livelihoods he had absented, he asked himself whether life might seem less transient had he now adult offspring, the rewards of his career made for an emotional distance that even time to reflect did not take into account, it was a breach of disclosure of having shored up a pension, which saved him, without that small pittance the mistakes of losing a home to dedication which had seemed great, matched by an erroneous fate of not having enough despite being drafted into a false consumerism, petty arguments, still pettier arrogance, replaced by consummate greed arrived to entrance his futility, humanity should correspond to sympathy, a resonance with a deepening chord, a universal hope impassioned of a bracing familiarity.

# 7 / Seven

SUSAN STEPPED INTO HIS FOUR ROOM ITALIAN-Austrian flat eyeing the walnut floors, the pink walls and stunning molding trim on the ceilings and french doors, three running the length of living and dining rooms overlooking a slate patio, swatch of grass and restive stone fountain of trickling waters and a small pond of lilies. These were a gracious living room made up of an oriental floral love seat and wood tables with lamps, a small cubicle of a walk-in kitchen with malachite green counters, glass opaque cabinets, and black Formica floor, a dining room with dark cherrywood dining table, a modest bedroom crammed with large bed covered by satin, a trousseau, a bureau with vanity and easy chair, and the last room, a tiny six by four library with not a single wall to spare of filled walnut bookshelves, wild red ceiling and fan with soft lights. She appeared to Jake glistening in European propriety, a classic beauty, her bronze brunette hair in a gold clip, thoughtful, a green crepe blouse and a grey green tweed knee-length ditty, her matching jacket and dark green lace scarf removed, and took a book off the shelf and leafed through it.

"How's your dad?" he asked her.

"Average. He has his job, his photography keeps him absorbed. An aide is with him in my absence."

"Does he know about Childress?"

"It doesn't concern him, I don't stay long."

"I'm surprised you're there at all, after that chilling description you gave."

"It's not as simple as you make out. With me he's perfectly under control."

He cleared the table of his Spode china, the dumpling soup had gone over well, the herring paste melted on the rye crackers, Susan had loved the long stem glasses half filled with frosted champagne, the small fudge drops and gold rimmed bowls with a scoop of coffee ice cream. He took her in his arms, felt her lips on his neck, her small breasts against him making him weak with desire for her, the promise of attainment feverish in its exacting ideal of longing, when he kissed her he found her neither reluctant nor cerebral yet surrendering as if no one but he could achieve her, he was seized by gratitude, by a weight of excitement as though to contain her were no subtle overture yet he restrained himself slightly, letting go slowly until she was the summation of his fluidity, capturing him, keeping her in finite tryst. Could he analyze this liaison, he could tell himself it was the idea of Childress that affected him, it caused him to question her sincerity, her needs, to be in an elicit union, she was a decoy, possibly a peculiar part of a triangle, one which contained too many ironies which he could see into clearly, he would despise her for a weakness, for having come to his table to begin with, indeed for having followed him to San Francisco or doing so at someone else's behest, for if her reasons were dishonest he was being seduced, and he knew he could be hurt. That pain of knowledge of her he would guard against, having her he would strike at Childress the monster and waking would lure him to confession, how many years had these trials taken, the search to uproot evil, to produce one tangible fiber of evidence and having found it eluded twenty investigators and two units? Was the knowledge even to be restored? He positioned her beneath him, her hands supple, his arousal dictating all thought, the soft dim light in the hall spilled onto a bowl of fruit in the dining hall, its luminescent promise an evening dream of fulfillment as damp as the wetness he felt emerge from himself, he was radiant, recalibrated, lifted from a depression of regrets. He searched in her gaze for a truth, for his answer, her desire for him acknowledged that in some way women were indeed like men. She wept, a mild confession. Words came to mind spinning him through a carnival of many weathered relationships, some readily tedious, quickly soured, others for a brief time momentous, still yet others a mismatch, disquieting. He was at once depressed, deflowered, cautious, integral, denied, capable, recalcitrant, resolute, filled with retribution, languorous, finite, sorrowed, ecstatic, astonished,recaptured, forgiving, amenable, retractable. He thought of his nomenclature — he was possessive, Anglo Saxon, brimful, conjured, confused by deceit, mired, affiliated, shorn, in an epiphany, garrulous, ardent, availing, a sense of domain, semi-conscious, spellbound, resurrected, ignoble, rigorous, joined, disparate without disparagement, bigotry, haughtiness, despicability. All of Childress he knew was a lie, the man was a void, a barometer of rejecting, minimizing arrogance, pejorative, hostile, some inward emptiness, a flamboyant unpredictable sloth, having a pseudo self, flat affect, demanding, fervent, glossy, withdrawn, brutal, a deviant, secretive, defensive, dishonest, clandestine, behaviorally incompetent, and elsewhere a militaristic, preachy, dependent, dallying vainglory. The contrasts rose up in a denial of passion and he shunned them knowing intrinsically that to give into them he was doomed in error while fulfilling his nature, with instinct driven out, replaced by a sordid defeat.

Susan was up. In the kitchen she prepared a souffle mixing cream and egg yolks with grated cheese, thin wafers of zucchini, tomato and broccoli and barbecued chicken and folding the mixture with stiff egg whites. Periodically she tasted the composite, chatting with him the moment he entered, gaily while describing her upbringing, her manner while pleasing and informative was appreciating, their dialogue energetic, gradual. She sparked in him a passage for awareness, an unburdening, a curious arousal, one that kept him whole, in his vernacular, he was aware of their differentness, of her individuality, her joy a normalcy of pride, of ownership. Unlike Roberta whose distinction was owing to a confidence born of working, of having run a corporation, such that her mind was continually attuned to deadlines, tasks, receivables, stock, Susan was leisure. Class was an epitome of refinement — it dictated avail of continued resource, of wealth not just jobs. Hanging onto money was a mystery, he had a dismal pension after thirty years of solid investigation, control was no longer what it had been, it was a tedium of fragile realities, of making due with a subsistent declaration of a small house, of weathering a bank loan, of service. Roberta might be destitute overnight once her inheritance was spent, the necessity of living lay for her in a causality of doctrines and gave her little choice for advancement, the store was still closed, her new store was hardware, for automobile parts, hugely successful without the glamour of convenient beauty, the relic a happenstance of someone else's corruption, signifying the monstrous effort of an insurance industry to consume losses, for what else could accomplish devastation as exacting in order to be funded for losses?

The private cop was a man named Height, a warehouse security man, he was in a handful of photos of Childress/Fersterhof and a tall thin blond with a stiff wave who could spot anything having aced for House of Winchester, doors were off, casino-like jeweled sights that looked into every room, some wealthy landowner's misery, a connivance of mirrors designed to kill anyone inside the house, if Height ran loose with Childress their association made no sense from the outside, one man smashed glass in convenience stores, the other destroyed lives, neither used a gun, the gun was always in the car with the dame, or in a desk in Childress' house.

Jake drove past the Arco plant onto Rim of the World Drive past the state park up a terraced road high above the national forest to the summit, the homes were extravagant, one story, the road up high enough to peer from incandescent, crowded squeezed in flock of renters, dwellings that looked down on ribboned mountains past a wall of steel reinforcement. The mountains were emerald and brown, a course of desert desolation, in winter a myopic myriad of glacial pools resplendent blue heralded by long drifts of snow, new pastures, breathless vistas, conquered mansions, a prism of reflecting surfaces, joined by orchards, farms, corrals and gravel beds. Francesca's house stood on the high line, what looked to be a one story cement and glass with a large cement patio, no tree anywhere. Francesca wore short shorts and a bathing suit bra, she was preserved, taut, winsome, all leg.

"I'm looking for Gone Williams." Jake said, showing her his retirement badge.

"Gaun Will. Not here, never has been."

"But you know him?"

"Oh certainly, we used to hang in the same crowd. He has a saddle room on the second floor in a senior high-rise off 215."

"What does he do for work?"

"He fences jobs for hire, small stuff, all for remodel."

A free standing collection of merchandize trays with glittering stones stacked in the corner left a mere impression of trinkets awaiting an armored van, possibly the van abandoned at the air base. Destiny was cheap, a detective's gun, a Luger, the real net.

"Any possibility you have a ring or two?"

"No, those items are all piece."

"Like in a bank?"

"That's right, all promised."

"Who was the jeweler?"

"Debut. He used to come in to Harris House on Wednesdays and Thursdays to set."

"What is their cost today?"

"Five hundred a carat. I don't have twenty thousand, the original size of the theft, maybe a hundred if that. They were reported as lost when the store closed down."

"Who is the shoe who wired the store? Your friend, Gaun?"

"He's done that type of work, but Harris Store would have been out of his league. Try a night watchman."

"Like Height?"

"I don't know his name," she replied, but she was already stumbling over her words, unable to talk quickly to produce the gems.

"The night security detective was a man named Tom Height."

"That may be but you're asking the wrong person. I don't know."

"Could we say you were involved in the store as a cashier?"

"I did work for Mr. John Hariff Sr. at Harris House, but by then he owned most of the shoppes."

"Why did he take over Harris?"

"That store was going bust, the way I heard. He was doing well at Patton and that was his thing, bailing out businesses that weren't doing so well."

"Who staffed diamonds?"

"Harris did. She had decided to mail order them and turn her store into a group of storefronts when her store was hit." She mused a bit. "I think she was a very savvy woman who was ready to retire. Her niece was in her teens so it wouldn't have worked to bring her in. Harris was looking at a retail chain in southern California on the coast at the time."

"Do you know who might have been interested in seeing her fold?"

"Possibly Hariff's son." She was doubtful.

"What about John Childress?"

"Mable's son? No way, he's a hired gun."

The back of his neck prickled. "Do you know by whom?"

"Klabbard." Seeing no name recognition, she explained, "They're the people who help you out when your income is down for a good long time."

"Did Hariff know them?"

"Probably. My guess is he couldn't be persuaded, he'd rather close a store, open a new one in another city. Klabbard gives you an advance, then throws in the demand when they're ready to go dot."

"How often have they placed demands?"

"Oh, I wouldn't know, I think they plan dot well in advance."

"Thanks, Fran. You've been great."

As he walked away, she called after him: "It doesn't have to be all business, does it? You could come up to talk."

"Can't."

He waved to her, and she waved back, looking oddly self conscious as though she were a teenager, half grown with false promises, idly dreaming of making it rich on a scheme of obsession.

The effect of having been implored shook him out of complacency, he wondered why it was that the degree of destitution made for a more commonly situated approbative ignorance than the finite simplicity that gave over the air of desire, for Jake the certain knowledge that an infinite universe joined mankind to the inexplicable preserved the ignominious to the unjust, the sense of inquiry would take note, the need for acquisition which gave men a stand for destiny created the stateliness which made one man poor and took in the wheel of abolished misguided detriment as though it were a need in itself, to understand men who convened in great halls knew nothing but conquest and governed by such forces were themselves rationally subjected to interior demands of convenience was to place within their ranks a viable plot for the mesmerizing evil that destroys civilization, the cornerstone of morality posed that in the absence of greed righteous ambition would shank a man of deplorable acts while less accusatory propositions would fetter circumspect correctness, numerous acts of evil afforded any society with accurate direction, violence deterred was the most hoped for of ambitions, the disgrace of the embellished identity gave rise to a strong willed immorality for its perpetuation, class became a fortified ritual for hostage politics, a prescription to adventure as a frontier negated the high-minded quest for beauty giving sanction to unilateral treaties, collateral government gave chase to ubiquitous forces without which peaceful delineations sought friendly trade, the insurgence of commodity factor, so grievous in essence, farmed for gain an acceptable species for designation, became a narrowly missed institution with less regard for dignified schooling than for transience. The enormity of a task which required a wire shoe, several murders, an armored van heist and an arson of three hundred homes gave an unhealthy dynamic of encouragement gone astray, a scheduled mishap might account for the timing of these three crimes staggered for deployment of redolent animosity, at least two crimes convened for immobilization held at bay a problem that began with store bought security hampering police so that unanticipated relief was impossible, the intention that a workforce was saved from being seen and identified had gone by the wayside in that act of destruction, these security aces consisted of a security detective paid by Hariff's, one by Harris Store, two seven blocks away at the train depot, one at City Hall and four at the county building, at Harris Store ten thousand three hundred diamonds were put in laundry bags, stuffed onto the armored van and whisked away to a van at the air base, nine aces on one plaza square, all known, one shot and put out of the way, the van was able to secure a satchel of goods that were easily disseminated to buyers, brought to a nursery of orange trees where they were planted in containers with dirt, sand and trees, gauze to keep the score tightly bound to the roots, seedling trees bound for foreign ports kept a steady traffic open to exports, carpets with strong backing shook them free of all reconnaissance security, air and export, a cement ornament.

Jake returned after a long futile day borrowed of an essence of fatigue, his search for Height unsuccessful, although vigorous. He discovered Susan gone, the page in her father's journal open — "The start of rebellion came with a covenant of wreckless psychological depravity, by a class that sought to create an aggregate of wealth over its own government, of a summation of history the learned became a corp of mistrust decreed by a faction of infidels, each village of fifty to a hundred homes was appointed by a roving band under a field command and variedly replaced when the U.S. Army arrived to restore stability. I sat in the vestibule ready at any call to enter chambers, yet was not called, the hours were on a nondescript quota mislaid by a tyranny of consequence, until early evening no one checked on me even to use the cooler, when the judge greeted me, I noted that Lisa's gun was placed on the desk, its brass fussed with until it shone like a winsome handle, I withdrew almost immediately, stunned by the implications, for how many judges left evidence in the open during a proceeding about a lost gun, a Colt chiseled to the size of a man's hand? The staging of a crime goes a long way if it cannot be committed in the place it began."

The show surrendered it for any offensive that had to view the coffin as the wire expense, therefore the cop in question had once been Guard, the caller would have known the gun and presumably would have known the cop. He had thought that Childress was the Colt gun, the driver was the Colt, the Luger went on the rifle, the gun itself was used for a robbery on Harris House. The Colt having traveled from England after it slipped off a Guard's leg named Gaun Williams made its destiny into the desert of orange groves for an eventual wire job, its sole association as a show piece for a celebrated event at-a showgrounds known as orange show on Dumas, or dumb ass; the Luger, known for no peculiar specialty other than its reputation to kill at close range, had once been in the hands of a sports car driver and when the Colt slipped the driver had fired Colt dummy spraying shrapnel over the pavement; the sawed off rifle Wadd committed a drive-by shooting with on Hollan, Harris and the Hariff guard carried a Stafford James sight and a Luger twist-off and emitted Colt dummy, the caller's concern was neither the Luger nor the shotgun which were well accounted for during the trial and admitted when the twist-off was found but the Colt which was rumored to have been seen on Mable Childress yet was still at large, he was even more confidant of his belief that the crime was not three separate events but one looming one that began with a diamond heist, the laundry bags placed in an armored van by the Harris security guard, the van was then driven around the corner where three people had been shot, two guards took money inside Hariff's while two attended to the wounded and then someone stole the armored van and made a dash to the air base where he gave the money to a pilot who recovered his own take, and that same day there was a major forest fire signatured by a movie producer. In all this the Luger was taken by the wire man and the Colt went on its way to the arson and then, who knew where, to a man's home where the revolver shot a man in the head, thereby ending an invasion and a trail of blood that led to Guadalcanal and distant lands, the gun was placed on the desk for a security guard who would take it to its original keep, it was not uncommon for a police jurisdiction in referring a case to the district attorney to strip down the case to that part that would bring in a conviction and leave out uncertain details that were not conclusive, Stratford on the Avon was where the evidence began but no one aside from a drunken man would fire into a Guard regiment and wound nineteen young infantry just to prove it could be done and then run off with Luger in tow for the purpose of giving the Luger a methodology to escape detection, with every constable in the chase the Luger as the gun for the law would become swiftly replaced by a slot revolver worn in a jacket holster, the nineteen never returned to duty and were replaced by necessity by show procession, Stratford at the Avon was where the changing of the Guard occurred and thus guards involved in the crime would not so readily expose themselves, despite this obvious extortion every guard name was dumped into protoplasm for conjecture as to willingness to commit a crime, his foreign correspondent desk gave Jake another tidbit: the exchange of pistols while fairly common was batched periodically for cleaning and disposition and suspected guards were then given pistols that could not fire thus bringing into consideration the rationale that if a trade had occurred those guards who politely permitted exchange, say by leaving their lockers open in the shower room, were ever ready for duty except for their inability to draw their weapon. This trend, not as alarming as anyone might suppose, nevertheless went far to explain a duty officer's companion when in a skirmish one reported he felt he had been set up because the other while covering him did not fire, the subject of the day was oddly not corruption but buy-offs and as everyone bloody well knew the right sort of money offered to a fellow in need lent a whip a whim of too much fancy, for the Colt to be the gun that landed on a judge's desk during a trial when it was known the gun that fired was a standard regimen Luger conveyed a denied capability that where one went so did the other like a misbegotten marriage of convenience, only two people would stand up to a rigor, that of the ballistics test and that of the oiling before the guns were returned for statute, either the Colt boarded a small plane with the Harris diamonds or someone at the arson took the revolver under consignment and buried it for future use.

He drove to Roberta Harris' flat, all the while asking himself what an attractive female did with the certain knowledge that her aunt had arranged a shuffle of pistol fire for a heist of jewels which had not yet surfaced, he decided after some thought that the proposition was made only slightly worse by the fact that the old department store was still retained under court order with no leverage of any kind, that although the parties were deceased the quagmire of opportunism had residually refused to acknowledge her young relationship with Steven Hariff, and that the owner of the train and its elegant depot had convened at least one train on the turnstile and could not set it into Rialto in time for a stash to be deported, costing local government the erection of a block of thin houses to resemble train compartments each with a window with small plants on the sill that overlooked the track. All access routes stymied, one to Rialto and Ontario with its own airport, another to Palm Springs, such as it was in those days — four blocks made entirely of spa resorts — another into the forested mountains, no cars nor buses, six avenues, two military bases, one at Patton with a club owned by Hariff, the other an air base with locked gates that should have been impenetrable, that one flew two Cessna planes a day, the desert at the edge of a vast lithic empire of spired red and golden stone, tumbling sagebrush and a few shallow creekbeds, and therefore the arson could have been staged to open the world to immediate development to get those diamonds to a trade marketplace, his guess was a batch went with a small aircraft, another batch went to Grand Terrace, another to a house on Highway 18, yet another allegedly the lion's share to a home that burned to rubble, the desert closed down for a long dry spell, the spread of the map filled it in all directions some twenty to thirty miles away in all directions by irrigated fields of wheat, crops, trees, and wildlife refuges while the government capably turned every stone and tile to hunt down a voracious new gentility and pushed them to the outer reaches of a tiny city, high above vegetation into concrete palaces where they were then held captive, unable to leave the city boundaries, routinely ostracized, damned as their age, without any avenue to jobs, shorn of marriages, bypassed; like tumbleweed, with nothing better to do with their minds or their time, this new upper class planned its new entries by city and map and laid down a grid structure to chart a handful of savoir faire arsons under a single title of deed for the sale of a new collateral, singling out Hollywood, Ventura, Seattle and New York. The train was no longer a passenger train, commodities once sold and shipped by train were rushed to new destinations by truck and air, and diamonds were sold under registry by certificate. The obvious answer as to use of a show revolver was that it had administered a fatal blow to the individual who owned the township's forests but because those lands were surrendered immediately upon knowledge of the three murders, he put that speculation out of his mind. The fact that the township rapidly matured in gestation also kindly de-evolved any contingency that the crimes were committed for the acquisition of land. With the state's permanent regulation of its clothiers as well as of its manufacturers, with a steady infiltration into movie making by state agents, with a growing bureaucratic regime signified by job rate increases, the sore subject lost its impetus and remaindered itself almost entirely to entertainment into which it plugged prostitutes, dentists who could later piercingly remove diamond teeth from citrine rock globs, nursery owners and a host of minimally contained entrepreneurs whose capabilities for catastrophe would be at best understated. Blue Chip vouchers for furniture left the popular market, soon to be replaced by stores of every type, most agent owned, and models went to work for magazines, no longer fashion houses, and were hired on the spot by rival movie producers to sell lines into retail outlets, the size and color glass of many skillfully chosen highrises were a consent by the steel industry to see rising costs be curtailed and although these buildings were quickly outmoded, for the years they stood as potential landmarks they were viewed as a legitimate way to dwarf individually combined resources that wanted to enter a trade market and collapse capital. In this government steel was king.

Jake parked in front of the elaborate home of John Childress, thinking he was ready for him now, nevertheless looking for Susan's car and feeling relieved he didn't see it. He walked onto the porch, knocked and having the door open, he hesitated before walking inside the cool interior. The hall looked immaculate, the bathroom was a glimpse of dark green and gold wallpaper, the living room a plush bachelor pad with all the accoutrements of comfort and staid conservatism, an upholstered high backed chair, a sofa, wood tables, a bookshelf, a plush carpet.

They were seated outside on the patio at a glass table beneath an umbrella having a mature focussed conversation. Susan was listening, Childress was explaining, they appeared a longtime couple used to a reserved distance, the calibrated heat not evident in his posture. In a single instant, forgetting any jealousy he might be capable of, he wondered how it was they were close, why she stayed friends with him, was it out of loyalty or protection to her father, he thought of the page she left open to be read, perhaps she required an answer only Childress knew, Jake stepped onto the patio.

"I'm apologetic, I thought you would be alone," he said to John Childress. "The front door was open."

"Did you leave the door open, Suki?" John asked Susan.

"I must have." She barely glanced at Jake, saying, "John and I have been at it for hours."

"I see you two know one another. Susan is my wife."

Jake thought he gave no indication of having heard. "I was told you can direct me to a man named Klabbard."

"Klabbard," said Childress, as if he had been caught red handed in the act. "He doesn't usually reside in Grand Terrace. Where is Lloyd these days, do you know, Suki?"

Susan laughed, sounding a bit high strung. "He's in Highland with Tom, they have a home on the ridge." To Jake she said, in a tone that was somewhat caustic, "Well, I'll be, you ran me to ground; was it necessary?"

"I didn't intend to, I wanted to speak to your husband," he answered, finding he was on the defensive and resentful of the events that had transpired between them. "I felt it would be best if I could ask him about the Harris diamond snatch. Did you hire in Tom Height?"

"Dear boy, that wouldn't have been me, not with ten thousand, three hundred diamonds in tow, I'm merely an errand boy. Now if you ask Tom himself how he was put in the mix, I'm sure Lloyd will tell you he wanted a few of his own."

"Was he licensed to carry a Colt revolver?"

"I'm certain it would be standard security weapon, if not a pistol then a cartridge, probably Magnum. He wouldn't kill anyone, though."

Childress gestured for Susan to leave, which she did, she was good natured respectful, a hint of graciousness which Jake was clear could be more exploited than it was, schooled for many emotions although possibly not biting betrayal or outright double-cross, Childress cleared the table surface with his sleeve, a sweeping motion Jake thought he would never forget having seen a quick motion of it at a smoke cafe when he scrolled through the trial tapes, he considered the luck that another detective had been impressed by the motion excellent judgement.

"We aren't going to get petty, are we?" John Childress asked. "If you have to know, that's one thing, but I'd rather Suki doesn't catch wind."

"Is she involved as a material witness?"

"No, but I have no secrets from her. "

"Does she know about the runs you take with your mother?"

He blanched. "I do it for my mother. She owns the gun, I don't use it."

"The gun in question was produced at a gun trial, not as evidence however."

"My mother's gun is a show piece."

"How could your mother have obtained the gun?"

"I would reckon since I've grown up with knowledge of her possession that my father gave it to her."

"Where is Fersterhof today?"

"Don't know, haven't seen him in about twenty years. We were last together in the canyon in his house."

Jake asked, "Where is the house?"

"It's no longer there. It burned to the ground in 1985."

"Did your father die?"

"No, he went to live with my stepmother, she lives near the county line past the airport. He's well into his seventies."

"Why don't you visit if he's nearby."

"He won't see me, we had a falling out."

"Over what?"

"It was a spat, he'd been drinking heavily and lost his temper. I'm not sure what we were talking about, he tried to corner me, really — must we go on about this? It upset Mable more than me."

"Your relationship with your mother doesn't make much sense."

"Then I'll spell it out. She wants a drink, there's no booze in the house, we go for a bottle and she wants the gun with her while I'm inside the store."

"Why when you go with her do you smash everything in the store?"

Childress looked unhappily at him. "I don't want anyone following us who might recognize us."

Susan wasn't around when he left. Jake looked for her, not finding her he understood her absence as a negation of common sense, a relenting to a subjective accommodation he found conducive to a lifestyle of deception. He had been warned. He had crossed a boundary he ought not to have relinquished himself to and having a knowledge of it admitted to himself he was less than adequate to coddle himself free of it.

Childress had lied about more than the booze, if he were a stumbling down drunkard himself Jake could see the context of such a lie, but he was more or less very self controlled, a iron hand inside a suede glove, a man who wouldn't flinch because he had walked too far in one direction without allowing the outcome of his erroneous thinking, if the gun were the missing Luger, then it seemed likely it was brought in by a guard already wanted for a heinous crime, the passions of crime were neither asserted to for reasons of persuasion or military tactics, such passions when fully comprehended breathed less for national defense offshore than for the stupendous achievement that men who sought to oppress might achieve, an unscrupulous aim to distort all human landscape to a small minded objective for that which, if made a declaration of commodity, would give power to the meek.

Men walked upright on two legs, beasts on four, the crippled with a cane, the truisms of living a purely aesthetic life hung around his ankles as a netting capable of snare, the child ought to learn his own method out of depth perception infancy and care to crawl as a certain knowing quest, the adolescent in shedding his ritualistic adoration would arrive to adulthood without a persona yet able to mask tasteful emotion and compile cognitive insights, to these mechanisms of frail tearful conjecture the maturing teen reinforced mastery with sometimes aberrational rights, taking from interactions a positive delight or a recalcitrant prejustification until experience, ruthless or conventional, was marked by retained wisdom, here lay the conjured elements of denial, stuffed anger, postulate arrogance, conceit, and marked sociopathy, here were the toe tags of adventurism, of fated will, of joined resurgence of altruism, herein lay the ambivalent features of discretion, illicit regression, decisive valor, tickled pleasures all motivated by a criterion for eminence, clamoring elation, a domain of inflicting pain, of viewing oneself superior with a knowledge that gave sway to prejudicial defeatism, the Childress conveyance had cost Jake a treacherous evocation, to commiserate his newly endured censure he was obligated to see a couple with Childress in his formerly captive radiance. He knew he might ask himself weeks later why he pursued Susan vigorously when he knew she had an unexplained flaw, he knew if he did nothing the torturous mindset that took other men's capabilities could claim him also, a choir of sojourn prayer filled his being as he drove on a straight course for Roberta Harris' home.

Roberta greeted him at the door dressed in flannel top and pants, her brown wavy hair pinned above her shoulders. Her face was smooth, her eyes shining, a narrow bodiced woman who would not seduce nor make light of, who seeing his haunted look took his hand and let him step against her.

"What is it, Jake?" she asked, a brevity of awareness in her voice.

"I've been had," he said simply. "I knew it was coming, that's the worst of it, I may have bungled the matter."

"I doubt you could bungle much, you have no deceit," she said, and wrapped her arms around his neck and kissed him without artifice.

"I've narrowed down quite a bit."

She unbuttoned his jacket, then his shirt, running a hand over his hip, posting her leg between his, her throat long and creamy white like a bird's warble at her collarbone. She took his hands and set them at her rib cage and moved against him, soft, grateful, and he responded, letting himself be taken to her, until he realized she was freeing him of a tormentor, vanquishing some inner need to be enveloped, he placed his mouth on her neck, his hands on her shoulders, tracing her arms, waist, stomach. He had to chase an image of Susan away, reassert Roberta in his gaze, yet when she nudged him he refused saying he couldn't act on his feelings.

"Don't I turn you on?" she asked him.

"I've admired you for a long long time. I had hoped I could run to you, I just can't go through with it right now."

"What do you want to do?" she asked.

He didn't answer, he didn't know what he wanted, she led him through the kitchen into the hall to the bedroom, a sensuous room with satin blue sheets and a dark blue quilt, a tan Berber on the floor, an open closet arranged only for organization, leggings, tops, blankets, pillows, dresses, suits and a long mirror with a step ladder, he allowed himself to lie on her bed, to have her take his shoes off, cover him and then draw the curtains and leave the room closing the door softly.

He awoke to the wind rustling the drapes and got up to close the window. He closed it, and then came across Roberta on a day bed, a blanket wrapped tightly around her, and sat beside her, lifting her blanket slightly and kissed her mouth, she stirred a bit, watched him in the dark as he lightly cupped her slightly pendulous breast and lay on her, kissing her collarbone, her soft warm skin, her nipple, her ribs; she pushed his head down her body, urging him to her abdomen, letting him beneath the blanket, he felt a pang of endurance, of urgency, and entered her, feeling her encircle him at the waist and hold him. He had no thought for moments, it was just her, a merciful waking, an honest pleading with a sense of completion like being emptied of tension, he was tense yet calm, renewed, a congruous group-ing of emotions, he cupped her body applying a consistent pressure, when he thought of Susan, of her shame, her denial, her clandestine ardor, and he asked himself why now, why was he seized with an idea of possessing her yet when he knew he could never have her enough, never achieve her surrender, Roberta turned toward him, her exquisitely lean body arching into his, her hand hurrying his motion and he looked at her, her soft face, and told himself she was without resistance, she wanted him, she was achievable, she went wet with desire, he thrust his fingers into her, she bit his lip, he was surprised at his re-arousal, at the fact that she was demanding, that for an instant he wasn't thinking past her, that when she sighed she took some part of him into her, he moved his arm behind her back and pressing her tightly to him he said her name again and again. He couldn't say he loved her, not after having poured his guts to Susan, he wouldn't ask himself why he thought at all about Susan, that he wondered whether she had let Childress handle her, he would come away from her, separate, let Roberta ease him from that edge of risk or devastation, he couldn't yet feel his way out of the night.

She had written him a note to say she had an appointment in town and he could help himself to whatever he found to eat. He made toast with butter and a cup of bitter coffee, then left her a note and dashed off.

The original petition described a gunman in a public square shooting Guard men wounding about nineteen. A few days later a driver shot and killed two adults before screeching down the street. These were the violent acts of murder from which other murders in a foreign country would occur using the same exact guns. The gun may have been a standard Luger, because the gun that slipped off the guard the same day as the shooting driver was a Colt and one gun could not be in two places simultaneously, both the Luger and the sawed-off rifle used at Hariff Department Store had an attachable piece, handmade, and both used Colt dummy, but only the Colt was seen with Mable Childress, presumably the Colt which was always in her possession was given to her by ex-husband Festerhof, Jake kept asking himself why she needed a Colt, maybe she couldn't adequately handle a larger gun or she didn't like a cartridge, Jake never had exceeded his middle class orientation despite the inducements of friends, he enjoyed a modest lifestyle having come to terms after losing a middle class house because he was injured on the job and was unable to work for four years catapulting him unprepared into near poverty, for four seemingly long years, ever more impatient to be wage earning, he shared a house with several men none who were law enforcement, one who was diagnosed affective disorder, the time was a period of endurance and because all through it he was not permitted to go out with fellow police it robbed him of dignity and felt like a sentence, he put up with numerous inconveniences the least of which was to find hours when he could be alone, he took up with discipline, watering the depressingly walled in strip of garden early mornings as his roommates readied for jobs, planning and preparing dinner which arrived in two shifts at six and again at eight, he read meditation, haiku, and Jung, the psychotherapist's doctrines on male/female psychic behavioral tendencies, his discussions on archetypes and on analysis, and then tried to compare Jung to Freud, Eriksson, Perls, and tried to understand discussions about transference, periodically he read John le Carre and struck out for Studs Terkel, infrequently he went shopping and for a brief two summers he went sculling before he parked his cap on the easy chair and surrendered to a seldom-known anxious waiting for the period of incapacity to come to an end. His narrow view of Childress was of a mother who may have retired from parenting, bored she was a cultivator of thinly veiled danger, with money she had an ability to behave capriciously although it was not her who manifested adventurism, likewise Jake's observations of son Childress was of a roving predator, a man who for whatever emotional needs took him to wreak havoc to mom and pop stores behaved with subjective terrorism in order to induce what was probably a dangerous compliance. The reason for living in cement city suburbs was likely because one could find a low cost expansively large home even if the cement foundation permitted only parquet or carpet, after a movie or a killing fee was made the sensible purchase was to derive a home with enough square footage to grow into it in ten years, a pool became a necessity, a large garden was desirable although not usually affordable, and where possible a small golf course in the backyard was considered a gracious life for a couple who liked their wine, the pitfalls for extravagance showered a desert habitation with at best a private airstrip, a pasture-worth of golf and a bean size swimming pool for the nanny and children to splash about, as many vehicles as a healthy income could maintain, a few palm trees, a Rolls sports car, these were the standard of preference for California living available to anyone who might afford the price tag, the Fersterhofs had exceeded their expectations by entering Dr. Childress' home, although he was semi-retired and his income did not make his stepson deed-wealthy, the marriage had given Mable a healthy joiner and there she retained herself, without the knowledge of her nocturnal activities she was the same as any housewife in the valley.

Jake floored the gas pedal down a breezy corridor into the high desert which until Highland had replaced orange grove orchards in 1998 had been a rustic scarcely populated gravelly composite of hills and some four or five small suburbs consisting of seventy-five homes apiece. The road from the airport led in a straight line to Church which led to Orange to the base at Patton. A Greek ranch or two sat on a lean hill awaiting something more than corrals and horses or swimming pools. The newly built Highland flowered with jasmine and deadly nightshade over high walls and houses erected in the Southwestern style for the Christos Mountains decently sectored red tile roofs, iron gated courtyards and shiny copper entrances for one story dwellings made of white or light tan stucco and opaque corner windows that permitted residents secure privacy. Tom Height opened the door and heard Jake's story before he cordially invited him inside a light airy home that took in a peach carpet, peach airy curtains and a vibrant plum wallpaper with cherry wood trim and a chartreuse wall, Tom was a typically handsome blonde, male, lean, strident, brown eyes, pale despite the sun, he wore short shorts, a raw T-shirt, floppy beach sandals, a red and black bandana tied around his neck like an insincere trophy; in the garden was a large orange flagstone tiled patio, a square of grass and flowering trees everywhere of different color blooms, white honeysuckle, small pink roses, purple lilac, irises along the border of a redwood fence that was faded with green moss, at a deck table sat the more esteemed of the two elderly men, a somewhat obese man with jeweled fingers dressed in pedal pushers and a silk black shirt and backless sandals, his gaze followed his handsome partner possessively, Jake stood at Klabbard's table, showed his detective license and sat.

Jake began, saying, "I'm looking for a missing Luger. It was last seen in London, presumably on the desk of Chief Constable. Might you know whether that particular gun was used here in the state in the last thirty years?"

Lloyd Klabbard felt his teeth with his tongue. "The Luger fell off the deputy's leg —"

"That was a Colt."

"I beg your pardon?"

"A Colt revolver."

"I thought for a moment you meant the horse."

Jake smiled. This would be like pulling teeth. "The Luger was allegedly used by a driver to shoot into a crowd. Previously a drunkard fired into a crowd with it."

"Perhaps the drunk found it on someone's desk."

"Could be. Have you seen it since?"

"No, I haven't, Detective. My preferred gun is a heavy gun."

"What about for Mr. Height?"

"Same," the man known as Tom Height said from behind him.

Jake hadn't heard his return. "What about a rifle?"

"That was Wadd's doing. He sawed off his sight, screwed on a spray and pumped out dummy. He got the idea from a shooter in London."

"Sort of like a demonstration."

"I wasn't there to witness him. He was a fucking nutcase."

Height spoke up, sitting down, lighting a fag. "Why do you want this Luger? It's not a Midnight Special."

"You're right, it was standard constable. A Luger disappeared from London, it allegedly sits below someone's desk today and accompanies a Mable Childress to the liquor market when her son goes in for a pint."

"Then it merely sits in her lap. What of it?"

"I was hoping you could tell me."

"Can't. Don't know enough about it."

Tradition accounting for its own military discipline capably defended law, law by nature shared no boundary, each rank was separate. Rank enlisted, the test of tracking incursion found a rapid response to strategic fire by ignition, the bullet never disintegrated, dummy looked the same except it had a red bank at its base and fired sparks.

When Jake left Klabbard's home he was in anxious knots, his mind ill at ease, his mortal sense of necessary accommodation wounded against the patterns of living he took for granted as his natural rights. He had learned long ago, scarcely youth far behind, that the language of betrayal hid an actual knowledge of circumstance, the individual who kept appearances often kept to himself for a reason not readily palpated.

The habit of living with someone made for the affections of partnership despite the enjoyment of brief releases, he felt with one or two women that he was in the way, that their life was far more encompassing in a spirit of deserved and blessed class than he could ever take bread with, the disheartening feeling of having been interested became somehow synonymous with being shunned as gauche, certainly as set apart, a meal for one, some way defined for self conscious candor, he could pine for Susan and she would yet overlook him, he would always feel tangled up in her nets, a brash effeminate lying in wait for a beautiful woman who beneath her skin knew nothing except deception.

It was late at night when he awakened in his small but well defined house, he took the dog for a walk on the path, and thought he would only fall for Susan once, the moon was over the canal with the horse heads, the canal bare to its white effaced bone, the water redirected.

He focussed on the empiricism of the investigation, its dualities, culprit tarnished weathering; had he been yet a working man he would take time in the strictest of fashions, collaborative briefings and field autopsies with sergeants his only contacts, narrative summaries by taped recordings over his lunch box in the post op, a perfectionist at detailed reports, everything measured, city maps, new retailers, new applications for permits and ownership, horse shoes and hand grenades. Height was a well scrubbed tall middle aged electrician of haberdashery ease to Klabbard's puffy mildly reclined state of wit as one might expect a nocturnal bicyclist used to tiptoeing on the pavement, an artistic carrying case to convey a tarp, spatula and putty, for a ten minute job. The man's previous dispositions said in his early years he liked the sort of woman other women envied, not a woman of independent means; the more dependent a woman was to become the freer he felt, a brief design with domain the winning proposition. Calibrated into monogamy lay a generous portent of prosperity based on a minute claim of despicability — she knowing nothing how this came about viewed in him a predisposition to extramarital affairs, an intolerance of her need to smother him with gab, were he a bit preoccupied instead of gregarious, he might be more intellectual, persuaded to melancholy or invention, but in her mind he was often catastrophic, giving into impulse or indigestion, a bigoted fussy man, her idea of comfortable companionship not meant to discourage him kept them at odds like two strangers across a garden, a square of grass bordered by a shade of maple and potted calla lilies, an occasional breeze their only whisper, a wire peacock lounge seat a sparse conversational piece, the boysenberries in bloom, sweet and stained like sickeningly pungent blood, a waste of space for potentially illustrious bulbs and hyacinths, a twenty foot rose bush climbed a trellis, pink yellow buds peeking through the grape vine, the drooping branches of the vine like long tusks, a lengthy twining of twisted trunk held upright by posts, chimes carrying a hint of tin resonance, the walking path overgrown with lust. Here he was, emasculated, an aging endearment, condensed of slanders, capably denied of pleasure, his heart clearly aching with the injury of having been misunderstood, yet blamed for all carnivorous lunacies, all around him his younger lad's cries of outrage, possibly of despair, until he incorporated it in his outwardly manifestations. Being of a single oriented mind he would have condemned himself, not for any knowledge but for his allowance for hatred aimed at those destroyers he had tolerated; in an attached photograph his young lad had fallen asleep over a book, his hair flecked with sunlight, his shirt having slipped to reveal his freckled skin, indescribably harmless and knew he had been brutish again, insensitive not only to his ex-wife but now to his boy, prickly and wished he didn't have to go through what he had to do, he had to leave for a long time, he might return cruel and would try to disappear from him, be unable to, not find adequate safety anywhere, he'd try not to show what he knew, where he had been, it was only in his presence Height was feminine, of that he was sure; otherwise his mannish tendencies were contained in an icy expression, a non interest in manipulation, much like Susan who would go about her day with prejudice, leggings and pinafores, a somewhat chauvinistic decline spoon-fed by indignity. Poor Klabbard who according to the voluminous file had to initiate affection lest he would be devoid of romantic inclination, he counted on Height's lacking nature over time, on his thinly cautious courtesy to regain his extroversion and shed his deviate unwillingness at entertainment.

He decided that the perplexing difficulty was that to define the problem for its source one had to categorize the vulgarities. To do that one had to take up each consideration conscientiously to break down what had occurred; always in this was an unexposed threat which often closed down the case and had it assigned to an unsuspecting workforce without backup, when an officer lost his life on the job the inevitable question was, could it have been prevented, the standard for safe investigation was to place the police elsewhere; in his department reports instead of field interviews made up the protocol of procedure, typically no one saw a crime scene in person, it was released as a set of photos, a photo developer was hired to discern what the photo disposed, to isolate activity from unclear blurs, once obtained the photos were sent to an undisclosed location where an Examiner attempted to match the body by evidentiary methodology, hair and fiber analysis; scars, marks, tattoos and fresh wounds; mottling and bloating; dentals; skeletals; length of body, width of wrists and ankles; ease of joint manipulation; the staging for discovery while intended to be innocuous sometimes reconstituted the crime, and herein lay the distress of culpability. Lingering in a bath in the field next to the turnstile, the corpse shorn of weight was pried loose from its disease by emptying the hardened mud; the tub recess measured and described saw no laboratory; the stranger who had entered the park had carried mud for the flowers, the perpetrator left by taxi in the dead of night, the body when it was delivered to post op was in a disgusting state, any state department employee now had to walk past a door that was always slightly open, anyone inside the building now qualified for being threatened despite the fact they were almost all health department personnel and not field investigators. This exposure to terror presumed fore knowledge of the crime itself, with Harris House the facts of the crime were alleged at best, the shoe to this day undetermined, the facts for a heist of Harris House stated in the file as follows —

*too dark*
*vehicle parked at back entrance*
*camera cut*
*lights never turned on*
*wire thread previously installed*
*vehicle left running at rear entrance*
*culprit walked out hooded*

The detective had made notes about his suspicions: works in the dark, likely the mechanism is small and easy to set up like a spool kit, shoes are rubber soled, busy store has too much foot traffic to identify any prints, diamonds gone, gun Luger 22 left on counter. The shoe had left footprints on the sidewalk, the street lamp photographed the person, a car picked up the shoe, the camera displayed Francesca at the wheel, took the car license, ran makes through Department of Motor Vehicles, catalogued all jobs that the shoe was suspected of, the incursions amounted to a long list of serious crimes —

*18 forest fires*
*12 department store wires along Topeka Kansas rail line*
*50 train depot stations*
*5 bridge closures*

Attached was a report given by a field detective: segmented for permanent rail failure, declined switch box relays, short-circuited narrow passage northwest train compartment wire hookups, joint passage communication shutdowns, creative box high wire with gun, paintworthy wire staircase celebrated wood ceiling skylights, the list covered hotels, trains and depots all situated in the Swiss Alps, leaving stunningly beautiful embassy type buildings looking like dog chow, Harris House adapted from Ritkva, Belgium, a sweeping aggressive entrance, mezzanine, upper stories, all grand for the music box, no Viennese waltz, the tent never went up, the floor remained intact, the glass turned brown, only the chandeliers loosened and hung slightly lower, the effect was for a fast moving train of hitches. But for Hungarian or Italian cases, the diamonds would have been blown all over the room, and the ampules inside the trays would have gushed crimson in upward streaks like fangs, some to the ceiling.

Collins's journal read: "Statues untouched, drapes limp, mortar exposed, carpets curled, no arson, only singes, a handsome auction of lamps, dressers, mirrors and jewelry, not a stitch of clothing sold at Harris; ten eye witnesses in flats next door ducking to avoid their windows of which the panes permanently glazed as though from flames, their own carpets pulling at threads producing a worn complimentarity. The getaway car was found in Rialto, its tires shredded, its Hapsburg contents limping, a third passenger picked up along the escape without so much as a cut; the brevity of the two lives of Francesca and Height readily apparent in nihilistic bombardment. I met Height in Orange at the air base, Francesca's front tire ripping. I had in my possession the gun he had forgotten on top of the glass mirrored counter, after I diligently stepped over the redhead female, obviously an unwitting match at love, a few trinkets recovered from the floor of resilient powder blue carpet, my innards very like sore aching guilt, knowledge which should have been banked directing my every step. Height's wrist veins stood out looking hammered by nails, his face as though contorted by clay. I took his laundry bags and paid him on the barrel. Then I labored to my plane, packed the fare into the cockpit and went to get a coke in the base lounge. The day was hot, the desert floor as bright as glass, granite specks to tell time by. In the distance a cultivation of orange groves extended as far as the eye could see. I told Height to ram the van into a hill, one tree would be indistinguishable from a landscape of orange fruit and a thicket of green leaves. Up in the plane the altimeter dropped once between the Dog and Monterey, I pumped shell into the valley throttling in at crankcase gauge, surrendered to pines and deleterious Demetered weather, a stony embankment made of loose stones and a marsh. The wind rustled with the thundering captivity of a conch, in no time I was ankle-deep in water, slogging my way with the laundry.

"I drove to Fersterhof's as we had agreed, to his smallish bungalow on the pristine Pacific ocean. The palms bent in a torrential rain, mud stuck to the wipers leaving fans. It was all drizzle by Los Angeles, almost nothing by Cuesta. I stopped into the Palms motel to my pad. The man was in the shower, blood watering from his head. I backed out and crashed into a small table on which the Luger was on the low rack, Height must have given it to Fersterhof, or it was his to begin with."

Collins had searched the newspapers once he was holed up in east LA for the dead man's identity and finding no reported death for late 1961 he consulted obits downtown, the factual database gave a Henry Adam as a dead on arrival, his possessions inventoried and bagged, a wife Amy was next of kin. He had spent efforts to find Amy Adam unsuccessfully. Finally he went to the authorities, the goods packaged into a bus locker box, and confessed. The officer who took the report was a John Jones, a patrol officer who was on duty at the times of both murders. Jones fingerprinted Collins, had a tech draw blood, and submitted a statement to his sergeant who signed it and filed it with the US Marshal, the District Attorney sent Collins and Height to the penitentiary for seven and a half years.

The fact that Collins was a broken man was not lost on Jake. Susan was attempting to restore her father over a falsehood probably to find those diamonds herself, a powerful invention of mislaid circumstance, unless the Luger were hers; however, no women had ever worked for the Constable Gun Registry Office in London. The medical lab to which all county findings had been documented sat on Arrowhead behind an architectural firm known as Turner & Turner which had been there when Harriff opened his store to provide fashionable inexpensive clothing, Harris was backed financially by Mayfield who lent Hariff startup funds in the mid 1950s on the say so of profiteering generated by sale of diamonds on the silver streak Kansas line, an individual who could separate boxcar compartments on the track and disable communications while a pony express robbery was in progress was indeed a problem, the Luger in question was the one piece of evidence to tie the man in the shower Adam to the redhead found dead at Harris House after a heist that cleaned out ten thousand three hundred diamonds, the only match for any person who knew enough about switchboxes and communication hookups was a female who had laid track for Belfast, her name was Josephina Webb whose father was late Chief Constable. As near as Jake could figure out Webb would have objected to a store bookkeeper letting them inside and wouldn't have chanced a problem when the redhead later added it up.

Per her mugshot Jo Webb was tall, definitely wiry brunette, slender boned, frequently seen in the Hariff lounge at Patton in Orange or at a bar in Belvatown, wearing tight pants and a low cut blouse with a string backing, she was hoping to break into film having just designed use of the scheduling monitor for radio sound and cathode tube in the home, in less than a year her product would revolutionize security along with entertainment and she would be virtually untouchable, every product advertised subject to excise. Only that getaway armored van sitting in a hill in the desert resembling an icebox would gradually infringe on her executive rights, its headlights smashed up against dirt, the would be robber crawling out for air as though he too were bereft of a magnificent heist, the goods having vanished into thin air, rumors might circulate for years that seeing the odds close in he threw the diamonds out the window onto the road, in the shadows a group of killers swiftly emerged from covered trucks and found the murderers and killed them, hooding them and with drawstrings strangling them, leaving two to be discovered by tourists seeking a bit of shade.

# 8/Eight

THE INTENT OF THE CRIME MUST HAVE BEEN FOR the actual shooters to pay the prize of the people who bought them, even the fences would lose at least a limb by some standard of criminality, the buyers assuming Klabbard was in that elite and not a fence, investor or a coordinator remained at large, the crime was originated in the style of a train holdup, no less nor worse than a heist on board the plank with at least two murders to get rid of eye witnesses whose participation presumably was negligent, Webb herself was alleged to be an upper class frigidere whose cousins gave British lords their mutual ambition, but for the puffy plaster knife the game was on to sort through the cement jungle for a spool kit junket whose comprehension of the Austrian finery market left the stage in the sand detached from its overnight coach. The large curled redhead who had been betrayed in the act was a Ross

MacDonald creature to the last, her shower cap Adam despite his rather odd Belgium looks of a broad forehead, wide face, coal black eyes, short neck, stocky build gave no association to the sleek Height or the modified Fersterhof, Europe's departed proved California's surfer crowd, keen, drugged out, concert has-beens who swore they would find the portal of youth and jetset back to the sand as soon as they landed a role in the bright lights, Jake let a former associate lend out his desk for a scroll through archived files for any connection he might find promising. Height had rotated in and out of jail on trumped by charges that hinted at a felony heist yet didn't actually sustain them, Adam received a shakedown in London after he was discovered altering a show pistol registry, he was tossed out to Belvatown on a pension and up to his death made the most of it living with a group of underage ballerinas whose night performances got him in the door as a small-time security post at the high school theatre, the permanently closed Harris House no contention for the shoppes opening in New York down to Maryland, the promise of European furniture replete for interior designers of apartments in a growing city of high-rises. Even the train would relinquish her attractive coach decor to a streamlined passenger coach, the years more or less subtracting the bed and breakfast look to make room for crowded cars and standing room.

Francesca was watering her bean shaped lawn and a border of trees, a few orange trees, a honeysuckle bush, and several rose bush trees, white and red, shooting skyward like blossoming climbers, their shoots falling over a fence on the hill side, she wore her hair in sandy blond curls, a pair of pedal pushers, blouse and backless denim tennis shoes gave her a look of fading beauty, she had barely touched the toast and coffee on the wood beach dark green umbrella table on the cement patio, her tiny house all glass to the west, almost no lookout to the northeast, a book on addiction splayed open.

"I understand you picked up Height after he pulled the wire job on Harris House," Jake said.

"Now you know." She shrugged as if to say even this small abode was worth the price. "I drove him to his plane. That's about all. We almost didn't make it."

"Did you drive him to the job?"

"No."

"What about Josephina Webb?"

"Oh, did she do it?"

"Yes, she hung the wire from the glass ball."

"I didn't realize she could handle that kind of job."

"Who did you think had?"

"Tom, that was his spoon. He held the pro championship."

"Why would he split the work?"

She thought it over. "There could be a thing or two I don't know about."

"Whose pistol was the 22?"

"I thought it was Klabbard's."

"He never served for the Guard."

"It may have been Fersterhof's or his mother's."

"No woman has ever served in the Guard either."

"Oh well, that may not mean much," she said, and put the hose down on a stake to drench the climbers. "Any of them could have taken that one gun, Wadd, Clerk, Adam --"

"He's dead, shot between the eyes in a motel stall."

"Henry, shot?" her voice was a tinny replication of itself. "He was having an affair with the Harris woman, she drove out of town every other weekend in her convertible Thunderbird."

The alternate weekend schedule reminded him oddly of Susan. "Why every other weekend?"

"Her ex-husband had the child on the other weekends and she wanted to be available in the event his girlfriend flew off the handle."

He had forgotten that menacing aspect revealed about Steven

Hariff at the trial. "Do you know who the girlfriend was?"

"It wasn't Dotty. The woman was a floozie Hariff picked up at his lounge in Orange. Her name was Cloie, Cloie Jones. She was a good deal younger than he was, something of an innocent."

"Not Dotty, then."

"No, Dotty was a trusted friend of both Steven and his ex, Harris. Cloie was the one who tumbled Steven, Dotty babysat when Steven needed time off on his weekends with his son."

"Does Cloie Jones live locally?"

"Yes, she resides off Church at the base of Highland. She lives with Klabbard's youngest nephew."

"Has she married?"

"Not officially. She wants to keep her house in her name."

"Did she by any chance know a large curled redhead?"

"We all did, that was Tom's contact at Harris House, she did the books, her name was Gena Harris, she was a cousin of the Harris family."

"Tell me, how did Tom strike up this acquaintance?" Jake inquired, lighting a cigarette.

Francesca joined him, cupping her hand around his lighter to block the sudden wind. She inhaled until she was certain it was lit. "Tom was hired to put in the chandeliers and outlets for the lamps." Seeing his look of consternation, she explained, "That's usually how it works. The people who put in the wires take out the wires. Tom took Gena for coffee every Wednesday at eleven thereafter."

"He may have killed her."

"Doubtful, that would have been Steven Hariff's inclination, especially if he's the one who bought the job. Was she found dead the night of Tom's wire?"

"According to reports. The authorities believe she let him inside with her key and then either Height or Webb snuffed her. She was found on the first floor, her shoes off."

"I think it's a possibility she had a heart attack. Sometimes that happens."

He made a mental note. "Did you know the plane owner?"

"Collins, yes, I met him that night. He paid us off."

"Was he a cop?"

"No, he was part of the franchise."

"Was the heist his arrangement?"

"No, Steven set everything into motion. His dad had just finished building a depot in New York City, and Steven's idea was to siphon off business and retail."

"Was Steven's objective strictly financial?"

"Probably not. He was dependent on a number of houses for rare commodities and he wanted to run a trade across the high ball with passengers off the train out of Miami. As it was his father arranged for modern era boutique for his sons and passenger fares, he just couldn't keep up with cotton costs."

"You give the son Steven more power than I think he deserves."

"Well, his father had those ambitions. He had a hotel at every depot station with a few retail shops. Steven wanted into merchandising and real estate. I guess he thought he could make a go of it if he could take over various operations."

"Yes, that seems about right," he said, hoping she would give him a substantial lead to chew on.

She took a drag and exhaled. "Steven wanted his son to inherit from his father. His father on the other hand wanted to staff model homes because he gained business from nearly every home owner. The problem, of course, was Hariff owned clothing and not furniture, which is what Harris captivated the market with. Steven wanted Harris out, the sooner the better, and then someone wanted Hariff's shut down and that wouldn't have been himself."

"Do you think Klabbard and Height went into business for themselves?" he asked.

"No, but I honestly couldn't tell you who took care of Steven after the Harris heist."

"Or the Hariff shooting."

"Or that either."

"Or the movie set arson."

She didn't make a remark, if she knew outside the social circle of wire shoe Heights, Dotty or Mable Childress, she couldn't speak to the subject, it was either too vague in her mind or the pronouncement of Adam's death had left her dazed, as such announcements left most people who hadn't realized at the time that involvement was a risk for loss of life.

When he left he was struck by the fact she had gone inside with the water spray still pelting the greenery.

Cloie Jones was still a youthful looking female, blond hair cut very short above the ears, a boyish trim figure, a high collared backless tan shirt and knit black pants with black pumps. The house while neat had nothing to recommend it. It sat five feet off the curb, a bit of emerald green grass with a cactus on it, a traditional floor plan, small walk-in kitchen, dining hall, living room and two bedrooms with sliding glass doors onto a yellow brick patio with gravel and cacti.

"I live with Jim Klabby, he is Lloyd's nephew by marriage but we don't see him and Tom often, maybe once a month if at all, I did live with Steven Hariff about thirty years ago and sometimes, not as much as Dotty, took care of his son, I was the person who found the gun part in the hatbox, I was the one who gave it to Dotty to take to the police, you should know I did not touch the gun, Steve's boy was too young to take it off the shelf, a friend was looking for a hat and came across it, Steve said he had never seen it before, fortunately I wasn't asked to testify on the finding of it, Steve's son wasn't asked either."

"Is Mr. Klabby around?"

"No, he won't be here before the weekend starts, he doesn't

know anything about the gun."

"Yet it ended that case."

"That's what I heard. There wasn't much as to Harris House though."

"Did you know about a heist on Harris House?"

"I learned from Tom the department store closed and hasn't reopened."

"Did you know what happened there?"

"Not exactly. Steve was irate for months right after that forest fire, he said he lost alot of old Sequoia stand. He said it might take years before he would see any money."

"Do you know whether it was his wood that made Harris House furniture?"

"That's possible, more likely it made Hollan his houses."

"Who may have produced the arson of 1959?"

"I don't know. Could have been the man who had the houses built if they were yet on a bank loan."

"The developer refinanced those houses he had previously built, the new bank wouldn't have any reason to kill off their loan since the loan could have made the bank alot of equity, thus it is more likely to have been someone who could cash out their particular properties."

"May be the movie financier," she said, taking a guess.

"That person did not obtain a permit to have an outdoor fire, it had to be staged on a set."

"That leaves an investor. Steve Hariff did not invest in his own wood."

"Well, you can't invest that way. Do you know whether Klabby's family could have invested?"

"I wouldn't know. I think Lloyd may have tried to get into lumber but I don't know that he found a way to do that."

"Thanks," he said, and he left.

The ride some few blocks placed him at the Klabbard home,

Tom Height let him inside, Jake asked Lloyd when he saw him outside on the slate patio.

"Wouldn't have been myself, dear fellow," Klabbard responded dryly, "I don't invest, really I can't, my business excludes it, whether I take home furniture from the forest is about all I would do."

"Did you ever conduct business with Jo Webb?"

"Once. Lost my shirt to it."

"Was it for a diamond robbery?"

Klabbard looked annoyed. He gazed at his garden while he debated. "It's a little more complicated than that, the diamonds had been taken off the train and were to get sold in the shoppes, that made a new problem, the train no longer was crowded with tourists, the tourists went instead for a tour of the studios and into Burbank for accessories, 1972 was a bad season."

Jake said sympathetically, "Wouldn't a resort have been possible?"

"We had one in the mountains off the train line, tennis, volleyball, a lake, boats, a stunning lodge with a pier lit up at night, everything we could desire."

"Then your problem would have been people didn't want to boat at a lake."

"It wasn't the boats, it was the number of movies tourists could see at the studios, ten movies if they had the time all day for a weekend."

"No movie houses?"

"Couldn't interest them without a live movie being filmed. Those diamonds had to be on the coach, it was the reason tourists went to New York, to show off their newly purchased baubles."

"Did you ever run into a man named Fersterhof?"

"Yes. That's Mable Childress's ex-husband. He was a cop, not for the trains though. He ran a racket on the side, he sold resales."

"Is he around?"

"No, he came from Florida and opened a gambling operation in Indio and staffed it with retired boys out of Coachella."

"Did he do this with Mable?"

"No, she had divorced him by then. It seems she thought distance would be the suitable way to leave."

Klabbard had confessed to hiring Webb and had in all probability fenced Height because he lived with him, Jake wanted to know who put out the job to Klabbard, Klabbard did not give the confidence of someone who purchases the job, he was probably just the west coast operator.

Fersterhof the cop followed his ex-wife to California where he established a small time racket of cards, roulette and dice, along with diamonds and glove accessories, soon he had put in a motel, twenty rooms each two doubles, a few bars, and a movie centre for afternoon and evening showings.

Susan stood in the doorway. Jake had not realized he could have such an aching longing, all senses converging to a single startling thought, causing him to regret with a swift pang that he had allowed the situation between them to affect him so deeply. He supposed it was her ease, not worrying about problems, perhaps a decision which if acted on could bring wealth to uncomplicate the things she might otherwise worry over, as though the world was a vast sparse place in which a real dollar could be made with a bit of partnership, however, they were in a place that did not hold out much for ongoing earnings, whereas one could strike it rich clipping dope or modeling swimwear at pool parties, the under the table pay would trickle out, after a purchase of a tiny flat and a few sticks of furniture. He knew only without Childress and his connections there would be no conflict, he'd look elsewhere, yet he stumbled into bed with her and thought she was the finest thing he'd ever seen, later when he asked himself what it was that drew him toward her, was it truly a synchronicity of strong emotion or a reciprocity of instantaneous identification of values, or was it a romantic notion, he could see he was falling, yet as he lay there thinking her skin was flawless and her legs like silk, thinking he was content to be swept away, to be carried by enthrallment, his wisdom at last superseded, he grew angry at himself for having been selfish. He could see that as time went on he would be telling her one thing and himself another, permitting no conflict to emerge in their moments, while the person he held onto had too much an illusory quality. He finally surrendered to his logic as he knew he had to, logic being a dominating force, and stayed the night, that same night, with Roberta, in whose arms and lacy bright grey and black short negligee passion came forward as regret. Despite Roberta being consistently encouraging, brave in her honesty to the point he had to ask himself whether there were any such realism to the belief that she knew better than he how best to employ the information he was in possession of, were he to withdraw Childress he would say Susan could have unwittingly acknowledged that her father had committed a felony, yet he was far from Susan right now and Roberta was stretching beneath him, a sweetly perfumed incarnation of desire and yielding and as she pressed her hands to his thighs her still lacy cupped breasts swelled to his rocking motion, he withdrew before she came and held her until he felt her quiver, hours had a way of distorting his belief of Susan, he had taken a step backwards to be less aware. Of Roberta he found he wished he could preserve their tenderness, keep it close to himself but loss again arrived unerringly, a need for the denial of the relationship itself, a methodology of its own, he would think her anything except cold or unyielding, his innermost Self ordained through scrutiny of the mindful objective of purity, seemingly an invitation to grace, he imagined how her house could look, and his heart sharply filled with a dearth of frustration to realize she had never taken him home, matched to the perfection of realization she could exist far outside his life, not as real as his emotion had led him to draw close.

Morning came with a surprise of dew and roses coming up in succession, reddish yellow and white, a confusion of barely emerged buds with languorous promise, inescapable definition, the path a garden in itself, a perennial sanctuary of delight adorned by limp annuals, each one green, he would pull through his own convalescence, seek his ideology in haiku, silence, possibly friends who had been through a similar denouncement, the barometer no longer measured, the stone houses above Edison were rebuilt, all cement, a few windows, in Grand Terrace, a cost of expenditure lay in a desert of empty dwellings, he could not discern Susan, she continued to speak of Childress as the man she had surrendered her complex needs to, still he was aware she elicited love in him, with her he had an absolute truth that he belonged to what he was born to, he was forever held in the highest esteem possible, every experience of her was fresh, new, he could possess no need that she would not meet, it was torrid yet did not allow him to sort through much but complicated, long built up tension, he was periodically aware of Roberta trying to create a distance in which he could discover what he was feeling, and in this uncomfortable out of kilter mixture of a sense of leaving someone behind, he thought he would like now to raise a son, extend his existence, make himself known before he too faded into a surreal landscape destitute by ravages of time. He would take his toddler to the precinct, teach him about cops, sit him down at a big detective desk, take him out on patrol, take him to funerals so as he grew he understood a cop's life while filled with rich satisfying investigations had a bittersweet grief to it that left an equal number of retirees unable to beat back the oppression of long often gruelling hours coupled with all threats of danger, he had made his choices, his wife hadn't wanted children and he only wanted her, he enjoyed their time, was possessive of her because she meant nurturance to him, they had their dinner parties, concerts, tennis, evening walks on the canal, morning coffee on a small deck overlooking the passage of a strong river, and then in a flash of a storm it was over. He had been single twenty-five years, as long as he had been married. Roberta could tolerate a child and him, he was not so sure about Susan who would fit in a child as sure as a schedule to relax. Could he accept her consumption of him and then put it aside without becoming moody, when he returned home intending to do some yard work he found her waiting and from a distance he could see she had not expected him not to be there, her chest was tight, her breasts strained against the light fabric of her tight fitting top and he thought she must have wondered what kept him, while she fidgeted she could have wondered about him the way he did about her and watching him pull into the drive had an overwhelming sense of relief, as she put a hand on his leg and let him walk into her, he felt her necessity to have him and it made him unable to resist, she was demanding as he hadn't known she was capable of and he went for her shoving himself against her finding her body taut and hard like his, backing her into the house, agonizingly responsive to her, he moved her against the wall and released himself on her, she offering no resistance, when it started to rain.

He drove her home following her inside the tiny three room house, a large living room with tan walls, white floorboards and tan Berber, black and white photos of natural landscapes in black metal frames marching across a wall, fashionable modern furniture, not what he expected of her, a Formica kitchen floor with picture window that looked at a wall and had plenty of glass cabinets, and a bedroom with a chest of drawers painted black and a poster bed, same tan carpet, tan walls, black painted floorboards, bathroom with walk-in shower, patio and pool, all told probably worth a fortune. There were people and style who drew you in, this was that sort of a place, he wasn't sure why but he had the sense of time running out, of a deadline, possibly she squeezed life in around her time to herself.

"Will he come here?" he asked her about Childress.

"He doesn't know about it. I come and go as I like."

"Will you drive down to see him?"

"If he calls first. He doesn't like me to just walk in."

He thought it odd as he kissed her soft mouth, she was malleable in his hands, without a core of contemplation, letting go of her needs for the briefest instant of a flash; for an odd glimpse of a moment he thought he caught her in a transparent mood, she was his, surrendered for his expensive pleasures.

"I'll call," he told her, making light of her relation to John Childress, and he left. He told himself the raw aspect of parting was that he had entered a world that was not of his capability and he ought to take himself out, act with nobleness, put it behind himself before it festered like an obsession, the better of him looking inward instead of for definition in another. Tell him the future, which was real, which wasn't, when would it materialize, a perpetual angst gnawing in the background that dictated action or passive waiting, had he written throughout his livelihood he could have entered the study of philosophy for a late-in-life career change into a ministry as many of his bosses had, but he was a cop's pro, a blanket morgue cop. Decisions were entered into anything but casually, for they took tremendous focus and deliberation and then a checking off of logic, weighing it against self insights to understand motivation, and all the while responding to the crime, designating prelim, talking to the sheriff coroner, casting the grid, sifting for an evidentiary path, the human dilemma and its enduring questions weighing upon him like a time pressure noose.

How did one get past the clobbering intensity of monotony after entering retirement, how did one maintain dignity. He knew that the years could become quite demanding without any real fulfillment as tedium doled out the day, affordability for dating lost to a meager allotment that barely covered living expenses. He drove with the long practised patience of one who must wait for hard-to-claim answers up Santa Ana Drive to Greenspot and high into the cement terrain of the wilderness above the Edison hydroelectric plant. The steep boulevard saw all of a few cars a day and otherwise hid a ramshackle of marginal homes mostly inhabited by people who did not fit in socially. At the summit was Francesca's small modern cement split level house with glass; in her driveway was parked a vehicle he knew he had seen in Highland. He parked and finding the front door open to allow a breeze he walked onto a mezzanine loft and gazed down at blond hardwood floors, opened sliding glass doors that led to a handsome deck, a small kitchen and presumably behind it an airy bedroom or two. Voices came from the deck — Francesca's and John Childress, she playing to him, he taking it in his stride, his voice somewhat instructive.

"You're quite mad to think you would get in so easily," he was saying.

"But do you have it covered? After all, Jo is no spring chicken, she'll use at least one backup."

"Won't make any difference, Chessie, it's the way I work, no eyes, they're too costly."

"What if I take Tom? He's good for the attention, it'll be five minutes."

"Can't, won't. It isn't as though we have to stick to a schedule, the way the mechanism operates, no one will respond."

She touched his leg bare foot, Jake had a momentary glance at that sleek firm foot and leg, John stretched bringing most of one leg into view. "Suppose we get found out? Suppose that backup of yours gets heavy?"

"It doesn't hold any consequence." He caressed her leg with his hand. She was obviously making time, enjoying it for all it was worth. It had to be worth a good deal if she knew about Susan; if she didn't, then to him she was a convenience.

"I'd like to know what you asked for from Ron."

"I didn't ask, I know better, he'd turn me down flat, blow the whistle on me."

She mused. "Will Joanie do it?"

"Joanie Klabbard? I haven't talked to her in years, not since that thing went down with Height, it was just too cheap for me, an aging divorcee looking to revitalize her life."

"She can do practically anything," she said, with a drawl which was meant to hook him.

"You can do everything, honey," and pulled her by the leg toward him, until she was partly in view. She was vivacious in a two piece denim swimsuit, breasts buoyant like orbs, her golden hair held back by a tortoise shell comb, she grabbed him by the collars.

"I haven't had a man in weeks," she said.

He wrapped his body around her and kissed her hard. "No out-of-towners, babe."

"I promise, just make me happy."

"I'll make all the arrangements, you just do what I say."

"Make me yours again."

He put his hands over her breasts and told her something that made her laugh. She slid her hands up each leg certain of him.

"Did you ever do this with Lloyd?" she asked, as though a bit drunk on the attraction of him.

"I don't do that, Chessie, men who do have little choice, they are succumbed."

She thought about his answer, then laughed and said, "He likes to watch, I wondered."

When he didn't respond, she said, "Old men with young men, women with women, no nudies, everything on VCR, if you're going to bring him on board you should know he has his favorites and he'll say yes if you have them too."

He sounded a bit tight. "Are you a favorite?"

"Joanie and I are his best. He said once he could spend all his time watching us."

"What do you two do?"

Jake left feeling like a regular peeping tom, as Francesca made a rather outrageous request to audition.

He found their entire set entirely preoccupied with affairs, the desire for conquest consummating. Although she was quite young, Childress had to have the availability of many pretty women for him to be able to relate to her so readily, Childress obviously didn't worry about Susan nor Susan about him, the open partner relationship was no greater an encumbrance than the necessity of arrangements he was obligated to make, and there appeared to be no misunderstanding as to how far she could expect him to go with her, even if he spent a night or two he belonged to someone else. Jake would have found this understanding difficult, except for now. It made him wonder whether Francesca was depressed by their lovemaking or whether she accepted his amorous philanderings because her choices were limited. She did not appear to Jake to be very demanding and Childress for all his seduction would not tolerate losing Susan. The grating idea Jake had of the man was his unusual relationship with a mother who had to be happily married. Despite the business of wrecking mom and pop liquor stores, it was not normal for a mother to accompany her elderly adult son on his more tyrannical excursions about town. Also her son was not significantly younger than Dr. Childress was and didn't meet any presumed age requirement to qualify as his son because he was a mere ten years younger; thus, the inherent gambit appeared to be that Mable in some way felt she had to keep her husband in check, and Childress obviously saw no harm in this, he was a real asshole and his mother as the sole person who might have any ability to intervene would not especially if it was she who insisted on being his lookout. Jake thought it was even more peculiar that Mable kept her daughter at arm's distance from being at the family home, if she was an attractive young woman it was possible Mable protected her from Childress' dominating intrusions but more likely she didn't want her son to affect her daughter, her daughter came down to see Dr. Childress when John was somewhere else. Jake had come across many abhorrent family relationships where violence figured prominently, and with every last one there was a residual of an earlier marriage still marking time. Fersterhof went into the rackets, it was likely his son John had plenty of contact with him, possibly he fenced to his father or someone his father knew, Indio was a half an hour away, Mable who locked herself up inside her house unless it was to drive her son downtown seemed not to worry that the outside world could encroach on her at all.

Jake dropped by the Klabbard residence. Klabbard was painting on an easel in the backyard while sipping iced tea and boyfriend Height was sunning on a lounge chair, his salad piled high.

"I was hoping you could tell me about your ex-wife," Jake said to Lloyd Klabbard.

Klabbard turned to him, paintbrush in hand. "Joanie is gay. She's the personal friend of a Francesca Harper except when Chessie has friends over."

Height pushed his sunglasses down his nose. "Several times a year we entertain. Joanie and Lloyd are still good friends."

Lloyd asked, "I gather you'd like to talk to Joanie. She has her own place in town but she's frequently busy, she's a data processor and works out of her home."

"I was given a rather indelicate description of your relationship with your ex-wife," Jake said.

"The fact is," Tom Height answered in his partner's defense, "Lloyd didn't really survive the divorce, Joanie was his closest friend for a long time, he still loves her."

Lloyd said, "I've made the adjustment, dear fellow, if Tom didn't love me so much, it would've been impossible leaving and staying apart. When you meet her, you will see why, she's stunning and she loves me still."

Tom said, "Lloyd never wants me to leave the house when they come over or I would, he's still very attracted to her. Many times he has begged her to take him back but her answer is the same, although she loves him she likes women more, and doesn't think her situation would be resolved, or at least that's what she says."

"Would you come with me to talk to her?" Jake inquired.

Lloyd glanced at Tom who shrugged. "I s'pose I could but you'd have to drive me back. What if I have her come over? You could talk to her here, couldn't you?"

Ideally he would have liked to see her in her own place, but her rapport to her ex-husband who was obviously involved in a new job was essential. "Would it take long for her to get here?"

"No, maybe all of ten minutes."

"I would greatly appreciate that," Jake answered.

Lloyd went inside to call her. He came out a few minutes later and said she'd be over straight away.

She arrived in a few minutes. She was a stunning raven. She was tall, very thin yet voluptuous, her black hair somewhat poufed and long, tumbling sensuously down her back almost to her waist, she wore tight stretch pants and matching heels and a tight collar-high satin blouse without a back showing off pronounced shoulder blades. She came right up to Lloyd yet did not kiss him, her breasts on him. She lacked any self consciousness. Lloyd put his arm around her waist and let it go limp.

"You look radiant, honey," he said tenderly. "My friend here wants to talk to you. I promise I won't leave you two alone."

"Is Tom around?" Her voice was lilting, without intention.

"If you like I'll ask him to join us."

She slipped her hand up his arm and caressed his chin. "That would make me very comfortable."

"Tom," he called out, "Joanie has arrived."

Tom entered placing his sunglasses on a table with a vase of flowers and went over to kiss her. "It's been so long since you brought Chessie up."

"She has her absences, it's hard to be away." She returned his kiss and hugged him and then sat on the easy chair.

Lloyd settled in at her feet. Tom sat on the love seat and Jake took the sofa. It was plain to see Lloyd was still taken with her. Tom seemed to encourage it, Jake found himself unable to pull his gaze away, she was strikingly beautiful, he could almost feel her pulse to her ex-husband, it was generous of Tom not to be jealous or flippant.

Jake took the lead. "I understand you know Francesca."

She smiled as though happy he knew a friend of hers. "Isn't she gorgeous?"

"Yes," he said, asserting control over the discussion.

"She's one of the most loving women I've ever known. " She slightly arched her back. "I met her through Lloyd who liked her as much as I did. Lloyd had fixed her up with a job and by the time it was over she made a huge amount of money. I threw a party and had Chessie do all the decorations. It went over sensationally."

She moved slightly and Lloyd moved with her, it was an unmotivated act but caused him to wind up with his hand beneath her leg, and she answered him by holding her heel to his large hip, Jake had a sense of them as a synchronistic pair, able to act on the other's thought. As she bent forward he stretched out his legs and crossed them and Tom got up to prepare drinks, she said to Jake, "I don't know how much Lloyd has told you but I used to bring Chessie over often until it was I who decided to act on it, I asked Lloyd if he would object and he said no. I was young, in my early twenties, I was trying to get into the movies, and I liked having someone around who could read me my lines."

Lloyd laughed. "I woke up one morning with a hangover and stumbled into a shower and was horrified that Chessie and not Joanie was there. It sobered me up faster than anything."

"It was awkward for a bit, until I asked her to leave. Now I make sure I'm not bringing anyone over who may wind up alone with him."

"Did you know she takes an interest in crime?"

Tom came in with a tray of lemonade drinks and set it down. They each took a glass and sipped it.

Joanie said, "No, I'm unaware of your accusation. I spend most of my time there and I've yet to hear anything incriminating."

He couldn't ask her about any involvement she had had unless he had a warrant. "Have you met any of her male friends?"

"No, she doesn't have any."

Tom was the wire, Lloyd the knife and putty, Joanie the celebration. "Have you ever known in advance of a crime that was committed?"

Lloyd said sharply, angrily, "Absolutely not, who the hell do you think you are?"

Joanie had paid a hefty price for her husband being the one with the pre-knowledge. She answered, before he was done talking, "We all did alot more than we should have in those days."

Lloyd said shouting, "Don't say another word," and raised himself off the floor.

Jake apologized saying, "I wasn't trying to provoke anyone. I am trying to learn how you would have learned about the getaway?"

Lloyd glared. "She's not a party, she wanted me to be happy and this is what happened, I left her!"

"I'm sorry I've offended you. I'll leave," Jake said.

Lloyd simmered down. "No, no, it's not your fault, I'm the one who is easily worried by questioning, I'm the one who suggested Joanie come here."

"Yes, that's right," Tom said. "This stuff doesn't really have much to do with her, she's an innocent bystander if only because she didn't ever really understand what was going on between us."

Jake was surprised Joanie stood up and pressed against Lloyd's back. He gave her an affectionate pat.

"It's such a complex twist of complicated events," Lloyd said. "You can see how incredibly beautiful she is," and inadvertently stepped aside to admire her. As if aware he had put too much separation between them he moved closer, then behind her, scooped her long hair into his hands and let it fall through.

Tom said, "Would you like to stay awhile? I'll put some steaks on the grill."

"I have to be going," Jake said, at which Joanie said, "Oh don't rush off, an hour of your time won't be giving up much, will it?"

He stayed. Joanie took him onto the patio and sat him on a lounge seat and sat beside him. She talked to him about her run-ins with the law as a teenager while Tom tended to the charcoal broil. Lloyd passed out drinks and by Jake's request 7-Up and laughed affectionately with Tom who yelled for Joanie to talk to him. She patted Jake, bent forward to kiss his cheek and he closed his eyes briefly, aware of her softness, and then watched her approach the two, come between them, and that they didn't actually move much, if at all; she circled Tom around the waist and told him something amusing and all three laughed, she hugged Tom a bit and he reached for Lloyd, drawing him close to himself, and Joanie slipped a hand down Tom's cutoffs and kissed Lloyd. Lloyd told her she was naughty and she replied she was getting drunk, Tom moved into her and said to bite his ear and she did. She kissed Lloyd again and letting go of Tom's hand he reached for her and held her as though he could stand there all night and at length Tom asked them to get the spice rack. Jake joined Tom at the grill and they chatted awhile about the sport page and once Jake traded places to flip the meat and caught a glance into the kitchen where Lloyd was seated and holding his ex and had his face buried in her chest and was crying.

"He loves her," Tom told him.

"No, he loves you."

"I'm his passion, she's his breath."

"You two get along well."

"She likes to tease and I want him to know I'll support him at all times and he knows it, but she is able to fix his mood, whatever is wrong. Lloyd is an exceptional man, he plans all his projects down to the detail and then gets headaches, bad ones, and nothing gets rid of them except her, it's a bit odd I guess."

They were missing from the kitchen. Jake went to wash his hands and passed by a guest room with the door slightly ajar. Joanie stood almost bare, that beautiful hair cascading across her body, her body nestled up to him, gently caressing his head, he motionless.

"She'll be here soon, it won't be long," she was saying.

"You really called?" he asked.

"Yes, sweetheart," her words overflowing with tenderness.

Jake stepped into the cool interior of the bathroom, its dark jade walls, night light, plush dark green carpet, thinking they were punishing each other, a mild taunt. A telephone rang in the bowels of the house. When he next re-entered the hall the door was shut. A soft crying slipped under the door.

He sat with Tom asking him about who he knew trying to elicit something tangible but Tom was alert to the interior. Finally he left the grill and went inside. Jake could make out indistinguishable conversation, then shouts, Joanie emerged dressed and said she was famished. Jake made hamburgers, slopped on lettuce, onion, mayonnaise, pickle, and gave her the first plate with a dab of coleslaw. He asked whether Lloyd was alright and Joanie said not really, he was feeling severely depressed, like he wanted to end it all, she had asked for a friend to come but at the last minute she couldn't. The others came out, Lloyd in a white terry cloth robe, Tom in jeans, and they ate and chatted about Lloyd in younger years, laughing gaily to humor him, until he felt better and walked her to her car.

Jake helped with dishes and then surprised at the late hour of ten he left. He thought their lives were a mess predicated on a misdirected adventurism. But for their sympathy for each other, they were isolated, and ruined, unable to sustain any whole or piecemeal intention, lost to the devil, never to recuperate. Despite his training he genuinely lamented for Lloyd who at the center of the drama yet had no common sense, who in all probability would die in his tracks, despairing. Jake drove to Roberta's with a pang of guilt, he was avoiding his feelings, hoping to create distance where only possessive desire had dominated, needing the relief from desire more than to find he had surpassed some fatiguing standard of adultery, insights were no comfort now nor was an informed realism all that helpful; seeing her flat dark he kept driving, bleakness setting in, his emotions raw, his sense of futility upswelling, his mind retracting to the pained Joanie, her notion of play dashed on a rugged shore. Even Height, the group's wire shoe, was menaced by his own ambivalence to recuperate the aging soprano, his harsh voice to Joanie a source of antagonism unintentionally leaving Lloyd defeated, the road to hell paved only by a fool's vain ambition that they were all sworn to, a buffoon tragedy.

The case pointed to the unexpected — of a severely compromising nature, that the women had planned the take on Harris, fenced the drivers, handled the abduction of the goods, how else would Joanie have arranged a celebration of presenting her husband with a charitable female if she had not known about the heist, her stupidity was she threw away her life on Lloyd and would probably do it again because life had dwindled her resources, in the dark corridors was Jo Webb, a dangerous enigma, she after all understood the lay of the land — of a small town, a railroad, ten thousand diamonds, four deaths, one of an unsuspecting clerk in love with Childress, her principal overseer neither Lloyd nor Height who she probably brought in, the gun responsible for wounding nineteen royal guard forgotten on the display counter like a signature — possibly meant for a weekend cop who relieved the slain security who worked for Hariff, the difficulty with the perception was no one looking at the landscape saw this group of women as anything but gorgeous pinups, certainly not as gun-toting molls, the real attraction to power few women would come to any other way. He ran clearances on Josephina Webb and discovered rather abruptly with a twinge of shock she had been assigned to the Registry of Weapons in London. She was to have an essential role as wire to Childress' capable electric shutdown, she brought the Luger missing from the Constable most reasonably for the Harris job and then reported it as stolen obliging the authorities to return it to her, the gun's hammer replaced the wire cork on satellite which suggested she had been part of a surveillance unit set up for sight and sound, their lead a brassy chick with rail wire experience. Why pretty females? His mind ached for an answer, it was much too obvious when he seized upon it, dumb in fact, they hit trains, cleaned out the displays of European gems, filled sacks on board a train during lights out as it sped through the Gulf into Appalachia — and dropped them off the train in dead night for a waiting van, the van hidden in a freshwater marsh was pushed onto a road as streams trickling to the ocean moved it out of place, the train like a lit lamp angled along a coastal route clacking over the tracks at high speed; no one would be aware of a heist until the fuse was changed, if the train was detained in St. Louis or Everglades to conduct a passenger check it was still too late to recapture the goods. Off shore surveillance would study its catch to identify the sting operation before command sent out its marshals to make arrests. They could have up to nineteen bandits, more or less, because the gun had fired on nineteen royal guards injuring them, at St. Louis a hundred marshals came through each compartment and turned all contents upside down, the robbers had jumped ship accounting for those missing, every last second instituted per their limited edition skeleton watches, Webb, Fersterhof, Klabbard, Height and four or five women, maybe Lake. Lake's name conjured up calm pristine waters for a jump off point, her one-time assistant a retired nurse, a man named Gladdis — Jake had worked for a lieutenant by that name, the guy could jump any fence no matter its height, knew the exact place to cut wire where the pulse hit the curve, a real pro for tournament fencing, a precise SOB who could outwit the best cat burglar, he was the detective who went into Harris the day the lights shut off permanently. The desert which he considered he knew intimately had become a stranger, the mother always on watch, the aging son always tearing up the joint, no one bothering to follow, no one ever stopping, a clear ride back to the lair. If the sheriff could not go on chase, it was because they lacked evidence or worse, had the wrong evidence. Another few calls told him Mable Childress had designed a balance wheel for a garage door, taking a picture of the car and printing the time at the top. Her ramp lift gave her protection into and out of her home as well as on the block on which her house sat, it gave her any vehicle that followed her. Because of the camera, because she would have to check her monitor, her eye was trained for entry and shadow. With this skill she might map out the job, bring in a watch restorer to tackle the choreography. Train delays were replaced, so there could be as many as eight trains running concurrently. Jake expanded the list — one to cut the lights, five to divert while one grabbed the jewels, one to throw the catch overboard, a team to pick up, a team to collect and take to the buyer or fence.

The BN & SF 1:30 never reported was the senior Hariff's only error, he never repeated it, each car got a fully licensed operative. He would have eventually hitched onto his son Steven's crimes, Steven would know the schedules for all the trains, Lloyd Klabbard was their putty man for stores, the electricians were Jo Webb and Tom Heights, the physician who might determine what to wear, Elisa Lake, a marine shipmate to latch onto satellite surveillance, Fersterhof, and a group of bimbos, Dotty, Francesca, Joanie, possibly Susan Collins, not to mention her father and the lookout from Harris, the same armored van man in the Hariff shooting. Added to the core group he put twenty others, unnamed, who rode the trains just to be there as spotters.

His thought froze with Susan. She represented something, a telephone call into the stationary contact who because of a problem would dispatch someone to get rid of it.

He instantly recoiled from this idea. There was only one place to take it and that was that he was for some reason in the way of a job in progress. He could no more see her initiating a call like that than he could imagine her taking a gun to a man's head. The fact that in Mable's hand it was never used had to signify a type of job, in Jo's hand it was left behind and in some unknown gangster's hand was a death warrant.

He left his car on the street. The day was a blustery wind torn Wednesday, by the appearance of the collection of clouds well on its path to a storm. The Childress home seemed no greater a fashion than any other of ten houses on the narrow winding canyon road lined with palms nor any less observant of the flats over which it dominated, its large window obscured by drawn drapes, all other rooms looking inward to the rear and the interior garden. Mable was polite, jazzed up in the tight tights of her social group, a silk pink blouse that showed off her shoulders and neck, her blond hair like a bleached manifestation of flamboyance. In the kitchen sat her daughter — a slender young woman in her early twenties, a college student at San Rafael or some such campus, in the face identical to her mother, dressed in an olive green sheath of a dress and black pumps. She was soft spoken, blue eyed, wistful, somewhat cautious, she instantly took up chit chat and asked him about his job and how he knew her parents. At length her mother asked her to sit outside which she did on one of four chaise lounge chairs with shades and a hat, a pack of Marlboro fags, and tanning lotion.

"She's a real beauty," he said, after she was apparently relaxed outside.

Mable said, "I used to look like her at her age. Fifty years ago."

"We all looked a hell of alot better fifty years ago."

"I hear you're asking about my gun."

"It's turned up as a party to a crime."

"Not my gun, of that I assure you. I have never fired it."

"Someone wants it thought that it has a twist part that fits on a rifle."

"I don't use a part. It stays close to my pants in the car."

"Why bring it at all when you drive your son?"

She cast a protective glance at her daughter as if fearful she would hear them through the glass. "She is training for justice, she can fire a weapon, because of that I can't afford to drag her into all this. I have the gun on me in the rare event something goes wrong."

"Has it ever?"

"I wouldn't know. John tells me to stay inside the car, I don't fuss about what he's asked to do, the person in charge pays him to do what he does, that's the way it is, I only want protection, after all we don't any of us really know what a scared person might be capable of."

"Whose gun is it?"

"My husband's."

"I thought perhaps it was your son's."

"Then he'd have it with him."

"Or one of his associate's. "

"That clerk did not let my son in the door, she showed up, it shouldn't have happened, my son took the fall; the other body attempted a double cross when he took half that was supposed to go into San Francisco, I don't have control over these things, those two ought to have had better common sense."

"Why wasn't a lookout posted to the back door for the Harris Store job?" She wouldn't implicate Webb ever, she certainly wouldn't identify how the stupid act went down if she even knew, and he was beginning to think she didn't know, it had been a complete surprise launched during the trial, possibly a district attorney foil to protect a witness.

"He ran off. He's the one who borrowed the armored van."

"So he was offered two jobs."

She looked tired. She gave her daughter a glance and looked back at him. "I raised her, she's a credit to me although she takes after her father in nearly every way, she's decent, she loves her life, she knows nothing of Fersterhof, nor of Hariff, she's just herself."

"Innocence is that way."

"I suppose. I keep them apart, she from John. It takes some doing."

"He's setting up a new job," he told her. "He is lining up the work. Harper, Klabbard, possibly Height, definitely Webb, not enough for a big job, what do you think it goes with?"

"Do I look stupid to you? Admittedly I am washed up, I'm old, I can't move fast anymore, the trains carry lumber or oil and we don't take a train for products, if my son wants to die, he'll choose his brand of poison. It definitely won't be Francesca, she's white trash, useful sometimes to Lloyd Klabbard."

"Do you approve of Susan?"

"Susan is faithful to John, she doesn't try to turn him around."

"If he has other women, perhaps she has other men."

"Susan keeps her father secure, that's all she wants. He made the mistake, he walked in on that fucking loser, he was warned — no motels, no stashes, no unapproved expenditures. She doesn't do diversion the way Joanie did in those days, the way Francesca is willing to do."

"Who was Adam?"

"No one anyone knew, not even Collins knew. He just popped out of a motel at a college." She eyed him and said, quite pointedly, "I meet all my child's interests, there's no telling who is going to try for me through her. Susan is not a dedicated daughter-in-law, I put up with Susan's difficulties but we aren't close, she sees John two days every other weekend and doesn't ask questions, if she is aware of affairs I doubt she gives it much thought."

"Does Susan know Lloyd?"

"Yes, of course, he covered her father's sanitorium."

"Would she have met his ex-wife?"

"I wouldn't know or care." But she considered it. "Probably she knows Joanie, but she's not Joanie's type. Not many are. Joanie likes women who are attracted to men. She likes their notion of femininity, it's not an intellectual attraction. Susan likes men, she's loyal, she detaches even from John, I suspect for her apart from her family she rarely has involvements of any sort, why I don't know."

"Is your ex living?"

"Yes, he has an estate in Indio in the valley. He has asked me to send her but I don't, he's the one who started me in this, I wouldn't welcome that complication."

The door opened and closed, the heavy confidant stride of a man could be heard, then John Childress stepped into the room, gave him a contemptuous look, and came over and dutifully kissed his mother.

"Where's Steph?" he asked.

She motioned to the patio. He stood debating, then dropped the mail on the table and went outside. It was hard to look at him without seeing the clandestine meeting he had had with Francesca but his manner with the young woman was clearly circumspect until she grabbed his leg and held on.

"She has a crush on him," her mother said.

John had successfully unclamped her hand and stood blocking her sun, she got up and put her arms around him, laughing at him, but he held her and pried her loose, at which she hung onto his shoulder.

"She's persistent," Jake said.

"She'll outgrow him. She thinks of him as her uncle."

"You didn't tell her he is your son?"

"It's how I've kept Fersterhof out of the picture."

It explained her concern. He watched the young Stephanie try to plant a kiss on his mouth, but he told her something and she backed off. She gave him the lotion and he put it on her back, neck and arms.

"Maybe you ought to tell her," Jake remarked.

"That's not a good idea, she'd want to meet my first husband and trust me, that could be a disaster. It's a harmless infatuation."

Jake suspected there was nothing harmless about it. The girl had backed into him on purpose and arched against him. He placed lotion on both hands, lifted her arms a bit and almost for her benefit lathered her neck and collar bone. Eventually they came inside, John sat near his mother and Stephanie sat on his lap.

"Do you think I'm pretty?" she asked Jake.

"Yes, you are beautiful."

She pushed into him. "He thinks I'm pretty," she said, her

tone wanting to know whether he might share the opinion.

"I didn't say you weren't, honey." He put an arm around her waist, reaching for fags in a ceramic dish and lit one. "You're just too young. We're almost forty years apart."

"I know but you're the only man I'm around all the time. I'm getting practice."

Jake had expected Mable to say something, he wondered why she might let it run its course. He needed a few more questions particularly on the subject of Adam but suspected the two had come in from the sun specifically to rescue her mother from having to say more.

"I know I shouldn't," she went on with a pout, "but I'm grown up now and he takes me everywhere, to the movies, the salon, to see my friends. He's always there to make sure I'm safe."

"I'd buy you a car of your own except I don't want you running off," Mable said.

Stephanie groaned. "Same old, same old." She got off him and flitted about the kitchen making herself a cup of cocoa. She came back to him and tussled his hair, saying, "I have friends who like you, they think you're cute."

He had begun to appear harassed. "Go to your room, sweetie."

She took her chocolate drink with her. "I'm in my room," she shouted, and slammed a door shut.

Jake asked Mable, "Do you mind if I ask you a few more questions?"

Childress answered, "Yes, I mind. I'd like you to leave."

Jake saw his way out. The family would stifle under the weight of dysfunction with its necessary and unnecessary secrets. Mable had turned over the limit setting to her son, when she ought to just kick him out.

Childress had not made the call to Roberta Harris but someone, presumably whoever brought Childress down from the mountain, had. Jake couldn't imagine how that worked unless a neighbor seeing him go inside the house had called Childress. It was either that or the closed circuit that Mable protected her home with was reviewed by another person.

Jake contacted an associate at the police department, his friend in robbery said he'd look around. The database search would take at least an hour.

# 9/Nine

THERE WAS NO BOYFRIEND IN THE PICTURE, NOR an overprotective friend, Jake looked up a cross index name directory by street address and parallel filed it to his name list, the one name that came up for a match was another cop, whose career had him transferred first from city hall, then from Arrowhead, finally to Rialto for a stint, then to the new station on Seventh, he worked burglary detail, while he worked for the superior court he went in as pistol to out-of-control, fired up witnesses, the fact that he didn't work the trial was of little consequence since it was he who logged in the gun part when it came in, the peculiar event was during the trial the evidence disappeared, no one knew where, the cop was a guy named Harper, not incidentally he was either Francesca's father or brother, he probably was responsible for getting rid of warrants on her.

The district attorney's office was gearing up for another big trial on a few blocks of warehouses who were processing stolen vehicle parts from over the border, the small office had brought in a pool of temporaries and the sound of typing dominated even telephone interviews, his man was in court, the supervisor was a touchy sort by the name of Acker Gessom who made it plain that if he had a perp's prints he had him bagged, and on a desk in his office he had a bunch of plastic bags each with a gun.

"Bad case, Jake, some lunatic opened fire on pedestrians in the mall, every last pistol came out of our favorite warehouse, the small town's losing to big suburbs because of it. I pulled in Webb, Josephina on a dirty bath, do you remember her? She was my chief suspect in that Harris murder rap thirty years ago."

"She's surfaced again, allegedly for a train heist around the time of that wire."

"Oh, yeah, we had a confession so we stopped looking. Guy named Callin was strapped to finger tubes on a lie detector test and was positive, we didn't have enough on the chick, not even a witness."

"What made you think she was inside the store?"

"Gun was left behind. We went to look her up, turns out she's reported it missing, but the slug in the body didn't match."

"What can you give me on a cop named Harper?"

"Nothing, he's alright, nothing out of the ordinary, pipeline to Edison though."

"Any family?"

"No, they're all dead. He had a sister, pretty girl, but with no brains."

Still had no brains. "I think Harper gave me a bum steer, does he have it in him to leave hang-ups?"

Gessom guffawed. "He wouldn't have made it thirty-four years in the precinct if he did, what's the angle?"

"Probably it's a burglary, few has-beens, Webb, Klabbard —"

"Oh, Klabbard, went to hell in a hand basket, guy turned florid."

"This would be his ex-wife. Harper and maybe a Collins."

"Oh that's the name." Gessom closed the door with his name on it behind Jake and drew the shade over it. "Too few people to pull a box job."

"Man named Childress is setting it up."

"Might be a liquor store, it's definitely not a Nordstrom or Macy, not enough players, you'd require another twenty, thirty people, diversions, unless they go in at night, yeah night might work, I can pull Webb in but she doesn't proof out."

"What evidence did we miss in the Hariff case?" Jake inquired.

"The shoebox. It was a kid's, but the case didn't have it for a kid, it was adult evidence which we couldn't prove, the address went to the station in Rialto which says trains, I mean what else, yet we couldn't get a ticket, it was just a wash, we got the rifle part but nothing else."

"There was a good deal to suggest they pulled Harris Store and then the Hariff shooting."

"Yeah, the fucks combined a getaway van that looked like an armored heist and wasn't, the guy took off in a two seater, and they bilked the state with a forest fire, there was that female found shot inside Harris and then some jaw up north dead in a motel, we figured it was a double-cross."

"Are you aware the Harris heir received a call?"

"That wouldn't be Childress' style, what did the caller want?"

"According to Miss Harris, the caller said the original case was not adequately researched, that there is missing evidence."

"Fan mail, we get that too, in all probability a bunch of bullies."

"This is a sex club, everyone switches. Seems to be what helps them best to retain diversionary tactics to pull a job."

"With Harris Store there was only gun diversion. Once the hammer was discerned, for some reason they couldn't get a read on the wire; when it was traced to an officer, nothing further was picked up."

"Who was it traced to, do you remember?"

"Mable Childress initially, but it isn't registered to her, it goes with a Fersterhof."

"I have the same info. This is a savvy group that's been pulling predominantly train heists for a number of years. My real question is who reviews the home surveillance and then sends in a bouncer."

"If their alarm rings into the precinct, your answer could be quite straight forward."

"Can you confirm that it is Francesca's brother, Harper, who picks up at the other end?"

When he at last drove to Susan's he was depressed. He had hoped their friendship was not an act of manipulation or diversion, the sadness he perceived as she opened the door and let him inside was crushing, a powerful injunctive against rational scrutiny, had she been younger he would have ignored her altogether and the visit to meet her father that first night would not have occurred.

"When you followed me to San Francisco that day, were you hoping to learn what I was after?" he asked, half expecting her to deny his query.

"You were investigating my dad, he's been through enough."

"In what way is he connected to the man at the motel? He merely walked in on him."

"You know perfectly what I mean, you went in for a handful of photo files on the getaway van. He was at the airbase with his plane."

"I didn't know that then."

She was angry, her entire frame steeled against whatever

he would say. "He went to prison for no reason as far as I can tell, took the rap for a handful of losers."

"Why do you stay? Childress has no interest in protecting him."

"John doesn't know where he is. I see John, he doesn't ask about my father, I don't say."

"He had Klabbard put up the money for your father's sanitorium when he was done with hard time. He must have some idea."

"None. I've done all one could possibly do to keep him away. I'm the person John comes to for certain protection, he doesn't go outside the group."

"Did you call your husband to ask him to break up my interview with Mable?"

"The girl was there," she said flatly. "Had she not been there, it would not have mattered."

"Who's child is she? His or his mother's?"

"Mine," she replied, her tone hard, as though a piece might flake off. "Steph is my child, John's been raising her."

"Well, she needs a mother in the picture."

"I don't need your fucking sarcasm, Jake. I do what I have to do, as long as my dad is around, he comes first, he gets me twenty hours a day. "

"I knew when I met you I couldn't see through you."

"Maybe you shouldn't have tried."

"Is that why you have Mable's camera in your flat here?" He strode through the house looking for it, pulling open closet doors, until they all stood exposed, then yanked open the garage door, popped the van door and got quite an eyeful at a surveillance unit, he grabbed the tape in the playback, in seconds had all the cupboards open and had flicked tapes onto the floor carpet. "You have any idea what a single mobile unit costs?" he yelled.

She politely took the tape from his hand, threw it on the

floor, and slid the van door shut, and said, "By the time you obtain a warrant, I'll be gone, the van will be on its way over the border where you won't be able to grab it."

Not knowing what she was capable of, he crossed his arms to prevent a physical confrontation.

"I'm not going to strike you, Jake, I'm not that kind of woman."

"Making certain your girl is alright is one thing, staging a peek at a job is altogether different."

Her gaze at him, far from being precociously wizened, bordered on the intolerable. "It wasn't me who ran the spool for either Harris Store or Hariff."

"But it was your van. Who's the cop? Harper?"

"Francesca's brother? I don't need him for what I do."

He'd like to twist off her arm, but he didn't make a move on her. "He work with Webb?"

"It should be easy enough, if he placed a call to the Harris heir."

"I place all calls."

It was a stupid boast. "Including the one that got Adam killed?"

"He wasn't shot."

"Yes, he was, that's what took your father."

She left the garage and he followed her.

She said, "Harper talks to John, he's his man, not mine, I don't buy cops."

"Who is the size 71/2 heel?"

"That's not a shoe size, Jake, that's a gun size. It's a Luger."

"That gun wasted nineteen Guard."

"That's all some guns are useful for, nineteen wire corks when it takes five for a job gives you three jobs it was useful for."

"A fourth job won't restore Joanie to Lloyd."

"It wouldn't matter anyways, the life of that gun is over; to recount, there were Hariff hit and run, that's three murders.

Harris Store and Adam weren't figured in."

She was a cold fish with a chilling serve. "I will be back with an arrest warrant, Susan, and you'll come in, like it or not. Your Steph doesn't know who you are, for that matter neither does Mable."

"Go fuck yourself."

"Not unless you can tell me who the 71/2 belongs to."

She debated the way criminals all did. "He might be someone like Harper. He's always got the picture, he's always got the show."

That would make him Fersterhof. Jake didn't think Childress would ever have tipped his hand that far. One thing he would have was a wall of monitors and surveillance into every corridor of the desert.

"I'd like my father's diary back," she said into an awkward silence that had grown around them.

"I'll stop by with it," he promised.

"It's peculiar, isn't it? You trusted him."

"I trusted you too."

The chatter was almost as thick as the smoke, it hung like indoor Santa Ana smog, a thick layer of hours at the tables, customers plied with drink and very little food. As soon as he'd entered the baccarat room the heavy duty security men walked up to him and told him the boss wanted a private chat. Fersterhof had the top floor penthouse, a thousand square foot suite socked into an all glass condominium that eyeballed Indio's downtown and agricultural zone. He was a medium height man with wiry brown hair cut to his shoulders, a full cheery face, somewhat stocky, the resonance of lower class Chicago in the flower mart, all knuckles, dark eyes that made one think that under the right circumstances he could be cross eyed. The monitors in an adjoining room showed every entrance, hall, door, window, roof, garage and elevator, conferences were well attended, floor shows were all lights and bare rump, the cashier had four consoles with a periodic gaze to the drawers.

Jake sat on a sofa. Fersterhof was anything but sociable, he bristled with aggression.

"Mable says hello," Jake said.

"Great. You know my son?"

"He's getting ready to move."

"Who with?"

"Chessie Harper, Jo Webb, Joan Klabbard — "

"What's the problem? They're still behind a gate with all that kitty litter. I wouldn't waste my time if I were you."

"I understand you're a size 71/2."

"The gun you refer to is a man's, identical to Hariff."

"Your Luger's out there too. It follows Mable or Josephina."

"I don't have a Lugar. It belongs to a nutcase who used to smash a display case on a train with a gun butt. Mable's gun sits beside her when she's seeing to the business of the hour."

He'd deny all avenues of responsibility, dodge the real questions of the setup of the jobs that relied on that piece of evidence, but his gun had killed at least once before it was taken into custody, logged, and then returned to Webb. In the final moment of truth the gun would be obviously irrevocably tied to the murderous acts and the cheat list of a killer would be brought to light.

He returned home before midnight. His flat felt empty, a clear sign that he had mislaid some internal awareness of himself, forgetting was not an attribute he permitted himself in his retirement, the daily newspaper had seen to that, a morning ritual with a third of a cup of bitter strong fresh brewed coffee, yet now there could be no unpleasant surprises as he opened the pages of Collins' notepad, only a sad reminder of the man who wrote them. We all have big egos, I thought the plan was carefully laid, even Suki didn't know, until I recollected the man

I saw leave the weapon on the counter, three were too many people for what we discussed, Childress a bigger liar than I realized, the man, that man, the one in the shadows who gave me a start, the weapon firing at a movement, and then the woman falling to the floor, I got a glimpse at him once, it was a shock to have to come to terms with him at the Lantern Motel, his face as discombobulated as the one who he had killed, I can only imagine that he sped here to meet me and someone arrived ahead of me, the shoes are the worst, they kill to quell fear, a small nameless interference, it won't let me sleep, this cataclysm of disaster that stalks me even as I approach it, who would have known except the man who let Adam inside? Collins was solitary in his act of taking the jewels and running, someone else's terror caught up with a slayer and ended the mishandled matter, he didn't have to talk, he could have simply stated the facts but he panicked, a dropping shadow busted his tether, a few spent bullets blossomed like roses on a woman's blouse.

Jake could have driven to Roberta's, he would have understood at last her detachment over men and love, he could have spoken to her about Collins, his daughter, her child, a generation of deceit and coverups all meant to repair the past, to introduce a decency or normalcy nowhere to be found, Fersterhof probably did keep the gun tidy under his desk drawer, chances were he reviewed Mable's tape and told her her best bet was to stick it anywhere but in her purse, he probably told her that one death at Harris finished her off, no more jobs, hustles, heists, she was in hiding for the rest of her days, then in all probability Fersterhof gave her a one grade up backup with a cop soon destined to be on the shelf, someone who could look in on them from time to time, handle some off season queries, botch curiosity and get Mable a look-good for the son. But he wasn't there quite yet, hadn't yet unravelled the stupid cheesecake, the fact that Roberta couldn't open her store wasn't the candy, it was the gun making its rounds on the promise of a solution, the bullets matched the Colt, solidly retired, and the twist off of the shooting rifle a slip on presumably made by Luger to attach to a Colt or a rifle.

The man who brought Childress down from Edison had to know guns, it would be a presumption that the camera tape must have automatically implicated the killer, the Luger alone was no big deal unless it had a piece put on, even a donut silencer would fix it up for another Adam, that had to be the point of the tape, Mable'd be carrying it on her until she or her stupid son unloaded it onto Webb or Height for another job, and then the cops would move in for the kill. Nineteen London Guard injuries at Victoria Station also sat in the limelight awaiting a piece of evidence which when found would nail Webb or a string on cop into the slammer permanently.

He was in his car waiting on the road when Childress came along, he honked him and the son taking no notice kept driving, Jake pulled behind him and followed him close enough to be seen down the cement jungle that was Canyon Road to the attractive sandstone corner on Barton and out Waterman past Blue Ribbon, along the railroad, past the mobile trailer homes, past Portland Cement over freeway 10 toward the orange show, all the while Childress driving like an automaton into the financial district to his stepfather's medical office.

"You're following me," he said, when Jake had cornered his car in the lot.

"I'd like to know about your liquor store outings."

"What about them? I have an escort with me at all times to make sure I don't get out of hand."

"I think when this started you were quite young, in your teens, and your mother took you along on trips you made."

"Could be but I don't see how that concerns you."

"You're the smashup guy."

"Not me, that's the one who cracked the cases on board the Santa Fe line."

"Had to be you, your mother kept it in her purse and you'd swipe it, give it to your fence who'd set it on the counter without bullets, and you'd pick it up demanding something and be emphatic with the butt, smashing the case with the diamonds inside, you were the only one who could get away with it because of your age."

"And I'm telling you it's not me. You go in there, ask him, he was always on the train, that's where my mother first met him, he and I played cards."

"How touching." He'd goad him into a confession. "Within sight of the display so later you could tell a cop just how shocked you were. Who'd you tell them you saw? Height? Scooping up the stones, his hands marred with cuts?"

"Every time he goes downtown for booze, we do what he used to do, two gins, a beefeater, then up to the display car to smash the glass before lights out, the liquor store owners all drunk diversion, bet you never figured on that scene?" He was genuinely peeved as though smashing up the inside of liquor stores were something he was forced to do and he didn't like having to talk about it.

"Does your stepfather know?"

"Haven't you been listening to what I've been saying?" he was shrieking.

"So who is it? The butt?"

"How the hell should I know? I didn't bring him in, I brought in the diversion."

"You bringing in diversion for this new job you're lining up with Chessie?"

He lunged for Jake through the window. "Stay as far away from me as you can! I know my rights! I don't have to put up with you."

He was a dumb blonde who'd never escape the trouble he had created for himself, nor would he escape the desert, he'd be stuck in chalky sand until he was too old to move. Only Klabbard would take pity on him, give him a go-ahead, and then set up some poor dumb shmuck to take the fall for all of them.

He made the climb for a last time winding his way from the airbase through the remaining orange groves in the direction of Patton, his car straining against the incline, he was certain that where hell lay the deceit of wire was and Height who could prove nothing short of moronic was sinking into an abyss of another sort, a pro's pro who once a job was done was a bundle of nerves until every final betrayer was dead, since it was he who laid the wire at Harris and the man who stole the armored van worked for him and had been his lookout for the Hariff shooting, he had to be the one who worried about the loose ends, only he wouldn't be figured in for the dead clerk he had invited into open the back door, a necessity he couldn't have operated without, he being the man to keep a watch on Klabbard as though he were a possessive yet protective lover, in all of life the mistakes that were made over time became the frets of those who had planned them.

Klabbard came to the door in a robe and slippers looking haggard and hung over, his hair disheveled, whatever medication he was prescribed having put him into a somnambulance. "Come in," he said regrettably, "I'll fix coffee." He shouted to Tom, saying, "Jake's here, Tom."

Jake sat at the breakfast table and let himself get waited on for a heated cinnamon roll and a cup of strong coffee.

"I've had a hellacious night," Lloyd said. "Couldn't sleep, was too hot, had sweats."

"I've been through that myself."

"Have you? I won't feel so bad then." He poured coffee. "So what's the good word?"

"You have a running tape on Mable?"

"That's Susan's department, it is after all her daughter, not mine."

"Does she call John down the hill when there's a problem?"

"No, Harper might if he's on duty all by himself, but chances are he isn't."

Tom came in, his white terry cloth robe open to show his chest, barefoot, his nails clipped precisely. "What's this about Harper?" Tom stood at the sink with a cup to dilute it with water.

"Do you call John when he's looking in on Chessie if his mother has a problem?" Jake asked him.

"No, why would I do that?"

"Someone drags him down the hill."

"Wouldn't be me, that's for sure." He eyed Lloyd as he sat down.

"Isn't me," Lloyd replied, but he was fidgety, aware something was in the wind. "I said it might be Harper."

"Yeah, could be he gets worried for that sister of his."

"What happened with the clerk at Harris?"

Tom made a face. "That's a long time ago, friend."

Lloyd said, "She walked in, saw Webb and made a stink about it."

Tom took a slow sip, then put the cup down. "Lloyd left after he was finished, that left me and Josephine. Elisa took a pulse and left, I guess that's when Karin came upstairs, she was all over Jo, didn't see me, Collins signaled we should get out."

"The clip I saw shows Webb working diligently, there's a glimpse at you, not much more than a profile and then someone else, a blur, fast in and out. Collins called someone, I'm pretty certain."

Lloyd grunted an assent. "Might'a been me, fergot my knife," he said, his speech slurring badly.

Tom hushed him up. "Collins admitted under oath."

"Not to the clerk, he got stuck with Adam, the guy in the tub at Cuesta."

"I remember reading about it. Adam did a cross, took half the haul. He was the van driver."

"What about Fersterhof?" Jake asked. "Couldn't he have seen that tape?"

"I don't know that he's ever met Susan," Height said. "He could've set Collins up once he realized Collins was given a bag, arranged for a slug."

"Whose gun was it? The Luger?"

"Jo's," Lloyd blurted out. "Took it everywhere."

"Who's the drunk who runs out of booze?"

The two were silent.

Jake had caught up to a truth, there were no more not-me's. "You?" he asked Lloyd, who looked away evasively at his coffee. "Who brought the clerk in on the job?"

"He did," Lloyd said, of Tom. "He brought in all the extras."

"Were you planning a double cross?" Jake asked Tom.

"No, it wouldn't occur to me."

"I think it did occur to you. I think the bag shoved onto the armored van was a powerful incentive, ample reason to kill Adam, ample reason to punch out the clerk who must have had an eyeful of what was going on, not just a wire job in progress but a gigantic swindle. Chessy has a handful of diamonds, you two have any?"

"We were paid off in diamonds, ours are gone, we bought the house with what we were paid," Lloyd said, sorrier than he had been the night he was with his ex-wife.

Jake said, "Something caused you to go back to the scene, what was it?"

"I passed her coming in as I was on my way out."

Jake gave Tom Height a hard look. "You left the safety under the rug undone. No one does that."

"That was Jo," he protested.

"Never work, Jo didn't use the gun for a gun, she needed it for the camera to fool any observers trying to discern the type of wire job she uses, she would never in a million years shoot with it."

"We don't leave eyewitnesses, everyone there is involved in the job or dead," Tom said coldly.

Height withdrew a small pistol which Jake knocked out of his hand, it was over before it was begun, he then withdrew a pair of metal cuffs and locked one on one wrist and grabbed for the other wrist snapping the other on it.

"Life's cheap, buddy," he remarked as he grabbed Height by the head and socked him into the hall closet and called 911.

By the time he made it back into the kitchen Lloyd was weeping, a labile man with a mood congruent disorder on his way to a mental ward probably into lockup. The world was filled with pathological veterans whose empathy for their victims gave them no real control to call off a job in progress any more than had they kept walking, gone to a telephone, called the cops and made a full confession right there and then.

On his return into town he called Harper and left a message on his answering machine. "No news is good news, but every stone has been turned over at least once and the girl is a hundred percent safe."

Roberta was walking on the canal overlooking the rooks when Jake finally chased her to ground. He told her her case had rolled in, the guy who left the nasty call a friend of a friend doing someone a good turn, the culprit a shoe who had left a messy trail of bodies in his wake including a bevy of unsuspecting constables who had been seriously injured in a shoot-out in a public square committed by a drunkard. He told her about Susan and the momentary fleeting idea he had had of changing his life. It was one of those things, he told her, to be attracted to someone you couldn't change nor could ever see enough into. He could call often, he said, and still have to look over his shoulder at an exhaustive list of men who couldn't be squared off right until a last moment or well into old age, neither which could prove to be an attractive bargain, it wasn't honest, the way he felt they had been together, at which point she told him he seemed to her to be awfully wrapped up in something elusive and the sex while good had not been lastingly tender to where she thought of him but without a concern that would gnaw at her until she had heard his voice, yet she was grateful to have the sense of being stalked well out of the way, replaced by the knowledge that the people who had shutdown her store might be put away and her department store soon reopened. He half wanted to tell her she was somewhat distant, smooth without being needy at all, but she wouldn't give them a chance and he wouldn't press her to try. He said goodbye and sincerely wished her the best. Women like Roberta existed around the state, the desert having its own fair share of up and coming entrepreneurs and bosses who wouldn't miss him, let alone know he was even there, the other myriad of females who wouldn't strive or push themselves to achieve were in most walks of life, he could see far down that lonely road that were it not for his own ambivalences there might not have been any wayward longing nor presumptions to cross either line, he would have ended much as he began, for the case at any rate, the tensions of peculiarity staved off, the women just players in a show, just waking mortality brimming with too much reluctance, straining to be free of the saddle, the crimes themselves taken into account long since past, all burdens equally duressed, the children of the conflicted set now blossoming with their own distinctions, some shadows, unable to become mature, others knowingly advancing fast into loss of purity and aging regrets, these children ambitious for unknown glitz, their gazes not yet acquired to the pitfalls of living, the roses blooming along the path spilled free of the metal fence in cascades of pink, yellow, white and deep red, an arch of peony like tiger eyes stretching like a veil over the path, always that tortuous yearning to know more than one knew advanced like a long neglected sentinel, ready for adventure, common sense fallen to a statue's unadorned feet, yet the vines of overripe pungent berries seeped to the pavement causing stains not quite purple to emasculate the cleanliness of the grass that cropped beneath the fence, he passed a set of young girls in short white pleated skirts going to tennis practice and thought how innocent they seemed, their laughter reminding him when he was their age, he was to the hill when looking back to see Roberta he perceived her as a gradually smaller figure in the distance, imperceptible by any standard of comparison, his longing beginning to follow her almost as certain as it had Susan and he thought how his training must have prepared him for the mindset of learning to know a person at that very moment he could lose them. All his striving, his attentions, were given to an instantaneous perception of knowing the case could be known, that the questions could be answered, that the long interminable hours of indecision and god awful fear were passing, stifling themselves from further complication, the alabaster bishops rose in the canal devoid of water, their ignoble presence distinct from the greyish white marble of the canal, their heads perfect shapes of horses, each pair reminiscent of a procession at a London overturnstile, his heart suddenly aching with ribbons of sorrow for the injured boys, their turning bodies looking for a route through which to flee, all time coming to an aching standstill, a fierce acknowledgement of agonizing surreal surrender, his knowledgeable idealism long ago in check now ripping apart from the emotional armor which had protected him against a lurid sort of mania manifested by killers, an invasion and penetration into the psyche, nineteen lives rendered in the span of a round of bullets, their lives sprayed like blood for a group on the take, the selfish hideaway from justice being the cement blocks of a city called Grand Terrace, the grandiosity of grand thinking that one set had a human right to steal the lives of another set, always he returned to the thinking that there ought not to have to be any bloodshed, that living ought to be sacrosanct and ambition not an immorality of deprivation, he saw that he had walked too far down the road and turning he retraced his steps to where he had parked his car all the while asking himself why these people — Susan, Francesca, Josephina, Mable, Joanie, Lloyd and ugliest of all Tom — why had an inner instinct, turmoil or disgust, not interceded into their decisions in order for them, one or all, to stop, what kept them going, what made their acts to their way of thinking acceptable, when they had to bend to the demands of the society that was driven to set them on a straight course, why had they not gone along and ceased their associations with one another, how did death not impede their functioning? At the bottom of his love for Susan, he could not comprehend why with any choices she hadn't chosen to leave Childress, he couldn't picture her in it for the money any longer, not with her father a modern day albatross, what made her maintain for Childress when he clearly would not keep her father safe, a hundred questions, none of them answerable, to say that was human nature was not adequate, to say she was running scared or needed to stand watch over the self serving Childress clan was barely plausible, even a need to have her child known in some pathetic way to herself was beyond normalcy, only Susan herself knew what her own vigilance signified and whatever it represented, it drove him to view her as unforgettable and irreplaceable, it made him feel sick to think about her, he knew he had almost renewed himself but was yet again struck by a sense that for him to have lost her was a denial of self, for her to lose to one man she may not have ever known and to a husband whose own metamorphosis was so incomplete, failed to leave him anything but bewildered, as long as he could palpate emotion toward her he was tied to her, as long as he knew where she was he felt confined to her, she was a desolate agony, and he wished as he drove home to his flat that he would not have the attraction he felt for her, he wished instead he could find solace in an empty place of drinking, yet knew solemnly he would not take a sip to quench this mood, he sat in his vehicle a long time asking himself whether he should try to see her and in the long run decided he was in a powerfully vulnerable state, too vulnerable even for himself, and was aware of the pressure to seek his own undoing. He would idle inside his house for weeks by the fireplace or in the living room at the large window, moody, suffocated by yearning, the books on the shelf unfulfilling, his journals, magazines, association news left on a table unread, he would think he were aging undesirably, becoming older, and he'd let retirement sequester him until he knew he was numb, lonely, disconnected. He'd lament on the past, attempt a crossword puzzle, smoke a cigarette, refuse to answer the phone. At last Roberta called him to inquire how he was getting on, he told her he was in trouble and would she come, she came dressed in a light summer black polyester dress, she was like a easy-going version of herself as she stepped through the slightly open door, an overnight bag packed, her hair in a pony tail, her body full of promise, his relief so great he thought he would cry.

THE END

# THE
# HOOD

# CHAPTER ONE

# 1979

O̶N SATURDAY JUNE 9TH IN A PARKING lot well after dark on Polk Street across from the city financial administration on Grove Street the cement blew without warning, a big bang with spitting pink and yellow fire and white smoke. Tumbling, a trunk cover from a black parked Chrysler shot headlong skyward, then careened into a plummeting dive like a plastic door burst sky high from a canon, come down fast, it landed on a mostly empty pavement thirty-seven feet away. The only witness to the scene was a beat patrol officer ticketing cars that remained parked after nine o'clock in the above ground of the civic center plaza. Approximately five minutes after the explosion the lights inside the police precinct next to the library and the courthouse dome shut off shrouding the plaza in complete darkness. A telephone ringing shrilly off the hook could be heard through an open window somewhere in the maze of lights above the second stories of city buildings.

J. Lea Koretsky

The time was ten forty at night by the public park plaza clock closest to the south entrance to City Hall at the Van Ness and McAllister intersection. A brown car turned the corner and sped past the court buildings up Van Ness on its way into oblivion. Uptown at Union Square the spools of history were about to be made as a series of film strips emptied into a photo bucket while simultaneously one frame a strip lodged at the nudie joints in and around North Beach. Oddly the catch of the night were a group of photographs of a notoriously known hegemony fund involving a male bureaucrat who had an affair with a female from dispatch. The pictures were salacious, wetly pornographic in intent, brassieres and lacy bikinis, to keep the drag queens and girlies intentioned to the youthful men inside their dungeons. By the time the police adjacent to the park baled into their patrol cars, silent sirens dousing the plaza with stipulations of warning, the dark cloud mass churning sky had again turned to Doppler predicted rain, a gushing downpour spilling into cement gutters washing to the flat basin where ships too sea battered to be put back out for midnight fishing received retrofitted sections to their paint-scrapped hulls. Immediately from the sanctum of Legion court chambers an edict was issued declaring a media freeze, a newspaper bullet head lead for the morning, and a single shift line staffing schedule for everyone but the Medical Examiner office. Hospital wards were informed to stay on standby; university campuses to release all color guards for the rest of the semester; campus radio and television to temporarily close. The City Architect was requested to review all seams for construction and prepare a bid for proposal by the end of the week.

∧ ∧ ∧

It was the second time in winter someone had tossed files on the pavement in front of a county welfare building on McAllister.

The files were the usual records in a welfare case, of which the county had barely less than twenty-two hundred. These would include AFDC checks to welfare mothers, young parents on alcohol recovery programs, food vouchers and rent checks for county unemployed welfare indigents. The petition signed by the judge, the declarations of children by name and assigned county registry number, monthly receipts, and court orders on change of venue splayed over the sidewalk as though an impatient data clerk had flung open a door and tossed them to an unlikely billing operative. The clerk scooped them up and carried them inside to the head secretary, assistant to the welfare director, who would look over the vandalism and file a report. As usual, as soon as the head secretary regrouped the information into their folders, she determined whose desk the files had walked away from. The files originated at the desk of a female who did intake, logged in each family member's name and then routed the files to investigators to conduct a verification for six months on a family. It was the responsibility of Risk assessment, not hers, to decide if there was a leak in the financial department or whether the damage was random. The day was a celebrated muckraker shooting for an illegal expenditure of a hundred in the shade, all burst water balloons hanging off gnarled leprosy trees, water from fire hydrants splashing into the gutters. Although it was slightly past four in the afternoon the long hand on the clock in the public square had fixed onto a rung with no visible mechanism to move forward. This time when Risk received the incident proof, signed and notarized, the counsel would duly note the public clock struck a finality and the welfare podium for some obscure reason not to be explained in chambers or in policy lost control of its previously envied instrument for increasing cash disbursements to welfare recipients.

San Francisco Ninth Street district saw little of the commonplace because unlike its warehouse debunked zones it shared nothing of Army Street, little basin or the new Rome basilica overlooking the speedway. Ninth was symphonic in its decorum, fanciful, marbled and marble inlaid terraces beneath a gold dome glorified by thirty ionic columns, photographed twiggy-looking models in skimpy sequins in flashing stars of falling lights annually at New Year's. County offices consisted of six marble buildings, the Courthouse where Harvey Milk had opened up a registrar to request a wiretap on an entire police headquarters for suspected enlistment of rostrum-ready bailiffs, the Office of Secretariat next door which archived all filings for the abridgments of law, adjacent to both county and police offices where Chief Moscone increased city staff to meet the traffic overflow from Geary and Market to the Ninth Street plaza where the library sat opposite the county offices across the green of the two block appointed square, the opera house, the judicial bench and opposite on a corner standing by itself the former art gallery, forty-four years in inequity the Registrar Offices of Live Births and Recorded Deaths. Uptown skyscraper banks filed for every corporation invited by the city to withstand permanent indentured servitude, six blocks from Market, past California to Stockton, short of Geary, Hyde and Fell, syncopated like stacked pile buildings only to hammer them down ten years later to make room for school plazas and apartment flats. To the west the piers gave the city its fascination of windows resting on the ocean, Portrero Hill now spoke of refinement and small corporate parks and China Basin was designing its emporiums to compete with its hotels. Ninth had never lost its dignity despite patron of arts replacing age-old battleships inside the covered docks. Ninth was, to a city whose face perpetually altered after its Presidio naval base closed, the honorable, rational plaza of indefatigable laws, freeways, bridges and parks. Built in the early Sixties, its architects chose to unite the city by its stately museum – the Legion – to her gardens and capitol buildings. Preserved by excellence, fortified by a lottery of police guards, the polished wood staircases and shiny reflective marble floor set forth a visible code of regiment that encapsulated in any image of pillar or cornice the majesty of purposeful institution.

Security patrol received computer tapes for the discard of files. At the top of the Mark Hotel, two agents looked through the night shift, janitorial men, and assessed which guard in dumping the garbage had spilled the files. He was a swarthy male in his forties, a quick finger through case stacks, someone who had been sent in with a mission to kill off a desk. The next person to enter the county offices at night left his vehicle running while he rode an elevator to the second floor and took a handful of files, locked the building and made a fast getaway in his car. Risk built the underground lot to be manned round the clock, all vehicles ticketed, removed the street doors off the courthouse, put a garden in where the top lot used to sit, and sent in an entire panel of detectives who spent a week at night at the start of every month to pour over eligibility files. Special arrangements were made for seven men to review several hundred files between the hours of eleven to four at night when neither the staff, guards nor janitors worked. They reported to an inquiry board, a discreet number of gavels knew the concerns, but the real terse indoctrination left the county in some other format, to be recuperated with changes within textural law or for insurance disposals. Risk sent Judge Ray Fellow their compilation with an apology, saying had the case not produced so many entanglements it should have been relatively easy to make foundation changes in the cement and assume the matter was tied up, but the case had overtones, dismal reluctances, there were legal witnesses, the case itself was scattered about in thirty cities like a paper chase which required an exhaustive sorting to find the destined target out of a mess of receipts for hotels and conventions, billings on credit, car rentals, mortgage lenders, department store purchases, periodic restaurants, cruise vacations, marriage license permits, and other, savory and semi-clad arrangements.

∧ ∧ ∧

The brown car sped through the rain on Market, its image flickering across mirrored glass panels of the county administration. It turned and drove north to Van Ness, screeched at a corner, whipping past an all-night lounge and Chinese restaurant and bar pulled up to a curb alongside the side door to the courthouse. An elderly man using a folded newspaper as a boat to protect his head in the rain stepped to the four door car and got inside explaining first which medical center he needed to be transported to. As the shiny transom took off, its passenger explained he thought he had witnessed a crime; of course if when he arrived at the hospital the man whom the ambulance came for was in the O.R., then he had to deduce if what he thought happened had in fact occurred. He fell silent reviewing the situation. First the shot, then the black Ghia taking off like a bat out of hell, then the shiny blue Mustang, its windows rolled down, rain blowing inside the vehicle, tossing the papers about. He reached for the slender cardboard briefcase and withdrew it before hurrying off, very nearly tripping over the unconscious man who lay bloodied sprawled out on the pavement, arms beseeching no one. He dialed from a pay phone in the park beneath a line of gnarled trees. An ambulance arrived in minutes, the attendant was quick, efficient, courteous, but he had a gnawing sense he ought to have left the man to sleep off his brutal attack. It wasn't until he went to wait for a medical van to dispatch him that he saw a light on the top floor of the county administration building go out causing him to wonder who if anyone might have seen the attack.

There were contradictory sources on Harvey Milk in Joe's clippings, Dan White reported shooting, why wiretaps on all police, when was last riot, 1969 People's Park, was there a riot on south side of bay? After a milk bath was stolen from the nearby mint, and the milk used to preserve gold, federal Mint deputies tracked it all over, each jar of bath cost a little over $1,161. One needed money plates, it was a big process, film to make imprint, glitter and this was gold flakes taken off rebar, and milk bath, all this to make it possible just to pour gold. Harvey's was gold before it is money; it was referred to as Harvey's Gold. Long Beach gave street signs to tell which other baths were necessary – orange and cherry – without both there could be no gold. Between 1950 and 1958 the only employment in SF was with the Mint; from 1958 on the Mint was relocated to Appalachia causing all potential counterfeit thieves to move to Nashville. As late as 1993 Nashville's Mint was invested in as Wall Street. Wiretaps probably were intended to verify voice.

∧ ∧ ∧

The case came through during the week Ray got his divorce. A dignified senior, splitting grey hairs like unwieldy star bursts, adapted to high society by virtue of his post, he held to a trim endeavor of black suit, stark white collar subordinated by the ruffle of a handkerchief peeking above a pocket, dapper shoes, tall hat, long cane with which he tapped the sidewalk as he walked from his office on Sansome Street to his small tan Mercedes coupe that he usually parked in the basement. He was elated, finally free of a tiresome list of petty objections he had attended to since he married Lorraine Sandpiper – her father George, an expert on retrials, sat uninvited on court call on all his Seventh District Court of Appeals work, his summations, torts and writs; and on a hearing about criminal pre-trials for protestors in blustery spring during intersession in Union Square, most who had chained themselves at high noon to park benches. Lorraine's father lectured him at every breakfast hall over any tiding of celibacy. They had begun as intimate friends with the same patches on the elbows on their dinner jackets, crests on their sash, and progressively turned a deaf ear over sentiments concerning public policy on corporate government holdings and on newspaper owned media stations. The X case looked to be a promise, certainty raising hair on the necks of trial attorneys who practiced at the Hunter's Point city center Hall of Justice, while across the bay in a nesting ground of provocateurs a confrontation had busted loose between police in combat gear and protestors at the Oakland naval base over the draft to send troops to Vietnam. The FBI had netted the protestors, tagged them and stuck them in unmarked vans, twelve each, and sent them to the south Berkeley Department of Health for hair and fiber specimens and interviews. The questions put to a group of a hundred and nine protestors added a sealed corridor to the collective din of prurient sobriety these rebels fleshed at a hundred agents. By the time Ray received a copy of recorded testimony he had one foot in a summation on the banner of county offices and the other foot in a storage inventory of police brutality up by the twenty three hundred crosses in Burlingame. The week of his freedom the X stipulation had advanced its way from the bus terminal where Beale & Trane, Co., through a series of thirty day windows as to forty-one counts, each held by junior defenders, eventually crouped its patriotism to the wayward esteem of one firm on Pacific Coast Highway 1 represented by his ex wife's cousin Barrister Beulah Sandpiper on a sole peremptory challenge. X was a dream case for any counsel who represented a female teen who had witnessed a murder, the teen herself of elegant bearing, a slender blonde au pair who while admitted to a University of San Francisco medical clinic, was idly gazing out a window when a male entered the garden and did something strange to a nurse who was on break.

The facts were a bit boned up to pepper a weak case. They were as follows:

A teen had a complication during surgery. A trial began as to the date when the patient was released;

A female lawyer brought in the post-op nurse who saw him sign to court to prepare her for testimony, then sent her to a motel until trial was over;

The trial became hung up on use of camera equipment, and court ruled counsel couldn't use filming of signature because of problem with vehicle back-fire, killing post-op nurse;

Rolling medication tray with surgical instruments was pushed down a corridor inside an OR, that means the OR is in the basement on ground floor, one below entry or pavement. At end of a shift aide is returning cart to supply room, cart was empty;

Light blue was aquiline, used only to soap instruments, it would never be in a syringe;

Blocker was assessed in report submitted by patrol night guard to be 3- 4 syringes that fed into one IV line/tubing; its medical use was for mother and in utero child. The type that fed soil by running alternate to water into pipe i.e. liquid nitrogen, plant feeder, carotene or bag-syrup liquid bark which enriched plants was sold separately in plant stores but otherwise referred to as the same content, blocker.

The rain flung a swirl at the sports coupe, coming down fast and furious in the night while Ray listened to discordant jazz sounds as he waited in his tan gray Mercedes to access the lower deck of the Bay Bridge in a freak snowstorm. The car was there before he heard it, a grinding meld of garish dark tan metal, the trunk a colossal sculpture of a fix of a rear-ender. Nothing he had done or was responsible for technically, except the court order said he couldn't return to work for a month until he passed medical requirements. His X case was in ruins. It necessitated all sorts of replacements – interim judges, possibly commissioners, summation counsel, Department of Health Juris-doctor administrators, FBI prosecutors. Ray thought life was premeditated. Felt cheated not to be able to return to work. The one thing he was permitted to do from home was to examine the wording of every question submitted to the defendant and witnesses.

There were hundreds if not over a thousand queries to be submitted. The questioning made a case, any case, every case. Every word permitted in an inquiry had to be approved first by a panel of attorneys who raked each particular type of situation for lawsuit potential and then usual questions were made into law. For the signature the case should have been open and shut but a minor had seen a murder while the signature was being produced. Knowing what she saw, she fled, when subsequently a judge looking out a window onto a hospital courtyard saw presumably the same crime he doffed himself with a pistol. If there were a connection there was no immediate way to know, unless it was the double murders in the shooting deaths of Harvey Milk and Police Lt. Dan White in April reported to officials all over the county plaza. Ray redacted all confusing circuitous paths of inquiry, removed inspections and interrogations aimed at hindrances that might obstruct justice, and revised his probe so that every question that would be asked was correctly posed in order to meet requirements of evidence in superior court as to validity should any link become established by reference.

^^^

Summer afternoon light streamed inside the cozy conclave of a living room with modern glass windows all around modifying the ash lacquered pine floor to a time-honored magistrate's sanctum. A hearth with pronounced veined black marble mantle was littered with gold framed photographs of all sizes, on either side built-in bookshelves crammed with hard bound law books, a handful of old cherry wood tables with plants growing inside silver containers, a black rug with a green accent squiggle and two sofas, one a rich deep tan and green stems and yellow flowers and the other a black background with golden yellow, toasted orange and wilted pink flowers. The front door opened and closed with a low dull sound, and a female stopped to examine herself in front of the oval wall mirror in the hallway.

"Lorraine, is that you?" Her younger cousin Beulah called out from the living room. "Can you come inside for a moment and tell me jus' what do you think about my design? Do you think this turquoise looks well beside that purple?"

"Beulah, why is it you cannot be more self-assured?" The friendly face of her cousin peered inside the room. "You are like one of those clinging vines, you never realize yourself what you prefer."

"I would appreciate some real interest on your part, Lo'raine. Give me your opinion. Ought I to plan a wedge of crimson?"

"Crimson could be a nice contrast to both turquoise and purple. Show us what you have in mind."

Beulah stood on spiked heels, a wisp of a crew cut red haired female, as she leaned over a pattern on the cutting table, her angular figure showed severely from a high waist light blue cotton shirt, buttoned down collar, and a navy A-line skirt with a single box pleat in the front. Of the two cousins she was the more detail conscientious, every denotation measured with a ruler and stitch up to the denouement, and whereas she would readily agree she possessed a bit of the tempest about her, she was the more dependable because she rarely left the house having garden cover and weekly groceries home-delivered. Lorraine on the other hand was a slight dandy of a golden haired tomboy who had a habit of sneaking up on people, rather a pest to enter a room in which others were deep in concentration and turn the place upside down without so much as a comment, as though to steer luff to a lugger, superb inside a courtroom where delivery accounted as much as strategy.

"You could at the least say a kind encouragement," Beulah remarked. "The design calls for dark green, a touch of chartreuse, a border of black."

Lorraine gazed upon her cousin's stitchery. The quilt was designated to consist of sixty squares, six across to form the width, ten along the length, each square measuring ten inches by eight inches, each which contained a fan of five colorful wedges on top a bright background of either crimson or white.

"Did you arrange the color scheme, or is it pre-arranged by the fabric company?" she asked.

Beulah gave an assent. "I did it myself. Like it?"

"It's lovely. Who will you give it to when it's completed?"

"John."

Lorraine replied a bit cross, "The comforter will be lost on him, better give it to Lisa."

"Your daughter doesn't need another gift; you've already spoiled her rotten."

"Well, cousin, your John is a bit of a destitute, never in one place for long. What use shall a pretty quilt be to him?"

"He has a studio rental on the beach."

"He leads the life of a bum, surfing every afternoon, staying up to all hours. At least Lisa works for an advertising firm."

"Lisa's not a man. The world expects more of males. Ought I to add a navy wedge?"

"No one will expect to give a damn," Lorraine declared. "For heaven's sake, why can't you have a conversation that's not chit chat? We're scarcely real at one another."

"Spoken by the person least capable of real," Beulah said, her voice barely audible. "What shall we discuss? Not John's all glass, five room condo? I imagine my judgment is better than yours."

"Who's talking? You're not anyone's mother."

"I never wanted to be. I've enjoyed my freedoms."

"That's the entire difficulty, the reason I get along so much better than you with Maman. Had you but raised a child –"

"For God's sake, that's enough, Lo'raine. Bite your tongue for once."

Lorraine looked utterly stunned to her very foundation. "I think that's your idea of providing for the family, you design the couch, select the fabric, sew the pillows, seams, drapes on occasion, put together the patio, the grass and garden. That seems to be your idea of life."

"You make it sound unbearable."

"Maman likes it because she enjoys being asked her opinion so often, but the truth is you have no life to call your own."

"That's not true, Lor. I was the first to go out and work, I kept the same job for twenty-four years. Clerking for a stiff lawyer is no idle task."

"But you've nothing to show for it. You have no house, no out-of-state property, no stocks, no photograph collection, and no children. Whose fault is that?"

"Why does there have to be blame? It is life. You have your divorce coming up, don't forget."

Lorraine removed four wedges on a turquoise backing and repositioned two white, two crimsons and a dark green. "That, I'm certain, will call attention to that brilliant backing."

"Why, yes, that's very industrious. Are the kids coming down this weekend?"

"All but Kenneth. He has a trial coming up on Thursday he has to prepare for."

"That's too bad. Maman won't see his trial as reason enough not to come."

"I was planning on us all painting saucer themes on egg-shells."

"That's a great idea. Did you purchase eggs?"

"Two dozen. I already pricked them and blew out the egg into a bowl."

"You should have waited. The kids'll want to do that."

"Oh, the kids won't care, they've done eggs half their lives. Is Jonathan coming down?"

"He might, depends on his schedule."

"Where did you say he works?"

"He's a surf board pro; he reviews film for Search & Rescue. It pays excellent during the summer."

"Well, who thinks anyone is in the water in winter?"

"Right, who thinks that?"

Beulah's mother Louisa pulled into the drive behind the house and came in through the garden, a long strip of grass bordered by purple clitella and marigolds and a brick laid path. She was tall like her daughter, so similar in style of hair and dress that from a distance they were thought to be sisters. She set two bags of groceries on the dark blue counter and began putting items away.

"Beulah invited John down," said Lorraine waltzing into the scullery flouncing a green and blue striped shawl about her shoulders. "He might be here if he has time."

"It will be nice to see him," Louisa said to her daughter. "It's been awhile."

"For us all," Beulah replied. "Last time was when he took Kenneth for his semester sessions. That was, what? A year ago?"

"Ten months and a week."

"Will we see Ken?" Louisa asked her niece.

"Not this June, he has trial work. The rest are coming down on the Silver Streak, I'll have to leave to pick them up in exactly," she consulted a thin elegant wristwatch on her right wrist, "eight hours, more or less."

"I imagine the fare is cheaper coming down so late."

"They prefer the night ride so they can study."

"Each to their own, I'd just as soon sleep. Will John want a room?"

"He can stay with me," Beulah said.

Louisa asked, "Heavens, where will we put everyone?"

Lorraine said, "I'm having mine in our living room."

"Oh, they won't relax sleeping on the floor. Best they stay with Mother."

"They'll be up all night on those bunk beds if Mother has them."

"Don't worry about it. They'll bag in all weekend anyway."

A car driving onto the grass beneath a cluster of magnolia trees staked Lorraine's attention. She ran from the room dashing into the hall, out onto the veranda, and shouted into the hall, "Oh, look, it's Ray come down. Why, heavens Ray, you sorely could use a towel, you are soaked wet to the bone."

"I've hand carried your dissolution. What do you think of that? You're a free woman."

"I didn't want even a separation. I gave you as much liberty as one can. We do reside a hundred and twenty miles apart."

"Tell your dad next time you visit that breathing his air is stifling, won't you?"

"I can hardly be expected to control him too."

"Don't call me daily either, or whisk me out of trial preparation to tell me about your hairdresser, or keep a book on who arrives for hearings."

"Are you staying over? The children are on their way in."

"Of course I'll speak with Maman. I hadn't planned on it."

Ray proceeded inside stopping to check his tie. He approved of his appearance, a pin-striped navy shirt, black suspenders, black tie, black trousers, he looked well rested, relaxed if a bit too thin, the weight of stress temporarily gone, his jet black hair turning white at the temples. He went into the dining room where he encountered Maman and Beulah, he gave each a peck of a kiss on the cheek, settling into an upholstered tweed easy chair he took up light banter with George's wife.

Maman said, "He scarcely comes down. Monterey's a wee tad far for him since he stopped driving nights. I did hear him remark he would be sitting on a big case involving an eye witness."

"That's intriguing. Did he say what court?"

"District court."

"They're all district courts. Did he say where the case was

first held?"

"Down here in the coastal valley."

"It would either be Salinas or Pacific Grove. Monterey is strictly fish."

"It must've been in the Grove. Judge Hyphen."

"He's all the way south in Channel Islands. He normally hears farmland. What is the appeal based on, do you know?"

"One detail. There was another similar car in another part of town."

"The defendant's trial attorney wants a piece of evidence unattached?"

Maman said, "Beulah saw the summary."

Beulah was diligently sewing crimson onto turquoise. "Daddy's case is aiming to amend prima facie. The sordid fact is a witness has appeared in closed chambers who described an injury habeas and the court's security officer with the evidence in dictum testified to another vehicle which in status contradicted an essential fact."

"Interesting," Ray remarked offhandedly, telling himself to act with caution in the future not to make Maman a stranger. Louisa Sandpiper, although no rostrum or juris-doctor, patiently accommodated hundreds of trial slates during her marriage giving her an added instinct for legal brewers. "What does the evidence leave out?"

"Minor gesticulations," Beulah answered. "The back-fire is explained in lengthy detail, the habeas is thrown from a moving car, and there are two other parked cars when this occurs, but a driver is not retrieved for the blue car in time for the trial."

Ray asked, "Is the blue alive?"

"Yes. It's a male who allegedly tagged his car with a flag to indicate a mechanical failure."

"Has the blue been inspected?"

"An objection was overruled."

"On what grounds? Egg on the pavement?"

Beulah said, "There's often that concern, that in preserving confidentiality through a tunnel, there's no good way to see what's on the shine, rain even worse. Here, the parked cars originally arrived to their spaces before it started to rain. Blue did not come while the attendant was present; the driver paid one of those night deposit boxes for a month. It still had time when the appeals was sworn."

Ray ambled to the bar in the under shelf on built-in wooden drawers and bronze decorous abstract corners and poured everyone in the room a whiskey neat in short crystal. Taking his, he peered into the kitchen where the warm smells of a pot roast had been spiced and begun in drippings. Always the inveterate consummate, Louisa had kept his interest tied to her daughter over many a maternity. He sat near Beulah as she stitched another crimson over the background color, sipping, deciding he could stay to eat with the kids.

He resumed the elaboration as to presumption, saying, "How many parties came across the blue car while it was parked there?"

"More than one person," said Beulah, who took a break to sip her drink. "Bit wry, David," she said calling him by his middle name. "The issue from the start was, did a car back-fire or was the sound due to a pistol shot?"

The skin on his neck prickled. "How was it determined?"

"The blue car reflected the car with the back-fire. The resulting picture was examined carefully for gun fire and ruled out almost immediately. Everything else was dark cement block."

"Except the courthouse."

"Well, can you see any car lights in those windows?"

"Only in the cube over the underground of cars on the street, I think."

"But it just finished being built. When all this started in spring there was no underground."

The three young adults crowded through the doorway at

once, conversing, laughing, a group unto themselves. Lisa was dark brunette, a young duplicate of her dad, the two boys a year apart nevertheless did not resemble each other or anyone in the family, Denis was a vivid blond to his shoulders, an athletic type who would grace the courts with his penetrating glance and precise clipped diction, and Randy, a shy shaggy, barely blond elbow, lettered in his grandfather's retrial torts, destined for college law.

"Hey, hey, look who's here," Denis remarked, and threw his arms around his father's neck. "Hey, Randy, come see dad."

"Be right there, bro," Randy answered, removing his sturdy boots in the hall. He jounced into the dining room, hugged his grandmother, and kissed her. "Kenny's studying, Lossie."

"I'm sorry we'll miss him. What's he studying?"

"Medical law. Hi, there, Bo, Bo."

Beulah grabbed him by the arm and they stood to admire her quilt. "Your mother planned eggs."

"Eggs are cool; I could paint a few eggs."

"And you have to study the books."

"We can do that, auntie Bo, can't we?" he asked his siblings.

Lisa and Denis agreed, eggs fine, law books fine. Lisa poured ginger ales for the three of them and they went outside, turned on the sprinkler low and sat on the grass wiggling their toes in the breezy droplets.

Inside Lorraine had joined her ex-husband, cousin and aunt and entered the round robin of discussion about the car that her father George Sandpiper had received filings on. Lorraine had her own ideas of prevailing honor and felt every after-hours officer should have been questioned as to time they left work and by which entrance; instead only the station guard was queried and officers were described as to what the video tapes in the hallways showed.

Ray was reticent. On the tapes as the door opened onto the plaza parking lot in the center of six square blocks the camera view flashed onto a group of cars, each beside the next, two white, two door cars, one a hatchback, the other a commonplace sedan, half a dozen attorneys from across the street standing around in the rain debating going to a pub or waiting for the shuttle to take them to Bay Street or China Basin. It was completely credible that the cars parked there at that one lot every day, that the officers who performed security by studying streets from camera street lights had all the answers anyway; the nature of the beast for a member of the judiciary was that one was constantly looking for what was out there, never able to relax for long, usually bothered by any little suggestion of fact, the whole barometer of the crime taking a toll in aging him, his neck sagging, his face becoming marked by weathering lines, any remark making a new dent.

∧ ∧ ∧

There were lots of unresolved prelims in which an older model late 50's car with only one back light was seen at night heading out of town. Easiest thing to solve, Ray surmised, if one knew about city hospitals. It was the coroner car heading out to answer a night call. He checked the dispatch triage record for a pertinent out call before he looked up for any other city and finding none but a derelict for Civic Center he searched for any finding of cadavers to one motel along the Pacific Coast Highway for which two examiners were requested. In the wake of a cloudless sky a TV-watch helicopter tracked a lone vehicle that had stepped on the pedal winding a pair of flashlight headlights down the coast, the coroner light its only significance, like a hound van on its way to detain a police dog that had wandered off south of the city limits. From the opposite direction a pair of fog lights swept over the headlands like one shore patrol seeking a lost skiff at bay. The motel sat off Highway 1 in Long Beach on the north corner of Long Beach

Boulevard beneath flapping palm trees. It was a yellow stucco and glass duplex building camouflaged to resemble physician offices with an adjoining restaurant painted orange stucco, two blocks from the major intersection of Orange and Highway 1. Prior to city developers erecting fifty, two story modern homes built with white wood and glass, balconies overlooking the sand and twinkling sea, there were only the sprawling Pacific Coast college campus surrounded by grass and oak trees, a few blocks of stone facing of dorm flats, and the Long Beach Motel & Restaurant for out-of-towners, weekenders and new college professors. The deceased was reported as a first year gridlock analyst named Beames Hadley hired by the state to evaluate traffic jams blocked by stoppage of cross town traffic, a plucky job for a recent business administration graduate from UCLA of any age. Nothing much was known about him except that his grandmother had paid his original tuition costs and housing fees. Depending upon which coroner reached his bedside first would determine which city handled the body and next of kin; it would then become the responsibility of the second examiner to field an investigation. South San Francisco John Davenport got to the scene first, wrapped the victim in painter canvas, tied him at the feet and waist around the wrists, leaving his head free in case he came to, and laid him in the back of the vehicle on a bed on the trunk. The driver left the dead man's prints with the officer at the campus motel and rode up to the county general morgue and took the canvas back to his office at City Hall on Grove near McAllister, two blocks northwest from Market Street at Leavenworth, before he headed to Grace Cathedral to give alms. The dead were defenseless, helpless in any true sense of the word, and it was bestowed into the hands of the county to make certain their route to heaven was unobstructed. In the meantime the Los Angeles examiner, a female named Priscilla Houghton, had taped all access to the deceased's room, removed his possessions, emptied waste baskets looking for signs of a

The Hood

last meal, and made a clean sweep of the closets, bathroom and car, a purple and pale pastel green Studebaker. From what he could determine, the analyst ate at the restaurant where he ordered the same roast beef dinner once a week on Mondays, paid cash, walked on campus, stopped in at the gift shop to flirt with a girl he liked, and then after having desert with her in the lounge, went to his motel room. Although the investigative narrative described the young woman as completely falling apart, there wasn't much that could be done for her, there was no engagement as yet, they kept separate residences, and she wasn't known to his family. His grandmother on the other hand received all next of kin actuaries including a bit of equity on a house on the beach fifteen blocks away which he had rented out, his payroll benefit and death benefit, and sports car, the total amounting to about eighty grand.

# CHAPTER TWO

AN INTERCEPT WAS CLEARLY RECORDED AT five minutes before midnight almost an hour following the explosion. The first spool was targeted on Grove and McAllister Streets at Ninth, another tape began picking up feed for Van Ness and Golden Gate, yet additional tapes played along Market from Sixth and Taylor all the way to Tenth and Polk; it was the seedy corner lit by three street lanterns at Polk and Grove that expunged the lights inside the seven city buildings that made the park plaza between Eighth and Ninth Streets. Over at California and Sacramento at Grace Cathedral the hotels experienced periodic failures, down Leavenworth and Jones traffic stop lights held to green for an hour like an expressway, from Geary to Golden Gate cops manually conducted speed signals until mid morning around ten. Because traffic backed up as far as Van Ness and Ellis, the city law leaving traffic duty were dispatched to direct vehicles into one of eighteen garages including at the opera house and symphony hall. A judicial order kept the lot at the Hall of Justice reserved for special administrators and police called to the plaza.

The City Architect sent a prelim upstairs to Ray's Department 92 at the courthouse recommending that the tunnel between the state and federal buildings be turned into a six tier parking lot for enhanced camera access, that reviews for cruising of van cam on the street be inserted at minute intervals, and uniforms be positioned at the exits to the underground walkways, one at the court, one three blocks away in opposite direction where the trolley picked up passengers, and one at the hotel station. Ray signed it and passed it on to the state building for permits where it could take all of a week to work through the required depth and egress for a satisfactory underground parking garage with elevators rising four stories to the street. Once built, the camera stations would be accessed through a complex interlocutory network of telephone systems and Outside Bay Area Motorized circuitry connected through both bridges, all highways and Metro links. BAM circuits, the newest panels installed for combined emergency road telegraph, had nevertheless failed to assure San Mateo commuters who drove to Half Moon Bay that they were able to obtain field operators of stalls and the like and as a result gave San Francisco an extension through San Mateo to its airport and best yet, its stadiums. Since he was the judge who approved the wiretap that had never gone into implementation due to the double murders, he had to appraise the Milk/White murders including the White cover up first in order to assess who in San Francisco or San Mateo might be adversely affected so that he could prevent a backlash of bodies falling on the Ninth Street plaza pavement. The item of particular distinction was the man who had fallen to his death the evening of the explosion; his fingerprints said he was James Mirage, 88, from Long Beach, his address 12788 Orange Avenue off Seventh Street below Highway 405, a beachcomber perhaps judging by the forensic report which revealed a last meal taken nearly three days earlier. The photo clip on Ray's database finder showed Mirage walking through a section of sandy beach assaulted in every direction with hundreds of new white Nissan's at the beach end of Orange directly below the Pacific Coast campus, his flat listed as an old warehouse on Long Beach Island at Surf City. As a matter of course, despite the knowledge that most males found without their wits about them clung to an inhospitable reality of odd sorts, Ray searched his system for previous whereabouts of Mirage only to discover the man had lived in numerous surroundings close by parking lots of all types and could be presumed to have been something of an expert. Such an interest dated back to 1963 when in Torrance he left his position as night guard to a movie studio, got into the last car, a brown model Ford, he would ever own and drove south on Highway 605 San Gabriel at night and exited to a mall parking lot where department stores, hotels and Long Beach City College of Liberal Arts shared twenty rows of parking stalls and left his car there permanently. He was seventy-four that year. Mirage took a part time job in the liberal arts building fixing radios in the radio and television studio. In fourteen years he would take a bus to any of twelve parking lots, eat a bag lunch, lie in the sun of any top tier and sleep a few hours before starting back to catch the evening bus. The lots were varied, each represented an altogether different slice of life – at an airport terminal, beyond an overpass with arrows for the shuttle, at a high school with bright lights shining on wet pavement, a lot in the country for hikers, six lanes and a single pump besides ten thin apartment buildings, at a theatre in an industrial lot, spaces lined up at forty-five degree angles to the back stage wall, at a Bed, Bath & Beyond mall, at a city center where the lot occupied an equivalent space for two city buildings where dining and entertainment dominated the street, at a high school with grass and bleachers, inside a ten story parking lot where a crane maneuvered cars one at a time to a tiny space like in Beijing, a small city lot marked by a P between buildings in the downtown area, beneath a solar panel shady lot of microchip tops beside Highway 405, in an underground of a department store and business college, and in a lot one block long adjacent to Driver's Education with one training car parked there. After riding the bus to the terminal on Fourth Street and taking a cab to the Civic Center, Mirage should have been unable to have been caught off guard, and thus it made more sense to Ray that the old man collapsed as a result of exhaustion due to age; or perhaps he slipped in the rain, hit his head, was rendered unconscious and died of cold. The question for Ray was Mirage's reason for coming to the Bay Area. He didn't strike Ray as homeless although it was definitely an oddity that the morgue had let their only coroner to a city where a male lying dead in a lot four blocks away had originated less than ten hours earlier. If the sought after wiretap of police headquarters resulted in the four deaths – Harvey Milk by Dan White, and White by Chief Moscone; Hadley the analyst in Long Beach and James Mirage – there was no confirmation available for them. Milk and White had offices on the same floor of the police department, that's all anyone could attest to.

Milk had the orders for wiretaps to every police officer in San Francisco County on his desk; White had received the cable splice instructions the preceding week; and Chief Moscone had just transferred from a Chicago Illinois precinct to South San Mateo when he was invited to step into the landmark offices in San Francisco by Senate elect Barbara Boxer. Boxer's husband was running unopposed in San Mateo for state assembly and Boxer herself intended to take over as incumbent for the Electoral College located in Burlingame when all this broke out. Meanwhile in San Francisco there was reported several heinous suicides, one was of a landmark house owner by a homeless man, another of a female electrician who allegedly died after replacing a single non voltage wire to a bridge box, and a third unknown male identity in a construction site under demolition by an approved demolition expert. The autopsies showed increased white blood cells in all; however, not a one had a fever. In morgue training, if a person died having a fever, the incubation thermometers always showed a fever; impossible not to.

^ ^ ^

Jean Jacques Figeaq, the county medical examiner, had the two bodies Hadley and Mirage to attend to, both from Long Beach within the vicinity of the Pacific Coast Campus. Flicking on the overhead light, he snapped pictures of front and back of each corpse, next washed their bodies for signs of debris or pebbles lodged in hair or fingernails, examined the neck, wrists, knees and feet for distal fracture, and checked each body for sign of contusion or other fresh or old scarring. No evidence of cyanosis or glaucoma, hematoma, major abrasion, cut with pus or other wound in less obvious places was viewed. Eyeglasses were removed along with false teeth, hearing aids, wedding bands, and diabetic necklace for Hadley. The oddity of similarity was not lost on him, that Hadley had slept into death while in that hour Mirage, a long time resident of batten down Surf City on Long Beach Island, took a bus up the coast to die in a lot. One fact nubbed him for its truth – in the Palm Springs desert the Mirage hotel was owned by Chief Moscone, entertainer Frank Perdue, advertiser John Saliner, and money Bob Idol for the resort use by police lieutenants and their families. From what he could see of night life in Long Beach, the place had changed from a sandy coastline with flowering cacti covered sand to a big easy of colorful bars and four story two bedroom flats crammed into boulevards between Highway 91 and South Street, a college town for wannabes into standup comedy in

Hollywood bars. It could hardly be that Mirage had come looking for the building where a few months earlier Moscone had worked and a valet had parked his car, but it was not too far a stretch for any medical investigator to believe Mirage was looking for a particular car, or for a certain parking lot valet or attendant, a student or instructor, or even someone he had been inside a radio studio with when he worked for the liberal arts industry in Torrance. That weekend the Symphony Hall began its new season with Vivaldi, the Opera House was still running its Italian Festival of five weeks for *La Boehm*, and the Asian Art Museum was into its twelfth week with movie backdrops for famous epics, among them *The Sweltering Sun* and the *French Lieutenant's Woman*, for images that deceived the eye, refractions, distortion, looming apparitions, scenes that saw through a dazzle, latent, swimming figures emerging through glare, a specter materializing, muggy dewy shapes of people walking out of thick humidity.

The canvas with the blood spattered across it which he had carried Hadley, gushing from a bloody nose and mouth indicating a complication of having obtained a bypass, in had dried causing particles, clots, stains and spots to require scratching off by diluting the trace. Since steam eliminated red blood cells and solvents could alter diagnostic properties affecting a probe, the material had to remain carefully controlled allowing nothing other than an occasional pepsin pap to come into contact with blood. Jean worked diligently into the afternoon combing Hadley's straight brown hair looking for any laceration which could shed light on a contusion; with Mirage since it was evident street dirt had affixed to the scalp, Jean took gauze collection before he inspected the dead man with a lens and retrieved some good deposits of unalleviated foreign matter whereupon he sent for an aide to give Mirage a shampoo and rinse. However, in his report he remarked near the bottom where he jotted his diagnosis, fatal accidental death due to extreme cold, that the victim smelled of dextrin typical of beer.

For Hadley, who showed mostly signs of fatal arrhythmia yet who had emitted far more blood than usually accompanied bypass, diagnosis was dry pleurisy.

He telephoned his secretary for a tape transcription and full body X-rays by morning with bites and occlusions. When he called City Architect Frankie Moser, cousin of Gay Spender and Giant nephew of both Jimmy Dean and mega builder Franklin Caper, he told Frankie, "Make sure you eliminate all the pavements. Dead man Mirage came to see an old friend known to Milk. Word at the dome is Harvey made a big mistake. He approved all drawers; that's brown gold." Brown gold was the end of the line if the Mint stored brown wheat. Gold for the Wall was manufactured from Harvey's with first orange bath and if approved with yellow which permitted it to crumble and be sold as Dow Brass. If the governor permitted gold stored beleaguers the next treatment after yellow was a violet mixture which permitted wafer thin security. On the Dow this was Gold.

When Frankie picked up his message he made a note to erect a complex for dollar value security somewhere in the vicinity of a corner paved lot closest to a highway on-ramp.

∧ ∧ ∧

Lorraine drove into the city from Highway 1 in her turbo charged Alfa Romeo having stopped to take a snapshot of every vineyard, coastal cliff and ocean inlet from Santa Cruz to Half Moon Bay to arrive for a short weekend with her newly divorced husband in Burlingame. The air circulated at blustery temperate, the sky gave no indication that the late spring rains might double back from the ocean drizzling pour spout, despite this, she rode with top down, her tightly coiffed hairdo wrapped in a cellophane, the stereo blasting out great classical music, the smallish brick homes with decks plastered up and down coastal green hills. She was considering a hop to Marin headlands to do a little window shopping in Sausalito before straying to Atascadero to visit a lawyer she used to date. The exit into the hospital sector came at mountains of vineyards and a tangled loop of freeways past marshes and low bridges into the back roads of Palo Alto along the Del Camino past plumes of spruce along stagnant fields and hundreds of crosses of a military cemetery into tree-lined Burlingame and walled manors. Lorraine pulled into a tiny half block alley in which she parked, grabbed a speckled powder blue sweater from the trunk, locked up and strolled through an alley with a salon and evening gowns to the rear entrance of the French restaurant where her sister took opposing counsel to lunch. White tablecloths, smoked candle holders, napkin fans, a full bar, liquid rival glass reflected in the mirror, she saluted the bartender, found her way through a lit hall to a private room. Ray perused the menu until she slipped into the booth opposite his, her subdued pastel blue as non intrusive as any apparel she retained from her marriage, Ray dressed in his usual flamboyant black double breasted jacket, dark brown trousers, crème shirt with expensive diamond cuffs, black interior soft beige lamb wool gloves folded on the table, and ordered his drink, a very dry martini. In a minute he would discard his bound writ, but not until she began babbling away at something meaningless. She promised herself she wouldn't focus on the hall traffic nor on which famous patron stepped out at the curb, and not on Ray either. She was unhappily at a loss, without thoughts on life, or dross of non permitted complaints about the numerous ways his life impinged on her.

"Have you ordered ahead?" she asked.

"I waited for you," he replied. "How was the drive up?"

"Few motorists, I had the entire road to myself, you know how that is, the road was dry, thank God, the kids had a wonderful time, it was thoughtful of you to come down. For Maman, especially."

"I had a good time too. It was like old times."

She smiled, looking fondly at him. "Divorce, Ray? Was that necessary? It's like you've hardly said a word to me in almost a year."

"Did the summons upset you much?"

She took a cardboard wine menu and fanned herself. "Not too much. I tossed it on the pile with the other brochures."

The waiter interrupted their repartee to take their order. Ray selected stewed cabbage roll hors d'oeuvre, lacy sharpened salad trim with sliced beet, tangerine and shaved beef, cannelloni, and spumoni wafer for desert. He topped off with a 1967 Merlot. The waiter returned with a non chilled Merlot and poured two glasses and corked the remaining bottle.

"Definitely splendid," she said after a sip. "I hate to ask but are you intending to offer alimony?"

"Two thousand a month in addition to mortgage. That should about do it."

"That should. Do you mind if I ask why?"

"It's the affairs, Lorraine."

She sipped her wine. She could feel the acrimonies swell up. "Yours or mine?"

"I haven't had any as you should know."

"You've stayed gone for weeks."

"No one asked you to stay in Monterey."

"It's more lucrative than Daly City. I can't compete with a thousand lawyers."

"I would've gone on supporting you. The children wouldn't have suffered."

"It was one stinking weekend."

He eyed her. "What does Bo say?"

"We don't talk. She's judgmental as usual."

"Well, now that I'm single, I won't have to worry. I'll have my trials and my friends."

"They run your life, your friends." The bitterness slipped into admission. "Who has the patience for your docket?"

"Apparently not you. I am however releasing you from child support. I'll put them through college."

The meal was set before them. The waiter dished out tiny portions onto three plates apiece and poured the last of the wine.

They ate the cabbage dripping with warm vinaigrette, sampled the beef and beet salad, snipped the main dish, Ray worked his way to the wafer, took a bite and resigned the palate while Lorraine fed on the salad marveling at the shavings of turnip, horseradish and spinach until she had supped down to the cilantro and yellow pepper. She reminded herself to keep their conversation free of hostility, any merriment would have to become her tasking, the past no longer mattered now that the affair was out in the open along with an abortion.

"I have changed the locks on the penthouse and had an attorney draft up a settlement."

"Why did you involve my sister of all people?"

"I didn't. The conflicts board drew her name from the rotation."

"You should have argued. Everyone who knows us will wonder."

"I'm disposed of from the case for a month."

"How credible is the girl likely to be anyhow?"

"She's old enough to be able to say what she witnessed, she took a deposition without character flaw, as far as summation goes the individual who took photographs reveals most of what she describes and therefore I admitted it in as fact."

"Defense will try to take her apart. First she said she saw a vehicle leave as the male suspect pulled a weapon on a nurse, the vehicle was captured two blocks away, then she said someone sat inside the car reading written material, but this is contradicted by a lawyer who works for city hall who described a male looking at pages flying around in a blue car, and then there are the varying descriptions of where the car is, not to mention who is inside the car alone, is the person male or female?"

Ray had begun taking notes in shorthand. For years in their courtship this was all she did – pointed out the inconsistencies of any workup to a major trial. When he married her it was she who delivered sections of extemporaneous law to complete admittance of evidence from one category to another.

"There was a scuffle during which the attendant chased the man off the lot and an unmarked blue jacket followed in pursuit."

"I thought you yourself flagged that incident as non substantive."

"The burglary of the parking box amounted to less than twenty bucks, all in ones. Whether he saw a driver for the Mustang is not determined, he couldn't correctly state the number of parked vehicles. He thought the madder blue was brown."

"The fact that he recalls a brown car should help establish time."

"On camera he is stealing from the lot safe while the attendant is parking a car."

"He can't be in two places at once and his burglary confirms it, but he is placed on hospital parking lot grounds approximately twenty minutes earlier by the girl. First a grayish blue car is seen by its tail light as it winds past the planters, then a black two door driven by a physician arriving after dinner who eventually parks at the plaza, after which a brown car Dodge is seen leaving by the street, then the girl witnesses the attack, and in that chronology a vehicle leaves the hospital parking lot. However, on camera the attack has already occurred hours earlier. I don't see how you're going to get your victim identified if he's not there yet."

"We don't know that when he arrives he doesn't get knocked over by the force of the explosion which we know occurs at 9:08 pm," Ray said, emphasizing, "because the first he's picked up on a lens finder he is lying unconscious, it would appear, near where a blue Mustang is parked which is seen on a building outside OCR at 8:26 pm."

Lorraine stabbed at the melted wafer. "How is it the chief examiner is out of town at that moment?"

Ray shrugged. "That's life. Long Beach is a college; it isn't approved for a coroner although it has a small physician training center on campus."

"When he returns, he learns he has two bodies?"

"That's right. This Mirage is the problem. He's an unknown."

"Is he legal counsel to a hotel chain by that name?"

"Not this Mirage. He was in liberal arts in Burbank."

"What is that? Radio and television?"

"Broadcasting, radio. He ran the first studio through Los Angeles Community College. He worked for a managing news editor who came out of New York."

"Did employees drive to work?"

"No vehicles were allowed on the set."

"Were the set locations on parking lots?"

"Probably," Ray speculated. "Everything was inside a big building. There were no actual outside scenes in those days. If a show required a garden it had to be staged in order to pick up sound."

"Here's what the Defense will try, the time is in dispute because the witness has identified a vehicle that is parked a block away when the explosion occurs."

The facts were still weak. "I can't account for what occurred when a wire is cut for the seeing lens that records the lot. The wire to the camera looking at the safe is also cut but its backup restores. The backup happens to record the robber and attendant chasing him onto the street. It should be easy to present for an actual chronology."

"Defense will argue for 'not yet known' to prove only an

inside camera was tampered with. They will go for separate crimes."

"They can try all they want but the fact remains the ground, not the car. Here's the technical feed, it looks like the car blew. That's why Sixth Street crime lab was built, but for this site it doesn't yet meet the condition for TIN, even though the ground is fractured."

She withdrew the list she had slipped inside her purse and handed it to him.

"What are these?" she asked, in a slightly critical tone. "I get these updates on my laptop."

He took the memo from her, his glance snagged by all of it. "These are not actual codes by which a CIA Intelligent lawyer can be required to fulfill trauma designations. TIN as well as AMA MD are never actuaries so TIN is likely to be translated as a market value if it pertains to structural metallic foundations, whereas AMA MD probably is actual, a group of physicians, a medical ward, trauma or incision, but the last two, COIN won't cross correspond or INK which conveys affiliation but may have no placement unless both COIN and INK go with STREET like Market Van Ness signifying the new Mint. You've come in on a major lane, not brown wheat, but equally commercial. I just won't know what it means until I index it."

"Are these files?"

"Yes, all. Doctor physician is a federal demarcation but does not cover insurance of any type, it is intended as morgue, County intelligence is state, Ink usually accounts for death certificates, and Street has all work orders. Brown wheat of course ought to be a type of situational code for files like brown auto coach or wheat thin. These are the type of files that come through the federal building."

"What was Dan White?"

Ray deliberated. Lorraine had no use of the material of

which she unerringly inquired, thus she was angered, leading up to some stomping indemnifier, once focused on anger gave a rather discerning spate. But he found a wise policy was to lead no secrets of a once opened gravesite. "Dan White, state file, name of a hotel industry, Caucasian suspect, no leads."

Lorraine toyed with the cannelloni, decided against eating more, and waved the waiter down for a cup of coffee with cream. After the coffee and ladle were served, once she prepared it to her liking, she took his stature in over the rim, sizing up her future against his desire to turn himself apart from their sore arguments. "San Francisco has a tiny Dan."

"It is a Dan nevertheless, just not in the vicinity, so there's no way to see what their loose change brought in. We cannot be sure there wasn't another wire on tap."

"Have you checked a match for federal stopover?"

"Once, if blurs include actual taping footage."

She tasted the coffee and drank most.

He said, "I can come up with no method to check roof exits."

"Your problem is civic center plaza is level, it has no sloping street above it. Pull up traffic photos for Ninth."

"City Architect did. He made his recommendation based on those prints."

"That's as good as it gets, throw your professional judgment to a sixteen year old."

Ray touched his mouth with the napkin, offered her a chocolate mint, took one, and covered the tab. As he stood, he said kindly, "I am assured you can survive on alimony of two grand to enhance your income of five thousand."

The tone was clear – any amount of yearly income exceeding thirty-two deserved a denial of alimony. "Until the children have graduated," she replied.

"I see no reason to conduct for any restriction."

She stood with him drawing close and kissed him. "Thank you, Ray."

He gave her one long lingering gaze and left her with cup in hand.

The fresh air alleviated his anxiety. Lorraine would survive, a footstool at her bedside if she could figure out a way not to get caught with a man in her bed. The Federals had all tapes. Whatever they could prove, if they had to overlook an obvious criminal injunction, the conviction might get tossed out. The spools were in place, the hammer jacket on a string, the cutter craft identified through a powerful observatory telescope, all sightings of any explosives expert visible as day, they had to be sifting through hundreds of quarantined district denials, each agent released from Mint duty to clear the magazine color off their trays. Sixty, seventy rounds of bulleted journal trays taken on the same miserable line, cut from every healthy tree, tacked onto any fence in a neighborhood, sentences slipped in as newsworthy print, shoe smudges bearing fingerprints, snow trails, bids on corporate, stains on stained glass, sheet after sheet impressions to anyone who had a bearing for unhappy treachery. Oddly, he suspected they had everything except his Mirage. Mirage didn't make sense, Ray didn't have him in a building, talking to anyone he had ridden on the bus with, no sandwich or fish and chips, no idea what took him there, the file for him was indexed as JAMES MIRAG, maybe that's all he had done in his late life, cleaned people's vehicle windows with Windex and a rag until he encountered a sympathetic female, the ludicrous outcome being the camera showed gigantic smudges over the glass blocking people's faces as drivers moved through traffic.

He paid the valet, sat inside his Nissan car rental and took off, a twinge of sadness creeping in, worked his way to an exit, let the top down, felt an exhilaration of driving toward the ocean, the spray winding through the air, the work at the office was certain to consume his attention, allow him to forget time and betrayal, while eventually restoring an immersion of good will. Although he knew Risk at this end of the county looked only at number of people to fulfill quotas, he pulled up to ivy court office where his desk man Alfred worked, caught him at his station on a console studying film of park plazas contrasting those to the plaza park lot which was partially inside a one story building overhead with time and green light on it, parking attendant in enclosed cashier office, cameras inside, wall mounts, bumper height, front and back, distance into the level lot, several carryalls – black, white and pink – a center row of four cars, and behind them in its own aisle, alone, the blue car, boxy and squat. The digitally stamped time showed as 06:48 pm, Saturday June 9, 1979, matching the real time indicator and date.

Ray said, "I am told there's someone in the back seat reading."

"We can't identify because the car window is smudged. It looks as if the party is a young man but since he doesn't own the car, we can't get prints. The worst of it is the cameras aren't fixed, they move so as to pick up the entire lot. What we do have is minimal. When the car enters the lot, we have only the rear bumper. We never have the driver or passengers, and we don't know who to look for. See here –" Alfred switched to another console group showing a blue van in reflection, small delivery van or bus, a side shot gave another eclipse of an oblong shaped car in the hospital lot. Through the foliage a car across the street in the same reflection looked like another car in the lot until a vehicle driving down street intersected through both. "Once that occurred we went over all film to see if they summarized correctly. When first car pulled away from the curb, we were able to see that the reflecting item was a pick-up. The setting still resembled a hospital lot. It doesn't occur what size last vehicle is until it finally pulls away, that's when we realized we were on the street. This is what your witness saw. There's no way she saw this other lot."

"I can't impeach my gal. She is the one who witnessed the attack. The subsequent scene was of the windows were rolled down in your car of interest, loose papers flying about, not much of a disturbance, the film was time stamped by a high resolution timing device so speed could be checked manually by calculating speed with dragon's teeth barrier calibrated lines painted on road surface.

"As it so happens when change was made from underwater photographic film to high speed technology, on which images are stored for playback, our biggest concern was that the camera was tamper-proof timed through a program called doctor-doctor to eliminate problems of intrusion; we developed a program that intensified camera bite sounds; integrated it with GPS police crime detection maps dated with time and tracked by motion tracking high resolution 480TVL and 23X optical zoom. At your particular lot we used a 10X digital zoom to bring actual zoom capability to 230X which because of this enhancement has a built-in automatic object automatic tracking feature."

"When does my blue car arrive? Where is it immediately preceding?"

"It enters the lot for the first time the previous morning at three something because the attendant leaves at two-thirty and reopens at six. The optical zoom reads and identifies license plate while car is in motion, but the problem is –"

"What do the scofflaws demand?"

"They state there must be high reading rates in all weather with full capability to transmit photos to Regional Video Closed Circuit section office monitors."

"Question – did the pipe disruption generate from a parking vent?"

"We have Volicom coordination of digital videos for a multi-channel system, that includes Remote program monitor

– com watch, closed circuit TV, view from the office with Intruder alarm, monitoring 24 hours, 365 days per year, audio and visual alarm verification, and call dispatch. In less sophisticated studios it is not uncommon for a transmitter station to consist of microphones, mixing boards, speaker, acoustics, tape console, sound board, broadcast to lots, and a com line."

"You have the plates."

"Address origin is not where the car is. We have to take the Bay Area apart."

"What about the deceased male? Mirage? Any known identifiers?"

"Plenty, for about twenty years ago. He's made a very quiet life for himself in a bungalow in Surf City," and brought up another file that showed a small stucco and glass on a hill overlooking the sandy beach. "Four rooms, neat. Long deck. Mirage paid $40,820 for his nest egg. He rarely left it."

"Nice comfy life."

"You know how it is, guy is single, divorced once, early thirties."

"Have you found any contact prior to him getting on Greyhound?"

"He occasionally went to any of twelve parking lots to walk around and have lunch."

"Did he take in a movie or see anyone?"

"No, he purchased lunch at a sub shop then walked in a mall and out the back."

"Did he sleep at any?"

"No. He walks, goes to the top, and looks at the area, and leaves."

"It's an odd habit. How often?"

"Every few months, no set day."

"Who is at the sub shop who might recognize him?"

"There are two students who work the counter, one who cleans up. Three total."

"Have you attempted to place any here?"

"One. He has studied management at LBPCC. He now works for a chain gallery."

"Does he drive?"

"He takes the Muni."

"Run a tag on him."

∧ ∧ ∧

Inevitably the cold lies of arguments descended into a reluctant desertion, without the semblance of possum heat. Ray had once decided the path he must follow was made of inconstancy perhaps but lived for the endurance of sunsets, passionate weddings given to indelible aging. If he had culminated an idea of hapless hedonism toward Lorraine he had discovered her to keep a seldom latch to whimsical fancy not surrendered by harmony of living but of some singular, somewhat selfish indulgence, a possibly discoverable long tendered yearning of the soul's awakening of newly arrived awareness which he might have kept cadence with but in her was a keen resentment aimed at withdrawing from a continual whir of activity borne of bench duties. Thus she who had reined him in had let him go through barely seething subconscious mishap, a release one would have to imagine had the stretch marks of impatient broodings. He found himself rejoining with a private encounter of guilt to imagine how she would fare, whether she might take to periodic absinthe if she remained alone for long, her destructive tendencies would burden her with a depression from which recovery was often challenging if it wasn't quickly rescued. Her impinging was to compare and therefore in desultory ideography practice her claws of wit demarcating foolish mannerisms to even less valued caloric cynicism. He would shut a door on the past, dilute a bitter strength of her objections with early morning coffee on the balcony of his penthouse, dining with a good friend after the rush hour had subsided spending his last on crumble cake and steeped lemon tea at a sidewalk bar down the street waiting for nothing but nighttime and twinkling city lights.

For hours after he read his trial notations he succumbed to the television watching any comedy switching from channel to channel to sample the relief after sleep seemed imminent when he reviewed his summaries and citations and decided it was unnecessary to assess. Sleep was not imminent, a convergence of thoughts crowding upon wearisome long well-charted discretionary encumbrances raising hoists of argument before principled edifices of memory. He recoiled to the child witness of a fatal stabbing on a charitable hospital foundations garden, her figure inside a marble arced window, barely protected by shadow much less by a copper canopy with green soapstone windows, as handsome a Byzantine architectural trumpet calling of angels on high reminiscent of Hood, Mississippi at St. Anne Cropolis strumming harps and all chariots of tractable intramural activity, an intricate compilation of intrinsic reductions. That the brown car sped between parking hedges in its speedy escape only to turn a corner in flashy wet rain had become an invention of time for the real problem of the ramp down at the Superior Court plaza. As qualifying as the pronouncement was for the crime, the law was exact. Child 16 was being examined, physician leaves the room, loud sound is heard and child runs to window and sees three people, someone who is fleeing; fleeing person sees child. Law 14002 says interviewing children in a child oriented setting; using a child interview specialist to conduct comprehensive interviews with children with mandatory use of videotaping of the said child interview; minimize and reduce the need for subsequent interviews. A certain desperation arose over the matter, the girl knew of nearly no hostel, residence or restaurant where a person coming through was safe from just anyone moving about, the closest closet across the street from the all night lot that closed at two o'clock.

In yet another disobliged short take which days earlier had the same girl walking home from parochial school on Bay Street, taking a short cut and walking into a tag of ten officers pulling a car out of the ocean by a hydraulic lift and subsequently after the all nighter lot blew two hundred riot police in gear to assist all departments driving to and from home, the sole photo tag that showed anyone inside the blue car was picked up in the angel's garden. Prior to this hostility the biggest crime in San Francisco was a high school gymnasium being thrashed usually with chemicals poured onto floor, that was about the most crime could merit. When San Francisco street detectives began digging around scratching below the surface they targeted a desperate man on run, the commission of a burglary, and a telephone call at 3:02 am to the parking attendant some twenty minutes prior to the blue car entering the overflow lot. There was a library, several clinics, sheriff station, vehicle garage, newspaper house, grass, courthouse with six court rooms and a jail. A typical Classical Eros seaboard block colonial town, Gumps, I-Magnin, and the trolley at Lane Bryant's, wine cellars, and clam chowder bistros for a fur wrapped downtown extending from the bus depot on Fourth to the Nob Hill Top of the Mark off Geary and North Beach and then in down a diagonal , a nursing college, two motels with restaurants, one for breakfast, one for dinner hof brau, some houses for town employees. On one spring afternoon sixty cops on Ninth ran battalion in combat shields from the station across the plaza to the stairs, ran down the ramp, marched to the courthouse and drew fire on a person holding up the courthouse. The law was vague as to use of firearms by county employees, on so many accounts the treasury forbade mint handlers to have weapons even to defend their lives. The law after all maintained a narrow shelf for jurisdiction and the difficulty with scrutiny was that once an environment had been defiled the necessary abrogative remedy might not be wanted. Having admonished so many times, as he fell asleep the law he knew so well kept him scarcely vigilant. *Hastings College of the Law, security officers shall have authority of peace officers only in city and county of San Francisco. They cannot carry firearms on or off duty.*

*830.5 firearms*

*(c) Parole officer of Department of Corrections or Department of the Youth Authority or any employee of Department of the Youth Authority having custody of the wards or any employee of Department of Corrections designated by the Director of Corrections may carry a firearm while not on duty. A parole officer of the Youthful Offender Parole Board may carry a firearm while not on duty only when so authorized by the chairperson of the board and only under the terms and conditions specified by the chairperson.*

*830.55 use of firearms in performance of duties*

*(a) As used in this section, a correctional officer is a peace officer, employed by a city, county, or city and county which operates a facility described in Section 2910.5 of this code or Section 1753.3 of the Welfare and Institutions Code or facilities operated by counties pursuant to Section 6241 or 6242 of this code under contract with the Department of Corrections or the Department of the Youth Authority, who has the authority and responsibility for maintaining custody of specified state prison inmates or wards, and who performs tasks related to the operation of a detention facility used for the detention of persons who have violated parole and are awaiting parole back into the community or, upon court order, either for their own safekeeping or for the specific purpose of serving a sentence therein.*

*(b) A correctional officer shall have no right to carry or possess fire-*

*arms in the performance of his or her prescribed duties, except, under the direction of the superintendent of the facility, while engaged in transporting prisoners, guarding hospitalized prisoners, or suppressing riots, lynchings, escapes, or rescues in or about a detention facility established pursuant to Section 2910.5 of this code or Section 1753.3 of the Welfare and Institutions Code.*

*(e) A correctional officer may use reasonable force in establishing and maintaining custody of person delivered to him or her by a law enforcement officer, may make arrests for misdemeanors and felonies within the local detention facility pursuant to a duly issued warrant, and may make warrantless arrests pursuant to Section 836.5 only during the duration of his or her job.*

*830.8 Federal criminal investigators and law enforcement officers; federal employees*

*(b) Duly authorized federal employees who comply with the training requirements set forth in Section 832 are peace officers when they are engaged in enforcing applicable state or local laws on property owned or possessed by the United States government, or on any street, sidewalk, or property adjacent thereto, and with the written consent of the sheriff or the chief of police, respectively, in whose jurisdiction the property is situated.*

# CHAPTER THREE

LARGE WEIGHTY DROPS SOON TEEMED falling from the air like a monotony of diffusion which once or twice in a half hour was interceded by reflecting light. The drenching rain was over within minutes, steam rising off the balcony in an impractical mist. A squandered missive, within minutes the air was cleansed, mitigated by a narcolepsy of a seeping, dripping mooch.

Ray's designee, a man from the uptown Seventeenth District in his mid eighties who had reared three generations of lawyers for legal firms in the Sunset, streaked white grey hair, bow tie, silk black leggings, satin shirts, loafer Jims sat at the sidewalk to the spoon of the coffee bar on Geary and Fulton awaiting Ray who he would bring up to date over eggs Benedict and a latte. Larry Blemsen rambled on the moment Ray joined him making a full complaint of a new appeals received at the start of the week with four other appeals, this one already a

day spent in examination of a slight-reference of witness having once been found had encountered the victim at the bay
front mall of Ghirardelli Park next to the Maritime Museum,
not as listed in the description encountered at the Presidio
Green looked to make a spectacle of the prevailing convicting
language in 1436.

"It's become a popular objection for grounds of appeal,"
Blemsen remarked. "Far more the curious than the findings
on direct, nowadays everyone wants the testing tossed out, the
SMTs listed as positive IDs of a jailbird, the cup an invalid
mustard for amphetamine or heroin, I might as well strike out
the DNA or saline on those uniquely acquiescent carpet stains."

They sipped their drinks, Ray sampling a crust of cinnamon, cream and vanilla before he made his meal from the
poached eggs and French bacon on English muffin.

Blemsen continued, his voice taking up a descriptive sauce
over the judicial presumptive. "The designated chambers reporter gave a summation of the day's upcoming hearings and
deferred to the rostrum whereupon I permitted discussions to
begin.

"The hearings called out by each criminal's name required
the calendar aides to rise one at a time, give a summary, presenting any failure to obtain consents and test evidence surrendered
by the police.

"Although I heard the prelims early between seven-thirty
and eight, the docket schedule posted late after eight-thirty,
because the county clerk had forgotten to list rooms, the regular
clerk sat in the large lobby of the dome at a desk dispensing
information and admitting in names of parties.

"The wheels of Appeals turn slowly, its lengthy cumbersome notice a procedure of intense tertiary confrontation as to
the count found to be non salutary. A stay of execution of judgment sought to reduce the death penalty to life imprisonment."

Ray asked, "Despite the conclusive evidence?"

"Despite all interlocutaries, the witness who ran into the murderer after he killed the victim was produced in a photographic document clear as day at a location other than declared."

"Proven to meet all chain of custody requirements?"

"In all ways."

"Then you can deal out life without parole."

"I've asked counsel to submit for placement in a Type IV local detention center as a "minimum security inmate" for the least restrictive placement possible."

"Defense will go for "low-risk offender", convicted to be placed in home detention monitored by The Board of Corrections. Have you given the sentence lately?"

"No siree, I'm completely in an objection. Man has murdered, he gets the basement," Blemsen said in postulate form.

By mid morning they moved from the sidewalk up to the sun porch to soak their choicest raisin, a chocolate toddy.

"And you?" Blemsen inquired.

"At this point, there's not much to bulk. Basically the crime is conjugated by a grouping of photo proofs from the bucket, the scene evidence is stronger than the stains and blood –

"A man left a parking lot underground through door to top ground dressed as the parking attendant, walked across plaza and grass to dome, then entered dome to hall, went up four stairs, walked down marble wax polished hall to an office midway, entered, removed a judicial docket notebook and left. That's one fact established. Subsequent item, someone in park uniform stood on grass with a food cart, local camera at City Hall got the shot, several other traps also caught photo, scene evidence, guess at length of time vehicle had sat there; at ramp garage a vehicle had just entered, gone down, taken a ticket, parked, a member of the San Francisco Bay Area Rapid Transit District Police Department arrived by car, parked in street, brought receipts to the office beside the courthouse. Point three, a security officer from the court left to go to City

Hall for evening shift when he was accosted by a man running through park, and state hospital officers with firearms were requested to come immediately to the courthouse to provide backup, their power extended to any place in the state for the purpose of performing their duties."

"Is the State ready to file?"

"No, the district attorney says not until a piece of evidence is brought in."

"What piece is it?"

"It's vague. A nurse rolled a cart into medical supply and rolled it out the door. The belief is she took striker supplies."

"Is she available to speak with?"

"No, she's been relieved. We are looking for the item on any number of networks. The problem is all the nurse aides return their carts empty at the end of that shift."

"Maybe the witness didn't work for the hospital. Perhaps she stole her cart. You may have to look elsewhere for an answer."

"We're prepared to tear the place apart."


After being shown into the drawing room with a mezzanine library, Beulah removed her gloves and handed her large, gray tweed nurse cloak to the manservant who promptly poured her a scotch before he drew the French doors and abandoned her to herself. Crystal glass in hand, Beulah walked to a stained glass window made of red, green, and purple glass overlooking a lengthy, modestly wide Victorian garden in the middle between two thin strips of lawn, a large white stone chimney at the far end. Through the reflection she could make out her broad bouffant, drooping lime green tear pendant, her grey woolen hoop skirt and stylish pink sweater, pointed patent heels, dozens of pink and reddish rust sparkling bracelets, grey eye shadow, darkened by mascara, powder and rouge, and painted mauve lips.

Lorraine was a fool to let Ray go, such a fuss over a house.

What had she expected from a split household? Nothing but insatiable wanderlust, she was a girl of illusion. Lots of wives like her these days, eager teens fresh out of college seeking a judge bachelor and once obtained with a group of kiddies onto the ramp of the career highway to follow signs to a once postponed secretarial law post. For the Lorraine who understood life so well to have herself tangled into a minor snafu there had to have been promising bench high water marks rolled into free condos and free overseas cruises of a month duration, an expense account of ten thousand, credit on gowns, business suits, dress wear, high heels.

Eventually Ray entered, his notepads and binder jackets under his arm, still outfitted in his morning's pin-striped brown and black three-piece trousers, a fresh crew cut, long jowls revealing a compensatory amount of sleep. "How're the kids?"

"It's been awhile for me. When Lorraine allows, I can take them with me down to La Jolla, but it's a far holler these days. I offered to take Ken on my next redo to the Bermudas but haven't heard a word."

"I'll call him. No reason to trench the communication lines."

"I stopped in to give you the pleadings and pick up the accusatory pleadings on Cap."

"Let's take a look. What does their defendant have?"

"No priors, no controlled substances, no violation of narcotics."

"Revoke parole?"

"We could. He was armed."

"Male, under twenty-five, killed with club, enraged, systolic reading way out there, two forty manual, negative for drugs, no priors."

She replied, "He sped off in his car, that's all we need, but we also have him on threatening, harassing, battering and disturbing the peace. Mitigating factors are all curtailed, rehab won't prevent him from aggressing. Trial to commence, and then you better give me assets, all real property, all trusts, records of corporation, et cetera so we know what we're disposing to the State upon mandatory in-custody."

"When do I get the cocaine base manslaughter?"

"We're still at prelim. They have to agree the report per cocaine grains was in excess of childproof safe amounts even though they have no children, they had enough meth and cocaine to shutdown the county, although he didn't test, he was found in possession. That's over fifty-seven grams of cocaine, they're in violation of the bodily injury – how deep did the knife go in – together they'll take under the influence for the umpteenth time, we don't know if there were firearms, fines were collected so it's there somewhere."

"It just keeps getting worse. Same old stupid stuff, it never decreases. We'll be in prelim a year."

Beulah set keys on the coffee table for him with an address. "Bungalow sits right on the sand on the ocean, nice hotel and coffee shop within walking distance on a hill. I paid for three weeks. I hope you'll like it."

His eyes watered. "That's very considerate of you. I'll call in a status."

"No phone, it's just to relax."

"Thanks."

"Don't mention it. It's a little peace, nothing like what I put up with from my friend John who really, I think, doesn't like to be weighed upon. He likes it that I'm colorful, I've told him every last little stupid thing about the family, about my closest friendships, and to this hour all he allows between us are these sometimes funny, somewhat thrilling slices of life."

"Most intimacy is based upon this neurotic suggestion of entertainment, quiet pick-me-ups of utterly no consequence, not insights at each meal or a deeply intellectual finding as to the arts or amusements."

"It's simply not me, it's not what I was raised with."

"Look at Lorraine, everything focused on the children, no time really on us."

"What about on your job?"

"Well, you know how it is, in the beginning we talked all the time. After the arrival of the kids, very little time spent talking about much of anything, their ballet school, little league, after school gymnasium, tutors, school pictures, PTA, symphony, summer rehearsals, endless, fatiguing."

"It's because she didn't work outside the home."

"Oh, she did, as a law pistol, every now and again."

Beulah said, "Everyone who knew Lorraine knew she was short on the string, patience went only as far as the strand. You ought not to blame yourself."

"I thought you knew. She had an affair."

"I didn't know. With whom?"

He was vague, saying, "Another attorney, bench cozy out of Atascadero, Channel Islands."

"She's never been given a case of prison."

"He resides down at Seaside, has a bit of a balcony snippet on the ocean. She just lost her head."

Beulah was silent, without further comment on any family matters. "This situation at the federal building – what does the county intend to do?"

"Not a thing for the time being. The city has to rebuild the police department and the state has put up a bid on the street park. Of the eight or nine jurisdictions, city lights has to pay the police department costs otherwise they are paid out of streets. Federal covers the stairs where the hospital ward pulled a gun on the guard, same with sidewalk where a patrol car rammed into the parking wall at an angle, tore out drive, and broke a window in the basement, the city detective team has to explain how the wall outside the precinct building blew; The library plumbing under the street also blew."

"That's shocking. Was this during Harvey Milk?"

"This year, a month and a half ago."

"This is the lot problem?"

"Yes. By the time repairs are done, the precinct, a side of the library and parking will be rebuilt."

"What in god's name went wrong?"

He gave her a weary, face turned down smile. "The usual. It's been happening for a while. Army Street is in competition with Noe for a few new tennis courts, any number of city halls, Palo Alto glass and dolphins, lots of new movie theatres and organic food marts."

"Army Street keeps adding other exit ramps."

"The area has been growing a few town zones per ten years. Condos are in demand among the young sets. Plus there's highway 280, it's been developing a lake mall every fifteen years. Life does not stand still."

"I only know the area by its church landmarks – Grace Memorial, Downtown Tabernacle, Delores Street, Buddhist Shrine and Pacific Union."

"That's a club. Fortunately it admits women."

"You know what I mean." She gave a sigh. "What ought I to do, Ray? About things, I mean?"

"I'm no better than you at answers. I haven't any idea. What does John say?"

"Oh, nothing, he says he's fine. He prefers to come when the kids are there."

"What about I adopt you one?"

"It's alright. He's moving in on Maman. Every time he visits he brings her favorite brisket. He's just so scarce, nothing I do tangles him up."

"He's a lawyer, toss him an ex parte."

"It would be beneath my dignity to ask him to contribute language for my torts. His field happens to be contract violations, he's comparing text to county dollar for agreed-upon materials. His most recent suit centered upon the sidewalks in

Chinatown's soup parlor for inferior grids."

"He can't be coached, each injunction probably takes him upward of a thousand hours to introduce."

"That's what I guessed you'd say."

"What do you say we have dinner in his Chinatown after I return from your rental?"

"Oh, definitely, that sounds like fun."


The complacency of a relaxing relationship insured insuperable sufficiency beyond which no fault could be justified. The easiest trifling of enmity having a deceptive jeer gave over to insurgency eventually. If there were no conjured or capable ink with which to view the covetous hankering of desire, then there was the desolation of anxiety in the moody, precarious reckless intent of calculation and cunning to hook one's plunder. It couldn't make sense, because there were no desserts to aspire to, every last litigant was given the litmus and lissome recitation to augment their compact. Ray was not one to mistrust nor to be made suspicious of in human nature, oddly he found living neither tedious nor spurious or stingy; he often extended the emotional perimeters not taking note of the periodic excitable intoxication, woozy impulsivity, or evasive, sometimes keeping an evanescent sequestered digression, Lorraine's constant voluble chatter, leaving him taken in, gullible, not in the least worried about infidelity. Never remote, she made all efforts to lay out his dinner table, make the house tidy, run the children to appointments and activities, and keep his calendar; who had so much exuberance for all that and an affair – derelict of duties first, he would have thought. At night, seated near the frosted lamp at her vanity, she applied an ointment to keep her skin soft, as he undressed to his garter, she seemed aloof, detached, unsympathetic talking about the day, the people she had encountered, until he kissed her; then it seemed to him that she traveled a distance to return, and was ignited. Who would have known?

He stayed on the balcony until nightfall nursing a warm lime currant brandy, always the high life in full swing around him, the distant lights on the cooling orange bridge, twinkling lights evident on rooftop bars, swanky music spilling into the street, the hum of steady traffic far below, a tall man on a corner in tweeds lighting a cigarette, pretty females with slender legs and thin arms in taffeta silks and bright ties. The single life would attempt to mesmerize him and he'd reject its callow, wastrel promise, he'd move against the traffic, return to his father's Sea Cliff mansion home to gaze up at the magnificent bridge, drink in hand, looking at the opposite coastline that sat on the Pacific, free of all structures which defined the bay, discussing his most controversial trial and finally, he could talk about his divorce to a man who believed no one ought to leave a wife with young children.

On the reverse camera the ninth district state bureau agent caught an odd picture of two unlikely bedfellows discussing plans to collapse the old Zellerbach building which in ten years would become redone as the famous Davies Hall – one was Francis Caen and the other unconfirmed looked like Arnold Herring of the station deck at Pier 10, an exit from Fifth. The agent captured a close-up of their faces and whisked it off to Phonetics for a dialogue transcript. Everyone knew that the plaza parking lot emptied into the basements of the Zellerbach, City Hall and the police department and except for Arnold Herring's 25th Street Office where he greeted one with a boisterous "hello," no one had an updated original docu-file to Case 56-813 for the city hall for which archives had moved to the mint office across town off California.

Beulah wouldn't leave her post for any reason until at least this case was tied up and she had had enough of typing, research and delivering documents to court for judicial signatures. The poor man who had lost his life at the college motel who had burnt his bridges behind him had last delved into the occult arts at a leafy tree condo complex on the other side of the freeway above a conundrum of stables and college buildings. He had left hill campus to decline his years as close to the Santa Barbara hub as he could afford and for some inexplicable reason had joined a fraternity of young adults who were still debating long term commitments. If they were found on occasion to be enlisted as hoaxers, swindlers, forgers, confidence trick racketeers – these were activities committed by goof-offs and blunderers, and being a notary he compiled his own little ford of potential blackmail. Even an honest man having discovered the unworthy compilation of immaterial adjournments would have experienced some hair raising chill from a sea coastal dungeon threatening to sweep across an inlet cove and batten every storefront. The occasion however that compromised his thinking was believed to have occurred roundly at hill campus in one of four open space classrooms for art expressionism where he had confided in a group of students that he could produce any document regarding provocation for examination and scientific note as to noticeable, recognizable, obvious detriment. Said to the wrong person who apparently had sought him down – obloquy of improper sentiment for him not to realize his position or place in reference to such an individual. Or perhaps it was a favor conferred upon the man as a debt that caused him not to readily understand the lowly disguise. In the least event the distracting discussion must have forewarned the jinni having discovered who might be able to jinx him took a swift advantage extinguishing Hadley.

It was at these moments when monotony struck its vexing decibel that Beulah took her sweet tea out to the porch for another languorous glint at a fault of human nature. An evasive dullard given to hallucinations as a result of imbibing morphine ice showed no ability to deter themselves of either a harangue

or harassment; the university listings however gave no indication as to weathered drifters seeking measurable mainstay work
for film or the movies making a remark syndrome of hanging
painted signs on the flats of condominiums up and down the
Pacific Coast Highway.

The law was specific as to drifters with children, all sorts
of Sections referenced parents who got up and walked away
from their obligations. Section 1500 of Division 4 of Probate
Code read, "Subject to Section 1502, a parent may nominate a
guardian of the person or estate, or both, of a minor child where
at the time the petition for appointment of the guardian the
other parent is dead or the consent of the other parent would
not be required for an adoption of the child" in which parent
has had financial care and custody but has committed any act
involving moral turpitude:

*1192.7 Plea bargaining; limitations; definitions*

*(a) Plea bargaining in any case in which the indictment or informa-
tion charges a serious felony, any felony in which it is alleged that a
firearm was used personally by the defendant, ... is prohibited, unless
there is insufficient evidence to prove the people's case, or testimony of
a material witness cannot be obtained, or a reduction or a dismissal
would not result in a substantial change in sentence.*

*(c) As used in this section, "serious felony" means any of the following:*

*(1) Murder or voluntary manslaughter; (2) mayhem; (3) rape; (4)
sodomy by force, violence, duress, menace, threat of great bodily injury
on the victim or another person; (5) oral copulation by force, violence,
duress, menace, threat of great bodily injury, or fear of immediate
and unlawful bodily injury on the victim or another person; (6)
lewd or lascivious act on a child under the age of 14 years; (7) any
felony publishable by death or imprisonment in the state prison for*

*life; (8) any other felony in which the defendant personally inflicts great bodily injury on any person, other than an accomplice, or any felony in which the defendant personally uses a firearm; (9) attempted murder; (10) assault with intent to commit rape or robbery; (11) assault with a deadly weapon or instrument on a peace officer; … (15) exploding a destructive device or any explosive with intent to injure; (16) exploding a destructive device or any explosive causing great bodily injury or mayhem; (17) exploding a destructive device or any explosive with intent to murder; (18) burglary of an inhabited dwelling house, or trailer coach as defined by the Vehicle Code, or inhabited portion of any other building; (19) robbery or bank robbery; (20) kidnapping," et cetera.*

*11171 X-rays of child; exemption from privilege*

*(a) A physician and surgeon or dentist or their agents and by their direction may take skeletal X-rays of the child without the consent of the child's parent or guardian, but only for purposes of diagnosing the case as one of possible child abuse and determining the extent of such abuse.*

*(b) Neither the physician-patient privilege nor the psychotherapist-patient privilege applies to information reported pursuant to this article in any court proceeding or administrative hearing.*

*11166 Report; duty; time*

*(a) …For the purposes of this article, "reasonable suspicion" means that it is objectively reasonable for a person to entertain such a suspicion, based upon facts that could cause a reasonable person in a like position, drawing when appropriate on his or her training and experience, to suspect child abuse.*

*(g) A county probation or welfare department shall immediately,*

*or as soon as is practically possible, report by telephone to the law
enforcement agency having jurisdiction over the case, to the agency
given the responsibility for investigation of cases under Section 300
of the Welfare and Institutions Code, and to the district attorney's
office every known or suspected instance of child abuse, as defined in
Section 11165.6, except acts or omissions coming within subdivision (b) of Section 11165.2, or reports made pursuant to Section
11165.13 based on risk to a child which relate solely to the inability
of the parent's substance abuse, which shall be reported only to the
county welfare department.*

*13823.11 Sexual assault victim examination and treatment, pres-
ervation and disposition of evidence*

Car – left in county above ground lot for three nights before
getting hauled away;

Scene – judge of writs witnesses the same crime while he
is doctoring a case to be heard on (c) (18) burglary of a trailer
coach of a peace officer for firearm;

Scene – priest chief of medicine glances out at corridor and
sees aide push empty cart to supply room; he knew the time
because of the empty cart;

Scene – Judge orders blue car towed out;

Analysis from weapons division:

Device removed from hospital is constructed with telephone plate harmonizer, which can operate a crowbar, thus
situation must go with a crowbar on a tow or a ferry;

Device clamped to telephone wires photographed by ex-
ternal bucket;

In 1958 women did not work outside anywhere;

Men could not work outside on hospital grounds unless
they were lieutenant anything;

If the male had stolen regulation uniform and was outside
pretending to work, they could be arrested if they used any

equipment;

Where would it surprise any observer to see a female civilian and a male nearby?

Redlands – train stops on tracks, walk 2 blocks up or 2 blocks across east through streets with houses; 2 blocks up is hospital and hotel, both have restaurants, go 3 blocks east from hospital, come to hill with a block of clinics, all brick, another smaller hospital, newspaper, radio. Today across the highway is a college for sports medicine, nursing, and gardening. At end of town down lane with palm trees, Hollywood houses, two old newspapers, Daily Facts, Oldman Department Store.

Other type train stop – train stops on track to let people off at town –

*12031 Carrying loaded firearms, misdemeanor*

*To any of the following who are completed in firearms training approved by the Commission on Peace Officer Standards and Training:*
*(1) Guards or messengers of common carriers*
*(2) Guards of contract carriers operating armored vans pursuant to Public Utilities Commission authority*
*(3) Private investigators and private patrol operators and alarm company operators*
*(4) Uniformed security guards or night watch persons*
*(5) Uniformed security guards and uniformed alarm agents on duty or en route to or from their residences*

*12101 Concealable firearm or live ammunitions; possession by minor*

*(a) A minor may not possess a pistol, revolver, or other firearm capable of being concealed upon the person unless he or she has written consent of parent or legal guardian*

*12020 (c)(9)(C) It is not readily recognizable as containing a firearm.*

"Camouflaging firearm container" does not include any camouflaging covering used while engaged in lawful hunting....

Man standing in window saw person and finished unpacking carton.

# CHAPTER FOUR

THE SUMMARY NARRATIVE ON BEULAH'S DESK read as follows: on the above date the petition was filed at City Hall alleging that one Ron Coventry, a person convicted of a felony violation of paragraph (3), (6) and (7) of subdivision (c) of Section 502 and a violation of subdivision (b) of Section 502.7 may be granted probation but in unusual cases where the ends of justice would be better served by a shorter period, the period of probation shall not be less than three years and the following fines shall be imposed. During the period of probation the said person shall not accept employment where that person would use a computer connected by any means to any other computer, except upon approval of the court and notice to and opportunity to be heard by the prosecuting attorney, probation department, prospective employer, and the convicted person. Court approval shall not be given unless the court finds that the proposed employment would not pose a risk to the public.

The tape displayed the parking lot with the attendant staffing the flow of cars having temporarily walked away from his station, a robber R. Coventry described only as a light skinned Negro adult male, probably aged forty to fifty-five, semi-balding, weighing a hundred and seventy pounds, five feet eight inches, emerged from a parked vehicle, was seen visually by the attendant who ran after him down the street sometime after which Mirage entered the lot, it had begun to rain, and he attempted to prevent papers flying loose in the blue car at which time he succumbed to death. The tape failed to show the driver and passengers, were there any, sitting inside or leaving the blue car. However, the vehicle was tracked back to its original destination of Larkin and California, two blocks below Nob Hill and three major intersections north from Grace Cathedral, to a section cramped with smallish flats, nine streets above the civic center. The vehicle was registered to a Nicholas Brendt from Indio who did not appear to reside anywhere in San Francisco and was found to be driven alternately by a Vren Gaccio, aged twenty-seven, or his fiancé Tiane Evvo, aged twenty-nine, a registered nurse who worked late shift at Polk and Sacramento and was presumed to have been the driver on the date the car was filmed. The Grove Street camera had the car coming into the lot, rear bumper and plate, automatic match to VIN, side panel, front bumper and plate but no driver; McAllister had the car in the rain with windows rolled down; Ninth Street backup gave the rear bumper, plate, rear window and top of vehicle, a minute and a half later the car in its numbered space, windows down. All other reading meters with time allotted for by day and date including year, time by hour, side of car, a bit distant, front of car, metered read of license, no person. During the burglary chase all windows were recorded for reflection and designated car gave no image. By degrees prior to arrival the vehicle was forced to enter by one direction only, down Ninth through a DUI corridor wherein only the driver's face was pictured. The picture revealed the side of a long straight haired redhead. Once the state bureau had a composite on Evvo, they would be able to draw out with chopsticks her image on any of official documents, notwithstanding driver license, employee decal, dispatch, government identifier.

This was no jurisdiction and misdemeanor, Coventry if he were a physician would have his license revoked, if he carried a deadly weapon he'd be sent up to a penitentiary, if he could be found splicing cameras prior to his act, he would be sentenced and convicted of a felony, but if as a part of his robbery he had committed the same act twice previously, his behaviors without a weapon would be a felony. Coventry had tinkered with the parking lot camera, adjusting the scope, hiking up the default such that any attempted interface provided a short range view of one familiar image, in the past this was City Hall East, the rim of the dome showing at the height of the photograph, and a false measurement designed to give a westerly street traffic of an easterly.

Since the Milk/Moscone murders at City Hall, the city had paid for high efficiency light switches, paneled doors, laser target bank posts for zeroing in on a gun to disable his gun, tinting which given any amount of light or shade projected shadow throughout the building and various additional violet rays. The numerous seventy-three lots had been rewired, surrounding apartments upgraded, soft lantern street lights could capably surrender any driver, street employee or pedestrian and reduce blurriness for close-ups shot far away; the McAllister/Grove lot on the plaza perked up its light system to display red stop for five seconds non flashing and green light with raising cross for as many seconds as a vehicle passed by the station, entered the street and made its turn, an entirely expert counter-espionage system with instant retrieval. So, how was it possible that the blue vehicle knew which camera picked up each view in order to schedule the vehicle for entire non disclosure? From time to time thieves utilized high band sector-proof high density waste makers that took in all decibels and thus eliminated image, but here with a narrow tube, ten feet wide across the plaza, used not for sending a retrieval for video or banking purposes to hone in on negative-draw feed, it probably was impossible.

There was a knock on the door to which Beulah glanced up at Maman holding a brown bowl making her way through vanilla ice cream topped with hot peach cobbler.

"Want some?" Maman asked.

"Sure, fetch me a scoop or two."

Maman left and returned in a few minutes with a delicious smelling dessert and coffee on a silver tray. Mother and daughter sat opposite the dark walnut dining room table accompanied by ten overlapping ribbed upholstered white satin chairs, Beulah's trial binder and separate pages splayed on the table. Dressed tidily in a conservative box pleated blue skirt with black trim and a Scandinavian navy and white knit sweater, she was nevertheless the more proper of the two, despite Beulah's all black velvet sheath and diamond and ebony necklace. To others who knew them well enough to say, they were each always ready to approach.

"It's just you and I tonight, Maman. I'm afraid you'll have to do all the talking."

Maman asked, "Are you seeking appeals on the civil damages?"

"Actually this one can't have an appeals and it's not because he doesn't qualify as indigent. He is found by computer warrant to have committed a crime against the state, thus he lacks the minimum standard that meritorious grounds exist for a reversal or modification."

They ate their dessert peaceably. Beulah inquired, "Did Lorraine tell you Ray has sued for divorce?"

"She told me when she hired an attorney, a little over a year ago. She originally asked for his residence."

"That's awfully cheeky of her. His residence? She's never been there."

"Oh, you're mistaken. She lived with him for a year there."

"Are you certain? Does your journal correspond, Maman?"

"I'm not mistaken. Lorraine's attorney asked for alimony, child support for Kenneth, all households, all ventures."

"It's not in fashion to show oneself off to appear impolite. Did you see the pleading?"

"Lengthy as any paper. The affidavit as to supporting declaration of the defendant's financial condition, I imagine, did her in. Lorraine earns more than Ray, so technically she doesn't qualify for anything."

"How often did she spend away from the children with this other man?"

"Not once. He took the kids out of state to visit his father. They were gone the entire summer," Maman replied. "It's a smart fight he's putting her to."

"I would've cut her off like that." She snapped her fingers.

"You wouldn't. You might think you could, but you wouldn't. He's getting back at her."

"She deserves it for breaking her vows."

"We don't know whether she actually did conduct herself inappropriately. She only said she did, but there's been many a hostility trial over mislaid facts. Lorraine may have perceived herself to have had to compete with his work. Perhaps she was seeking to grab his attention."

"It's a neglectful thing to have said, willful."

They ate to the last, picked up their mugs, and sipped.

"You may as well know, I paid for a week on the shore in Ventura for Ray."

"That is a mistake."

"I felt sorry for him."

Maman winced. "In time it won't be easily separate if he has to look out for you too."

"He does anyways. He's all my appeals work." She asked gingerly, worried about treading on her mother's toes, "do you know who Lorraine had the affair with?"

"He's another counsel, I think, in proceedings for prisoners."

"That should be lucrative. How much do they make?"

"At least a hundred a year."

"Is there any talk of them getting together?"

"Heavens. What a morbid thought. If there is, Lorraine hasn't said. What did Ray say?"

"He's relieved its over. I would imagine he's been in litigation since the contingency was filed and that it's been stressful but it's hard to know because he hasn't said a word. Where's Lorraine?"

"Who knows? She took off."

"Where're the kids this weekend?"

"With Ray. He has them alternate weekends, every summer, two weeks at major holidays including Easter, and by arrangement for the month of May. He informed me when I asked to take them up to Tuolumne with Scouts."

"Is that when she has her affairs?"

"She's a grown female, she may do as she likes."

Lorraine traveled to Loon Lake on the Oregon coast off Route 138, a vast swamp possibly four to forty feet deep with no sign of waves, ancient petrified trees sprouting with sapling fir, hundreds of yellow brown marbleized trees docked in gentle waters, canoes beached on the grainiest sand, the least remote town about ten miles west to London Bridge, a clandestine fortress of stucco hotels over a drawbridge lined up on one side of the river. She secured a hotel room with a porch beneath which waves lapped to shore causing the thin trout boat to bob in the eddies, a log cabin two hundred foot long room for a king size bed, a sofa and low magazine table in front of a burning ember and between the interior and kitchenette a sliding glass door onto a deck with table for four where she camped out the first night on a hammock and thereafter slept with the door open to the stars and howl of distant owls. When she had slept two days and two nights, she drove to London to The Carriage House, picked up a man and paid for a hotel. A night later she was found at a bar sipping whiskey straights for three dollars a glass, alone, spouting ribbage to the arsenals of law, citing every comical downturn of chapter and docket she memorized, most ceremonials on murder, aggravation, forcible rape, and fitness.

While Beulah heard the citation anticipating a hopscotch over marital rights with mixed prohibitions, she assessed a rather haughty culmination of entitlement, no doubt a cover for however numerous culpabilities that could be named, a strike at advisories that might yield her a repeal of limitations to which Beulah said Lorraine was lucky not to have to confront penalties for willful use of drugs or negligence as to an untoward diagnosis of venereal disease.

It was after nine that Beulah came upon the section in the almost six hundred and twenty-two page trial transcript for the reference to firearms –

Q. How would you as a firearms authority for a local ballistics control unit define a firearm?

A. The accepted legal definition of firearm states that any of the following: a cane gun or wallet gun, any plastic firearm, any firearm not immediately recognizable as a firearm, any camouflaging firearm container, any ammunition which contains or consists of any flechette dart, any bullet containing an explosive agent, any ballistic knife, any multipart trigger activator, any nunchaku, any short-barreled rifle, any belt buckle knife, leaded cane, zip gun, shuriken, any unconventional pistol, lipstick case knife, cane sword, shobi-zue, or any instrument or weapon of the kind typically known as blackjack, slung shot, or sap or that which is carried concealed upon one's possession.

Q. As to the object presented to you at the start of this court-room inquiry, can you explain to the court its use?

A. The material proffered before the court yesterday morning as Exhibit 3 is technically neither a pistol of conventional description nor a multipart trigger as these devices are commonly known and must fit a metal piece listing carriage capable of expending a shell out of a trajectory barrel. The material also cannot be legally said to consist of a device such as what I have described by the immediately preceding question. The item is made up of three syringes that feed into one intravenous line tubing and is used allegedly for a mother and her in uteri child. In gardening this use of three syringes is to feed the soil by running alternate lines to water into the pipe such as liquid nitrogen, plant feeder, carotene or bag-syrup like liquid bark which enriches plants.

Q. On the date in question of the year 1979 what spillage or incident must have occurred for you to have suspected the nature of the device to have been similar in use to this three syringe line?

A. The sewage pipe broke, the entire lot was plunged underwater, it looked like a major flood in front of the pipe, flooding occurred instantly up to ten feet covering the gardens.

Q. Is there a term you experts use to generally refer to a device that does this?

A. Yes. It is a blocker.

Q. Are you familiar with what happened at the hospital two city blocks away?

A. Are you speaking of San Francisco Charity on Ninth?

Q. Yes.

A. Yes, a blocker was fed by another metal part attached to the tube that instilled some type of nitrous liquid inside through a sewage fault.

Q. How long does it take to produce flooding?

A. About an hour if the sewage goes directly from the soil outside into a basement.

Q. Did your answering taps pick up any sound, commotion or other disturbance?

A. Yes. Approximately two knock-about, one loud sound coming from an employee bathroom on the first floor and a second louder sound toward the back exit to the grounds and drive.

Q. Is knock-about a lawful description?

A. No. It is what we call it.

Q. Could you describe what you are terming a knock-about?

A. A knock-about is frequently heard along the upper ramps of a parking lot when a low grade explosive is set off in the street alongside an attendant's station. When it occurs from inside a building we usually hear it emanating from within a basement that has a chief industrial heating unit.

Q. So what would you infer as a result of what you heard?

A. First I checked meters and found the indicators had gone to zero. Then I checked the hoses including fire hydrants. I discovered no water emitted from any hosing but that the hydrants were in good responsive shape. Leakage was beginning. It appeared to rise from nowhere.

Q. Did the hydrants wash out at any point?

A. Yes, the sewage lanes emitted up to fifty minutes.

Q. From how many directions did water appear to come?

A. Two, front and back.

Q. Were there any other sites on that day that sprouted a flood?

A. Yes. There was also the police department at the end of the plaza on Grove.

Q. On this date did you happen to see a crime involving a firearm shooting?

A. I did not observe this myself, but it was recorded.

Q. Where did it occur?

A. On Grove Street before Market Street. A robber apparently stole money from the parking attendant station on the plaza.

Beulah was buried deep in the two volumes of trial transcripts looking for lead points, when her man friend John whom Maman called The Guv ambled upon the front porch and peered inside between the slats of glass rapping with his fist for anyone inside to come running.

Beulah opened the door in a wild breathless motion. "Why, Big Daddy, we had no idea you were driving down. Do come inside," she said, reaching for his arm.

The Guv was six feet two, dwarfing poor Beulah with a newscaster noose of an unpretentious thin weight capable man in his early sixties, his eyes masked by crow's feet so much so he seemed to wince permanently. He plainly doted on Beulah, even she could not deny his intentions, yet he had that unmistakable air of marriageable uneasiness about him that rang clearly to a distance that she scarcely held toward him.

"I believe, Beulah, when I saw on the state docket an appeals bearing your name and title, I doubted my only upstanding concerns for your aging tenderness and drove with all speed."

She linked her arm through his and together they marched to Maman's room at the back of the house at the last of the dining room, the pantry to a small room with windows overseeing the arbor where in teen years she slaved over her books. Maman was sipping tea and having ice cake; John bent to kiss her very smooth soft cheek, whereupon he took her hand and they exchanged pleasantries. Beulah poured tea, sliced the crumpet onto a saucer and explained the appeals problem.

"It's on a vice merit awarded after a security guard transferred from Hastings Law College fired at a male dressed as a surgeon seen shoving a nurse to the ground and then inserting a clamp calking remover attached to a spray net."

"Can Hastings carry firearms?"

"If assigned to the police, then off duty; otherwise it's never."

"Then he was off duty."

"Here it is, since he was awarded for excellence in the course of duty, he therefore was either detained or he was on overtime. However the court found the occurrence two hours later after he assisted a friend officer in measuring the amount of rising duct. Although merit states well beyond call of described duties, the issue is pertinent to the firearm."

"If he was on duty he could be dismissed?"

"Yes. He would have been suspected of acting with premeditation. He would have come to a situation where although he was assigned to City Hall during his working hours he was diverted after the other guards received a telephone call."

Maman said, "How many hours once a state of emergency is declared?"

John answered, "No that constitutes special hazard pay at double and a half. The declaration of statement of facts won't be the problem nor when as during day and time of day. The issuance is the problem itself, it says by inference the vice is at the squad lot attending to patrol cars in the street when the camera at that time takes the infrared of the plaza lot cashier robber. That's the item."

Maman inquired as to the chronology of circumstances to which her daughter answered: first a nut-case assaulted a guard at city hall and had to be suppressed, then a robber waiting until the lot attendant was occupied robbed the drawer; then a rumble occurred in the plaza lot presumably taking a man's life, and set off a chain reaction popping an underground pipe in front of the police department and up two blocks between the state building and the hospital.

John added matter of fact that he thought the situation was very serious for a hit on the alley adjacent to the hospital. It was unheard of that after an attempt on the mint the previous year, anyone wanted a portion of street chopped out.

Maman interjected, "Unless it's to go after all those underground telephone pipers; you know, the sounds that rattle the com lines when twenty calls connect at once."

Beulah said, "I pulled the underground electrical maps for telephones that supply government and they're all lined along pier walls from Market to Sutter and Seventh to Polk Streets." John gave it to jurisprudence, "The switch breakers from China Basin all the way to Market were recomputed after the Fourth Street ramp was expanded. My hunch is that the function of the Basin was moved across town to Bay allowing for additional lines to be put in along the streets."

Maman went into the kitchen to make cups of Kona coffee. From the kitchen she shouted, "Those one person parking attendants have to stay inside their huts or they might miss their camera shots."

John said, "I thought the ones that did that were basically lazy. Those cams are fairly small."

"The more assertive ones are outside handing out tickets as drivers pull into the lot."

"Have we interviewed the lot man?" He asked Beulah.

"Yes, we are flawless. He had to testify. He remembered every car except the ones which entered after he chased the robber."

"Did he say whether he reviewed the tape?" John asked.

"He actually stayed after closing 2pm. He retrieved vehicle with windows down, papers flying."

"Man on the pavement?"

"Not there yet."

"So where are the tapes which show the crimes?" Maman's tone was impatient. The kids would stay up all night talking, she was used to this. Normally Lorraine would poke her head in at ten or later and would leave just as a good debate was starting, but Lorraine was out of town drinking off her woes most probably.

Beulah answered. "The precinct picked up all tapes except the hospital alley which is monitored by hospital security. There were six tapes, just three were reviewed, two were seen when the crimes occurred. The transcripts newly filed consisted of a corruption across town in the vicinity of the financial district along the wharf, we called it blondes in mink, these salacious babes, many were Chinese, arriving in Packard sedans to Portsmouth Square near Chinatown and North Beach, lots of money in Asian skyscrapers, property coming out of their ears, selling dope and prostitution, many youths still in high school earning moonshine on the side. Then there was the pipe raider crimes along the coast near Sea Cliff beneath the bridge, the file went to the grand jury and twenty-five men were sent up to the Q, and then there were the mint bribes referred to as tea leaves in one's fortune and that case never saw the light of day."

"What I heard was there was a bad run, batched and distributed to all the businesses from Union Square to Civic Center, and that by itself caused a scene," John said.

Maman said she was going to sleep. The clock read eleven-thirty, far past her bedtime. John stood to kiss her goodnight and Beulah said she would write her schedule and leave it on the dining room table.

Beulah poured two glasses of Grand Marnier flavored orange chocolate brandy at thirty-two bucks a bottle. "There were two junkyard profiles turned into State the month of the shooting – the first ten feet in the air above a cement water canal through the mountains to Daly City; and a second, a view of a cement curb of a water canal and center dash of a street."

"What was the significance?"

"The State Bureau regularly dumps a bunch of pictures into the net bucket, the robber too, that's how we learned his height, weight, and hair style."

"The district attorney started with in a search of any person who imported into the state, offered for sale, lent or possessed a device capable of splicing film off citywide."

The brandy produced a burning sensation in her throat

going down. "Here's what the state bureau thought about its catch – it was an advisory, mountain showers, get off to a speedy run, find a doper, stop a speed timer."

"Speed timer?"

"They work radio, they're the ones who have to demarcate the tape."

"What would that tell?"

"A good announcer would memorize the numbers that each song begins."

"Could he also complete an inside track for a find and replace?"

"If he knew it was there. It depends on a digital spool. That wouldn't have been there yet."

John said, "These are focus, find your camera tape, post to time, otherwise they would get away with holy shit all the time;" explaining further he said, "The moment tape is spliced even by robber it enters a new tape automatically."

Beulah replied, "It raises a good many questions, I should say. For starters it suggests for the 1978 Milk/Moscone murders to wind up spooled onto new tape in another city, say Surf City in Orange, was an inside job with an insider sending splice somewhere."

"Or that someone, a broadcaster at the college for example ran a rinse on all film boards to filter out certain sorts of imagery."

"Maybe Mirage took down sound applets."

Mimicking a chief sound engineer at the controls John did a spoof, "Hey, Sam, what d'you make of this can? Milk's inside the nose cone, can you spray a bytes worth of silicone over the cylinder?"

Beulah laughed. "If he knew the device was used only for three-story parking garages or higher, maybe he knew who had the patent for it. It's entirely possible he could detect origins of sounds based upon the tier and length of wave detectable by camera."

"Who is Moshe Cone?"

"Is that like how many mosques should there be for Muslims? There is no hidden file name in Moscone's name the way there is in Milk."

"Impossible. All are files."

"If it isn't first mosque, then it's moss cone in an island somewhere, lush paradise, mist and rain."

"Or Muslim bread bakery." John gave a weak smile. "I should've gone to bed when Maman retired. My preferred is still – can I have another scone with my tea, please?"

"To make a good biscuit you need an ounce of milk. This no doubt must constitute a bakery. There is Greens at the base that serves a high class meal for reserved lunch four times every Saturday; there is Noe Valley cough drop which high end bakes medicines like hardened sauces; there is green tea ice cream cone, I'm afraid at midnight I'm not much good at this."

"Oh, to hell with it, let's go to bed."

^ ^ ^

The sunlight was dense, it looked as though the house had smoked all night over booze and a card game and come morning the air was packed in. Outside the pavement was saturated with rain from sometime during the night. On the computer rain teemed in the streets pooling generously on sidewalks and in city lots deep enough to be non-traversable leaving vehicles in water to their fenders. Internal Affairs Division over at State Bureau on Polk was getting chilled over a brough-ha-ha as to who was listening at the other end of calls from police informants, upset over an incessant ringing in the background which reflected all the way along upper Polk, as far east as the wharf. They had shut down piers on the bay to the Presidio seeking a series of computers capable of storing police telephone calls through dispatch to patrol cars. The other police came up for detention once the corporations were listed – a bunch of Chuncys whose offices after five became hammer-heads ready to respond to any disturbance that might not yet have registered on the central computer some ten minutes arrived. With thirty-four hundred suites and fifteen million telephones it seemed unlikely the break-ins and perjuries were without manipulation since when the tape was reversed there was no one there. On the night of the problem at the Ninth Division when a patrol car rolled right up onto the curb and slammed in through the files room breaking windows and mortar the only clue was one answering ring which empirically dialed to its list showed a sophisticated entrenchment starting at Pacific Bell and ringing at planned offices as telephone trunks went on message lines for the night. It was a real bug to realize the snag snappers in fact were contained within a five block radius. That gave the Civic Center its entire component except in five blocks there were no residential apartments, so the bureau shut upper story firms down, retrofit them for landlord tenancies and moved in its own Internal Affairs Bureau. The retailers changed hands at an alarming rate; when the IAD was called out of town the place became a ghost town.

Miguel Chancery was in custody appeals with old man Sandpiper seven hours a day springing free after three to run uptown and plug in a few trunks after the action turned on. He had handled a prejudicial number of embezzlement and listened to stagecoach parlors for Brinks bangs long before he walked easy street into the juvie cellars. The city had fashioned its whistle on laundry and kitchen parlors bringing in teen prostitutes of both sexes so that now when the trades slowed for respectable high society holidays the teens wound up homeless, a needle jammed up a vein or cleaning some couple's house. Although he was known to every bailiff and chamber, he could place them at their shifts by lunchroom and time of day, out on the avenue, or in the limousines as they advanced to the curb.

He was seventy if he was a day, salt and pepper crew cut, neatly attired in navy pin-striped suits, trimmed, reserved, usually taciturn. The millionth rock cocaine test had swum the channel and lost for failing to come in at the acceptable minimum of a hundred and sixty grams of guilt, and again the court in its wisdom had kicked out the test that read in nine grams. High Judge Sandpiper whose son-in-law could now walk into court a proud man, no longer servile to this acrimonious honor, was pissing all the counsel off with his florid jokes about gays but in his chambers he was the only one who would put his reputation in newsprint to pass laws banning prejudice. Miguel had his papers ready, the guardian had pulled a straight lineup, the JV-123 was verified, notarized and kissed, and the Exparte orders disallowing skin patch testing, febrile heat bracelet and droplets on a chicken plate all scratched with a demand that said no to lie detector readings, the goddamn polygraph scratchers spilled ink at non asked questions too. The sole comment Sandpiper dismissed Miguel's case was on, leave the child out of the courtroom if you're going to subpoena on the paternity test to answer why dad is not real dad.

It was after four when Miguel tore through the tunnel leaving Chinatown and emerged in the Buddhist section of the city out where cinematic theatres and family restaurants lined the modern industrial complex originally meant to flow to Daly City. The IAD situation promised grids every which way with no off-line switch-eroos and by now crooks had set up obvious camps trying to get arrested just to figure out where their files with their identifications went to. After extensive bugging and routing circuits from hotels and multi-story residence buildings to newer buildings, the city finally said to hell with it and removed sections of the mint and reframed their wall posts as telephone taps. In twelve short months after the murders at City Hall, the city had expanded to its last available space on the ground, had seized the Bayshore corridor and was taking bids on its peak zones above its freeways. Internal Affairs knew its officers were moonlighting and putting in graveyard shifts anywhere they could get work to make ends meet, but despite this had received telephone calls to move evidence lockers to storage throughout the wharf zones from the bridge to Ghirardelli Square and on the other side of the towers to Half Moon Bay. Although the procedure was relatively straight-forward – bag the haul, cellophane and duct tape it, dial the warehouse meat shelf it was to get refrigerated in, secure a telephone lock to the goods and transport the load to the building site where state agents would eventually arrive to break it down for disposal – despite this typical efficiency, evidence locker goods were lost, sent to other cities, placed in bus lockers and so on, until by themselves they represented a bulk of street valuables.

Surveillance meant sitting at a desk inside a small storefront listening to bugged companies in a five block radius trying to identify voice and dialogue, typing up conversations and shooting them across town to state bureau and obtaining photographs and identification from the federal building. For IAD the tie-in was to match the suspects' fingerprints, determine where they had lived and worked, and then catalog complaints and cases by precinct. Internal caught officers with their underwear down in photographs in the act of arranging crooks to gain access into Pacific Bell, accepting pay-offs and handing over mug shots on file of the crook as well as arrangements to meet executives of various corporations. Miguel would mention to Sandpiper every so often usually after he had to match an invoice with the evidence in storage that the stuff was crawling around the city in trunks of all types. Sandpiper's usual reply was that he would send the inquiry to his son-in-law, but no one had hopes that admonishment could do much given the fact that the federal boys had to initiate all investigations before an order to slap a few hands could be issued. One could play taps to the bottle sounds coming over the filter, Miguel decided. The popping

corks were not evenly distributed. Despite the alarming number of them and the belief they were relaying to the precinct
lines, Miguel issued a closure on every line except dispatch
and reordered tunes to the churches so he could assess distance
capability for the neighborhoods that tested.

The shadow of a man appeared once lurking about emerging
from the basement loggia of the hospital wearing what was
in all probability a blue or green surgical nursing gown. He
was seen leaving a laboratory holding a whistle and for an
instinctive reason the nursing aide witness was correct in his
presumption when they came across a pulsing meter that read
a police incoming line across its digitalized path, a wire dan-
gling suggesting because it couldn't be set off at the morgue the
saboteur had to be someone who worked at the office. Under a
lens caption the man was identified as Vren Gaccio, the owner
of the blue car. Gaccio would die after it was over and done.
The number rang nevertheless to the precinct, confirmed with
a send back, and posted red high definition to a television out
there somewhere. That's when the state bureau decided they
had lost an hour on relay dragnet. They were fairly certain if it
was a dragnet the series of sequences would call into a central
avenue such as Ma Bell, to register and protect the series a
department of trunks had to be separated and this was done
inside a half hour with no repercussions; once logged off, it
took a week to assess no daylight savings, that gave them their
response, it was a delay reel to circuit showing Gaccio returned
in a night and removed it. A detective wanted to know, why
did he abandon his car? Federal said, it had to be he required
no finding, his compartmentalized open windows kept him
from being snapped on camera, despite the car coming up on
the tape two days sequentially the needed information had to
be researched through the ADDRESS computers which were
by far the most readily available to find a JIM to match the

thumbprint; the fact that he never returned to his vehicle told them once it got removed to an impound it could be tagged for disposition, and tagged it was by every viable row in the city, instantly sent to undisclosed sites, interpreted by every cross-translation for any match. Both state and federal would guess because there were no prints on Gaccio; who the hell knew who had provided the vehicle to begin with, they'd be searching every border as to where he came in and where he went after he was checked through. Could be any tag – he could've come as a child with a family or as a translator for an industrialist who had been accepted to a high profile agency.

∧ ∧ ∧

Ray saw no easy way for matters to end smoothly, having received Lorraine's hotel bill for the four days at Loon Lake. He considered the numerous complications to consolidating debt rather a remorseful entrenched parlay of negative holding, although he was clear she would balk to learn now he was entitled to her checking balances. What had been so intriguing in the beginning was a tiresome thing with split ends and reluctant acquiescence. In the past he had hired a dick to tail her and any interlude went into a photo bin until Ray had more than substantial cause. He had hundreds of photographs, Lorraine and this guy – dark hair trim Latin type, heavy in racquetball – an easy scoop at the race track not to mention candlelight dinners at restaurants, pickled hot dogs at baseball games, ice capades at the rinks, quickie conversations in shopping marts, coffee bars, but their affair had apparently started with an overnight at a coast highway motel after a grueling month reviewing discovery for a trial, and here she was again, starting over with a pickup at a motel joint. It struck him that he did not understand the pattern; but he found himself morose, astoundingly saddened by the degradation of the act, it occurred to him she was escaping into a din, an ether existence with many doors and far too few improvements. He did not see her as worn out, at a low ebb, she was after all in his presence a spontaneous wit, no matter the amount of havoc, a vivacious chatterer, clever, charming, educated. Such an emotionally skeleton of a decline was not an appeal he associated with her; but here she was, wreaked far past any morality. The hardship of it would be he could expect it to resurface and reach out for him in a manner he wouldn't see coming. The repetition of the irregularity surrendered in him a sense of transience which he rebelled against wanting no further knowledge of it. He did exactly as he often did, he threw himself into conscientious activity to take his mind off petty annoying grievances. He took out the thick folder on the City Hall plaza and upon retrieving an abundance of files and orders on dozens of filings he decided the time had arrived to figure out how many files had been collected for wire taps. Judging by the line items under costs there had to be hundreds of camera-arguable failures just within that geophysical pyramid of building structures. The city's preference was a speed DSLR caption, a fast frame no-pixel sensation of exquisite pictures, because with the short view it turned everything into a picture. Once the state detectives had Gaccio on tape, the rush would be to place a make on the street in an effort to catalogue where the blue car began the day of Mirage's death.

Ray called Blemson and arranged to meet him at the only café where he could hear himself think, this small upbeat place with black tablecloths and tan lights on racks, a very comfortable parlor below the 2nd Street Galleria Mall at nine at night, after the energetic pulse of the downtown had left.

"What do you think this guy Mirage figured out?" Ray asked.

"I've asked myself that very question half a dozen times. It must've had to do with Surf City studios being basically for sound boards, because there's not much TV until one gets to Santa Barbara campus to the art workshop where adults primarily are studying backgrounds for color."

"Mirage worked Surf City thirty-one years before he took a university job doing taping."

"We know he walked around parking lots, all types, put himself at every last one there, the State thinks he's party to a bud system for which he knew entire radio along coast and wanted filter draws for smaller stations at college campuses in Long Beach," said Blemson. "Mirage is in the surf, did you know he worked the cars that sit all white on sand each summer and then had to drive them to car lots? I'm sure that isn't what made him the expert on what each level sounded like. As to radio in high fog, one can't hear it, it's like rain falling on tin; rain pounding water sounds like a devastating downpour, can't see which one it is, picking up what each sound is in that sort of high volume drenching fog qualified him for search and rescue of boats."

"Probably that's all the college needed out there."

"Inside a house where communication with boats at sea or with station the density of fog flooding over Surf City requires more than one VCR, the responding light candle off larger boat sizzles but does not warn during a gale, light should flicker so wattage has to be higher, sound has to be able to create an amp as far away from 0 as 2 3/4 mile, that's an essential to have that distance, Surf City is on a ½ mile wide island that acts essentially as a reef barrier, and 2 ½ miles puts boats along the ocean/island deck."

Ray gave a nod, sipped a glass of dark amber. "He probably could identify any series of water sounds and attribute them to off course large yachts."

"No doubt coroner car as it emit from mist, past cacti with purple flower spears, if coroner was in communiqué all the way to Long Beach then the college radios became essential to road traffic and staying visible, they don't have high spectrum satellite dish there, thus they have to rely on campus stations inland for which there are approximately six, two are private and four beep from three campuses."

"After all that length of time Mirage had to be recognized as a pro; San Francisco may have wanted anyone who could say what their precinct after-hours problem is, with water possibly ocean dumping into sewage extension pipes, it is entirely possible the pipes handle a too small percentage water to explain recordings of filtrations. It could explain why inside a year San Francisco decided to remove the telephone box in the square and put it in China Basin on other side of Market after erecting a convention center off Ninth Street."

"Except he never got to it because he died."

"But answering the question is essential, the girl at the campus who dates the dead man Hadley has no idea as to what Hadley learns about the campus station except that it has television."

"Only system that has radio and no television is Maritime off Bay Street and it is used for Ghirardelli in event an outage kills everything ie light, sound, dumbwaiters, trolley, sprinklers."

"Hadley knew the campus – he worked at Long Beach City College North in computer programs, he worked at Santa Barbara college in art building adjusting television, he knew all frequencies that override radio, so although there were FCC-approved overrides for securing sensitive transmissions these were not allowed to be used by non federal bureau technicians."

"It's obvious to detectives that the timing of both deaths runs in tandem with series of wire taps that were installed and linked to telephone units where technological imputing has occurred."

"People often think what they have come across is escaping gas underground but it is not this at all nor is it actually water being released too far into the city; it is solely a micro dish clanging if traffic supercedes all footage of camera technology and to manage it requires upgrades that permit frequencies as high up as sixty stories."

They talked until closing, then walked two blocks to the swanky bar on fourth and ordered up dirty martinis and salted plantains and drank until morning when the street sweepers came down the hill. Ray talked mainly about Lorraine's pickup and Blemson who had married and divorced four times listened with the devotion of a wise owl. It was difficult to articulate, still too close to home, Ray drew blanks as he did in this moment, he floated off unable to stay focused on the feeling that she had walked away, every so often he riveted to her strengths to isolate his legal problem and once having determined it unearthed dozens of potential battles and fumbles, he was just starting to try to replace her, so used to partner discussions had he evolved himself, but he knew he would worry for her also, she was not choosing well, all encounters were left to chance, not that he should admire her choices nor appreciate her new need to be single again, while it was true he was judgmental and she had triggered an over response he believed she was too old for this sort of whim and considered whisking the children right out from under her. But he couldn't do both, languor on her behavior and plan a trial, the complexities of building a case on an interlocutory series of chain of custody could involve months of review, there were proofs to be prepared based upon intricate detail of routed telephone junkets and the boards they rang to and which boards were assigned to an actual officer, and then there was danger; if the shooting murders were any indication of how bad things could get, the murders having occurred the moment the collection of evidence produced a police suspect, then with more suspicious deaths, Hadley and Mirage, and the tentacles of a desperate mastermind reaching all the way to Long Beach and Surf City Island to eliminate linkages to knowledge before it was assured the suggestion of guilt was adequately erased.

The spectator evidence on the eye witness had him particularly concerned, he had asked the nurse registry to alter its policy, combining with a county registry that served war victims where the security was beefed up and the hospital personnel could without posing inquiry select a nurse and post them clear across town, Ray researched this carefully, the occasions during which the court had a problem, Madison County being a center consideration, fourteen boys vanished off the planet without explanation other than an officer driving by a coffee shop in dead of night saw a hurly-burly sort of officer in a booth with a kid both sipping milkshakes; the red brick institutions where these boys attended secondary school claiming major claims when their gymnasium was flooded judiciously bringing about a new all basketball court gym with bleachers, the town moving hotels, city government and its two high schools to the far end of town to prevent railway transients from sleeping across the country and then jumping from a train compartment and befriending the first recalcitrant youth they laid eyes on. The fourteen were found in trenches in far country, having been abandoned by a custodian, believed to have been victimized, they found their way into cellars where they died. The law provided for a vulnerable witness to enter a witness protection plan but since the deaths of Hadley and Mirage, Ray wanted nothing to do with it, and instead he searched for an innocuous party where the nurse could surrender her career after the depositions on her testimony had been notarized.

∧ ∧ ∧

What would he do with the distance of time after the witness had been thoroughly hunted down by the mob, thoughts came to Ray through the muffled environ of sleep awakening him, single words flit through his mind – diuturnity, duality, postponement, too late, leisurely, inopportune, sit up all night – he turned them over telling himself it was still too early to arise, he had nothing to do in the morning and he wanted to enjoy the freedom from the urgent necessity and flurry of journal review. He was in no hurry to read the IAD report that he had received from the county clerk and skimmed, the contents were an abomination, the Mission precinct mess was an inside job of a beat officer, they had sent in twelve teams at night to put in feeds and the taps were clicking away all over the city; not only team recording tappers reading in ten hours a day, the analysts had determined the felt-tip hammers made seven innings a week placing the problem in a garden bed of roses immediately outside the Saint Francis Hotel which recorded bottlenecks of wharf stations. If you didn't realize what you were getting into until the moment of awareness arrived, you would try to determine how the involvement evolved, who began it, which piece you entered, what was seductive; and then if you left and met up with a group of people and didn't want them to know anything about you, you might not choose things out of your life, you might borrow, practice someone else's hardship, never allow anyone to see the true nature of the lie, a walk from the beach, up the mossy incline, to the bar on the road daily at eleven for a dirty olive and fries as a method to anchor the semblance of flightiness, turn the tide for a new identity. Ray's problem with Internal Affairs lay in how best to decide when these people who were seen reappeared, the fact that IAD had made their case was far from the problem as to whether the insider cop knew any of the ring that the spin landed on, it was the one disagreeable item the appeal had to counter in order for Ray to reverse a lower court's decision.

Certainly IAD was as convincing as 99 episodes in five years of the film movie City Streets that went looking for the identical crime ring on the streets identifying the thumbnails to Tarantino's and Scoma's on the wharf into Chinatown's neon lit district to Ray's on Grant Street, in 2010 actress Jill Clayburn bit the dust and the shipping pilot's office got a boost, at the corner of North Beach and Hayes Carol Doda's strip joint was lit up along with Joe's pasta and clams, Sharazad Restaurant and Cable Car Hotel, "jump in the back jack, have a good ride Joe, don't have to discuss much," Art Garfunkel was singing as a wife was getting taken for her worldly goods in a mansion on Nob Hill, its night light looking from a distance on the wharf like a very respectable presidio, the old brick SF General Hospital off 24th was a converted high school and the ramp inside like a train station to a hotel past a salon and post office to a lobby, the Hyde Street pier with ferries to Oakland, and out on Van Ness Tommy Jones and a long view of Alcatraz, Sak's Fifth Ave, Mason Street trolley, all logos on the pavement for which the city was known, the usual suspects anywhere where money was trading hands.

An Initial inquiry posted the problem for the Civic Center having oddly enough begun with a race course gambler in South Carolina, on Bissell Road, cross street Lavender, standing 1-200 feet from corner with a slide scale measuring distance across the street, this reference came up in Alabama 2 ½ weeks prior to Mirage's death with the notation, Southern gulf 1 mile in from Yucatan north are referenced on computer file to Audi 1, downloaded to Concord New York, gold tone Y//...Tribune, SF tan only, 1 bar matched to 30 wt. gold, call card, reed feed picked up at oil corporation, all blue Exxon, site of read Tiburon, stock market broker Allen, pre released to FBI, the question still the same, why SF precinct Dan, Milk, demarcated by 2nd indent paragraph, column heading, focus, numbered; reply SF Idol in town, coliseum, reply Dan top of page, reply Milk, top center of page, decider focus; Covington track, one horse leads, still chimes into Civic Center, seek other columns, Daly City, Burlingame, salt flats, mountains, bridge, Golden Gate. The image of a slide scale lifted from the feed showed directly to

Cow Palace, Civic Center, probable reason prefixes were the same, controlled by telephone box, only way to pull out Civic precinct city needed a large building on the square that was all glass, following Davies Hall wild impulse no longer rang in through dispatch, so the question was how did impulse enter a number that was not dispatch? State Bureau found impulse could ring in through parking lot, which might be where cables were. Original designs called for a site that could be used to expand additional buildings to. There was a problem if a building were to be erected there, lines could go down and come on late at night when lights went off, a jumping bean signified a phone dispatch no longer able to pass through because there were too many impulses drawing on those numbers at the same time.

Ray found he could not dispense to City Audit because glove box on Grant had a bar lit with his name and because of it he could not sign an order to bring anyone on. The city couldn't put in a box underwater or on manmade landfill. That left orders designated through another city, Atherton might suffice. Palo Alto was geographically too far.

Atherton had a lot of curious items, manmade shorelines, an overabundance of bridges – it had five, Dumbarton, San Mateo, Hwy 17, Half Moon Bay, and Woodacre Bridge at the NASA junction – insufficient colleges, wooded gulfs, too many towers and no airport. If an airport wasn't attached to a major city there was no way to redirect storage sheds once a business leaves. That meant Atherton was primarily for retired Stanford professors. A bizarre item that identified criminal intent were the height above the city without towers enshrouded by dense fog, here in everglade apartments, four storied, on thin balconies suggestive of hot summers sat the new Mecca entrepreneurs whose lonesome hours were dedicated to taking distance photos by telescope lens of pilloried stone of two story Tudors where the foundation had cracked along uneven hilly pavement. Here lived a black Polish man born in Germany who entered US in 1953 with an uncle who was later found guilty of tampering whose mother drove a large chugger van for a bakery with racks stacked inside, who made a name for himself when he proved why an aircraft malfunctioned when it did not gain height. He was known as the catcher's mitt, because he evaded camera capture with a white van driving past reflecting windows is lost when it passes last of reflection and moves past long white jeep, this problem vanished camera control, glass was next to lot but couldn't see lot, lot was surrounded by high rise with balconies, detectives had to determine the interest, who was it? The person who came in for intent resided above city, that person wanted to tie off rings, allow a certain number calls to get through, engineer which department to concentrate on, save phone calls, delay some, presumably they were looking for someone, possibly the officer who responded to the call at the hospital, civic precinct was presumed to be primary intake, the precinct itself began as a hospital, when it changed the former hospital guards remained as police patrol, lots of hospitals became other institutions such as UC Extention college, the other issue as to who had authority to possess a pistol would not have been a hospital guard, only Hastings officers could carry so they trained the police.

Someone had needed a man in a black rain tarp coat inside a dark building to look injured. The telephone in hospitals prior to having lights in rooms other than OR needed to be started with what was called a saddle which consisted of a receiver and a crash cart EEG mechanism used to overload the phone prior to a syringe wipeout, one had to assume all mechanical failures were done by people familiar with the interior who perhaps went there. When the camera was not seeing what was sitting there, the question as to moving traffic, if one stepped away from the camera and in meantime a silvery white pulled further down and one across street turned corner you would think previously parked van was one of two when in fact they were each different, when security went to run tape they would see parked van leave, they wouldn't get the reflected item until wharf view which indicated a warehouse near wharf.

Ray poured boiling coffee into a flask when his eldest son showed up for his exam prep. "Were you dropped off?"

Kenneth was stylish, a blond in a shag reaching to his shoulders, green eyes that often filled with amusement, an upper class thin nose boasted from his mother, a kid who spent every summer on a bicycle pedaling on coastal highway 1 to his father's penthouse. He was meticulously studious, hard at the summations, a senior who had already been accepted to Brain, Brane & Bard on Sansome as soon as he passed the bar. "Mom dropped me off. She's in the car."

"She's going to wait all morning?"

Kenny shrugged. "That's what she said."

"Better have her in."

"She won't. She claims you stuck another dick on her. You're supposed to be divorced. Isn't that what you wanted?"

"I'm sure she's mistaken about being followed," Ray replied as was his habit to never involve the kids. "I for one wouldn't need to at this stage."

"That's what she says. She has talked about nothing else since she returned."

"It's not me. Let's get down to work. How's the last tort?"

"Well I passed but it sure wasn't easy. There's no way to excuse bad medical behavior, but then on the other hand the party was warned, they had to wait two days after signing the contract requesting the procedure, and they had already compared three providers."

"Despite the disparate problem that they received informed consent the medical community is still bound to its ethics and moral conduct."

"I wanted the physician's medical history bared. Could I have asked for it?"

"Not without the party being surrendered to a coma."

"It's not a coma but the party has to have the surgery again."

"That's common with knee replacement. You shouldn't ask about what's typical. It's experimental, but lots of people are signing up anyways."

"I missed a count. I said the physician did not require additional tissue, he could have used thigh."

"What did the instructor state was asked for in litigation?"

"Since the individual was very thin, tissue was called in in advance. Lab testing revealed an Rh positive factor which could indicate moderate to high risk."

""Okay, physician anticipated muscular difficulty arising despite pre-op. So, let's review consequences. Did body reject transplant? Although it seems possible, on account of the bone marrow becoming regressive, the law won't allow your supposition. It is entirely feasible that the rationale behind a repeat is the replacement tissue does not bind quickly enough."

"It's not class action."

"No, there is no malpractice. These ops will forever be performed in exactly the same way. What is recommended bed rest?"

"Two months off your feet."

Ray shook his head. "These patients probably know what they're doing, they are more than likely walking after a month."

"Then there was the assignment I turned in."

"Okay, this would've been open book."

"Yes. Also medical. A physician fell asleep during a procedure rendering the patient with a complication."

"The law requires the physician in charge of a medical training program to post all surgical hours performed. Where a malpractice charge arises the first consult goes to immediate prior hours worked. Should he have performed the operation?

Was he ready to handle his job? Do his schedules contradict common sense? How did you do?"

"A-plus. I figure I know my way around medicine enough to file on routine complication."

"Let's not charge ahead. There's a whole series of adjudications that become questioned if the reach is too ambitious. I would stick predominantly with contracts. That way you deal only with law."

"So, can I borrow your civil rights persuasive contingencies?" Kenneth asked.

"I very nearly forgot." Ray went to fetch the text, handing it to his son when he returned from his library. "How are you fixed for dough?"

"I'm pretty good. Mom gives me sixty a week for minor incidents."

"Need a business suit?"

"No, really, I'm doing fine. I have two quite expensive tailored suits, not a closet like yours but I don't need it until I start work."

"I'll expect you to accompany me when the time comes."

His son slapped him on the back and disappeared out the front door into the hall and elevator. Within minutes there was a knock on the door.

"It's open," he shouted.

Lorraine walked inside. "It's bigger than I expected. How large is this?"

"It's two thousand. What do you require?"

She sat opposite him at the formica. Lighting a cigarette, her hair fashionably topped, dressed in a white jacket and navy skirt, a wristwatch on her thin boned right hand, she tapped the ashtray with her usual standard of impatience. "When do you expect to call off your detective?"

"Not for a while, Lorraine. You appear imminently in danger of making an irretrievable decision."

"I don't think you should be allowed that sort of expenditure. I haven't the children with me."

"You are still their primary authority. They ought not to be exposed to your behaviors at all. They have exams to pass, degrees to obtain, if you feel you're not up to it, certainly you could have notified me."

She placed her cigarette in the glass flat ashtray, unbuttoned her jacket to her bra, went over to him and slipped a stocking foot between his thighs, and smiled at him while pushing her skirt up to reveal the crimson garter. He permitted her to seduce him, running a hand up her leg to her thigh and unsnapping the garter, rolling down the stocking, kissing her waist, allowing her to position herself on him. She was as she usually was, insistent, rocking him quickly, cunning in intent, holding his waist as she exacted his pleasure.

"I can't see you until the weekend, if you'd like," she said, standing, arranging her skirt, pinning her garter.

"It's a bit out of the question," he said.

"You couldn't have many objections now, or are you seeing someone?"

He held her jacket for her to slip into. "Do you know anything about the man you had sex with?"

"I know a lot about you, that should be enough," and kissed him on the mouth.

"Do you know his name?"

"Kerry something, I forgot. How's that big case turning out?"

"It's what it is. Standard appeals."

"Well, that's good. I peaked on Beulah's desk. Here's what I think if you're at all interested, IAD knows where the origination call rings in at, there's the law and proof of crime, there was at least one witness, the plaza lot robber was convicted, State detectives have several suspects, this Gaccio being the strongest, the files that are involved are known, the police precinct/hospital basement investigation for flooding is possibly completed, you have key identifiers – blue car in lot, witness, camera record, backup; and then of course you have to look for suggestible evidence, Mirage, what brings him into Civic Center, and you know how I think, I'd return to the first San Francisco landmark, the Hyde Street Pier and look up who wanted a slice of pie."

"Don't return my verdict for me, Lor."

She threw her arms around him. "What is the last word on Mirage? Daly is a partner to Mirage Hotels in the desert, who's the movie connection?"

"Who is Mirage Productions in the movie Havana? You tell me."

"It's Mirage Street, don't you agree?" She walked out on him.

∧ ∧ ∧

What was a mirage street, Ray queried of Blemsen over evening coffee-chocolat. Blemsen outfitted in wool grey trousers, a pale pink shirt and a black corduroy in good humor gave the question his straight-off-the-table response – optical illusion, refraction, spectrum, false light, mist before the eyes, see through a glass darkly, or apparition, to which Ray gave his own, an ethereal fog through which gradually recognizable shapes emerge out of obscurity, like a hazy view of the mountains. They bantered back and forth as to their ideas about Mirage's name and any connections he might have to Mayor Daly or Police Chief Moscone and their ownership of the Mirage Resort in the desert at Shangri-la, Indio and Palm Desert. Odder still was Mirage's fatal curiosity about cars or parking lots or concealed files from his broadcast days, possibly certain ocean sounds, misty spray, motors on the ocean, ships entering too close to the shoreline. The lot that sided his studio was tiny, enough for seven cars. Whatever came across the sound pans when dilutions were washed to hone in on particular tinny or clunking tones, wet weather would of course change the way sound was picked up, Ray and Laurence heard these fluctuations all the time without realizing what they were hearing, Hadley no doubt had some sort of sound display at that studio of his in Long Beach but he was inland, nowhere near the sea. If there were something to tease out, they had no idea if they were on track, Hadley had seized upon the female student so there was something there to be gleaned, but Mirage knew Hadley by way of a campus television studio where technically sound is matched to image, whereas Mirage's only reference point was a boat lost at sea. No boat in a parking lot, Larry Blemsen remarked stirring dregs of chocolate and when he had a sauce spooning it out with a dash of pepper.

A man at the next table gave Blemsen his newspaper, and Blemsen divided the sports section from the front section which he distributed to Ray. Ray read with plum regard, taking his espresso fairly much as one who having pondered the drizzle outside debated if he should hail a cab or brave a downpour when he was ready to go home. The news broke out with an early afternoon edition that showed falling graffiti over giant fans crowding the streets and a rowdy group of a hundred or more pouring from bars onto the pavement to join rowdy passers-by. Across the street near Bart square on a billboard stood exact frames of Thomas Hawk's thin iron man statue standing on a large puddle that reflected the statue upside down called Fallen Angels. On Post Street cars dallied up a hill to rows of apartment buildings that towered above the city, five apartment buildings twelve stories tall squished together, balconies and large windows on one side of the street and across, seven apartments vying for front row access, each providing skyline views of the two pinnacle towers and clock of Columbus Church and west, a dome spire cathedral. On an interior page the Chronicle still operated by Hearst despite half a dozen takeovers and mega bids by aspiring corporate shell-entities the ornate Ferry building, usually a favorite photograph with the yellow early morning 6:45 am bus dropping night fliers to Marin at the three-arced promenade, was featured for increased funds for its tugs, stronger engines to outperform a twenty hour on-deck management to its islands, cruising from Hyde Street Pier to Alameda Harbor Bay, dragging the shallow depths at Bay Farm Island on the estuary, out to Farallon Islands to test toxic wastes, then to Alameda Island, six miles sitting at 37,45,55N and 122,14,30W, and twenty-two acres of Alcatraz Island which had been a military prison until 1963 when a demonstration closed it permanently. Other bay islands maintained by the coast guard from Coast Guard Island were listed, Angel Island, Ano Nuevo State Reserve, Bair Island Wildlife Refuge, Belvedere Island which housed the wealthiest in the state, Bird Island off Rodeo Cove, Brooks Island Regional Park, Brother Islands lighthouse south of Richmond, Kent Island in Bolinas, and the old Mare Island base where streets of buildings had flooded with a rising ocean tide. The old man who had built a mansion on Nob Hill was still leaving Hyde Street Pier at five in the morning on Tuesday s and swimming with the current two miles to the flats of Sausalito every week.

"Powell Street trolley," Blemsen said, folding the newspaper intelligence-style.

"What about it?" asked Ray who did the same with his A-section.

"That's Powell Street's attraction. Geary is the theatres, Van Ness the hotels, Grove the library, Ninth Davies Hall and so on."

"Mirage didn't see the sights."

"Oh, I'm not talking about the sights. In this world of hidden dilemmas, if you lose it on that plaza square in the vicinity of City and County Halls, you have the assurance it will empty into a chamber on any of three basic thoroughfares,

Hayes, Sutter and Hyde. Hayes is a hazy sight, Sutter is Mother Lode because that's where the digital picks up the pan wash, and Hyde is hidden. If your ring goes to Hyde you can't get it for weeks. The streets directly correspond to Long Beach on the map – there's Orange, Cherry and Carson, also references to a mint. Powell is the Pinkerton detective of the wharf days, Ness is the old New York marshal coroner driving his morgue van with the red light on the trunk, and Hyde, depending upon how you look at it, is the old laboratory physician."

Ray asked, "Where are you placing Mirage?"

"Hayes. Both landmarks Pacific Coast Campus of Long Beach and San Francisco City Hall plaza land on the same respective square of a map."

"But that's just co-incidence if accurate and I'm not convinced. City Hall joins to Ninth, Orange to Seventh. I believe the streets are just names."

"Well, that is where the names are situated on maps, it is a mint heist that allowed its thieves to remove orange and cherry milk, hide it at a mosque. No one but Mirage identifies a garbled sound; the only reason to come to San Francisco by bus to study a lot problem is presumably due to the area. The Civic Center plaza has a telephone box that crosses through every trunk rotator. Where is there a telephone box in Long Beach?"

"The largest sits on the Angel Highway."

"Is that San Gabriel?"

"Right," Ray replied. "Gabriel is 605 going north, nine major thoroughfares across town west of Long Beach Highway."

"So, maybe Angel received a dead call from whoever is on Hayes, it wouldn't be Federal, they're on Geary."

"It should be easy to find."

"I'd be willing to bet a mint ship left Hyde Street Pier and sank wherever 605 begins and the state filled in a park island to prevent further difficulties; I'd even venture a guess they've had radio stations along the coast in case a ship loses sight of course in the mist."

"I've never heard of it, but it doesn't mean one didn't go down at 6:05 am trying to make the pier and that all parties didn't sink with it."

Blemsen gave a shrug. "They do have their ship."

"Yes, they do. Here's a puzzler. I have a reversal on the precinct battery charge for the guard who fired on a burglar who cut the junket before he stole the drawer. Hastings sent a man over originally to handle a crazy at City Hall and dispose him in a restraint at County Mental but when he arrived he ran into this burglary. It was an assigned guard who brandished a weapon."

"Anyone see him draw or fire?"

"Sure, most of the officers. In the conviction the burglar took twenty-two counts. His appeal lies with the technicality that city hall can't carry a weapon on the job."

"Stupid loser. Who's his counsel?"

"Hyde."

"The old man took it on as defense work?"

"Two files, the browser and the other, public tray."

Blemsen sat looking stymied. After a refill on his choco-lat, he opened a tin, took a licorice and putting the tin away, very frankly, all doubts put aside, said, "Tell Hyde it's nothing personal, he can't have it on the browser."

"I have to concede language, he's bent his fuzzy stick at precisely the second the camera would have snapped the car pulling to a stop in the rain, his hand is on the money a second afterward."

Blemsen leaned against the table and said, "Tell Hyde you're going to kill the fucking prick."

"How's it looking on the Q.T.?"

"Like Lombard Street, top to bottom."

"My only misgivings are that if the feds know where the

striker originated, why I can't have a confirmation as to whether this file bears some involvement."

"It's possible they are still making tests."

"Well, that's just it, I can't delay much longer. Who do you suppose they're all working for?"

"I'd put my money on the black mint off 280 Skyline or the red arrow at Hills Brothers."

"As long as you are not sardonic in court," Ray said.

"I'd only be saying this sort of thing to you. I'm a polite individual."

# CHAPTER FIVE

THE SOPRANO FILE WAS NEVER SUBMITTED. Content involved a witness to both the culprit who trenched the box from the park and simultaneously a line that rang when a wire was cut and went on recorder. Circuit sounds squealed onto the tape and zipped to silence. It wouldn't be until spring long after the banded sounds were produced as a table of spike information that the sounds would have been relayed as photographic units displaying transfers, wire wraps and a host of other telephone identified stations in and around San Francisco. For one they now had in excess of ten minute, less than four second resounding sequences which displayed in Daly City at the palace generating a big question as to which landmark was of interest to anyone and a ten-nine-nine seconds sequence involving at least three posts. When the digital tune was sequenced to a map, there was a pause of about four seconds followed by a light sequence for the palace, surrounding streets and businesses. On a computer the sounds gave text which as they moved across the page dipped over the sentences below as though melting.

Ray reserved a few days off his court calendar with his tape man. In the studio booth packaged between two walls less than eight feet apart with three of twenty-four monitors playing they reviewed the soprano tapes. The underground lot was dank, dark, sinister in chilly winter without sufficient overhead light, and although nearly seventy vehicles faithfully parked there every day if not every month, the way into and out of it was depressing, walking with cars speeding past, or taking two flights of stairs in almost complete dark to the busy intersections on McAllister or Ninth. Soprano was unseen, a concealed voice presumably hooked to a carry-pin with good voice control. A single tone cast found a dark haired, tall dark male somewhere near Bay Street. They were all fearful he had proved the binocular path of the cut wires, that he had a cut-trap-wire into all sorts of authoritative non clearance locations, the idea the state bureau had approved to send top notch agents into dank parking lots was laughable, but it had to be done, one couldn't just sit idly by as hostile threats were logged into dispatch caller-without-ID tags. There it was on high resolution, fast you-tube quality camera recorder, one deep throat after another, each male's voice acquired to a Voltaire microphone capable of picking up any nuance, but all were same height, Caucasian, wiry-thin aging adults, it made one wonder, they watched an endless plethora of ten, twenty minute tapes, waited out the waiting, heard the man leave, footsteps hurrying away, peered at the screens as the sight-viewer immediately snatched the dude out of the shadows, put him on visuals, and waited for him to emerge into broad daylight which he never did, or he wore platform shoes which he ditched, hours later every last person was tagged and followed to their flats on the basis of occurrence.

"Who did you decide this man might be?" asked Ray, when the errand boy arrived with their coffee and clam and stuffing rolls from the sandwich shop which was wedged between a bookstore and a small garden across the street.

Degas fix-captivated the three monitors and turned down sound before he answered. At fifty-five, he was weary in appearance having put in forty hours at the studio without a shave, hair trim or bed, his somewhat large rolled curly brown hair getting scraggly, dense stubble soon to form a beard. It didn't take long to resemble a stranger, he often told the interns from the state building. In a small wakeup room behind the pipes he had a hard mat bed, a livable shower, stacked washer dryer, refrigerator, a sink and counter for a one cup coffee which he relied upon late in the wee hours, a nail clipper, razor, handheld hair dryer, change of shoes and a poster pinup of a semi-clad Connie Sellica.

"I put a voice-on the image of this slease and got him out near county hospital, all the way to Glide Memorial Methodist Church, at the ferry building, on Bay Street and one afternoon at the Legion of Honor. He's educated, suave, wears a business suit, knows his way around. I think he's a physician-turned-priest because of the hours he presents himself." It was Vince Degas' opportunity to wane philosophical.

"Height?"

"Five, ten. Reddish brown, very wiry hair, no motor, resides somewhere high up because of what he described during any of a number of call-ins, leather shoes that scuff a bit, no accent."

"Did he contact us first? How did he get started?"

"He talked to an agent as our man was walking to his car, a convertible dark gray two-seater."

"What did Soprano want?"

"Come here, I've a bag for you."

"Our man actually took it from him?"

"Not on your life. He told the man to kick it into the open and leave."

"What was inside?"

"It was a tape of a conversation between two men. One alleged they had a probable of the witness watched the placement of spikes to wires in the telephone box."

"If they have a probable, they know her. What else?"

"He claimed the saboteur used .11 indicator spikers to receive only."

"How long a distance did we end up tracking?"

"Two miles distance not capable to camera."

Ray asked, "Did this soprano ever make reference to distance in order to set it up as a telephone grid on the computer before the jack goes in?"

"He's not a splice, that much we do know, he's a leg man, able to go up a pole, because we ring for equipment on his body. We thought at the time he was making contact that he had knowledge as to which precinct the relay was intended."

"Was he ever traced to one of our agencies?"

"No."

"Then how did he know an investigation was in progress?"

"We think he was told by a suspect whose home was under surveillance."

"You're saying he jotted down someone's license plate or followed someone into work, or what?"

"Followed Grazi," Degas replied. "Grazi was doing Burlingame development at the time for company clearances, we thought the soprano didn't qualify to obtain a liquor license on a nightclub."

"Was Grazi on anything other than town and country?"

"Street muni, he signed all contracts for San Francisco. I know it's not much of an answer but this guy insisted on hiding in the shadows and we didn't see a reason to look him up despite the fact we think we had him in an ambulance on one occasion."

"Was he admitted to county?"

"Yes, on 24th Street, for an ulcer."

"Was he a heavy drinker?"

"No, it was drugs, he used heroin. At that time he was new in town staying at the YMCA."

"How many times did he talk to someone?"

"Four total. Always at night around eight, always with an accurate up-to-the-hour ad, all three posts said he had inside information. He told who in the state arranged for non funded use to be disrupted in such a way that another project use could be funded. He said Oakland ferry had to retire, San Jose sewage couldn't sit on the shoreline, there should not be storage at landfill exit and Marin on-ramp had to be final exit. When we last put him on a map he came up for San Mateo off Bayshore."

"Who wants Black Pole?" Ray asked.

"Who doesn't?"

"What brought him in?"

"He bought a building in San Mateo for around a mil."

"How'd he finance it?"

"He sold two houses and a time share for a sum of nine hundred and twenty-five thousand and wrapped it into a loan. Next thing we were aware of, everyone whose equity had gone up substantially was tying a loan on a building. The east bay went up in ribbons."

"Is Black Pole established in the east bay?"

"Very little, a warehouse or two, maybe he'll open a mail merchandizing center, more likely it will be car parts."

They were starting the city grid all over again. One point one per building around Fourteenth or close to the lake made an expert tax appreciable loan for seven years before retail had to kick in overhead.

Premiums on a building ten stories tall were three thousand a month. Canvassers could readily determine where customers resided and either build inexpensive condos or direct competition.

Ray gave him a sober glance. "What occurred when we

discovered he wanted an entire mall?"

"We gave it to him for cheap in the middle of nowhere, off the beaten track, outside city limits, with even lower rates for mall parking. Here's the thing," Degas said, stacking decks of packaged cards. "He was downtown California at Pine having a hard time. He asked for China Basin at ridiculous rates and we said no. We looked around and decided he could have it all for relatively inexpensive if he were similar to a cow palace. Lots of developers jumped at the opportunity for land, the mall itself, and interior goodies, movie theatre, a dozen restaurants, mattress, books, auto repair, banks. It was a time that had finally come of age."

"What do we know about his financial profile?"

"Half a dozen homes picked up through liquidation for a few grand, remodeled and some partially rebuilt per area, five areas of average affluence. Only managed to purchase one mall; otherwise he traded all areas for building ownership; sold two buildings per five years and put a little under two to enhance his mall and pocketed four million, lives highly affluent. When we ran him through a ledger, his headliner flashed black line twice to empty gray meaning he was solvent with high end retainer to $75,000 giving him a quick pickup, speedy withdrawal, but if he did any of soprano's list as rumored, two ends at third, then he's dead."

Beulah sat by the window in the dining room on the lookout for John. Maman rattled on about the bouquet of long stem salmon roses he had sent her with the afternoon courier to wish her well on Mother's Day.

Primped to the height of elegance Beulah wore her hair chiffon style with small glittering combs tucked here and there, eyeglasses hanging at her chest, still dressed from the morning in trial courtroom garb of a severe black box pleat, white stiff starch with long sleeves and black double breasted jacket and low black pumps, her mother in a lavender polyester one box panel in front, a soft white turtleneck sweater and dark purple two-inch heels, her glossed silver jewelry and all five rings, large ornamental jewelry with round and square turquoise and citrine stones embedded in gold.

"We began at eight-thirty and went straight through lunch, all testimony from a therapist. She's very good, precisely what we like to see, calm on the witness stand, thorough in answers, exactly what is asked. She said after her client arrived to work, she set up the charts per the admits, the phone rang and at that moment she glanced outside and saw a male dressed in workman's clothing in the park."

Maman said, "Doubt her client was where she said to have seen his face. The only windows that can see the park plaza are the county building on Fulton, second floor of city hall, and possibly across the street at the concert hall. The teenager was more credible coming out of the basement and seeing the male digging the grass near the underground. What does Ray think?"

"He's in favor of the teen; after all, she passed the poly. For the poly she describes leaving the hospital after getting a blood test and walking down to city hall for a pre-trial conference with an attorney by eight fifteen."

"She'll testify in closed chambers and have to be escorted to a limo and that will be the end of her life. Even witness protection won't be able to get her out securely."

"It won't get that bad, Maman."

"Where did Ray put her?"

"He doesn't say. We're more worried about who knows she's made an ID."

"It's a bad situation if you can't get to them first. Do you expect her to point the person out of a line-up? Old photos are too misleading."

"John's here," Beulah said, and went into the hall to open the door.

He walked in, stepping into her embrace, he set his briefcase on the floor. He was dressed as usual in tennis shirt, casual jeans, formal white dinner jacket, black tie, white tennis shoes. She kissed him, and steering him by the arm led him into the dining room. The table was set, fine dark red china plates, glassware, cups, dark green napkins with shooting red star flowers, the chilled snapper grinning on its green platter, chilled lime ambrosia spiced with dill and cream cheese. They sat, and Maman served portions of mulled wine and hot garlic bread sticks as starters. He talked all night through a second helping of fish about an upcoming winter surfing tournament, buying a new wetsuit, hiring his own photographer, practicing weekends, doing a little windsurfing to help retain posture. He was in rare form, not dogged or tiresome, but having regained his distinguished airs for which Beulah originally brought him home to meet her mother. The current was fast, two headers to the wave, straight course on a curl, swerving pipelines a graceful momentum. His body could sail, he was a statue on a crest, the ocean could raise forty feet off the incline as it shot toward the shore but he was fixed, at one with motion, aware of nothing but the feel of a sailing board under foot. Discipline was rigorous, the task was uncompromising, the waves were a tyranny, he had to be a martinet for detail, every degree of crouch made the relentless stiff stance a driving necessity. These seditions were lawless, the mulled wine further loosened his tie, he had no doubt that a man in his seventies, although toned, had a bargain with fate for which strict practice made the nearest resistance to the revolt of waves. Throughout dinner and sour cream apple pie for dessert, warm spiced red wine kept his bib permitting him to elucidate upon the submissive nature of man to the coercion of the sea, a forbearance of obedience that he resigned himself to while dismissing potential terror of getting pulled in an undertow out to sea from his thoughts. Late into the night in bed with Beulah he kissed her fingertips, her bare shoulders eliciting uncommon emotion and promised her he could do no more than attune himself to her; as he obeyed the uncontrolled sea so he willingly answered her, not a restraint was there to be forced from him. As she fell asleep her thoughts drifted to Ray and the physician approval permitting him to hear the whole segmented file.

^ ^ ^

A District Court of Appeals brought two categories to be heard. The first was it could overturn a former decision made by a judge under a due process disagreement; and the second was it had to hear any convictable evidence whether the evidence could impart prejudice to a case. From time to time Ray supposed he ignored his indecision on an appeals. There were classic venue-holds and then there were laxities, a proposed absence of authority such as not having street lights at an intersection because those would interfere with the trolley turning around, and then there were ministerial bureaucratic interference, the catholic charity hospitals that gave all funds to their district archdiocese for salary payout which under any other restriction, eg it served as retention for overflow from county hospital, would have imposed a fifty percent tax for state collection. The idiom of favor often struck to that which could institute a fair minded polity, for without broad interpretation the more mundane of leverage controlled all implementation, reasonably or otherwise. State of the realm kept language at a fundamental doctrine, the subway matter – should a subway stop midcourse to permit passengers to wait even in partial darkness if a fire broke out on board – controversial because the transportation board disagreed. Its own commission held that only in the event of flood should disembarkation occur since the tube had been built to prevent containment of ocean water. Ray kept a tight berth of disinterest, his scepter sought to join necessity to individual rights, not acceptable practice. The norms of merit were skepticisms that depended upon inexact standards judged for correctness when much of the time it was deemed less worthy than another avenue of advantage. Long adherence to considerations of error and outcome tightened the reins, until aged on the strengths of pronounced judgments he easily abandoned severity leaning strongly toward seignior prerogative, and as the years dispatched farther and farther from syndicalism, ergatocracy and autocracy. He was of the belief the witness ought not to be brought forward, that the evidence without her strongly established flooding to the hospital and incident to the plaza garden square, but her testimony would establish without prejudice the fact that two wrongdoings occurred. He had already accepted her lawyer's reasonable foundation to permit her to testify which gave him incontrovertible proof of both crimes. Whether she dispelled the permitted proof as to identity was not at issue; he might decide to suppress with the presumption that the defense should not be permitted to possess any of the testimony. He could do this. His chair was granted any authority he believed necessary to maintain the public conscience. He was able to go so far as to implement rotation of a new judge but that was a risk of making public the very information he wanted curtailed.

Now that he knew what the testimony consisted of in prima facie he knew also there was an eventual problem. The street showed that the man removed a blister syringe and while inserting to a circuit clamped the attached wire. Technically Ray did not require one iota more. At this point he had the case locked up. The lower court allowed only the camera tape of the blocker saddle to be shown but not who assembled it and struck for reasons of prejudice who the tape showed inserting the blister. The attorneys filing on the evidence showed the man's arms and hands and to demonstrate scrutiny of fingertips for prints on file. They had a film of the man leaving his workplace, of picking up the saddle, of removing it from the trunk of an uncorroborated vehicle, of entering the hospital and of emerging from an elevator into the basement and of entering the women's bathroom with his device in a pack. Although this was enough for the hospital crime, the fact that the city hall plaza square film took a frame of the saboteur and a separate frame of his hand manipulations was inconclusive both frames were of the same male. Even with the party in the parking lot who saw what the man used, they would have to introduce an evidentiary expert to discuss likelihood. This could take days to present, any inconclusive evidence was often enough to ask the court to dismiss a proof. It was the stocking over his face that got rid of the girl, even had she observed it and described facial distortion she could not state with any preponderance that it was him.

It didn't add capable description to less direct evidence to learn that the sequence of events for just what was there held the blue sedan pulled up into the lot when the underground was full, two days prior to the black robber who shut off the camera on the lot, a nice looking grey-silver vehicle parked in the space in which three cameras snapped photos of the car hourly, a dark brown truck hood in complete sunlight looked like dust in a reflection until 1015, the rest of truck accurate at 0850 on that winter December morning, or underground twenty-seven cars filled almost half the section behind the elevators and were photographed every one and a half minutes. The plaza lot was slated for remodel into an underground, four level lot with no spaces available on the square in the open and a stairwell to below. High speed, maximum resolution cameras would as-sure film of passengers and vehicle license plates on vehicles identified by make and model, up to three blocks away upon departure. Because the driver didn't return to the blue sedan, it was towed off the lot at the end of the third night and sent to a state bureau garage for a report on the reason the camera could

The Hood

not select out the driver or possible date and time of arrival. Ray had an expert he used many times who knew everything about cars when the riders did not take on photographs, too much salinity, rain at a 45 degree slant or more, too much glare, a stain residue on window due to chemical, and the photo bin had been tampered with, but his guess was that someone on the staff who watched for duration of minutes when spaces were not photo-filed had tipped the driver. That suggested a photo bank or federal officer, but the FBI had never altered tapes, it was out of the question, impossible, they weren't the ones who combined tapes or hid scenes or studied sequences anyways – those were longtime agents, and until soprano showed up there was no understanding of a leak. Yet soprano obviously had obtained in-depth information as to scheduled building use by unauthorized groups, far worse were offices opened by dirty money for grievous portent, known ex-cons photographed on sites, state funds flowing to small contracts in troubled areas, Ray went back in his mind to Mirage; here was a man in his late seventies who had spent innumerable time at an out-of-town college campus at Santa Barbara to set up several studios for them for both radio and television for live series, and Hadley who picked out a female from Santa Barbara who was keeping tabs on an unfaithful husband who was playing around with a dean at Pacific campus, poor Hadley had gone from Long Beach campus to campus until he found the object of the erstwhile husband, and then there was his young clerk friend at the bookstore who knew all about the times the husband went to visit his mistress, and he was still waiting for an opinion as to cause of death on Hadley and suspected it would get written as fatal injection; the other crime was Mirage whom Ray suspected had caught on to mob law involving a man who took an adolescent to a gymnasium and killed him, probably the worst Long Beach crime ever committed because the teenager had had his mouth taped and his hands taped behind his back before getting ditched into an old house on the beach. Long Beach was known for her witnesses to brutal acts; cops died faster there than anywhere else in the U.S., once every five years. She had the most underserved cop force, police were tough to recruit and average age death was under fifty. That was the reason swanky Long Beach didn't get a morgue – deaths when they did occur were gruesome, picturesque captures of betrayal lacking common sense or indiscretion and the money was the wife's. Long Beach didn't have a soprano as far as he knew, soprano was alone San Francisco, there were no indicators the male in the shadows knew a thing about broadcasting, he had it on good authority the fund structure emanating out of South San Francisco intended to fund both the Hayward and Atherton shorelines and hang a shingle at the north end of the bay, all dubious marshlands better left permanently to wetland green designations.

The fact that a line of inquiry touched two severe crimes did not worry him, much less obvious were locations the federal arm required for new buildings, and while he saw the request for bid pass over his desk infrequently he was disconcerted that the soprano had as much information about designations as county builders, even the tip-off that the police precinct was going to be thrashed triggered suspicions about leaks. He called Beulah at home.

"Better find me a solid detective who can give me a link between Hadley and Mirage," he told her.

"What about David?" she inquired about a radio announcer with a license at Allioto's.

"Try to get someone from out of the area. Consult an attorney board."

"Should the person have any particular expertise?"

"No numbers, race course betting or casinos."

"That leaves out most private investigators."

"Look for a retired police officer who's kept his ear to the industry; maybe he can tell us over the phone." Ray took a sip of coffee. Then: "How's Maman? Have you discussed things with her?"

"I never bring the work home. I saw Lorraine. She indicated you were patching things up."

"No, I'm suing her over a new infidelity."

"Why don't you ask her what she knows?"

"What would Lorraine know?"

"I understand she's friendly with counsel on the state board of medical staffing. It's a boon for us that that person has actual camera photo prints of the lot meter on the surface. Here's the reference: clamps attached to telephone wire were trying to determine what they rang to; if wire doesn't ring in it has to go to center lane and it will get rerouted. When ring can't get through, it lights up red, when entire circuitry loses ability to put through, have to remove those circuits handling most units, per tab, if all mall lights depleted and unable to ring through, then you knew you had a problem."

Ray said, "Good info. Get a hold of these if you can. There was a person who went in as a parking attendant, he must have been picked up on several cameras, he had to have pick experience, stop and reverse, shut the lights down, shut telephone lines down, don't go near Lorraine. We have him on tab having pulled out wires somewhere else and then nothing responded, shut down metro, no effect on metro elsewhere. Original plaza lot built ferry style, one lane into one floor and two man station, cameras everywhere, above small lot, around corner down street Van Ness small parking with attendant, west on Market two lots back to back, ticket purchase all day all night. The station that was affected subsequently was not Pacific Heights as originally conveyed, it technically was a downtown station, it has no parking, it shares a wharf, it has a muni line it can access into, but the muni stops in the opposite direction. One side faces a street, the side door leads to the wharf, the other entrance goes to ferry terminal, access to a boat. On the day of the lights out two boats were called out to Angel Island to investigate a trespass into the museum and were gone four hours, and last we tracked a telephone operator for a department store.

"Each person seen on plaza has to be assessed. That produces the man dressed as a parking attendant, the uniformed man with a food cart, verify who was called out including the security from court, state hospital officers and nurse and you'll have to identify if her cart had any medical supplies such as a three-prong syringe. As to a striker find out the patient who reported temporary loss of sight."

Lorraine sounded tired, a bit shorn around the edges, the usual high in-bound enthusiasm clearly on the wane.

"You're losing your flex," he remarked. "Maybe you should pay attention to your energy and get some sleep."

"I'm alright, nothing a final preemptory won't fix."

"What are you looking for?"

"A little humility for starters."

He was in the hot seat before he realized she was bumping up her energy with argument. "Lorraine, we can't discuss this. It's not fair to me, and it should be beneath your dignity by now."

"What have you told the children?"

"Nothing. Why?"

"They've started asking questions. It's a little sudden to bring home a girlfriend for the night."

"That's my business. What are you up to?" He asked.

"I was a dutiful wife to you. I typed all your documents, filed a fair percentage of them, and investigated your side ruler commentaries. My entire life with you was spent waiting for my pleasure."

He kept a poker face enduring the hardship that he had inadvertently chased her to another man. "You were a calculating girl, Lorraine. I didn't make you what you are, that's your notion of survival."

"I am what I have to be for myself to win – most of my cases have to be upheld, minds changed, the bench convinced; you forget, I entered your court for you."

"Not for me, young Lorraine, you only did what suited you. You could have been made yourself more amenable."

"I was home every night, eight-thirty sharp. You weren't. You came home nine or ten; often times you stayed at a hotel."

"I didn't stop needing you."

"I needed a man who could coach me, turn me into an approbate."

"Last thing I'd be up for." He stood, putting on his overcoat and leather gloves. He asked, although he'd had an answer when he first raised the subject at least a year ago, "How many cases before you retire, Lorrie?"

"I'm young – I'll wait to lose my first case before I decide," she answered, put her pens into the pen holder on her desk, scooped up unattached clause work and stacked them neatly, and withdrew a cigarette and lit it. "I'm in this for the long run, you know that; I want to have won on every major appeals that exists."

"Then I suggest you get busy. It's a long wait list for Russian Hill, Basin to wharf on federal land, sidewalks, and let's see, what won't you have submitted on? There are one-way streets in a county jurisdiction, or sub-entry for boats into pier house docks, or the street limits of Chinatown, or when a police station can be converted to an elementary school as was done on Eighteenth. Then you'll be about done and have one of everything under your belt."

## THE END

The Hood